THE GLASGOW GIRLS

Frances Paige was born in Glasgow between the Wars, but has lived in the North of England for many years. Domestic life absorbed much of her time until her forties when she took up first painting, and then writing, with great success. She is the author of more than twenty-five novels, including, most recently, the popular *Sholtie* series.

'Written with the sure touch of meticulous research, with wholly believable characters, it is an amazing insight into middle-class Glasgow between the wars. Frances Paige is an exciting, vibrant writer'

ELIZABETH ELGIN,
author of *I'll Bring You Buttercups*

'Beautifully and sensitively penned, and the pain and poignancy felt by her characters struck chords deep in my own heart. This is one book I'll treasure and read again and now that I have discovered her I'll want to read more'

CHRISTINE MARION FRASER,
author of the *Rhanna* novels

FRANCES PAIGE

The Glasgow Girls

Lines from 'The Isle of Capri' © 1934, reproduced
with the kind of permission of Peter Maurice Music Co. Ltd,
London WC2H 0EA

This edition published by Grafton Books, 1999

Grafton Books is an Imprint of
HarperCollins*Publishers*
77–85 Fulham Palace Road,
Hammersmith, London W6 8JB

First published as a Paperback Original 1994

1 3 5 7 9 8 6 4 2

A catalogue record for this book
is available from the British Library

ISBN 0-26-167353-X

Set in Linotron Galliard

Printed in Great Britain by
Caledonian International Book Manufacturing Ltd, Glasgow

To Helen, Eric and Molly

ONE

June 1934

THE PENDULUM OF the beaten brass clock swung rhythmically within its perimeter, there was a whirring, a stirring, for all the world like a hen about to lay an egg, Anna often thought, then the chime began its staccato sound, one ... two ... three ...

'Those sisters of mine.' She spoke to her father who was wiping his lips on a voluminous white napkin. She got up from the breakfast table and went to stand at the foot of the stairs. 'Nancy!' she called. 'Jean! It's eight o'clock!' She came back and sat down again. 'Nancy thinks she goes to the Art School to impress the men.'

'You and Jean will be above that sort of thing, then?' More than half his life spent in Glasgow had not subdued the soft tones of Angus Mackintosh's native Ross-shire. And as Nancy, his youngest daughter, came into the room with her usual flurry: 'Well, will you look what the wind's blown in?' His glance was admiring. Anna thought Nancy's resemblance to their mother enabled her to get away with murder at times.

'Like it?' Nancy posed in front of them, one hand behind the smooth golden bob. 'How would I do for one of Pettigrew and Stephens' mannequins?' She swivelled on her hips. Her short, accordion-pleated skirt whirled provocatively.

'That outfit's too fancy for an art school, isn't it, Father?' Anna said.

1

'I'm an architect not a shopwalker. Leave me out.' He got up and pushed in his chair. 'I'll say cheerio to your mother and get on.' At forty-six he was young-looking and proud of his litheness. He covered the steep slope of St Vincent Street every morning on his way to his office as easily as he might have attacked Ben Dearg. 'Where's Jean, by the way?'

'Bessie got her to take a cup of tea to Mother in bed.' Nancy was buttering her toast. 'That Bessie's beginning to rule the roost, if you ask me.'

'Privilege of the old family retainer.' Anna was the joker of the family. 'She and Mother have been together now . . .'

'. . . for forty years . . . !' The two girls burst into song together.

Jean, Anna's twin, had joined them. 'I heard her sympathizing with Father the other day about being surrounded by "wum-men". "An' no' even a wee male dug to keep you company, Mr Mackintosh."' She laughed, her teeth a flash of white. She had the dark Highland good looks of her father, with a flamboyance which wasn't apparent in Anna. Her dark mass of hair was longer than the usual bob of smart girls of the thirties. Anna's, although darker, was shining and short, and her complexion had a thin, china fairness. Her neatness of dress contrasted with the theatricality of Jean's, who liked scarves and dangling ear-rings.

Anna was uninvolved with her appearance, unlike their younger sister, Nancy, who was intimately acquainted with hers on account of long consultations at her bedroom mirror. 'Oh, I wish I had hollows in my cheeks like Garbo's, and *soulful* eyes, not pale blue saucers like Tumshie's milk.' Tumshie was Bessie's beloved cat, her familiar, Anna said, which led the life of Riley in the kitchen.

'I'll have another cup with you, Jean. I haven't any classes until half-past nine.' Anna was leafing through the *Herald*, which their father had left. She looked up. 'Bessie wants to know if you two are having something cooked.'

2

'Not me. I'm slimming.' Nancy was nibbling daintily at the corner of a piece of toast.

Jean glanced at her. 'Men like curves. I think those people who started the craze for Ryvita have a lot to answer for.'

Nancy stopped with her buttered toast halfway to her mouth. 'I *told* Bessie to put some on the table!' She looked up as a gaunt-looking woman with her hair brushed behind her ears appeared in the doorway. 'Bessie! Where's the Ryvita? I *told* you –'

'You don't catch me putting skliffs of cardboard on the table for anybody, miss.' She put her hands on her hips. 'Ony orders for bacon and eggs?'

'Don't let that mangy old cat in here for a start,' Jean said. 'It's got fleas.'

'Whit rubbish. On you go, Tumshie.' Bessie's face softened as she looked at the tabby at her heels. '*You* know when you're no' wanted.' It turned and walked away obediently, its matronly bottom swaying from side to side.

'They don't want anything, Bessie.' Anna looked up from her paper. 'Away and have a cup of tea at the fire before Mother gets up. This is her bridge afternoon.'

'Don't I know it! *Rolled* sandwiches noo! Rolled roon bits o' asparagus. Ma Goad, whit next? Nae porridge, then?'

'It sticks to your ribs.' Jean laughed with her sisters.

'You lot will laugh on the ither side o' your faces some day.' Bessie went away. She had never believed in the smaller courtesies of service. That would have been 'kowtowing', and she was as good as the next one, or the Mackintoshes come to that, much as she liked them as a family, and their Granny and Grandpa before them who had taken her in as a girl of fourteen.

'Funny how that cat's desperate to come in here,' Jean said in a dreamy voice. She had both hands round her cup and was staring into space.

What is she really thinking of, Anna thought, watching her. She had been secretive last night too, not even remembering

3

the picture she had seen – or, she thought now, was supposed to have seen. 'It might have been that Fred Astaire and Ginger Rogers one,' she'd said. *Might* have been, when everybody was queuing up at the Regal to see it.

'Listen to this!' She stilled her unease by letting her eyes fall on a heading in the paper she was holding, '"Bonnie and Clyde shot in police trap . . ."'

'Bonnie and who?' Nancy was spreading some more butter on her toast. 'I'm not having a cooked breakfast so I can –'

'Clyde. Like the river.' She read out to them, '"After a four-year partnership in which they killed at least twelve people . . ." Can you imagine, twelve people? "Clyde Barrow and Bonnie Parker drove at speed into an ambush in Louisiana. Minutes later Texas rangers found their bodies riddled with over fifty bullets, a revolver and shotgun in their lifeless hands,"' Anna read in a hushed voice. '"A half-eaten sandwich and a saxophone were found in the car . . ."'

'They were fated,' Jean said. 'I can see the inside of that car, the detail helps. Like the skirt of that woman in the Dutchman's painting we were shown. Remember?'

'Onnes. Mr Kleiber showed it to us.' She watched Jean's face. 'It had been painted . . . with love, he said.' Too calm.

'I don't see where the sandwich comes into it,' Nancy said, 'or the saxophone for that matter.'

'Don't you?' Jean's dark eyes were suddenly glowing. 'Can't you imagine Bonnie and Clyde in bed together? They would laugh, and hug,' her voice was almost inaudible, 'and love . . .'

'It could never happen here.' Nancy looked horrified.

Anna got up. Her vague unease was back again. 'We'll be late. Come on.'

Jean got up slowly. She shook back her hair, lifting it from her collar with long fingers, let it fall, slowly. *She* could have done it, Anna thought. She could be infatuated, bewitched, even. Not murder, but almost anything for love . . .

* * *

4

Anna sat in the Theory Class at the Art School. Listening and looking. She had noticed how since she came to the school she observed people more. Like this morning . . .

Of course, she wasn't a painter like Jean, nor had she a natural facility for watercolours like Nancy, who had never troubled herself about learning techniques but who produced delicate and appealing watercolours as if they ran through her fingers onto the paper.

Mother had the same talent but had given it up when she married and had children. It hadn't been demanding enough, she said, not like Jean, who was recognized as the gifted one of the family. Anna's beaten metal pieces were never mentioned. She suspected her mother thought it was infra dig to use a hammer, and had once been upset when Anna said that perhaps there had been a blacksmith in the family. If there had been, she had inherited his strong fingers and an eye for design, but little sense of colour.

Great-aunt Jessie at Kirkcudbright had been more faithful to her art. She had studied here, at the Art School, and had known the Glasgow Girls, that talented band of women who had been among the first female pupils to attend. Her eyes went back to the man on the podium.

They said he was Austrian and that he had fled from Vienna when the Nazis were clearing out Jewish musicians, writers and painters. Ritchie, who admired Mr Kleiber greatly, said he felt sure he had been connected with the Bauhaus, because he'd talked of knowing Kandinsky.

You could believe it all. He was foreign-looking, with a debonair manner, and his voice had the rich rounded timbre of many Jews. They were ten a penny in Glasgow, mostly furriers and jewellers. Mother thought their wives were too loud in their dressing, not 'Jaeger-genteel'. Anna liked them. Their voices caressed and persuaded when you went into their shops. They had the same dark eyes, the same charm of this man who was speaking.

5

'I am so glad to have come to a city where there is such a love of design. This building we are in, for instance,' he waved his hands, 'do not take it for granted. Look around you. True avant-garde, a functional structure designed by an individual mind. But what did you do to him? How I can sympathize! I too had to flee my home. But in here,' he tapped his forehead, 'I carry pictures, the *Beethoven Frieze*, the bustle of the Graben – art can be in the marketplace too, art is universal. Please appreciate it, realize your good fortune that you are free, un-molested.'

He was a charmer, there was no doubt about it, not looking persecuted at all, but full of gaiety, Byronic – that was Ritchie's word for him – dark, thick hair brushed back from a broad forehead and longer than worn here, finely set eyes, broad-shouldered, sturdy build but not fat . . . and that captivating, broken-syllabled voice. Had Jean been captivated? She had been strange this morning, as if she were concealing a secret – or thinking she was concealing it. She should have remembered their closeness; 'great minds with but a single thought,' they sometimes said of each other.

'You will know here of your fine heritage, of the European trend for brilliant colour which pertained in the Glasgow School. Not for them the gentleness of the English water-colourists. There is room for both, but I know which *I* prefer.' His short, caught-in-the-throat laugh made the girls nudge each other with delight.

'Did you know we have our own Glasgow Girls?' His eyes were dancing. 'I see you are looking puzzled. Well, we have, the Mackintosh sisters! Surely it is rare to have three in one family studying together. And bearing the same name as the man who built this school, Charles Rennie Mackintosh! Ah, I see you looking around . . .' Anna bent her head.

'Oh goodness,' she whispered to her neighbour. 'I could kill him.'

Later, she said to Ritchie Laidlaw when they were having

6

coffee in the Regal cinema café: 'I was covered with blushes today.' She told him of the incident. 'Who told him of us?'

'Use your loaf.' He smiled at her, and her common sense almost left her. He was often in her thoughts, his teasing smile, his total lack of shyness, which let him say the most outrageous things, his black riotous curls, which only lay comparatively flat the day they were trimmed, the uniqueness of his talent. He was the school's shining star.

'Use my loaf?' she said. 'What a rude, common expression.'

'I am rude and common, didn't you know? I live in an old grey tenement near Hamilton where the tenants wouldn't know the difference between the Bauhaus and Barlinnie Prison, my father's on the dole, my mother takes in closes, but you wouldn't know what that means in Clevedon Crescent, Kelvinside.'

'Of course I do. I'm not daft.'

'Just overprivileged, poor soul.' His smile disarmed her. 'Half a crown a week they give her.'

'Well, there's nothing wrong with that. It's honest work.'

'She knows that. There's only one thing she's afraid of.'

'What's that?'

'Meeting you.'

'Oh no, Ritchie!' She stretched out her hand to him. 'I'd be proud to meet her, some day.'

'That's a promise.' He still held her hand. 'I tell her all about you, how . . . great you are, how beautiful.'

'Oh, shut up!' She took back her hand. 'So how did Mr Kleiber know of us? Was it Nancy?' Nancy's doll-like prettiness was a favourite amongst the staff.

'Not Nancy. He wouldn't be seen dead in her class.'

'Jean?' She was suddenly sure.

He nodded. 'They're alike. I've seen them talking in corridors. There's a . . . wildness – no, that's too much – a feeling they wouldn't bother about convention if it suited them.'

'What's his first name?' She knew he was right.

'Frederick. He's married. We call him Fred. He likes it. He's

7

happy-go-lucky, natural. You could imagine him in leather shorts and alpenhosen dancing in one of those beer cellars, slapping his knees.'

She laughed at him. 'He's married? Oh gosh. He's just the type who would attract Jean, strange . . .'

'Don't think of your sister.' He captured her hands again. 'Think of us. Are you nearer to loving me?'

'I might be.' She had to lower her eyes before the love in his. 'When will you know?'

'The first wet Sunday after the fair,' she teased, thinking: when I was doing my ironing in the kitchen yesterday the feeling came over me, and Bessie, who misses nothing, said, 'Have you got a pain?' The pain of love. His forefinger moved round and round in the palm of her hand. 'I have a class at two,' she said. When she stood up she felt her thighs moist.

Going down the Regal's regal staircase he said, 'I've tickets for a dance at the Union on Saturday. Coming?'

'Should I? That lounge, most of the lights off, and the long sofas.'

He laughed at her. 'You mean the sitooterie. Come on, you liked it!'

'What gave you that idea?'

'You told me.'

'I never said a word!'

'Your body told me.'

The pain was there again, that pleasurable, thrilling pain as they half ran down Sauchiehall Street and climbed the steep hill to the Art School.

TWO

ROSE MACKINTOSH LOVED her bridge afternoons. She felt she deserved them. When Angus had been making his way they had lived in a flat in Claremont Street and she had been busy with the children. There were only two years between the twins and Nancy. They had hoped for a boy, but when Nancy arrived, pretty as a doll and feminine from the moment she opened her eyes, Angus said, 'Three daughters will do me fine.' He had seen how trammelled she was with the little girls, getting them dressed, putting the three of them in the pram every day and trundling them over Sauchiehall Street, past Royal Crescent, and then into Kelvingrove Park to feed the ducks.

She was a conscientious mother, but not motherly. Angus came first with her. She was far too busy to gossip with her neighbours. Besides, she was from the *real* West End, and the Argyle Street end of Claremont Street was only on the fringe of it. She wouldn't be living there for ever. They planned happily in bed after their protective sex.

As it happened, events moved quickly. Angus was made a partner on the death of the founder of his firm. Rose's parents died within six months of each other, and as she was the only child she inherited their spacious house in Clevedon Crescent. Kelvinside was the only place people recognized as the *proper* West End. She had also inherited the property which her parents had owned all over the city, not alas so profitable now that the rights of the tenants were safeguarded at the expense of the owners, but it put jam on their bread. She had also inherited Bessie. And, regrettably, Tumshie.

Yes, she liked her bridge afternoons. A house such as this ought to give pleasure to others as well as the family who occupied it. The only friend who wasn't impressed was Grace Binnie, but then she lived in one of 'Greek' Thomson's terraces. Rose knew when she was beaten.

She and Grace won the first rubber comfortably. Bessie had wheeled in the trolley with its burden of rolled asparagus sandwiches – the secret was in the freshly baked loaf wrapped in a damp tea towel for half an hour – the home-made strawberry jam in its cut-glass dish for the buttered scones, the Dundee cake, rich with cherries, angelica and fruit (Sunmaid raisins were a must), the home-made meringues. Bessie was a dab hand at meringues, of a rich, pale coffee colour with cream to match. It was worth while putting up with that terrible Tumshie for the sake of those meringues.

'And how are the girls?' Nessie Muir trilled, adjusting her felt cloche. Hats at afternoon bridge parties were *de rigueur*. She made a point of enquiring about everyone's children because she had none of her own and didn't wish to appear envious. And she never took off her hat because she wore a wig. Grace had told Rose, swearing her to secrecy, how they had both come off at the same time at Una Simpson's – a cousin of the Simpson in Simpson, Hunter and Young – in the bedroom, fortunately. 'You can imagine the conster*nation*, Rose,' Grace had said, long-vowelled, chin pulled in.

Angus had suggested, when she told him of the incident, that perhaps alopecia and infertility were linked. She was prepared to bow to his superior knowledge in that department.

'Blooming, thank you, Nessie,' she said. 'They're doing very well at the Art School, Jean particularly. Nancy has a gift for watercolours, just like me.' She gave a little laugh to show it was a joke. 'I've never thought much of *my* endeavours.' She let her glance drift towards one of her best, which hung over the

10

china cabinet. 'Nor of watercolours *per se*, to tell you the truth.' As a young girl she had greatly admired Turner.

'Oh, I don't know.' Nessie, thus directed, looked critically at Rose's *tour de force*. 'Look at Sam Bough.'

'Ah, but he came from Carlisle,' Lily Cunningham pointed out. She was considered the most travelled of the four, making frequent sorties to England where she had a married sister.

'How about Anna?' Nessie still exuded warm interest and even enthusiasm. 'Still at the beaten brass?' Some said she wrote down every detail of her friends' children so that she could ask intelligent questions.

'Yes.' Rose sighed at having such gifted children. 'She brought home a photograph frame the other week for me. Beautifully tooled with a trailing design, icanthus, I think she said. It was my birthday. Don't ask me what age I was, girls. Life begins at forty!'

'So they tell us', 'I hope they're right', 'Downhill now all the way' – they all contributed with commiserating laughs.

'Have you got it handy?' Nessie asked, still sparkling, and anxious to use up the last of her sparkle.

'Yes, somewhere . . .' Rose looked vague, could see in her mind's eye the exact shelf in the spare room cupboard where it lay. 'I have to find a photograph to put into it, preferably one taken twenty years ago. Now who's for more tea? I insist on you sampling some of Bessie's meringues. We have another rubber to play, and Nessie and Lily have to get their revenge.'

'Have you got any of *Jean's* work?'

Nessie Muir is trying to get at me, Rose thought. It can't be just that she's jealous of the girls. Is it because she drew Lily Cunningham as her partner? Or is it the house? It's the way she looks round when she comes in. As if anybody minded her living in that flat in Byres Road, above a shop . . . She would have to be polite but firm.

'They're too big to move about and she leaves them in the Art School most of the time. Not that we haven't enough room

11

here, too much, I'm afraid,' she sighed. 'Of course, she gave up figurative painting long ago. You have to search for the meaning in them, she says. But, I'll give her her due,' Rose's long dormant painterly nous surfaced for a moment, 'she has a singing sense of colour.' Nessie's sparkle wavered and finally died. She took a bite out of her meringue. Rose saw her chest rise.

'Is she going *out* with anyone, though?' Really, this was not proving to be one of her best afternoons. Now it was Lily Cunningham, who had no time for painting, who said she preferred bare walls except in the case of her panelled dining room . . . now it was Rose's chest which rose.

'Too many, I'm afraid.' She glanced fleetingly at Grace to whom she had confided only last week her worries about Jean: 'There's a certain . . . lack of caution about her – do you know what I mean, Grace? – a lack of willingness to conform . . .'

'Not like Anna. She's more or less going steady, isn't she? I remember you saying –'

Grace took the matter in hand, wiping her lips delicately with her lace-trimmed napkin. 'Delicious meringue, Rose. Isn't she lucky, girls, to have a live-in maid?'

'I inherited her with the house.' Rose grasped the straw gratefully. 'Yes, I'm lucky. Although I sometimes wonder who *is* the mistress.'

'What does this boyfriend of Anna's do?' Lily was as persistent as Nessie. Were they *both* trying to annoy her?

'Do?' This was the sore point. She didn't want either of the twins to marry painters. Artists were a feckless lot. She should have thought of that when they first decided to send the three of them to the Art School. 'Talent should be fostered, Rose,' Angus had said. She didn't have to worry about Nancy. She was like her and would choose unerringly an architect like her father or a nice, safe businessman who would hang her watercolours in their pale-walled rooms and be proud of his artistic wife. 'He's a painter.' Come right out with it. 'Oils. He already gets commissions, Anna tells me, in London, no less.'

12

'Well, you certainly are an arty family,' Nessie said. Her tea, to which she had done full justice, two asparagus rolls, a meringue and the outside slice of the Dundee cake, must have softened her. 'And I expect Angus has to draw in his work, plans . . . and things.'

'Oh yes. Some of his drawings could be framed. In fact they are, in his office. That big assignment he has at the moment . . . well, I mustn't tell tales out of school. And I mustn't talk about *my* family all the time. Is Annie still in that office in Bothwell Street, Lily? Well, at least the hours are good. And girls get married anyhow . . . Have you all finished? No more tea? You're sure?' She rang the silver bell which Bessie had placed on the lace-covered tea trolley. She was a snob. She admitted it to herself, but if there was one thing she liked on her bridge afternoons, it was to ring the wee silver bell and have Bessie appear and the others pretending it was an everyday occurrence. The only thing which sometimes spoiled it was that Tumshie's face appearing round the door too, hoping to be invited in and purring like a steam engine.

'Shall we move back to the bridge table, girls, and let Bessie clear away the debris?' That was clever, 'debris'. 'You should have eaten more, you really should. Are you all slimming?' Her silk afternoon dress slid round her silk camiknickers as she rose.

THREE

THEY WERE HAVING their usual autumn holiday in Kilcreggan, a little resort on the Gare Loch. Father had bought Cowal View when he had been made a partner in Keppel and Armstrong, Architects.

It was a stone house, Firth of Clyde Gothic, with its church windows and doors painted white, its fretted iron balconies, its steep roof. Anna thought it looked like a prim woman with its neat apron of lawn running down the hillside. Generations of walkers had made a path cutting through the wood at the foot to reach the coast road more quickly, and many a steamer had been caught by using this route instead of the gritted side road which went downhill to the post office and the pier.

The pier was the hub of the village, stirred into activity by the arrival of the steamers from Gourock and Craigendoran, or as far away as Broomielaw, and this particular morning in August Anna stood on the wooden boards along with other intending passengers waiting for the steamer going to the Kyles of Bute. 'Is it a paddle or a turbine?' she heard a child ask of his mother.

Anna didn't care what it was. It was bringing Ritchie. He could only spare one day from his holiday job in a fruiterers in Hamilton – 'they give me their rotten fruit for still lives.' He didn't write love letters, rather vignettes of his days, a painter's description of what struck his eye as he went about his duties, the early morning stir of the fruit market, the piled-up crates of bananas, oranges, hairy coconuts, rosy apples. They generally ended with a terse, 'Remember, you're mine!'

'Mammy!' the little boy shouted, 'It's the *King Edward*!'

Along with the other people she strained her eyes to see the great turbine forging towards them. Only if you were a Glaswegian could you appreciate the sight. It spelled the freedom of the Firth, sunlight, bands playing, handkerchiefs waving, grey cottages nestling round piers, arrivals and departures.

He had told her to wear something distinctive, and her red and white striped cotton dress was partly covered by a white cardigan. Under her indispensable waterproof draped over her arm she had a securely wrapped brown paper parcel which contained Skipper's sardine sandwiches, ham sandwiches and two slabs of Dundee cake.

Bessie, temporarily installed in the Cowal View kitchen much against her own wishes – 'nae shoaps and nothin' but midges' – had grumbled, 'If he canna gie ye a fish tea on the boat like ony decent person, he's no' worth havin'.'

Bessie lived in a permanent bad temper when they were 'doon the watter', mostly caused by Tumshie who seemed to go mad with the foreign sounds and smells and had to be carefully watched in case she took to the woods and didn't come back. 'She's a town cat, not meant for open spaces. There's no sayin' what she'll meet.' Tumshie's reproductive system had been taken care of long ago. It was a question of her keeping bad company and unsettling her for the quieter and more refined pleasures of Clevedon Crescent.

The *King Edward* had edged sideways to the pier with a loud clanking of its bell. There was a respectful silence for the rope thrower, then the passengers were galvanized into action, nudging, pushing and shoving to get onto the gangway. Anna saw Ritchie instantly. He was clowning for her benefit, registering delighted surprise, clapping his hand to his forehead, pretending to swoon, jumping up and down, waving his arms. 'You're a

15

daft devil,' she said to him when she had gone up the gangway and been claimed at the top.

'Chance is a fine thing,' he said, leading her off towards the rail. 'What's in your parcel?' He had sharp eyes.

'Mind your own business.'

'You're my business. And my love.' They turned to look at each other. 'Imagine,' he said, 'a whole day of you. Will we get off at Rothesay and take the tram to Port Bannatyne?'

'I haven't brought my costume. No, I think we should sail round the Kyles. It's safer.'

'What do you mean, safer?'

She didn't answer him. She was enjoying the familiar sensations in her body. She hadn't thought she would reach this stage of loving so soon, her heart beating faster, her knees trembling, the heightened appreciation of everything round her, the blueness of the water, the whiteness of the gulls wheeling overhead, the bright colours of the passengers' clothes.

'How do you like your job?' She tried to be matter-of-fact.

'It's labouring, that's all, sacks of spuds and crates of fruit. But the smells are better than in the meat market. It's useful to see what some folk have to do for a living. Soul-destroying.'

'Yes, we're lucky. We've been doing a bit of sketching. Nancy is the only one who turns out any sort of picture. Pretty colours.'

'But she has a black and white mind.'

'You wouldn't suit her, I can tell you that.'

'But I suit *you*. At least our minds do. We've still to find out about our bodies.' She met his eyes and he bent and kissed her lightly on the nose. 'Not much of a kiss,' he said. 'Passion is for darkness.'

'Mother would think kissing in public was common.'

'Your mother thinks you've chosen wrongly, but a banker with a cash till for a mind would be terrible for you. You'd spend your entire life not understanding each other.'

'Painters haven't a monopoly on creativity.' She was pleased with that. Sometimes he was too sure. If they were married she

16

would have to point that out to him. Love didn't mean you had to lose your critical faculty.

The band was playing, a concertina, a fiddle and a tinny piano. It was a seaside kind of day, of soft breezes and sunlight. The gulls were trailing the boat, greedy, raucous, beating white wings. She heard laughter in the voices around her, and the occasional long, low boom from the funnel as the captain on the bridge warned a yacht or a rowing boat that might cross their path.

'Are we going in at Hunter's Quay?' she asked him. 'I love watching the palaver at the piers. It never palls.' They laughed, saying together, 'Alliteration.'

'Aren't you having a holiday this year, Ritchie?'

'No.' He looked away at the Cowal shore.

'Why?'

'That's the kind of question someone asks who lives in the West End.'

'Sorry. I didn't think.'

'It's mean to tick you off. My father's been laid off again. He's a throwout from the Industrial Revolution, a last pathetic remnant, and he's not aggressive enough to find anything else.'

'That's sad.'

'You can imagine how guilty it makes me feel when I'm able-bodied enough to get work but choose to paint instead. My mother understands. She's clever. Completely uneducated. She left school at thirteen, was a skivvy in a big house when she met my father. I think he must have stuck to her like a limpet. I know he sometimes makes her mad. I see her frustration, but they never row, at least, not when I'm there. She has dignity.'

'I'd like to meet her.'

'I told you she was scared, but I'll sound her out. You'd have a lot in common. She buys scraps of velvet in Paddy's Market and paints roses on them with paint from any of my squeezed-out tubes I leave lying about, makes them into cushions and sells them. God knows where. When she hasn't even that she

17

varnishes pieces of wood and makes designs on them with a red-hot poker; sticks on a calendar, or writes some rubbish on them, "Ne'er cast a cloot till May be oot." It would wring tears from a dead donkey.'

She looked away from his eyes. 'You'll be able to make it up to her,' she said.

'That's what's spurring me on. You first, then Ma. I don't want her to die before I give her a fur coat.'

'We're not going into Hunter's Quay after all,' she said.

'It will be Kirn, then Dunoon. Hey!' His face lit up. 'There's dancing! Come on!'

The band had thrown themselves into a potpourri of Viennese waltzes, and they ran hand in hand to where some people had made a large circle round the musicians.

'Leave your coat here,' Ritchie said, pointing to an empty place on a bench. 'We'll keep an eye on it.' She covered the parcel with her coat. It was becoming an embarrassment.

'They've killed Dollfuss,' Ritchie said, when they were dancing. 'Now that man will have a free hand.'

'Hitler?'

'Right. By God, if he stops me from painting I'll kill him!'

'Don't start feeling bitter already.'

'Anyone who uses their head nowadays is bound to feel bitter. We had a talk with Mr Kleiber in the Life Class the other day. He asked how many of us thought we would be conscientious objectors if a war came.'

'What did you say?'

'I said I wouldn't. I feel rage.'

'What did he say?'

'Not much, but he's bitter all right. I hadn't realized how much. He makes us laugh a lot but when he isn't laughing there's bitterness in his eyes. "I shouldn't be here," he said. "I should already be fighting by any means in my power. I tell you, young gentlemen, do not give hostages to fortune."' He whirled her round with a strong arm. 'I saw him today.'

'Mr Kleiber?'

'I wondered whether to tell you.'

'Tell me.' She felt her heart squeeze, she even imagined a little cold wind had sprung up.

'I had to deliver a parcel to the main shop – they're at the foot of Renfield Street, and I thought I'd cut through the Central Station. I saw Jean.'

She'd known it. 'Go on.'

'She was looking around. I was going to go up and say hello, then I saw her face change. She took a few steps forward . . .'

'Kleiber?'

'Right. Our Fred. How did you know?'

'I just know. I didn't think. She said she was spending the day in Glasgow with a schoolfriend, even gave her a name, Margaret somebody. Did you speak to them?'

'No . . .' He hesitated. 'It would have taken a brave man. They were just standing, looking at each other, not touching, not speaking. I passed by them. Quite close. They didn't see me.'

'Who the hell d'ye think ye're bumpin'?' a man in a cloth cap said.

'Sorry.' Ritchie looked round. It had been Anna's fault. Her feet had stumbled. 'You're upset,' he said. 'Let's go down for lunch.'

'All right.' They stopped dancing, and made their way through the crowd who were watching. When she went to get her coat she threw the parcel overboard. The gulls would have a fine time with Bessie's sardine sandwiches.

'It's a shame you spending all this money.' They were eating their haddock and chips, drinking their orange-coloured tea, rich and strong. She needed it.

'Mother gave me the money. "Don't be mealy-mouthed," she said, so I took it. She'll get a great deal of second-hand pleasure knowing we're having lunch on the *King Edward*. You're not eating yours. Is it Jean?'

19

'Yes. He's married.'

'Three children. She's daft.'

'Daft's normal for Jean.'

The *King Edward* sailed majestically up the Kyles of Bute, turned tail and came back on the other side to show its versatility. There was some rockiness going round Toward Point, but no day's sail was complete without it. Anna forgot Jean for a time. She and Ritchie were in that enclosed land of lovers, talking obsessively one minute, falling into abrupt tender silences the next.

'Here's something to cheer you up,' Ritchie said. 'I've been chosen by the school for a fellowship.'

'Oh, Ritchie!' She turned to him. 'You should have told me earlier.'

'You were too worried about Jean. There's a grant, and possibilities of shows in Glasgow and London.'

'It's great news. I'm really glad.'

'The Director says if I don't make a fool of myself he thinks there's an exciting future ahead of me. I can't tell you what else. I'd blush.'

She kissed him, her arms round his neck, not minding the other people near them.

The chill wind of early evening had sprung up. The band had stopped playing and were sitting in a huddle with their jacket collars up to their ears, cigarettes in their mouths. The passengers were quieter. Now they were in the Firth again and steaming towards Dunoon. She would soon be home at Cowal View and she wouldn't see Ritchie until they were back at the Art School for the winter term.

She walked down the gangway at the Kilcreggan Pier and turned to wave to him. He had put on a jersey over his white shirt now. Under his arm was a box of chocolates they had bought for his mother. It would be dark and cold when he got to the Broomielaw.

20

Angus was waiting for her with the car. 'Hop in,' he said. He looked handsome and youthful with his striped silk university scarf tucked in the open neck of his shirt.

'You shouldn't have bothered, Father.'

'Why shouldn't I bother? I was glad to get away from the Lumsdens.' These were her mother's friends.

'Is Jean back?'

'No, she's coming across by the ferry. I told her just to get a taxi. You know what school chums are like when they get together.'

She looked at him. He seemed hardly old enough to have three grown-up daughters.

'Did you have a good day?' he asked.

'Great!' she said. 'Just great.'

She didn't challenge Jean that night. She lay sleepless in her bed while Jean apparently slept peacefully in the other. Yes, she'd had a fine time with Margaret. Margaret was a scream. She seemed to lie with consummate ease.

The opportunity would come, Anna told herself. She would watch and wait. But the real reason was that she was afraid . . .

FOUR

GLASGOW HAD RECOVERED from its sortie 'doon the watter', nights were longer, as were cinema queues, the girls were back at the Art School and the University Union hops had started again. It was Saturday evening and Rose had suggested that Ritchie should call at the house for Anna. 'She wants to play her Lady Clevedon role with him,' Jean had said.

'Did Ritchie *want* to call for you?' They were both in the bathroom where the light was better. Anna was titivating herself at the mirror and Jean was sitting on the mahogany lavatory seat rubbing at her newly washed hair. It fell about her face in a black mass as she emerged from the towel.

'He doesn't mind being patronized. He has a strong sense of his own worth.'

'Anyone who paints like Ritchie Laidlaw is bound to have a strong sense of his own worth. Annan's has got one of his in their window.'

'I know.'

Jean was nonchalant. 'I was speaking to Mr Kleiber the other day and he said Ritchie and I have something in common.'

Anna's anger flared. *Mr* Kleiber! She thought she was clever. 'You seem to have a lot in common with *Mr* Kleiber.'

'Who wouldn't?' Oh, the coolness of it! 'He's so interesting. He was saying we don't know how lucky we are here, whereas all the brilliant people he knows in Vienna had to give up their jobs. Jews. Thomas Mann's books were actually burned, and then there was the composer Schoenberg . . . remember we

22

went to St Andrews Hall and some of his stuff was being played? Marvellous!'

'And Father said he'd rather have a ceilidh. But we're all ignoramuses in reeky old Glasgow.' She saw Jean's eyes flash.

'You're trying to get at me. I know you. But you're not interested in anything that matters. I know why.'

'Tell me, then.'

'Your mind's full of Ritchie Laidlaw and nothing else.'

'Is that so? At least he isn't married, like *Mr* Kleiber!'

Jean stared at her. She read Anna's eyes, the suspicion in them.

Anna stared her out, thinking, she's going to attack me, claw my eyes out.

'You bitch, Anna!' Jean suddenly shouted. 'You horrible bitch!' She dashed out of the bathroom, banging the door behind her.

That got her dander up, Anna thought wryly.

'And where *exactly* do you live, Mr Laidlaw?' Rose said. They were all sitting in the upstairs drawing room, which was considered by Mother to be one of the assets of living in Clevedon Crescent. She had offered coffee, but he had refused it. Angus had suggested a dram, which Ritchie had agreed to with more enthusiasm. It wasn't a good start, Anna had thought.

'It's difficult to say *exactly*, Mrs Mackintosh,' he said, straight-faced. 'It's on the main road between Glasgow and Hamilton. I don't think it has a name like Kelvinside, or Hyndland, just *between*. It's a grey stone tenement above Brechins, the butchers. They make great sausages.' She would kill him when they got out of here, wring his neck . . .

'I only like Coopers',' Rose said. 'They're all beef, absolutely no bread, that's the point. I get them in their Great Western Road shop. Of course, it isn't exactly handy, but Mr Mackintosh will run me down, if necessary, and they deliver. Twice per week.'

'Is that one of Nancy's watercolours?' Ritchie asked, dismissing Coopers' sausages which were all beef and absolutely no bread.

'No, it's my effort, I'm afraid.' She giggled girlishly. 'Maybe one of my best. What do you say, dear?' She looked at her husband. 'Dear' was used in company when she didn't want to be too familiar by saying 'Angus'. It was a smile of love, nevertheless. It never failed to surprise Anna that Rose, who could irritate her beyond measure at times, so obviously adored Father and was adored by him. He was completely uncritical of her. Anna herself wasn't like that. She could see faults in Ritchie while loving him. He was egotistical. He was sometimes rude. He was playful when she would have liked him to be intense. He was sure of himself. His painting reflected his sureness.

Jean came into the room. She was wearing a scarlet dress with a wide Milanese collar, which she must have tacked on. She never left dresses as they were. She wore black patent leather shoes with stubby toes, and a broad black patent leather belt pulled through a fretted silver buckle which matched her long earrings. She was pale, haughty. There was no sign of tears.

'Ready for your date, Jean?' Ritchie said.

'Why should I have a date?' She looked at him coolly.

'Well, you're all dolled up and ready to go.'

'It's in your honour.'

'I'm flattered. I can hardly take my eyes off you.'

'Just as well Anna's dragging you off to the Union –'

'I remember those dances,' Angus interrupted. 'So do you, Rose.' They exchanged glances. She looked young and rose-like.

'Yes,' she sighed. 'Mind you, my mother insisted on me being back by ten thirty at the latest.'

'I hope you don't say the same to Anna,' Ritchie smiled at her. Anna saw her mother melt.

'As long as my girls behave themselves, that's all I ask. My husband and I move with the times, although it might be difficult for you young people to believe. We were both at the Art School, Mr Laidlaw. My mother and father knew Mr Burrell, the shipowner, and that may have given them the idea.'

Angus nodded. 'Glasgow was a prosperous city in our young days. There was a great call for design for the buildings that were going up, and their interiors. Architecture was left to the men.'

'We'd some really interesting people at the school,' Rose said. 'I was hobnobbing with a coterie of gifted women, many of them sisters, some with their own studios. I didn't know the Macdonalds – Margaret married Charles Rennie Mackintosh. Oh, those women *made* Glasgow with their style, the Willow Tearooms, Miss Cranston's, Miss Buick's – it was all so elegant, the Glasgow Style, so different, strange . . . like an Arabian Night's dream.'

'You've got it too,' Ritchie smiled at Jean. She looked sad, Anna thought, yet exotic, beautiful with the bold eyebrows and dark eyes, that mass of hair . . .

'At least we've got a clock in the Glasgow Style,' her father was saying. 'Margaret Gilmour did it, another of those talented ladies.'

'I'll show it to you on the way out,' Anna said. 'It's time we . . .' Then the idea struck her. 'Why don't you come with us, Jean?'

'That's a great idea. Come on, Jean.' Ritchie seemed to approve.

'No, thanks.'

Rose sighed loudly, but didn't say anything. Angus got up and stared out at the Crescent pavement, the stone flags shining in the rain. The light from the wrought-iron lamppost on the stone wall (one of the many distinctive features according to Mother) was reflected in the flags, making them look like smooth slabs of coal. There was silence.

'You're welcome to come, Jean,' Anna said. 'Father and Mother are going out, aren't you?'

25

Angus turned from the window. 'Yes, to the Armstrongs'. A duty visit.' He said to Ritchie, 'My partner.'

'We'd better get off, then,' Ritchie said, getting up. 'Get your coats, girls.'

Jean's eyes were cold. 'I never said I was going.'

'You'll break my heart if you don't come.' His smile was beguiling. 'And there's a good band booked.'

She capitulated suddenly. 'If you can put up with me.' The shadow hadn't left her eyes.

'What do you say if we walk the whole way?' Ritchie said when the three of them were hurrying down Great Western Road with its sweeping terraces.

'Will you listen to the meanness of the man, Jean?' Anna laughed. 'We've our dancing shoes on!'

'Okay, I give in. Here's a tram.' It had come swinging along the tramway tracks behind them like a brightly coloured galleon, stopping beside them with a double 'dunt' of the driver's foot on the brake. They jumped on and clattered upstairs. Anna sat in a seat behind Jean and Ritchie.

'That was a piece of luck.' She leaned forward between them, her elbows on the polished wooden backs. 'We'll take the white car at Charing Cross to the University. It'll save our legs.'

'Does she always boss you like this?' Jean said. He leaned back so that his cheek brushed Anna's.

'I love it. I'm putty in her hands.'

Anna laughed and looked out of the window. Great Western Road bordered by its terraces, the busy hub round the Botanic Gardens gate, Byres Road, a tributary shop-lit in the darkness, then over the bridge at the Boys' Academy, then St George's Cross, a crossing place of tramway lines. Now they were clanking along St George's Road, here they were at Charing Cross with that imposing red sandstone cliff of tenements like a French château complete with mansards and towers. 'Here we are!' she said and they got up.

They clattered downstairs again, laughing, talking, falling

against each other. Trams always made you feel good. Perhaps it was their unsteadiness, the feeling of riding rather than merely travelling, of danger where there was none.

Jean was snatched away from them almost immediately they went into the hall by a tall young man with smooth dark hair, a smooth, slightly red face, even a smooth smile. One of us, Anna thought, noticing his good manners, his good suit, his Glenalmond tie. I'm class-ridden, yet how can I be when I've chosen Ritchie?

They danced together, closely, exclusively. No one would have dared to butt in. They were 'going together', they were sacrosanct.

'I'm glad we brought her,' Anna said as Jean danced past with the stranger. 'I'm worried stiff since you told me about seeing her with Kleiber. She flew at me this evening when I mentioned him. Do you think there's anything in it, Ritchie?'

'Come into the sitooterie with me and we'll discuss it.'

'You're thinking of those six-foot sofas, not Jean. No thanks. I must keep an eye on her.'

I'm so lucky, she thought, compared with Jean. There would be nothing in her friendship, or whatever it was with Mr Kleiber, but sorrow. She thought of the copy of one of Frances Macdonald's paintings which Ritchie had given her, an elongated, sad-faced woman with her long blonde hair in a horizontal line from her head. Strangeness, poignancy. Like Jean, except for the colour of the hair. And there had been another one which he'd told her about – *'Tis a Long Path which Wanders to Desire*.

'What are you thinking about?' he asked her. They were dancing a quick foxtrot. He was a *gallus* dancer, Palais style, good.

'Painting. The Glasgow Girls.'

'I'll educate you yet.' He showed off with a few little running steps, *very* Dennistoun Palais.

At eleven o'clock Anna looked for Jean. She was still with

the same young man, and when they danced past her she called out, 'Jean, it's getting late. We'd better make tracks.'

'All right.' She seemed more cheerful. The four of them stopped dancing and walked to the side of the dance floor. Jean introduced her companion. 'Robin Naismith. My sister Anna. Her friend Ritchie Laidlaw.'

'Are you at the University?' Ritchie asked him.

'Yes. Engineering. Look, I have my father's car. I could easily run you home.'

'Isn't it out of your way?' Anna asked.

'Anything's out of my way if you don't live in Kilmacolm. It's no bother, really.'

'Okay,' Ritchie said. 'We'll drop off the girls in the West End, and then if you can run me to the bus station it would be a great help. I'm on the north-east side.'

'Right.'

In the cloakroom Anna said, 'Well, you didn't have to wait long for a partner. Is he nice?'

She shrugged. 'Rich. His father's in shipping. Quite simple under the smart exterior.'

'Don't be so critical.'

'He hasn't half the strength of character Ritchie has. You knew what you were doing.'

'It's not all roses. He wouldn't be Mother's choice. But keep your hands off him. He's mine.'

At the entrance they found Robin Naismith and Ritchie sitting talking in a sleek, olive-green car. Ritchie jumped out.

'You go in the front, Jean. I'll go in the back with Anna.'

'You could have stayed where you were,' Anna said when they were together.

'And miss a chance like this?' He put an arm round her. 'Home, James!' he called out to Robin. 'And don't spare the horses!'

'Your wish is my command, sir.' Something in his voice, a slight slurring, made Anna wonder if he had been drinking.

Even if there were no licence at the Union he could have had a flask with him. She, Jean and Nancy had been at a birthday dance recently, and their host had put a liberal tot of whisky in their cups of coffee. 'Irish coffee,' he had said. 'Sorry, no cream.' He'd been known for being fast.

But Robin drove well, chatting amiably as he did so, telling them how he'd been bored and had decided to drop in at the Union. 'Best thing I ever did, I tell you, Anna, your sister is in a class of her own.'

'Great.' Ritchie was kissing her, stopping any further conversation.

Robin was singing as he drove: '"'Twas on the Isle of Capri that I found her."' Jean was quiet. '"'Neath the shade of the . . ."' The car slid sideways as he suddenly swerved. 'God! A cat!' Immediately there was a sickening crash, Anna felt her head thrown backwards violently, then forwards. A few feet in front of them there was a buckled lamppost. She heard Ritchie's voice in her ear: 'Anna, Anna! Are you all right?'

'Yes.' She blew out her breath. 'Gosh! This is terrible! What about you?'

'Okay. Robin?' He had his hand on Robin's shoulder. Jean was whimpering softly beside him.

'She's hurt! Get out, Ritchie! See to Robin! I think he's fainted.' His head was slumped on the driving wheel.

A small crowd had gathered. Surprising, Anna thought, at this time of night. She opened Jean's door, at the same time picking out a man from the crowd. 'Could you phone for an ambulance, please?' she called. He nodded. The crowd pressed closer, unwilling to miss a thing.

'What is it you've hurt, Jean?' She bent over her. She looked deathly pale but there was no sign of blood.

'My shoulder . . . it's broken or something. Sore enough.' And as Anna bent further, 'Don't touch it!'

'Oh, I hope it isn't broken. Sit still. I've asked a man to phone for an ambulance.' She watched Ritchie lift Robin Naismith's

29

head gently from the steering wheel and lay him back on the seat.

'I think he's concussed,' Jean said. She had turned to look, her face screwed up with pain. 'What a thing to happen! It wasn't his fault.'

'Don't move. Ritchie will see to him.'

'It wasn't his fault.' She didn't move her head. 'It must have been that black cat. I saw a black shadow streaking across the road in front of us. Robin braked. Nobody wants to run over a cat. But why people don't keep them in . . .' Her voice trailed away.

Anna saw that Ritchie was slapping Robin's face gently. 'Robin! Wake up. You're all right. Open your eyes.' At first there was no response then his eyelids flickered, he groaned, moved his head, and slowly opened his eyes. Thank God he isn't dead, she thought.

'What happened?' His voice sounded fairly normal, but his eyes were unfocused.

'A cat ran in front of you,' she said. 'Does anything hurt?'

'Just my head. Splitting headache. Seeing stars . . .'

'There's a large bruise where you bumped it on the wheel. You're sure nothing else hurts?'

'Don't think so. Concussed, maybe. Once, at Rugby . . .' He muttered, then fell silent. Ritchie looked at Anna.

'There's a man phoning for an ambulance.'

Someone in the crowd said, 'A telt him to dial 999. It's as easy as winkie. We once had a fire . . . See, the organization in they places . . .'

Ritchie said to Jean, 'Are you bearing up? It won't be long.' She was weeping a little, probably with pain. She was usually stoical.

'Are you and Anna all right? I didn't ask.'

'We're fine,' Anna said. 'Don't worry about a thing.' She saw the little crowd of spectators move, heard the squeal of brakes. 'Oh, thank goodness, here's the ambulance. And a policeman as well.' A figure in blue had materialized, pushing his way through the knot of people. 'Here's the polis,' she heard someone say.

'Away to your beds!' He scattered the onlookers. 'What happened?' He spoke to Ritchie. Robin answered him.

'Trying to avoid a cat, officer.' His eyes closed again. 'Sick-making, that.' He kept them closed. 'If I hadn't swerved . . .'

'The road was slippy with rain,' Ritchie said. 'But quiet. There was no other vehicle involved.'

'No other vehicle involved,' the policeman repeated, writing in his notebook. 'Aye, it's easy done. You should never swerve to avoid animals, though a wouldny like to run over a moggie myself. Here they are.'

The ambulance men were suddenly there.

'Stretcher cases?' one of them said, and to Jean, 'Can you walk, hen?'

'If you don't come near my shoulder.'

'Let your friend help you.' He looked at Anna. 'We'll see to the driver.' And to Ritchie. 'You two will be going with the injured parties?'

'Yes,' Anna said. 'I'm her sister.'

'What about the car?' This was Ritchie.

'It'll be towed in or driven. Just give me your names and addresses. I can let your folks know.'

'Do you remember your address, Robin?' Ritchie bent over him.

'Oak House, Kilmacolm. Simple.' He smiled faintly.

'Could you get at his licence?' the policeman asked Ritchie.

'Sure. Licence, Robin?' He pointed to an inner breast pocket. Ritchie got it out and handed it to the policeman who flicked through it.

'All present and correct.'

The ambulance men looked restive. 'We'll take the driver on the stretcher. He looks as if he needs it. How about you, Miss . . . ?'

'Jean Mackintosh.' Anna replied for her. 'We'll help her in, but do you think we could phone home and tell our parents? My father could pick us up from the infirmary if she isn't kept in.'

'You can phone from there. In you go with her. In you go too, sir,' he motioned to Ritchie, 'and keep her company.'

The crowd had melted away. The show was over.

In the ambulance, sitting at the end of the stretcher where Robin lay, Jean resting on the other side, Anna looked at Ritchie. 'My mother will have a fit.'

'It'll be the talking point of her bridge afternoons.'

'You bet,' Jean said.

FIVE

IT WAS THE WEEK before Christmas. The girls were on holiday from the Art School. Since the accident Jean had been unusually quiet, sitting on the window seat reading most of the day. Her face was drawn and pale. The ligaments were taking a long time to heal. Robin Naismith, who had made a quick recovery, often came from Kilmacolm to visit her, bringing gifts of flowers, fruit, chocolates and books.

Rose welcomed him with undiluted pleasure. 'His father is a well-known figure in shipping, Jean, and he's such a nice, well-brought-up boy.'

'Would you say that if we'd all been killed?' Jean had glanced up from her book.

'Really! It was that cat. People are so careless.'

Bessie, who had been clearing the table had bridled, saying that her Tumshie was never allowed outside.

They were visiting Great-aunt Jessie at Kirkcudbright for Christmas. Bessie's friend Mary Pollock would keep her company at Clevedon Crescent. 'A change of air will do us all good,' Rose had decided, 'and you girls might get some sketching done. Those old painted houses in Main Street make good subjects.'

It was a crisp winter's day when they set off in the roomy Vauxhall, the three girls in the back, Angus and Rose in the front. Rose was in her Otterburn tweed suit and nutria fur jacket, the girls wore jerseys and kilts, their camelhair coats laid carefully in the boot. As they sped along, Rose said, 'It will do you good, the change, Jean. And we'll take Great-aunt to the Murray Arms for Christmas dinner. She'll enjoy that, and it will save her doing any cooking.'

Anna, looking at the winter hardness of the Tinto hills, could only think of how much she was missing Ritchie. Once she had thought of these expeditions with pleasure, the drive through the hilly country, the stop at Lockerbie for lunch, tea at Dumfries, then veering off to the green low-lying Rhins of Galloway, painting country.

'Do you remember we all went to Portpatrick Hotel for your sixteenth birthday, twins?' Angus said. 'Nice hotel, that. Dramatic situation on the cliffs. We might pay it another visit.'

'I remember the dinner dances,' Nancy said. 'You danced with each of us in turn because there were hardly any men, only old codgers.'

Anna said softly to Jean, 'Do you remember what we wore?'

'Green. Chartreuse, she called it. Reminded you of sick. Our first long ones.'

'Strapped silver shoes and shingled hair. What sights we must have looked!'

'But the cliff walks. And the sunsets.' She said under her breath, 'I could die, die . . .' Anna looked quickly at her, saw the anguish. Her own heart hurt.

'Is it your shoulder?'

'No. If it were only my shoulder . . .'

'Lockerbie,' Nancy sang out. 'Overdone roast beef, gooey gravy and watery cauliflower.'

'Their apple tart's good.' Angus was a connoisseur of apple tarts in the many restaurants where he had wined and dined his brood.

Great-aunt Jessie was a very good seventy, inasmuch as her hair was untouched with grey. Her hairdresser probably used henna on it. She wore it marcelled in a low chignon set off by a variety of earrings from pearly studs to swinging jade ones. She favoured Jean's style of dressing, if anything more eccentric, and her narrow barred shoes were made to order from a Sauchiehall Street shop that kept a record of her last. Jean was her favourite amongst the girls, perhaps because she recognized a fellow spirit.

'What's this lovely lass been doing to herself?' She embraced Jean first. 'Your eyes are falling out of your head.' Anna thought so too, but Jean had shut up like a clam since their quarrel in the bathroom. That had been a mistake, she recognized now. Jean was as proud as Lucifer.

'A very nice young man was driving them home,' Rose said. 'It wasn't his fault. A cat ran in front of them. He was concussed, poor soul. His father's in shipping too.'

'Should that have saved them?' Aunt Jessie caught Anna's eye. They shared a sense of humour. 'And your poor shoulder, Jean. Well, come in and make yourselves comfortable. It's good of you to drive such a long way.'

'We shan't be a nuisance, Aunt,' Rose said, laying her nutria jacket carefully over the back of the sofa. 'Angus has booked us in at the Murray Arms and you'll join us for Christmas dinner.'

'That's kind of you, Angus.' She smiled at him. 'As long as I have my wee pills with me I'll be as right as rain. My,' she said, looking around, 'you have a fine family of girls. It's going to cost you a fortune, all the same, to get them married off.'

'It will be worth every penny to get rid of them.' He laughed, at ease. 'Now, this is a nice cottagey place after Clevedon Crescent. It reminds me of my home in Ullapool.'

'You never go back?'

'Not since my parents died, and my brother, Calum, went off to Canada. I miss those grand mountains.'

'Roots have a pull. Mine are here now. I never liked Glasgow the way you do, Rose. This is the right size, and there's a painting coterie to hobnob with.'

35

'Aye, you're well settled, Jessie.' He stretched his legs to the fire. His face was wistful.

Anna had begun by feeling desolated at the thought of not seeing Ritchie at Christmas, but she also found herself settling in. The pace was slower. Sometimes they lunched at the hotel, sometimes they had car runs in the surrounding countryside, which was gentle, restful, and even the hoar frost which rimmed the hedgerows had a clean smell.

Jean was quiet, her eyes often unfocused as the others chattered. Once, when they visited Sweetheart Abbey where Lady Devorgilla was buried, she surprised Anna by saying, 'Would you go to that length? Have your husband's heart buried with you?'

She shook the question away. 'I don't think of death.'

'You're lucky. I do. I feel tragedy all round me . . . like a great black bird.'

'Oh, Jean!' She tried to lighten her mood. 'That's a bit far-fetched.'

'Is it? You haven't grown up, then. You think your life with Ritchie is going to be one long dream of delight.'

'No, I don't! But I'm practical, not pessimistic.'

'I'm in the depths of despair.' Her voice was flat. 'I wish I could die.'

Anna became exasperated. 'You're always talking like that. If it's because of Mr Kleiber you should put him out of your head. He's married. You know there's nothing in it for you but unhappiness.'

'You don't understand! It's useless talking to you!' She looked around, as if desperate. Angus was plodding up the hill ahead of them. She called out, starting to run, 'Father! Wait for me!'

Anna watched her stumbling over the rough grass. Her heart beat uncomfortably.

They called a kind of truce. Anna buttoned up her lip, as Bessie would have called it, and Jean's pallor was put down to the fact that she was still suffering pain from her dislocated shoulder. It was probably true.

A few days later the two of them were having tea in Great-aunt Jessie's cosy sitting room with her. Anna liked it, with its view of the back garden sloping down to the river, the spars of the fishing boats showing above the wall.

'I'm surprised you never married, Great-aunt,' she said, 'a beauty like you. Oh, I'm sorry! How clumsy of me.' She remembered their mother telling them about Aunt Jessie losing her fiancé in the war, presumably the Boer War.

'It doesn't hurt now. Jamie and I were like you and this young man you've been telling me about, young, artless, thinking everything would go on the same as ever. He volunteered. Men! He was a good painter. He threw away that too.' She shrugged. The lamp gave a red gleam to her smooth hair, her jade earrings swung. 'But I found the Lady Artists Society, and that compensated. My talent was for watercolours. I haven't your gift, Jean.'

'I can't even paint. This arm –'

'It'll heal. Be patient. It meant a lot to me, the companionship of other women with the same interests. My mother thought they were a bit fast.' She laughed. 'So they were. We had life classes, but I told her the models were draped. You get good at telling lies when you have to.'

Anna met Jean's eyes. Jean turned away as if her sister might see something in them. Their aunt was still speaking.

'Anyhow, they taught me independence. My parents gradually got used to me staying overnight there from time to time.'

'You found out that it was stupid to bow to convention?' Jean looked at her.

'I suppose that's it. I became my own woman, I met interesting people like Jessie King, Anne MacBeth, the Macdonald sisters, all that crowd . . . the Glasgow Girls. They were bristling with talent and gaiety.'

Anna said, in spite of her resolve to keep quiet, 'Mr Kleiber, a lecturer at the school, called *us* that. "We have our own Glasgow Girls," he said.'

'Good. Kleiber? That's not a Scottish name?'

'No, he's Viennese, married. Isn't he, Jean?' She looked at her.

'You know very well he is.' She looked back at Anna with dark eyes, then turned to their aunt. 'Did you ever . . . throw convention to the winds when you were with the Lady Artists?'

'My, that's straight from the shoulder, Jean.' She nodded. 'I suppose I did, in a way.'

'You mean you threw your cap over the windmill?'

'I never said I did.'

'*If* you did, would that include married men?'

'Is this the Inquisition, Jean?' She shrugged. 'Painters are often married.'

'Did you ever say to yourself: "This man attracts me, but he belongs to someone else and I mustn't think of him"?'

'Don't answer her, Great-aunt. She's being cheeky,' Anna said.

'No, she isn't, and so I'll tell her. There was a married man, not long after Jamie was killed. I suddenly wept one evening when I was with him – grief is no respecter of time or place – and he comforted me, and . . . I forgot about Jamie.'

'Did you . . . ?' Jean was bending forward. Her eyes were brilliant.

'No, I didn't. My upbringing stopped me and I'm going to die a virgin. I bilked at the critical moment, I who was going to experience everything. Maybe that's why I never amounted to much as a painter. My work lacked passion, and eroticism, and you'll get plenty of passion and eroticism in the Glasgow Girls' work behind the stylization. Good gracious me!' she said. 'I've got a load off my chest and no mistake. More tea?' She lifted the teapot.

Jean got up. She looked distrait, shaken. She ran a hand over her hair. 'It's suffocating in here. I've got to get out.' She looked around, white-faced. 'Got to get some air.'

'It's nearly dark, lass.' There was concern in Jessie Craig's voice.

'It doesn't matter. I have to get out. Excuse me.' She seemed to stagger as she made for the door. She wrenched it open and shut it behind her.

'I think I'll go after her.' Anna was on her feet.

'No, leave her. She's a troubled girl. It's a man, isn't it?'

'What do *you* think?'

'Could it be this Mr Kleiber? I thought she changed colour when he was mentioned.'

'I was crazy to bring his name up. I'll go and find her all the same.'

'Maybe you should.' She saw her great-aunt lean back in her chair.

'All those questions. You're upset. Is it your angina?'

'It's nothing. Away you go and take care of your sister.'

She found Jean at the harbour. There were some fishermen getting their boats ready and she was standing looking down at them working on the decks, in the yellow light of lanterns at their feet and hung on the masts. She was very still. Anna went up and stood beside her. 'I shouldn't have mentioned Mr Kleiber.'

'Frederick Kleiber.' Her voice was flat. 'I shouldn't have quizzed Great-aunt. It doesn't matter.' They looked down at the men, busy, chatting as they worked. Did they have hidden lives, or was it all plain sailing?

Anna said, 'They're mending their nets for tomorrow.'

'Yes.'

'Father is due to pick us up at five o'clock, Jean. It's that now.'

'Is it?' She turned slowly, and their eyes met. Jean's were filled with pain.

'Is your shoulder bad?'

'That . . .'

'Come on, then.' The Jean she knew wasn't there. She was more like one of those sad women in a Macdonald watercolour. 'They called Kircudbright the little town of Never Weary,' she said.

They walked together, not speaking.

SIX

1935

ANNA WAS HAMMERING busily at a brass plaque in the school workroom when Frederick Kleiber stopped beside her.

'I like it,' he said. 'I see you have gone back to Nature. It always pays.' She was pleased, embarrassed, and rushed into speech to cover it.

'I made some drawings when I was on holiday recently, sea shapes and land shapes, rocks and winter vegetation.'

'I see you have been trying to look beneath the surface.' He lifted her sketchbook, which was lying on the seat beside her. 'Sensitive. Winter reveals, sun obliterates. The Scottish dark days can be useful.' His charming short laugh made her look up at him. He had good features, they had a boldness of contour, but his attraction lay beyond that. He had presence, a vitality, she could feel his maleness. 'Sometimes foliage is fussy, like an over-dressed woman.' She smiled, giving in to his charm.

'We don't see a lot of snow in Glasgow. It's a temperate climate. I expect you get more of it in Vienna.'

'Ah yes, Vienna . . .' He sighed. 'A crisp coldness. Why do you think so many ladies wear fur coats there, fur toques? I tell you, Miss Mackintosh, one of the greatest pleasures of my life used to be my Sunday trips to the Viennese woods. As a student we used to take the tram to Grinzing and then pile into a bus which wound its way through the woods to the restaurant at the top. What a view from there! Especially when the city was

41

lit up at night, and especially when we had been imbibing the *Heurige*!' He lifted an imaginary tankard to his lips.

'It sounds like Strauss,' she forgot her embarrassment, 'music, and students with tasselled caps – do they have sword scars on their cheeks? – and waving tankards of beer and singing.' It must have been a film she'd seen.

'I can see you know it all!' He was laughing at her. 'But you are right. The *Bierkellers*! Such fun and merriment, such singing and greeting of friends, and gargantuan quantities of food – sausages, dumplings, *Apfelstrudel* and *Schnitzel*! I do not find the same atmosphere here, morose men sitting staring at their glasses and spitting in the sawdust on the floor.'

'Oh, that's not fair! Those are low-class pubs! We make up for them with our tearooms. Haven't you heard of our famous Miss Kate Cranston? She actually got Charles Rennie Mackintosh to design the fabric and wallpaper for them, not to mention the furniture.'

His eyebrows went up. 'I find it strange that a man of such stature should take on such assignments.'

'Perhaps we're not so élitist here.' She was proud of the word, less proud of the carbon mark on her cheek which she could see out of the corner of her eye. She wiped it with a handkerchief she took out of her apron pocket.

'No,' he said, his eyes twinkling, 'you have missed it. Allow me.' He took the handkerchief and rubbed gently at the mark. Near her, listening to his breathing, she could feel that presence again. No wonder Jean . . . Still close to her he said in a lowered voice, 'Your sister is unable to attend the Art School this term?'

'Unfortunately.' She tried to speak calmly. 'She's very frustrated. She was in a car accident. Perhaps you know. Her right shoulder was dislocated and it isn't healing very quickly.' She saw his face become suddenly grim, as if to hide his emotion.

His voice was still low. 'The pain . . . one feels it . . . for her.' How foreign he was. No Scotsman would speak like that. 'Your sister is gifted.' How deep and dark his eyes were. 'One or two always emerge. Mr Laidlaw, he is already being talked about. Dark and strong. Good painters must be strong. They treat their canvas as a battlefield, not as a way of passing a wet afternoon.' He looked at the brass plaque she was working at. She was sure he didn't see it. 'Would it be in order if I wrote her a letter of condolence? I would not like to offend her parents.'

'Our letters are private.' She could hear her mother's deliberately casual voice: 'I didn't recognize that handwriting, Jean? Is it someone we know?'

'Thank you.' His charm went like a blind being pulled down. He became an art tutor, impersonal, critical. He examined the plaque. 'Too crowded. You must keep your idea firmly in front of you. Eliminate the inessential. Simplicity should always be the keynote, but a stylized simplicity. Let your motif emerge. You are not embroidering a cushion.'

'Thanks for nothing,' she said to herself as he walked away.

'Have you clicked with Mr Heart-throb?' Nellie Cox, working beside her, said.

'Not my style.' She took up her hammer.

'They're all dippy about him. Pity he's married.'

'Pity.' I'm standing on the brink, watching, she thought, unable to do a thing. Watching a tragedy rushing to happen. It could be called a tragedy because of its inevitability.

When she was going down the outside steps at the school she found Ritchie waiting for her.

'You look very solemn,' he said.

'I'm worried.'

'Have you had a bad day?'

'No, but Mr Kleiber spoke to me. It was an excuse to ask about Jean. He didn't think much of my work.'

'You're not worried about that?'

'No. It's the thought of him. When he was asking about her his eyes were so intense, as if he was . . . tortured. Does that sound soft? I've seen the same kind of thing in hers, a sort of anguish.'

'Anguish?' He looked bewildered. 'You're sure you aren't imagining all this?'

'I've been sure for some time. And worried. Since before Kirkcudbright.'

'Come and have a coffee and we'll talk about it.'

'I haven't time. He asked if he could send her a letter, a letter of condolence, he called it. That's odd, isn't it, from a tutor, a married tutor?'

'These foreign blokes are more formal.'

'I suppose so. I think he'd already made up his mind but he thought it would look better if he mentioned it to me first.'

'No.' He shook his head. 'It's your imagination, Anna, and your closeness with Jean. He'll just be disappointed she's missing a term's work.' He said in a cajoling voice, 'I never thought you'd turn down a coffee offer from me.'

'I'm too unsettled.' She met his eyes, remembering Mr Kleiber's description of him: dark and strong. 'I'm melting,' she had to smile. 'Oh, all right, you've talked me into it.'

'That's my girl.' He put his arm round her waist and bore her off like a hunter to his cave.

SEVEN

'WHEN I GOT YOUR LETTER I could hardly believe it,' Jean said. They were sitting on the upper deck of the tramcar which went to Rouken Glen Park, one of the longest routes from the heart of the city. It was Frederick's idea. It was less dangerous than sitting in tearooms or cafés where they might be known, and tramcars reminded him of Vienna.

'I felt I had to tell you how I missed you. Each day you weren't there, my heart was like a weight. I could not stop thinking about you.' He had his arm across the back of the seat as they swayed along. 'Did you think at all about me?'

'Oh yes. I've thought about you from the first month you came to the school.' She felt shameless. There was a young couple behind them and she lowered her voice. 'I don't know how to be coy. Nancy could teach me. I thought about you, constantly. Anna noticed it. She would.'

'My darling.'

She trembled, drawn to look at him. 'You shouldn't say that.'

'It's how I think of you.' His eyes held hers, deep, dark, compelling. She must look away. She heard Anna's voice in her head: 'It's ridiculous, Jean. He's married . . .'

'There's your wife, and your children, the little girl you told me about.'

'My little Hilde? Yes, I doubt if I could live without my little Hilde.'

'See,' she said, despair making her look straight ahead, 'it's

45

no use. I told you right at the beginning, when we had coffee in that terrible place –'

'So terrible?' He was amused.

'Cowcaddens Road. Mother would have a fit. That's darkest Africa to her!' Her sense of humour came back for a moment. 'I can hear her saying, "If you have to meet a married man, at least make it the Malmaison!"' She saw his uncomprehending look. 'That's just me being funny.'

'The English sense of humour.' He was prepared to learn.

'No, Scottish.' She stared out of the side window at the bustling people round the shops, Pollokshaws Road, the South Side. He hadn't a clue, really. They were poles apart, except . . .

'But I was wise, don't you think?' His voice was light. He never remained gloomy for long, he was a true *Lieber Augustin*, a merry fellow – he had used that expression when he was describing the wonderful times he had had in the Viennese woods. She had a good ear. Kahlenberg. That was the church up at the top with the black Madonna. Would she ever see Vienna with him? It rose in front of her, a golden city, unattainable. 'I asked your sister if it would be all right to send you a letter. What a fragile-looking girl she is with that pale skin and the darkness of her eyes and hair, such precise hair compared with yours. But sharp eyes, oh yes, sharp eyes.'

'Anna's looks are deceptive. She's tough, practical, it's I who am the dreamer and yet I look strong. I'm more –'

'Womanly. A painter's dream. The colours of your flesh are rich and warm. Could I paint you sometime?' His arm slipped down round her waist. 'Please, Jean?'

She turned to him, laughing. 'No, you can't. What an idea. Nancy's been asked, all the same.'

'By the undiscriminating. Pink and white and gold, like the little angels on some of the Ringstrasse buildings. Too sweet, like pink fondant icing. Anna, your other sister, was disdainful to me. She said all your letters were private property.'

'She told you off? She's right, of course, but it doesn't stop

Mother being nosey. I told her yours was from the President of the United States.'

He squeezed her waist, laughing. 'You little liar! No, that makes you sound like a coquette. Vienna has plenty of those, taught by their mamas how to charm men. Elizabeth, my wife, was like that when I first met her.'

'Isn't she still?' The dull pain was suddenly sword-sharp. He shouldn't have mentioned his wife.

'No.' He shook his head. 'What was between us has gone, as the Viennese life we knew has gone, the laughter, the talk, the music, always the music.'

'It sounds so different from dull, grey Glasgow.'

'I don't consider it that. Certainly Vienna is light, but Glasgow to me has a slow, powerful atmosphere, it's like a sleeping giant. Different, strange, just as you are different to me, strange. So young, so unaware of your womanliness, the female power that is in you, the power to love. You are like your own river –'

She burst out laughing. 'Oh, stop, Frederick! Our dirty old Clyde! And I'm not strange at all, I'm an ordinary Glasgow girl.' She stopped speaking as their eyes met. *But besotted . . .* Her lips shaped the words.

'You feel it, don't you,' his eyes were still on her, 'in bed at night?'

'Yes, I feel it,' she said slowly, 'in bed at night . . .'

She was suddenly aware of the suspicious silence behind them. She put a finger to her lips. They listened to the whining voice: 'We could take a rowboat out, Andy, eh?'

'I told Mother the truth.' Jean tried to speak sensibly. 'I said it was a letter from my tutor who was worried about my work being neglected.'

'Sometimes I am a little jealous when I see how well you paint.'

Still the silence behind. She could imagine the whining girl nudging her Andy.

47

'I'm just in the Kailyard School.' She laughed at his expression. 'Kail's a Scottish vegetable, like an overgrown cabbage. My mother would call it common, wouldn't have it on the table. Only fit for cows.' A wave of love swept through her, looking at his widened eyes. 'Actually she was pleased at your interest and said she was going to ask you and your wife to visit us.'

'She knew I was married?'

'Oh yes, she ferrets out things that matter.' She laughed again. His presence made her feelings change from second to second, from amusement and lightness to that strong, slow, strange surging like the Clyde . . . She was becoming poetical like him. 'She would ask Nancy.'

'It makes no difference, does it?'

'To us? To this?' She turned her hands outward. The couple behind were quiet again. She had forgotten to keep her voice lowered. It was the boy's voice now.

'If we didn't take out a rowboat, Cissy, we could have two nougat wafers. *Chocolate* nougat wafers, if you like.'

'Some treat!' She could imagine Cissy, her pouting mouth.

'Is it me or ma dibs you're after? I'm no aw that fond o' gold-diggers.' The girl's voice rose. She was voluble in her anger. Jean used its cover.

'Of course it makes a difference! I shouldn't be with you at all. I shouldn't be hiding with you in miserable cafés, going on long tram rides –'

'I like you when you're angry. Look at me.'

She looked and knew she would never give him up. She saw his brown, glowing eyes bent on her, his smiling mouth, felt his foreignness, which appealed so strongly to her, and knew she would die for him. Why did death come into loving? She remembered once saying to Anna, 'I could die . . . die . . .'

'Some day we will be together in Vienna.'

'You're married. It's impossible.' She was sunk in gloom, like the muddy waters of the Clyde.

'Marriages can be broken. Or ignored. We can plan, and

48

meantime enjoy...' She looked through the window: Kilmarnock Road busy with traffic, then Rouken Glen Road quieter. 'Let me tell you what it would be like in Vienna.' His voice was cajoling, that broken-syllabled voice, because it spoke an unfamiliar language. His arm tightened.

'Tell me.' She leaned back in its curve.

'In summer we would sit in the Graben under coloured umbrellas. In winter in the Café Halwelka. All the world goes there to talk, to smoke, to read their papers, to set the world to rights. If we were feeling a little cold we would each have a *Fiaker* in a glass with a little rum, and if we were celebrating, say, our love, we would have a *Kaffee Creme*.'

She repeated the words, trying to copy his foreign intonation, '*Kaffee Creme*...'

'But,' a delighted chuckle, 'if you had sold a picture and made a lot of money we would certainly have a *Franziskaner*.'

'A *Franziskaner*.' It was like a spell. 'What is it?'

'Coffee with whipped cream and chocolate sprinkles. Ah, how homesick that makes me feel, the rich dark taste.'

'How do the women keep their figures?' She straightened up. She'd had enough of this day-dreaming, this giving in. 'Haven't they heard of slimming? It's all the rage here.'

'That is a waste of time. Every man likes his woman to be soft and round like the *Schönbrunner*, opulent, fecund...'

'Is your wife... opulent?' She turned to him, haughtily, and saw the laughter die out of his face, his eyes go flat.

'She has had three children. She likes food and cooks well. Yes, you could say so.' What was she thinking of? It was Anna again. 'Wasting your time with a married man, foreign, three children, opulent wife...'

'*Was* she, before she was married?' She hated herself for her curiosity about this woman, her jealous, prurient curiosity.

'You are hurting yourself, and me. Don't do it, please.' He took up one of her hands and kissed it. 'I have told you. We were very young when we were married. Students. We rushed

49

into it. The future was unclouded then, no one hated us, wanted to get rid of us because I was a Jew. Look at me, Jean.' She saw there were tears in his eyes. 'Believe me, my dearest, this is different. I never thought I could feel like this. It is with me all the time, this *overwhelming* feeling. You are with me, your dark beauty, your *frightening* youthfulness. It was my passion for you which made me speak to your sister, made me write. Your mother wouldn't mind, I thought, or suspect.'

'Not yet, but you don't know my mother. She's polite, cool, but she keeps what we call here a canny eye on us. Her aim in life is for us to marry well. Father only wants us to be happy. She said to him, who doesn't take any part in her machinations, "Perhaps we should include Jean's tutor in your office party. He seems to think a lot of Jean. He's written to her." I saw Anna, sitting back, listening and watching. Oh, she's clever, Anna. She brings up your name to tantalize me. But she knows me through and through, she shares my pain, my unhappiness, my happiness. I'm the same with her. I knew she was in love with Ritchie Laidlaw before she knew herself.'

'Ah, Mr Laidlaw. Yes, she must be clever.'

'Mother's hedging her bets. No, you wouldn't understand. Ritchie isn't quite . . . Now I come to think of it, it *was* Nancy who said you were married: "Will you ask his wife as well, Mother?" She's jealous of Jean and I being twins. She thinks it leaves her out.'

'Young ladies with doll-like looks are often spiteful.'

'Don't think Anna and I are paragons, far from it. We're both impulsive, which sometimes lands us in trouble.' The sword slid through her heart. *This* was trouble, here and now, in this man sitting beside her. 'Mother was quite pleased to know about you. She collects people for her parties.'

'I thought it was your father's office party.'

'It *began* like that, but she's appropriated it. She wants you for her salon. You're distinguished, foreign . . . we laugh at her.'

'You are always critical of your mother like this?'

50

'It's Scottish. We don't like to be considered "soft".'

'Then I will tell you that already Elizabeth has received the invitation and she is delighted. She wept when I said I would rather not go, so I told her to accept. She is perhaps a little like your sister Nancy. Does *she* cry if she doesn't get her own way?'

'Quite often. So you are both coming?'

'Yes. Elizabeth has arranged for a student to take care of the children.'

'That's that then.' *She* wouldn't weep.

The conductor came running up the stairs, whistling, went out to the uncovered front deck, and, taking off his green peaked cap, leaned out to turn the handle of the indicator box.

'Ur ye stayin' on?' he said, coming back past Jean and Kleiber. 'That's the end of the run.'

'When is the next tram back?' Jean asked.

'Every hauf oor. You'll have time for a walk in Rouken Glen and a cuddle.' He gave them a wink and went clattering downstairs again, whistling. They were the only two on the top deck. The young couple had gone.

'What is this cuddle?' Frederick asked. She smiled at him but didn't answer.

They walked about the park, he marvelling at its non-park-like appearance. 'In Vienna we have the grand design. The gardens are as important as the buildings themselves. The Schönbrunn Palace demands formality, as does the Belvedere. Rowing boats would disfigure the total effect. This is like the Viennese woods.'

In a quiet lane when they sat down on a bench he took her in his arms and kissed her. I could die, she thought again, shaken. A married man's kiss was different. She had been taken out a few times by Robin Naismith, and she had been scarcely aware of him, or his overtures. He was a well-brought-up Kilmacolm boy. Frederick touched where he hadn't, and his tongue explored until she was breathless and longing and almost fainting with love for him.

51

'I was stupid to meet you,' she said, pulling herself free. 'I promised myself I wouldn't . . . not again. And my arm aches.' She pretended peevishness.

'Your poor arm.' His voice was tender. 'But you have such love and passion in you. You are meant to express it. It would go into your work. You have so much to give, my dearest.' She knew tears were streaming down her face.

'I'm going to *die* of shame when I meet your wife.' She wondered why she used that word so often.

'How do you think I'll feel?'

'Do you still sleep with her?' She couldn't believe she was asking such a question, sitting in a Glasgow park with young couples strolling about, unattached young couples. In Glasgow girls didn't go out with married men, at least, she had never known it.

'It is a small flat. There is no room. Small and dark unlike the spacious one we had near Steffi.'

'Steffi?'

'St Stephen's Cathedral. It is the tower.' Jealousy flamed in her that she had never known that part of his life, that it belonged to his wife, Elizabeth. The blood was pounding in her cheeks. She put up her hands to cover them.

'I'm just someone . . . to pass the time with. I blame myself entirely. Anna thinks I'm stupid, that it's pointless, that there's nothing in it for me but heartbreak.' The pain was unendurable.

'You're wrong. There could be pleasure and delight and passion.' His eyes were deep, boring into hers. 'Elizabeth has had a hard time. Your city is strange to her. But I will tell her soon about you. I am making enquiries about a choir she might join. She had many happy times in Vienna when she sang in a choir.'

It was fanciful. She didn't believe it would be so easy to make his wife happy if he deserted her, singing in a choir to console her! 'What about your children?'

'The boys are already happy.' He smiled, shrugged. 'They

love the football at school.' He stopped, said in a different tone, 'But little Hilde . . .'

'See,' she said, 'it's no use.' The blood had left her cheeks. She felt cold and determined. 'There's my painting. I've been painting in my mind while my arm has been in a sling. I *long* to paint. That is the only thing I think about.'

He took her so gently in his arms that she couldn't reproach him. He didn't kiss her. 'You will paint,' he said, 'and you will love. One will help the other. You will live fully, gloriously, completely. You must accept that we are meant for each other.' She stayed in his arms, but her unhappiness was great.

They ran for the tram when they saw it standing at the terminus, and would have missed it if the conductor hadn't rung the bell twice to warn the driver who was at the wheel.

'Cut it a bit fine, eh?' he said, when he had helped them on. 'There's nothing like a cuddle or two to pass the time, know what a mean, eh?'

EIGHT

NANCY ENJOYED Father's parties. 'I like to do my best for the lads in the office,' he invariably said. 'I can well remember how lonely I was when I first came down from Ullapool.'

This time, as well as the usual people, there was Ritchie Laidlaw – he might as well see what he had to live up to if Anna stuck with him – and, this was exciting, Mr Kleiber and his wife. Mother said it was because he had sent a letter of condolence to Jean when she was off with her dislocated shoulder. Nancy thought that was a bit funny peculiar, actually, but she would wait and see.

Still, it was fun to dress up, she thought, surveying herself in the full-length oval mirror in the door of her wardrobe. She didn't think the heavily beaded dress was too sophisticated. Mother had been dubious. The weight of the beads made the scalloped hem sway and tremble round her knees. She foxtrotted a step or two, humming – it was a 'Tea for Two' dress – and felt the little slap of the weighted chiffon on the silken backs of her knees. Lovely!

Anna and Jean, of course, had made a point of *not* choosing a new dress for the party. Typical. They always said they were totally different from each other and hated to be called 'the twins', but they didn't realize just how alike they were.

Jean was a mystery. She had that rich boyfriend Robin Naismith, who was always hanging around, but she and Anna laughed at him behind his back, calling him 'Mama's pet' and Anna saying never trust anyone who wore an Academical tie.

They hadn't realized yet that the way to judge people was by how they dressed, if they had good manners, if their parents were in a good position, if they had gone to a fee-paying school, if they played rugby instead of football, and if they were members of a tennis club and didn't hire a court by the hour in a public park.

There was that quite nice boy James Robinson, whom she had rather liked, and then he had taken her to play tennis in Kelvingrove Park with dirty children on bikes staring through the wire netting at them and sniggering and shouting, 'Who's for tennis?' And the man who looked after the courts had told James when he paid that they were ten minutes over their time and given them a dirty look. She had felt so affronted that she had told James she didn't want to see him again.

She looked over her shoulder to see if her stocking seams were straight. Of course the women from Father's office would be there: Cathy, his private secretary, definitely cut out to be an old maid; the women tracers, dowdy-looking creatures, hump-backed with bending over their boards all day . . . She frowned at herself in the mirror, 'No, Nancy, that's unfair.' They *had* to work, and Father said their tracings were as good, if not better, than the men's.

After the last party Anna and Jean had had an argument with him, saying that if their work was as good as the men's they should be paid the same. In her heart she had agreed with them, but Mother had said if their fathers were earning good money that had to be taken into account. The twins said that was nothing to do with it. It was a question of equality and what had the Suffragettes been fighting for after all, and it had ended by Father saying he would put it up to the partners.

It was difficult to know whose side to take because Mother had put the tin lid on it by saying girl tracers were taking a man's job away from him, except she *hadn't*, because the twins then said that the women were being exploited by firms like Father's.

The only difference between Anna and Jean was how they dressed. She thought that was deliberate, so that they wouldn't be taken for twins. Anna wore simple clothes and raved on about 'line', while Jean always looked as if she had been rummaging through that old ragbag Bessie kept in the kitchen, and ending up looking *like* an old ragbag.

Once she had even made a little jacket out of some of that rubbish and put it on Tumshie on the evening of one of their parties. Mother had had a fit when Tumshie came strolling into the drawing room in her green velvet jacket tied with purple ribbon, and Grace Binnie had said, 'You're nothing if not orig- . . . inal, Rose,' with that accent you could cut with a knife.

There was that exciting moment just before the door bell rang when they all stood on the Persian carpet at the fire and she tried to see what her hair looked like in the mirror – she was trying out a pageboy – and Mother kept on touching the ornaments on the mantelpiece to see if Bessie had left a speck of dust anywhere and Father kept on saying, 'Everything's lovely, dear, don't fuss.' He had checked the decanters on the side table at least half a dozen times.

'There's someone!' Mother held up a hand with rose enamelled nails and her three rings, her diamond solitaire, her eternity ring and her sapphire with pear-shaped diamonds on either side.

She had been looking at Anna and thinking how she managed to look pale and healthy at the same time and how lovely the shape of her lips was. Her own were rather thin and she had to make a Cupid's bow with lipstick. And thinking how daring Anna was to wear a black dress composed entirely of layers of fringe, but, black on a warm evening in August!

She was just going to say, 'I really like your dress, Anna. Only you could wear it,' when she saw Anna's face light up like a rosy pearl and her eyes fill up, not with tears. She followed their direction and saw Ritchie Laidlaw, at the door, see her and make straight towards her, and there was the same kind of look in *his* eyes.

'Hello, Anna,' he said jauntily. 'Am I the first?' He looked as if he would like to kiss her, but Anna said quickly, 'Somebody's got to be first, haven't they, Father?' and soon he was shaking hands all round, completely at ease.

'I never think of parties at this time of year,' he said to Mother.

'It's a tradition with us,' she said. He looked as if he'd stumbled on some quaint custom and turned to Jean.

'Hello. Long time no see.'

'I've been off because of my arm, silly,' she said. 'You were there too, or has it slipped your mind?'

'It's a blank when I see Anna.' His eyes ate her up for a second, then he was back to his teasing. 'I hope you've learned a lesson, Jean. That's what comes with picking up blokes in fast cars.'

'Where *did* you find this clown?' Jean said to Anna.

'Jean!' Mother said. She never missed a thing. 'That's no way to speak to guests.'

'You tell her to treat me nicely, Mrs Mackintosh.' He wasn't at all abashed. 'And how's the baby sister?' Now it was *her* turn.

She had to admit there was something unusual in Ritchie Laidlaw, a feeling of strength, not strength such as a weight-lifter might have, but an inner strength which came from being sure of himself. And he certainly had lovely eyes, a deep sort of indigo brown, a colour she would never use even for shadow, deeper and richer than sepia. 'None the better for seeing you!' She couldn't help laughing at him.

'What am I going to do with these girls?' Mother sighed dramatically, but you could see that in a way she was captivated by Ritchie.

The room was filling up now. 'You offer the anchovy ones and the smoked salmon,' Jean said, pointing to the silver tray of vol-au-vents. She really looked beautiful tonight in a kind of patterned dress, deep reds and purples and blues. Only someone with Jean's rich colouring would dare. The red poppies of the pattern were matched by her lipstick and nail varnish, and the white background made her skin look even darker. Father's Highland colouring, Nancy thought.

Tonight Jean seemed to be in a flamboyant mood which matched her dress. Her deep blue eyes were sparkling, her warm dark skin glowed, she was laughing, talking, her teeth very white against her lipstick. She painted in the same way, not taking time to think, splashing on the colour, 'trying to empty the painting out of my head onto the canvas,' she had once said.

'That's the bell again,' Jean remarked. They were near the open door and she stopped talking. Bessie appeared first, padding upstairs with that long-suffering face of hers – 'her party face', Mother called it – followed by Mr Kleiber and his wife. Well, it must be his wife. Jean remembered Mother saying they had both been invited.

They looked foreign, she thought, dark, un-Scottish in some peculiar way, his suit was a different cut although his shirt was very white, and her dress was dowdy. She could imagine the rather dusty ruby velvet dress with its lace sleeves hanging in her wardrobe and only brought out once or twice a year. Still, she had quite a nice little face. Jean had gone forward as they stood hesitating at the door.

'How nice of you to come, Mrs Kleiber,' she said, holding out her hand. 'And you too, Mr Kleiber.' It didn't sound like Jean at all, that party talk.

'Thank you. We are delighted to be here.' He spoke in that deep rich voice which made them all swoon in the School. Jenny Drummond thought he was like Fredric March, but Mrs Kleiber was certainly no Garbo. And she had a bad skin. 'This is Miss Jean Mackintosh,' he said, 'and her younger sister, Nancy.'

'So lovely the skin,' Mrs Kleiber smiled at her, making her blush, 'like porcelain.' She felt awful. She noticed that Mr Kleiber had put his hand under his wife's elbow, and Jean was standing looking at them, all her vivacity gone, her eyes drained black. What on earth had upset her?

There was a youngish man with greying hair speaking to

Mother and Father, when she took the Kleibers over to be introduced.

'James, this is my youngest daughter,' Father said. 'Nancy. We've three daughters at the Art School.' Her mother was chatting to the Kleibers.

'Are you interested in art, Mr Pettigrew?' Nancy asked.

Her father laughed. 'If he isn't, he should be. He's with Pettigrew and Crawford, the architects.' She remembered that Keppel and Armstrong had tried to induce him to join them. 'James has come along this evening to show he bears me no ill will.'

'I'm a magnanimous bloke, Angus.' Mr Pettigrew smiled. It lit up his face, making him look younger than his age. What *was* his age? Thirty-five? He had a look of authority.

Somehow she found herself standing at the flat triple windows of the room with Mr Pettigrew, their drinks and loaded plates on the window-ledge. She was nervous.

'Didn't you win a competition recently for a new church?' he asked.

'Yes, we did. That was just before my wife died. Blood poisoning. Everything was going so well.' He stopped speaking abruptly.

She felt shocked and looked away, unable to say anything comforting, or right.

He put a hand on her arm. 'That was crass of me. Sometimes I just hear . . . my own voice . . . speaking. It's probably my way of coming to terms with her death.'

'It must have been terrible for you.' She lifted one of the plates and held it out to him. 'That's yours.'

'Thanks.' He took it. 'Vol-au-vents? Guaranteed as a panacea for all ills?'

'Oh gosh, I'm really stupid. As if they mattered . . .'

'But they do.' He lifted a vol-au-vent and bit into it. 'Mushroom?'

'They seem to be the favourite.'

59

His eyes smiled at her over the plate. 'You must be barely twenty?'

'That's right. My birthday's in September.'

'I'm thirty-five. Does that seem very old to you?'

'It does and it doesn't. Father can be quite youthful sometimes, jumping over rocks and things when we're on holiday and he's older than you. A lot.'

'That's a relief. Now, tell me about yourself, Miss Mackintosh.'

'Nancy. "Miss Mackintosh" makes me feel about –'

'Thirty-five? I'll call you Nancy if you call me James.'

'Not right away.' She smiled at him. 'But I might come to it.' He laughed, looking young.

'I knew Angus had three daughters. The other two can't be any prettier than you.'

'It depends what your taste is. The three of us are quite different.' She looked round the room. 'There's Anna with her boyfriend, beside the fireplace.'

'I should think she's spoken for.' He had followed her glance.

'Yes, she's in deep with Ritchie. Then, Jean. She's romantic-looking, I'd say.' She scanned the room for her. 'She's over in the corner there, speaking to Mr Kleiber.'

'They seem to be in deep too.' That was ridiculous, and yet when she looked there was a tense, absorbed expression on Jean's face as she listened to their art tutor.

'Oh no, Mr Pettigrew!' He was pulling her leg. 'You met his wife. They're from Vienna.' She looked around. 'I don't see her. Maybe Mother's showing her the house since it will be so different from her own. Give Mother half a chance and she's showing people the house. It was built by John Burnet Senior in 1876. You'll probably know all that. She inherited it from my grandparents.'

'I've read there's some doubt about it having been J. J. Burnet's.'

'Oh, don't for heaven's sake tell her that or she'll have a fit!'

He was still looking at Jean and Kleiber. 'There's a sadness in that man's face. You said he was Austrian? I wonder if he came to Glasgow by choice?'

'No, I don't think so. You know how that man Hitler is hunting out the Jews?'

'That's what I meant.'

She looked at them again. It was as if they had made an island of themselves. Mr Kleiber was slightly bent over Jean as he talked. She had a strange feeling that she was watching something happening, something dangerous. Mr Pettigrew was speaking again.

'She seems absorbed.' He shrugged. 'Well, I'm lucky too, talking to the prettiest girl in the room!'

She laughed. Why was she trembling? Was it because Jean had upset her in some peculiar way? 'Mother told me to be sure and circulate. Would you like me to introduce you to anyone?'

'I'm more than happy, if you are. Tell me, what do you do at the Art School?'

'Watercolours. Anna does metal-work and Jean does oils. She's good. The twins say I have a fatal facility.' She laughed. 'I don't care. I could drop it like a bent pin if I got married, or anything.'

'Lucky man.'

'Oh, I haven't got anyone yet. I just mean if. It was Father's idea we should all go to the Art School. He's dead against any of us marrying just as an escape route. Do you agree with that, Mr Pettigrew?'

'James.'

'It feels funny, but it might slip out. Learning to paint or draw, to explore something with a brush or pencil helps you to explore yourself. It's contemplative, you see. You can't contemplate in most jobs for girls. You can't *grow* in them.'

'That's profound.'

'Oh, I'm not profound, James,' she said. 'It was one of the twins who said that.' She laughed. 'It *did* slip out.'

NINE

1936

IT WAS AUGUST and the family were in Kilcreggan for their holiday. Nancy was 'a bit mournful' because James might be too busy to visit. He was courting her on a regular basis, much to Rose's delight and satisfaction. Anna more or less accepted the fact that Ritchie had to work during the holidays and seemed secure in her love for him. Neither of them was in the turmoil which Jean constantly found herself in.

The last year had passed in deepest misery or rapturous delight – delight when she and Frederick managed to meet, misery when they were apart. Her guilt was constant.

Strangely enough, or was it strange?, she had never painted better, large canvases full of colour, 'explosions of colour,' Frederick called them. 'Remember form,' he would say, bending over her in the studio, and whispering in her ear so that the other students wouldn't hear, 'my dearest dear.'

They had managed to have a quick coffee together on the last day of term. 'It's going to be more difficult to meet you now,' she said. 'The school was a cover.' And suddenly feeling the pointlessness of it all, 'I'm beginning to think I should stop seeing you altogether. There's no future in this. I constantly think of your wife and children, the harm we're doing them.' She could never bring herself to say: 'You must choose between us.' She had seen Mrs Kleiber once again at the Art School and she had had little Hilde by the hand. She had run to her father . . .

He took Jean's hands across the table, his eyes agonized. 'Don't say that. You'll break my heart.'

'How about mine? You're going to the coast with your family for a fortnight and then I'm going with mine. When the school begins again it's back to these furtive meetings. I can't stand it any more. It . . . diminishes me, Frederick.' She had put her face in her hands, and then ashamed that she should do this in a public place had raised it again. She felt cold inside. 'I can't break up your marriage. I would never know any happiness.'

'I'll speak to her when we're on holiday. There will be time.'

She shook her head, looking at him, feeling that she was being crucified by this love. She got up and left the café swiftly, let the door swing behind her and ran through the city streets for a long time, mindless, until she stopped at Charing Cross and waited for a tram . . .

'Jean!' Now she heard her mother's voice floating upstairs. 'Jean! The telephone!'

'Who is it?' She ran down from her bedroom, fearful, yet hoping. She hadn't been able to sleep at night. Her mind was full of Frederick, his features, his eyes on her, his hands on her. She had been too hasty. Was he feeling like this, on fire when he thought of her?

'Hello!' she said, feeling breathless. Her heart had seemed to throw itself about in her rib cage and had now lodged in the back of her throat, choking her.

'Jean, I had to phone. My life is no good without you. I can't work, eat, sleep . . .' His voice had a new huskiness.

'Of course you can! You have your wife and children.' She tried to sound authoritative, the way she sometimes spoke to Bessie . . . 'Bessie, that nice hair-band of mine. It's been chewed to pieces by that cat of yours! . . .'

'They don't count. I tried hard to talk to Elizabeth when we were on holiday, but the children were always there. When I say they don't count I don't mean the children. Oh, we have to

63

talk! Could I come and see you today? I'll make some excuse, anything.'

'We have friends here of Mother's, the Binnies.'

'I'll meet you in the village. Only to see you, to talk.'

She made up her mind. 'All right. I'll tell Mother that you want to paint the cloud formations over the Cowal shore. That we had talked about it in the school.' This was true enough.

'What is the destination of the train I take?'

'Gourock.' She spelled it out. 'And then take the ferry. Don't wait for a steamer.' He didn't have a motor car, something about the difficulty of getting a licence in this country. 'Are you in your house?'

'No. I telephone from the railway station.'

'Right. I'll be waiting at the pier,' she looked at her watch, 'at eleven o'clock. Goodbye.' She hung up and stood where she was until her pulse had calmed down. Anna wouldn't have been weak-kneed like this. She was disgusted at herself and yet the anticipation was sending thrills through her body. She swallowed, pressing her tongue hard against the roof of her mouth.

Her mother and father, the two Binnies, Anna and Nancy were having breakfast when she went into the dining room.

'Come on, lazybones,' Nancy said. 'Anna and I are nearly finished. We're going in for the American tournament. You have to get your name down early.'

She spoke to her mother, keeping her voice steady. 'That was Mr Kleiber, Mother. He's coming here for the day to picnic. And paint.'

'With his family?'

'I suppose so, but he doesn't want to be a nuisance to you.'

'We could surely manage to give them a meal. They seemed very nice. His wife thought Clevedon Crescent was lovely.' She looked at Grace Binnie, cool in her blue silk shirtwaister, 'the night of our party, Grace, last year. She's Viennese, so it was quite a compliment.'

'Vienna?' Grace raised her eyebrows, turned down her mouth.

64

'We didn't really spend much time in it, did we, Stewart? We only went for the music.'

'A wonderful opera house all the same.' Her husband was judicious. 'We were told they have a grand ball there every year. They take the seats out. It must be quite a sight.'

Jean sat down at the table. She avoided Anna's cool look. 'I don't think they would push themselves on to you at such short notice, Mother. It's more likely they'll invite me to have lunch with them. Maybe at the Pier Hotel.'

'When have you to meet them?'

'Eleven o'clock.'

'Is that the *King Edward*?' Her father looked up from his paper.

'No, I told him to take the ferry. And, of course, maybe the whole family won't come if he wants to paint.'

'Well, we'll make it like this,' Rose said. 'If he's alone, bring him up here for lunch; if it's the whole family, see how it goes. It *is* short notice, not that I haven't plenty in the house. How many children do they have?'

'How should I know?' She got up and filled her cup from the teapot on the sideboard.

'Someone's got out of her bed on the wrong side this morning,' Grace Binnie, with not a hair out of place, said.

There was a silence as Jean ate a piece of toast which seemed to stick in her throat, washed it down with a mouthful of tea and got up again. 'I'll go upstairs and make my bed, then get down to the pier.'

'Well, remember what I said.' Rose looked up from her eggs and bacon, 'Bring him here for lunch. Hospitality has never been a problem with us. I think you can bear me out on that, Grace. If he's going to spend the whole day painting, your father and I might wander down and have a word with them. It will look better.'

'Oh, Mother!' She was at the door. She shut it behind her and ran upstairs, her mind in a turmoil. Anna, just sitting, and

65

that Grace Binnie with her snide remarks. She should have said no to Frederick and then she wouldn't be in this tangle of lies and half-truths.

She was brushing her hair at the mirror when Anna came into the room. How trim she looked, she thought, with her short tennis dress and those socks and sandshoes dazzlingly white against her brown legs. And yet her face never tanned. She always had a look of fragility but she was as tough as old boots. She threw herself down on the bed, her hands cupped behind her head, her feet crossed at the ankles.

'What's this ploy you're up to?' she said.

'I don't know what you're talking about.' She was lofty as she searched in the drawer for a hairband. 'That cat *lives* on my bandeaux. I'll tumshie her.'

'Don't avoid the subject.' Anna got up suddenly. 'I've had an idea!' She opened the door of the wardrobe and peered in. 'I *thought* they were here!' She reached in and brought out two furry-looking tennis balls. 'Better than nothing.' She threw one of the balls in the air. 'Father's incredibly stingy about buying new ones. We'll need them in the tournament.'

'There are two in the pocket of my tennis case. You can take them.'

'You're going to miss the tournament, then?'

'Yes.'

'You could have walked away with the prize. You're much better than Nancy and me.'

'Rubbish!' She wished Anna would go. She knew by her eyes that she hadn't finished with her.

'I don't even have to guess.' She sat down on the end of the bed. 'It's in your face. You're crazy about him, aren't you? And he can't keep away from you. You're a fool, Jean. He's married. Mother would be furious if she knew what you were up to.'

'She does know, doesn't she? I told her.'

'Oh yes, you're clever. But she doesn't know you're playing with fire.'

66

'What an expression! Like a cheap novel or something in the *People's Friend*.' She got suddenly angry, fanning it deliberately. 'What are you doing in here anyhow? Is it just to annoy me? Get on with your own affairs. Go up to the club and put in some practice before the tournament. You could do with it!' She tidied the dressing-table quickly, sticking the comb in the brush, taking a sapphire ring from its silver tree stand – they both had said they would prefer a ring rather than a twenty-first birthday party. Who wanted to be labelled as twins? Anna was now standing behind her, but in the mirror Jean saw reflected her pale face, the black straight hair, the red lips. She was real Art Nouveau. She should have a greyhound on a lead.

'Jean,' Anna said, 'I don't care about that old tournament. I'll come with you.'

'Come with me!' She pretended surprise as she put on the hairband, saw how it made her hair rise from her forehead and fall becomingly on either side of her face. 'What an idea!' 'Lovely, lovely hair,' he had said to her not long before she had run out of that café. 'I shall call you Lorelei.' 'You mean you want to hang around with Mr Kleiber and his family instead of enjoying yourself at the club?' She veered away from her sister's eyes meeting hers in the mirror.

'I bet you he'll come alone.'

'I'm not in the mood for betting. And stop pestering me, Anna. I don't go on about Ritchie Laidlaw to you!'

'He isn't married, with three children.'

'You make me mad! I don't know what I'm doing with you standing there behind me like a public executioner.' She swept lipstick, vanishing cream, handkerchiefs into the drawer. 'I'm going now. I'll have a walk before the ferry comes. And don't look at me with those eyes. Just leave me alone!'

'It's you who's mad. You're obsessed by him. Of course he's charming. Of course the girls at the school rave about him. He's different. He makes the boys look uncouth, but he's *married*. With *children*. He is experienced, the way you'll never be, nor

67

will I, nor will Ritchie, but don't say I didn't warn you.'

Jean looked in the mirror for the last time, saw the glow under her skin because of her annoyance with Anna. What did Anna know of the longing, of reliving the delight of having been with him, of the slow delicious thrills which went through her body, took hold of her so that she had to go and walk, walk until the fever subsided? She looked at her mass of dark hair controlled by the hairband, so different from the trim shortness of Anna's with the points lying on her cheeks. She had no need of a ribbon or clasps to keep her hair in position. Anna looked controlled, *she* looked wild – there was that word 'abandoned', which was better.

'I'm off,' she said. 'See that you come home with the trophy.'

'I'm going to get Nancy.' They went downstairs together in silence and parted at the dining room door. 'Remember what I said.' Anna put her hand on her bare arm but she shook it off.

'If I tried to remember all you said, I'd never be done.' She went out of the front door, down the steps, walked across the lawn and into the wood. It was dark, like her soul. I'm aching for him, she thought, but it doesn't make me happy. Anna was happy when she had been with Ritchie, eyes sparkling, playing the clown, dragging her or Nancy into a daft dance in the kitchen, with Bessie and Tumshie looking on. 'Daft-looking lot, aren't they, Tumshie?' she would say. Tumshie would lick one paw contemplatively.

She was standing on the wooden pier when she saw the busy little ferry forging its way towards them. Of course he wouldn't be on it. His wife would say she didn't want to be alone all day with the children, or she would ask him to do some shopping for her in town, or to take little Hilde for a walk. She saw in her mind's eye a chubby little angel of a child with shining curls, not all over her head, but in ringlets on either side of her face, rather like Shirley Temple.

But he was on the ferry. Alone. He was standing beside the engine house wearing his wide-brimmed hat. When he saw her he took it off and waved it. She must tell him not to wear that hat, it made him stand out in a crowd, look foreign. But on the other hand, she reminded herself, he was coming here to paint. He probably needed it to keep the sun off his eyes, like Cézanne.

He was first off, running up the steep wooden stairs towards her. He took both her hands, laughing, speaking rapidly. 'I made it! I followed your instructions to the letter and here I am!' His eyes were deep, like a well, with a diamond sparkling in their depths. She marvelled that she had ever thought of giving him up, but she was circumspect.

'You didn't bring your children?'

'No.'

'Nor your wife?'

'She wouldn't have liked it. The ferry, you see. She's easily made seasick. No, it was better to come alone.' His eyes engulfed her. 'Why pretend, Jean?' She was still circumspect.

'You haven't an easel with you?'

'No. Only a sketchbook in my knapsack. I'll make notes. I've never been one of the *plein air* school. My work is done in my studio.'

'So is mine. It's the impact I'm trying to paint.'

'The *frisson*.'

'That's it.' The conversation was going the right way. They were walking down the pier as they spoke, and the wooden boards made their footsteps loud. 'Do you want to start right away? Mother says I've to bring you for lunch if you're alone.'

'Then you must tell her I was not.' He took her arm, held her closely against his side. 'I come to see you, not your family. I was desolated when you ran away from me. I have to look at you. When I'm away from you I forget the real colour of your hair, which can be purple in its depths – no, don't laugh – the way the nose goes, but it is always your eyes I want to see again, the pale brown lids, the depth of the blueness . . .'

'They're ten-a-penny eyes.'

69

'I like it, "ten-a-penny eyes". But you're wrong. They're unique.' They had reached the shore road now and they stopped. 'This is a peaceful place,' he said. 'Even the hills are tranquil.'

'Would you like to walk for a little?'

'Could we get a view from somewhere, look down on the water?'

'Yes, if we climb through the wood we come out on the high road, and then you get the feeling of height, the great curve of the sky. Are you thinking of Turner?'

'Oh no, he is too romantic for me. Cézanne, perhaps, and those cloudscapes above Mont Sainte-Victoire. Or some of your Scottish painters who are so French – Guthrie, Macgregor, Hornel. They knew how to build in colour. I have a fellow feeling for them and your Mr Charles Rennie Mackintosh. *We* had the sense to give them more acclaim than they got here.'

'We cross here, Frederick.' Mother wouldn't object to this, a painterly conversation. 'Perhaps it was the greyness of the Scottish weather which made them adopt such a colourful palette.'

'Perhaps.' He put his arm round her as they joined the path through the woods. 'You and Mr Laidlaw are following in their footsteps.'

'I'm not used to compliments,' she said, pleased.

'Then you must change. You have such a rich heritage in Scotland, Mr Mackintosh who built your Art School, so gifted and yet so unappreciated. I always feel his watercolours although fine were a poor substitute for the great buildings he might have designed.'

'Life's unfair,' she said.

He stopped, put his arms round her and drew her towards him. They were in a green darkness in the depths of the wood. 'My clever Jean,' he said, his face close to hers. 'Are you talking in this erudite way because you are . . . afraid?'

'You started it.' An absurd trembling was making her voice shake. She pushed him away. 'But you're right. It's the only

70

way I can keep sane. I should have told you not to come. I would have got over it.' She walked on but he quickly made up on her.

'You don't feel anything for me. You're right. I should not have telephoned you. I should not have come.'

'Don't feel anything for you? I wish you were right. But I can't forget that you're married! At this moment my parents are quite content because they'll be thinking you have brought your wife and family.'

'It was impossible. I couldn't share you with anyone. Don't you see, you are my real love, always will be? Elizabeth is my wife, but there is no understanding there, no real rapport.'

'She is also the mother of your children.' She felt utter despair. He hadn't spoken to her.

'Could you understand, my dearest? In a young man's life his sheer virility drives him into marriage and procreation. He becomes sadder and wiser, finds he has taken on commitments. He would willingly shake himself free –'

'From your children?'

'That is the great sadness.'

And hers. She ought to shake herself free before it was too late. She had done it already, walked away from him in that café, and then hadn't had the courage to stick to her decision. 'Oh . . .' The pain in her heart made her groan and she turned from him, at the same time catching her foot on some low-growing brambles. She stumbled and fell.

'I should watch where I'm going,' she said, bending over her foot, close to tears.

'Let me see the damage.' He was tender to her as he crouched down beside her. 'Is it bleeding?'

'I don't think so.' The ground was velvety with moss. 'It's nothing,' she said, mopping the beads of blood which had oozed through her stocking. She hid the handkerchief. 'It's not even bleeding properly.'

'Wouldn't it be better if you took off your stocking?'

71

'There's no need.' She thought of the embarrassment she would feel if she had to raise her skirt, undo her suspenders.

'I see the idea doesn't appeal to you.' He smiled. 'You are a shy girl behind your Bohemian exterior.'

'I'm glad you think I have a Bohemian exterior.' She smiled up at him and then looked down at her foot. Only one bead of blood now. She would ignore it.

It was very quiet in the wood. She listened and heard the sweet clear call of a robin in the thickets. She thought how well she had come to know this holiday place of theirs over the years, like a well-fitting glove, this wood with its primroses in spring, followed by its bluebells, then the soft fat raspberry fruit on the canes, now the blackberries. Kilcreggan had never been a tourist resort like Dunoon or Rothesay. It offered nothing to visitors except its quietness and its proximity to Glasgow. It had not the grandeur of the Highlands – Father had accepted that the way he accepted most things Mother planned – but the soft lines of the landscape had their own charm.

The inhabitants didn't stir themselves for the visitors, but they recognized the regulars who came year after year. They, she felt sure, were docketed as the family with three daughters in Cowal View. Mr Robinson, the grocer, stirred himself to enlarge his stock – Gentleman's Relish for Mr Mackintosh. And Mr Robinson was careful to keep the right brand of sherry for Father's drink before dinner.

What would he say, that quiet father, if he could see her at this moment sitting in this dark wood with a married man? She stole a look at Frederick, his imperial profile, the dark sweep of his hair, his sensitive mouth. He turned and met her eyes. 'What are you thinking about?' he said.

'My father. And this place, and the people in it. Decent people who know which side their bread is buttered on. Gardening for the men, and little retainers for their wives to keep an eye on a holiday house in the winter. Quiet, respectable lives.' No heartache like mine. Father would be disappointed in her.

'How quiet it is,' Frederick said. He had taken off his hat and jacket and laid them on the grass beside them. 'Quietness such as this is unknown to me. My background is urban. I spent my time in coffee houses or beer gardens with other students where there was constant noise and laughter. Those were good times. Sometimes we would go to the Prater and ride on the Ferris wheel. I invariably left my stomach at the bottom!' He threw back his head and laughed. 'Crowds and laughter, that is how I knew Vienna before the trouble started. Music. Everyone singing, these were happy days. Now it is an uneasy place to be, the light-heartedness is gone.'

'It's different in Glasgow. Men would go to the nearest pub, but not people like my father. He drinks at the Conservative Club. Women go to tearooms, Miss Cranston's or Miss Buick's. If a girl was seen in a public house she would be thought of as a fallen woman.'

'Perhaps you don't have as many galleries as we have. As a student I spent a lot of time in them. It was part of our culture, to be *au fait* with art, to be able to discuss it.'

'What is your favourite picture?' she asked him. She was now at ease sitting in this green darkness with the sunlight splashing through the branches of the high oaks, making her dress look blue-white where it caught the sun. Dappled blue-white. Her trembling had gone.

'Well, you know,' he turned to smile at her, 'I am a Modernist. Klimt, Schiele, Kokoschka. I feel an affinity with them. From figurative expressionism to abstract expressionism to Klimt – the *Beethoven Frieze* in the Secession. What beauty of line.'

'Like your hat?' She laughed at him.

'My hat makes a statement. It says I am foreign, I am an artist. My favourite picture? *The Kiss* by Klimt. Do you know it?'

'No, not even an illustration of it.'

'It is magical.' His voice dropped. 'He holds her in both his arms so beautifully, so gently, from behind, wrapped in his coat

73

of many colours. So pure. He protects her from the world as he kisses her. I became a man on the day I stood and looked at that picture. It was suddenly clear to me.'

'What was clear to you?'

'That in a real love the man protects as well as loves. It is unique.'

'Is it . . . unique?'

They fell into a silence, a deep, anticipatory, joyous silence. She felt close to the trees, to the thicket behind which they sat, to the birds rustling, to the mossy earth. There was a slow ticking noise, perhaps a bird, perhaps time passing. She knew his arms went round her, that he supported her, gently, as they lay down on the grass, which was soft, like a bed.

'Don't,' she said, making no movement to rise. She felt as if she were fainting in his arms. Now she was looking at the sun finding its way through the tall trees, trying to reach them, and then it was blotted out by Frederick's head. 'I don't want . . .' she said, but the words were strangled in her throat as he kissed her. There had never been anything like this, never would be, it is not, she thought, with the last shred of sanity remaining in her, like *The Kiss* by Klimt, 'I must . . .' she struggled, or put up some pretext of a struggle. 'Frederick, you must stop before . . .' You must stop . . . She knew she hadn't formed the words, that they were in her head only.

'No, no . . .' His voice was gentle, his arms gentle as he pinioned her. 'We are too much in love . . .'

'You don't understand!' She was suddenly strong. 'I don't want this! I don't want this.' The sun slanted on his face as he turned it, and she was disarmed. She heard herself say in a voice unlike her own, clotted by emotion, husky, low, 'You must help me up.' She held out her arms to him, weakly, and her hands came to rest on the back of his neck. She felt the strength of him in his hair in her hands, thick, curling, black. She felt its blackness.

All doubts left her, or were washed away by the closeness of their two bodies. I am in the centre of a terrible, wonderful dream, she thought. I am not here in this green-dark wood, I am with Anna. I have gone with her to the tennis club. She heard the smack of the tennis balls on gut, the cries of the players, their ritual cries, felt the satisfaction as one of the cries became, 'Well played, Jean.'

There, with Anna, she had judgement, awareness, a mutual conception, here she had none. 'My judgement is gone,' she said, looking up at him. 'There is only a pounding . . .'

'Lie in my arms,' he said. 'We will just lie quietly in each other's arms. The world will be shut out. We will escape to our own world.'

She gave up struggling, or pretending to struggle. She watched like someone outside herself, watched and heard the small movements of clothes, felt anguished delight as flesh touched flesh. I should be remonstrating, she thought, but this is not a rape, it is a mutual need.

And then it was no longer gentle, it was fierce and inevitable. She was weeping with joy, pleading with him because of the tremendous surges of joy. She raised her body to his, making it easy for him to enter her. She hardly knew what was happening until she heard him groan, knew they were on a gigantic Ferris wheel together – in the Prater, he had said – which was whirling them round and round.

This was what she had been made for, she was thinking. Faster, faster, faster, and then as if the speed and the lights and her body were one she heard herself groan, like Frederick.

Now it was very quiet except for her quickened breathing and the small rustle of a bird in the thicket where they lay. Of course, she remembered, her mind asserting itself, she was in the wood, lying on the mossy ground in a little room made by the thickets. This place was familiar to her, she had walked here often with Anna, picking the rich blackberries for Bessie's jam. But she would never be the same. She wept feebly because there had been no cloak to protect her like the Klimt.

*   *   *

After a long time they went back through the wood towards the pier. She couldn't speak. Once or twice he stooped to kiss her gently. 'You are angry with me, my darling?' She was slowly becoming herself, weak with their shared loving, but now she had her own head, her own judgement and a deep, bitter realization inside her, worse than regret. There was no going back. And there was a bereft feeling as if she had been cut adrift from Anna, a coldness of finality.

'How could I be angry with you?' she said. She was now adult. 'I wanted it. I've wanted it since I met you.' What would Anna think if she heard her? She would know the same passion with Ritchie – she was her sister – but she would hold closely to her judgement.

'Ours is love as it is meant to be. I will ask Elizabeth to release me.' She looked at him and saw the sincerity in his eyes. 'I cannot live with her any more. It would be hypocritical. She is a good woman in many ways, but she doesn't stir the pulse. We were too young.'

'You have three children.' She too had forgotten them, been greedy, going from one delight to the next, always confident she would stop before . . .

When they reached the shore road she said to him, 'Mother may be expecting you.'

'No, that was always impossible.' He looked at his watch. 'One o'clock.'

'Lunch time.' Ordinary words had no meaning for her. 'I am suddenly terribly thirsty, Frederick.'

'Not hungry?'

'No. I couldn't eat. But I have this thirst. My throat seems parched.' She looked at him. He hadn't changed. He was handsome, handsomely foreign, as he had been before. Why should he change?

'Is there an hotel?'

'Yes, but you are expected to have three courses.' She pulled a face and his smile was Frederick. She knew him.

'What about this café? They'll have liquid refreshment at least, if that is what madame desires.'

They stopped at the entrance to read the placards propped up against the wall. It was also a newsagent.

He read out: '"Hitler Bans German–Jewish Marriages."' How strange to read that in this little Scottish village where they do not understand what it means. Next stop the Concentration Camp. His distress deflected her thoughts from herself.

'That's terrible for you to see that!'

Juden unerwünscht. Jews Not Wanted. Vienna next. Do you know what the Nazi word for Jew is? *Untermenschen*. Subhumans. People like me, of the art world, adding to the culture as we go about our work – we are subhumans! It is not to be borne.'

'I can understand how you feel.' Her eyes fell on the neighbouring placard. 'Sun and Prosperity Lured Holiday Crowds.' *Did* she understand?

They sat opposite each other at the red cloth-covered table. She looked around at the adverts for beer written on mirror glass, the ugly vases of paper flowers, the dusty-leaved aspidistras. 'Would you call this Art Nouveau?' she said, smiling at him, trying not to think.

'When you smile like that I forget everything.' His eyes were warm, with a liquid brownness. They held her. She forgot her question.

'What would you like, please?' A stout young woman was standing at their table.

'Two coffees, please,' Frederick said. 'That is all right for you, Jean?' She nodded.

'Fancies?' the young woman said.

'Fancies . . .' Frederick appealed to Jean.

'Small sponge cakes with coloured icing. Viennese cakes.' She laughed.

'We'll have fancies,' he said, smiling at the young woman, 'a large plateful of fancies.'

Jean saw how the waitress's front teeth rested on her bottom lip and that she had the expected carroty hair. She would be good to paint.

Their table was at the window, and when the girl had brought their coffee and cakes, they looked out on the calm water. It was a quiet day with little or no wind.

'Was there any risk in what we did?' she asked him.

'No, no. I'm sure not. You're a . . .'

'A virgin. Or was.'

'You make me feel ashamed. But my love –'

'Mine too.' She took her eyes away and looked out. The yachts hardly moved. It was too calm for sailing. A rowing boat came into her vision, manned by someone who was making it bound over the water, someone young and vigorous, possibly a schoolboy on holiday.

'That's the only way you could move today,' she said. 'See the boy? He'll probably have a favourite spot for fishing. Everyone fishes here.'

'A halycon day.' His face was wistful as he looked. He was far from home.

'A good day for midges. That's what we say when it's a calm day like this. A family saying.' She remembered sitting up in bed comparing weals on their legs. 'The dirty devils,' Anna would say. 'Pass me the camomile lotion.'

'I've got an idea . . . My God, isn't this bizarre?' He was referring to the two-tiered cake stand the girl had brought with a variety of cakes arranged on it, chocolate éclairs, iced cakes, currant cakes. They called them fly cemeteries at home.

'What were you going to say?'

'We could go on the water. It would be peaceful, calm.'

'You mean in a rowing boat?'

'Yes, why not? It's a long time since I've been in one. In the Danube Park, possibly.'

'Why not?' If you had become adult, you had to get on with living and she couldn't in any case go back to Cowal View at

78

lunch time without him. Nor with him, with the mark of Cain on her forehead. What a stupid thing to think! She hadn't killed anyone. 'You might even have time to sketch.' She smiled mischievously at him. 'There's a ferry over to Gourock every hour more or less.' She looked at her watch. 'You could get the three or the four o'clock and you'd be in Glasgow well before dark. That would give us a couple of hours.'

'Clever girl.' He was admiring. 'Besides, I'm here to observe the cloud formations. Had you forgotten?' Evidently he must seduce girls every week since he could be so light-hearted. But, then, to a married man lovemaking was usual, it could happen every night. She remembered having a conversation with Anna about how many times their parents 'did it'. They had felt very bold and modern having the discussion. Anna said she had once heard a groan, she thought, from their bedroom, but it could have been Bessie, who snored in her sleep.

'You must seduce girls every week since you're so light-hearted,' she said. She felt very bold and modern, saying that too. He took her hands across the table, love in his eyes.

TEN

IT WAS LIKE A MILLPOND. The hills on the Cowal side had a soft bloom on them, the loch was milky, with wavelets which creamed on the shore. She had taken the oars first. She had more experience in rowing than Frederick, they decided, and it was good to have something practical to do. She couldn't have borne to sit with him on the pier and wait for the ferry to come in.

She looked at him as she rowed, the full brown eyes with their liquid softness, the strong features, Levantine perhaps. To call him Fredric March as they had done in the Art School had been apt. He was the hero of any film she had ever seen in La Scala (Glaswegians always said *the* La Scala). He filled her life as her heroes had filled the screen.

He had been looking around him, but as if he realized her scrutiny, he turned and met her eyes. 'You regret it? Your face is sad.'

'No,' she said. 'It happened. I'm not one for going backwards. Even in painting I hate to alter anything. The next step is for you. This is new to me.'

'You mean the next step is to ask Elizabeth to release me?'

'There can't be two of us,' she said, and thought, how naïve, how *young*. Am I ready for that kind of situation? There would be great hurt on both sides. 'I wouldn't want any pressure. Perhaps I'm simple. But if you love me, as you said you did . . .' A coldness struck her. Perhaps he had no intention of telling his wife. She felt cheap, like something used, not important . . .

80

He leaned forward and put his hands over hers on the oars. 'I'm ready, Jean. Do not doubt what happened. You are necessary to me.'

She went on rowing, her face turned away from him. The used feeling persisted. There had only been one time. Experienced women didn't expect their lover to rush back home and ask for a divorce right away, did they? But this was different, there had never been anything like this before. She put effort into her rowing as the boy had done. It was necessary because of the calmness, and for the relief the exercise gave her. It took a certain amount of concentration to avoid the anchored yachts.

Rowing was like cycling. You never forgot how to do it. Would lovemaking become the same, a pleasant exercise, insignificant? She saw the steamer crossing the loch, recognized the *King Edward* by its funnels. Father had made sure that the girls knew them all by the colours, especially the paddle ones. It was a part of Glasgow history, he had said. 'Some day you might be the last person to have been on the *Columba*.'

'I'd forgotten about the *King Edward*,' she said. 'If you had been on the pier you could have taken it instead of the ferry. It would be more comfortable. Anna's boyfriend loves them.'

'Mr Laidlaw?'

'Ritchie Laidlaw. You don't have to be so formal.' She smiled at him.

'The Viennese are formal. I do not feel sorry that I will not travel by the *King Edward*. It would have given me less time with you.'

'Do you really mean that?' she said, resting on the oars. They gave her confidence, even a sense of power.

'I always mean what I say. I want to be with you always. It is quite clear in my mind. I tell you, it will be difficult saying this to Elizabeth. We do not have intimate conversations, only practical ones. She is not interested in relationships, ideas, ideals. She was so young when we married that I had not found that out.'

'My sister Anna is practical too. She would steer through a situation like ours like a hot knife through butter.' She laughed, remembering. 'Once she told me that Ritchie had tried it on . . .' she saw Frederick's puzzled face. The expression was too colloquial for him. The word came to her, dredged from some novel she had read, 'that he had been importunate.'

'Ah yes,' he nodded gravely. 'English is such a rich language. I haven't as yet mastered its nuances.'

She decided not to tell him what Anna had said to Ritchie. Not under the circumstances. She felt cynical, thinking that.

'I know enough of it to say that it is you I love, you I want to marry.'

'Ask me again when you're free.' It was Anna speaking in her, for her. She wanted to weep. Of course it was impossible. Anna would have told her so, would have warned her about her heart ruling her head. Why should his wife with three children ever agree to let him go? In a week's time what had happened today wouldn't matter. It was happening all the time, a married man having a flutter, making promises which he would never keep, especially someone like Frederick who adored his children.

'Don't worry,' he said, 'we will be together, you'll see.'

'I won't see ever.' She knew it as she spoke.

'You are so young and beautiful, and I am thoughtless, selfish, but I promise, it will turn out all right and we'll be together all the time.'

She met his eyes and was comforted. They could go and live somewhere else if there was any scandal. She thought of her parents. What would they say, especially Mother, who was so conventional that she became silly at times. Her daughters had to marry well. There had never been any hint of a divorce in either her family or in Father's. What would Mother say to her bridge friends, to Grace and Stewart Binnie who were her yardstick for decorum? And Father? How could he possibly say to Mr Keppel or old Mr Armstrong, his partners, 'My daughter

Jean has been having an affair with a married man. There will be a divorce.'

She became agitated. She skiffed along the surface of the water with the oars and nearly lost her grip on one. She mustn't weep. And what kind of weak-kneed girl would allow a married man to make love to her and then cry about it? Like crying over spilled milk, although that didn't seem so terrible. The tears ran down her face. Through them she could see the steamer coming nearer. How proud it looked . . .

'I am usually good in boats,' she said, 'but I seem to have lost the art.'

'Would you like me to take the oars for a little? I am not as skilled as you, but it would give you a rest.'

'All right. If we're going to change we're better to do it now. The steamer's coming nearer. The turbines go at an amazing speed.' She could make out the people on the deck, even thought she heard the band. What a happy sound that had always seemed to her, so evocative of many trips they had made. 'Don't stand up!' It was one of the precepts for changing places.

But he was already on his feet, and she felt the boat rock alarmingly under her. The *King Edward* was running parallel with them and making for the pier. Now it was leaving them behind. 'Get back to your seat!' she shouted, remembering the wash it would make, but he was too near her, bent forward and reaching for her seat. She rapidly changed her mind. 'No, don't! It's too late. You'll only make it worse.'

'If you could slide over . . .' She had confused him.

'Right. Take my hand. It will steady you.' The boat had swung round, and the frightening thought struck her that they would take the wash from the steamer broadside on.

With the thought the boat began to sway dangerously in a sick-making way. Frederick stumbled, lost his balance and fell to the leeward side. As if some monstrous fish had reared up from the loch underneath them, the boat whirled like a spent match in the current, and they were both decanted into the water.

It was so sudden, and so simple, that she couldn't believe it. The water wasn't even cold. Did fear kill one's senses? Now the boat was floating overturned a few yards away from her, and incredibly the *King Edward* was already well past them.

'Frederick!' she shouted. 'They haven't noticed us. Frederick!' She looked around wildly, treading water. There was no sign of him. Panic made her thrash around madly, calling his name, then she made for the boat. Perhaps he was on the other side of it. 'Frederick! Frederick!' She was shrieking his name. 'Where are you?' Oh God, she thought, he must be trapped underneath. She was filling her lungs ready to dive underneath the boat when his head bobbed up beside her. 'Oh, thank God, thank God. What's wrong?' He was thrashing the water in an unco-ordinated fashion, gasping, blue. 'Hang on to the boat!' she said. 'Are you all right? Have you hurt yourself?'

'I can't . . . swim.' He went under as he opened his mouth to talk, and she pulled him up again by his collar. His longish hair was streaked down on either side of his face, his lips were blue.

'You really can't swim?' He shook his head. Mother had sent them all to the Western Baths, a club . . . 'Support yourself against the boat.' She guided him. 'That's right.' She tried to sound reassuring. 'Someone will see us from the pier, or from the shops. I'll wave. They'll be here any minute . . .' He couldn't swim! She looked towards the shore. It was deserted. The pier was a magnet. Everyone would be there to see the *King Edward* coming in.

'Perhaps someone on the steamer . . .' He had got back his breath now. 'I'm sorry. I never learned. Bronchitis . . .'

'Never mind. Someone will have seen us from the pier.' She swivelled round in the water and saw a small crowd waiting there, but their backs were towards them. She even made out the red lifebelt at the end of it. What use was it to them hanging there? Her panic came back. 'Help! Help!' she shouted. Her voice dissolved into thin air. She tried again, cupping her hands over her mouth. 'Help!' She saw that the steamer was now sailing into the pier like a visiting dowager. Its arrival was monopolizing the attention. Even if you weren't an intending passenger it was always fun to go on to the pier and watch the steamers coming in. Father with his three little girls – how often they had done that.

'Frederick!' She went close to him. 'We must shout together. They're bound to hear us. I'll count up to three and then we'll shout. Ready?' He nodded. His lips were still blue. He was shaking. 'Now,' she said. 'One, two, three! Come on, shout!' His voice was strong enough. 'Again!' she urged, 'Help!'

'It didn't work.' He was shuddering with the cold. Strangely enough she didn't feel it. But then he couldn't *swim*.

'They'll be too busy.' She knew from long experience all the pleasant bustle when a steamer came in, the gangway being put down after the heavy ropes had been thrown . . . Father had always made sure they were well out of the way, taking Nancy's hand, telling Anna and Jean to hold on to each other . . . 'Maybe I could swim for the shore.'

'Don't leave.' His voice changed. He looked deathly pale now. She couldn't leave him.

'I tell you what,' she found courage from somewhere, 'I'm going to right the boat. You'll have to help me. But keep beside it, remember. Then I'll climb in and pull you in too. It will be easy.'

He nodded. 'Whatever you say.'

'But when you see me raising it from underneath you must pull it strongly towards you. It works. I've seen it done.' She had *heard* about it being done, which was quite a different thing.

She had to dive under the boat three times before she got the knack of it, forcing it from the water with her arms stretched above her. Frederick helped. He seemed to forget his fear of the water in helping. Quite suddenly after she had tried for the third time, when she was becoming very tired, the boat bobbed round, looking harmless, an ordinary boat. But without oars. They were floating somewhere. She would think about that later.

'Good, oh good!' she encouraged him. 'Now you must hold tightly and keep balancing it while I climb in on the other side.'

He nodded. 'I understand.'

She forced her body out of the water and clambered in. 'Oh God,' she said. 'Oh God, it's worked!' She lay flat in the bottom for a second and then looked over the side. Yes, he was still there. 'Frederick, we did it!' She touched his hand on the edge of the boat. The fingers gripping the wood were deadly white. Had he the strength left to clamber in as she did? 'Come on, Frederick! Force yourself up. I'll help you.'

Something was on the edge of her vision. She turned and saw two men in a boat vigorously rowing towards them. Purposefully.

'We're all right! Look! They're coming for us!' She saw they were gesticulating, waving, she could hear them shouting something like 'Hold on!' The boat was fairly leaping over the water towards them. 'Oh, Frederick!' She was almost hysterical with relief, 'We're all –' He wasn't there.

She knew she didn't make sense when the two men drew alongside. Also that she had vomited in the bottom of the boat. The mess swayed gently with the motion. 'My friend,' she said to them. 'Oh, quick! He isn't there now. He was holding on.' Their faces were blurred, but one she thought she recognized, a local fisherman who sometimes worked on the pier.

'We'll get him,' he said kindly, and to the man who was holding the oars: 'See any sign?'

'No aboot here.' He was peering over the edge of the boat.

'Right. Well, it's in we go!' The fisherman stripped off his navy jersey, kicked off his shoes and got into the water. He disappeared under the boat. She remembered someone once telling her that a lot of fishermen couldn't swim. She was lucky.

'Here,' the man at the oars said. He had taken off his tweed jacket, and held it out to Jean. 'Pit this roon yer shoothers.' He had on an open-necked shirt.

'Thanks.' She stretched out and took it. 'But I'm not cold.' Nor was she shaking, she was sure, as Frederick had been. She had the odd sensation that she was watching herself in a dream.

'Hughie will get your freen,' the man said. His jacket smelled strongly of tobacco, and was badly worn at the elbows. Not one of the summer visitors. Possibly a gardener. 'Is it another lassie?' he said.

'No. Just . . . a friend.'

'Hughie'll get him. Swims like a fish.' He had a tow rope in his hand. 'Catch this.' He threw it neatly on to the bench beside Jean. 'Tie it through that ring at your back. We'll be giving you a tow.'

She did as she was told, clumsily. A reef knot? Long ago memories of being a Brownie surfaced. She had hated it.

'Whit did a tell ye!' she heard the man say. 'Here he is wi' yer freen. Quick work, eh?' The surge of relief was so strong that tears ran down her face.

The swimmer was certainly back with Frederick, a pale Frederick with closed eyes. 'Oh!' Now her heart was contracting with fear. 'What's wrong? Is he all right?' The fisherman wasn't listening to her.

'Help me in wi' him, Jock,' he was saying. 'Aye, oor boat. The other yin's in a bit o' a mess.' That was the vomit.

'Did he knock his head, or something?' They were ignoring her.

'Aye, maybe.' They now had Frederick prone on the bottom of the boat and the fisherman had turned Frederick's head sideways. Water ran from his mouth. He didn't move. His eyes were still closed. He would be unconscious, that was it, unconscious from shock.

The two men were looking at each other. The one called Jock said, 'Is he gone?' Quietly. She saw Hughie frown, looking meaningfully in her direction.

'Get crackin' for the pier. They'll have sent for the doacter.'

'Aye, right ye are.' He began pulling strongly. The tow rope became taut and her boat seemed to be skimming along the surface of the loch.

'Will he be all right?' She tried to steady her voice, to push away the fear which was threatening to smother her like a black blanket. The fisherman in his soaked vest and trousers was now sitting astride Frederick, pumping at his chest with spread hands. She cleared her throat. 'Is he all right?' Why weren't they answering? She looked away towards the Cowal shore. It was hazy, like her own grip on reality. The only real thing was the pool of vomit in the bottom of her boat. There was a small storm in it because of the speed. She must talk, ask, face up to what was happening.

'He'll recover, won't he?' She made herself shout so that the fisherman would hear her. He seemed to be laying a rug over Frederick, to keep him warm. In spite of Jock's thick tweed jacket she was beginning to shiver. The smell of cheap tobacco from it made her feel nausea in the back of her throat. Hughie, the fisherman, looked back at her.

'He's nae sae guid. You said he wusny yer man?'

'No, just a friend. Good thing you had a rug.' She felt light-headed. You could hire rugs like that on the steamers, along with deck chairs. Mother always liked one to tuck round her legs.

'Aye. Where dae ye stay, hen? You're no' a local?'

'No, we live in Glasgow, but we have a house here. Cowal View. We come every summer.'

'A thought a kent yer face. You're up on the high road, then?'

'Yes.'

The men were talking together now, quietly so that she wouldn't hear them. She saw Hughie shake his head.

'Has he moved at all?' She spoke the words loudly, desperately. 'His name is Frederick. Frederick! Speak to him.'

'We've done all we can, lassie. We're nearly there.' She saw the pier clearly now. The *King Edward* had gone, proudly steaming across the water to Craigendoran.

There was a little knot of people at the top of the steps. Jock was slowing down, manoeuvring the boat to the foot of them with practised strokes. 'We'll get ye to yer hoose in no time,' he said. 'Wull there be anybody in?'

'Yes. My mother and father. They'll have finished lunch. My two sisters, maybe. And friends, Mr and Mrs Binnie.' As if it mattered.

There was a small scrunch as the boat hit wood. Two men were waiting. She watched while Hughie and Jock – they were like old friends now – handed Frederick wrapped in the rug up to them. He couldn't help. His head was covered with the rug.

Someone else had pulled her boat close to the steps by the tow rope and was helping her out. He was an older man wearing a cap with a peak on it. He had a walrus moustache. She had often heard of a walrus moustache. This was the first one she had ever seen. 'An awfy thing tae happen,' he said. 'The doactor says I've to drive you hame. Leave everything to us.'

'Thank you,' she said. 'Are you the taxi man?'

'Aye, that's right.'

Now she could see clearly, but her legs were like paper. You often got that feeling when you stepped off a boat onto dry land. Frederick was lying there, on the wooden boards of the pier, under the rug. A middle-aged man was getting up from looking at him. They all seemed to want to cover his head. How could he get any air that way?

'I'm the doctor,' he said. She could see that. He was well dressed, he had a black bag in his hand and he wore a hat which he raised to her as he spoke. 'Mr Forrest will drive you home. You're a summer visitor?'

'What about Frederick?' she said, 'Mr Kleiber.' She knew with a swift stab of reality that he was dead, then dismissed it. It was too painful, like a sword being thrust through her heart, a

89

double-edged sword. The reality had to be banished. 'Could I see him?'

He gave her an assessing look, then turned back the rug. Frederick's face was drained, white, peaceful. He could have been asleep. She hadn't ever slept with him, wakened with him in the morning . . .

'There's a mark on his forehead,' she said.

'Yes. He must have knocked it on the boat, perhaps concussed himself.' He gently covered Frederick's face with the rug and put his arm round her shoulders. 'I'm afraid he's gone.' He began walking with her, propelling her slowly along the pier.

'That's what they said on the boat. Gone where?' She leaned back against his arm, resisting, shouting, 'Gone *where*?'

'The blow on his head,' he spoke softly, as an example to her, 'asphyxia –'

She interrupted him. 'If you took him to the hospital?' She looked and saw the real man in his eyes for a second, the pity, his confusion.

'I'll do everything that's necessary.' They had reached the road. 'Here's Mr Forrest. He'll get you home. I'll follow in my own car.'

She was sitting beside the man with the walrus moustache. The doctor must have helped her in.

'Bear up,' he now said from the window. A thought struck her. She knocked. The doctor opened the door.

'I have Jock's jacket. Would you give it to him?'

He smiled. 'You keep it meantime.' He shut the door again.

'It's just that he might want it,' she said to Mr Forrest who was putting his taxi into gear.

'That's the least of it.' He steered into the road. 'Don't bother your head about a thing. We'll get you to your folks in no time. Cowal View, isn't it? Fine house. Fine view. Old Miss Chalmers had it for over fifty years. Ninety-one when she died.' He suddenly stopped talking, as if he had said the wrong thing.

'Perhaps Kilcreggan is noted for the longevity of its inhabitants.' Her comment seemed to silence him further. He didn't speak again until he had driven up the drive and stopped at the front door. The pebbles of the drive were shore pebbles. Perhaps old Miss Chalmers had collected them over a long time. They made a pebbly noise under the wheels. 'Here we are,' Mr Forrest said, getting out.

Bessie opened the door to them. She took a quick glance at the taxi driver, then burst out, 'In the name o' Goad, Jean, whit have ye been up tae?'

'The doctor will be here any minute,' Mr Forrest said. 'I'll leave her with you.'

'Whit happened?'

'An accident.' Mr Forrest looked uncomfortable. 'She'll tell ye. All right, miss?' He spoke to Jean, doffing his peaked cap.

'She's far from all right,' Bessie said, 'and fair drookit into the bargain.' She put her arm round Jean and drew her in. 'We'll square up with you later, Mr Forrest.' She shut the door on him.

'Where is everybody?' she asked Bessie in what she thought was a normal voice. She was being led down the passage as if she were an invalid.

'They're in the parlour. I was just going to take their afternoon tea in. My, those Binnies! They would talk an arm off anybody.' She propelled Jean to the door, opened it and pushed her in. 'Look at the state this one's in!' There was consternation in her voice. 'The man says there's been an accident!'

Faces raised, alarmed faces, Mother rising, coming towards her, taking her in her arms. She started to weep because now that she was here, with her own family, she didn't know how she could ever tell them. Because if she admitted it, in this room, she would die of pain and grief.

'Bring her a hot cup of tea with lots of sugar, Bessie,' Mother said. 'Fresh.'

'Put a tot of rum in it.' Father was there too, hovering beside Mother. They got her into a chair, Mother was kneeling in front of her, trying to be jokey, which was the way she always acted in a crisis. This was a new one for her. 'Fancy a big girl like you falling into the water! At your age.' She stroked her cheek. The hand was loving.

'Luckily she doesn't seem to be any the worse.' That was another face somewhere, Mrs Binnie, and beside her, Mr Binnie. She noticed his domed forehead, Nancy, excited-looking – she liked drama – and Anna, bending down beside her, putting her arms round her.

'I'll take her up to bed, Mother. That's the best place. Come on, Jean.'

They helped her up, and she allowed Anna to take her out of the room, up the stairs and into her bedroom where she had dressed just a minute ago to meet Frederick.

'Clothes off,' Anna said. 'You're soaked to the skin.' She helped her off with the tweed jacket – that wasn't hers, surely? – her pretty blouse, her dirndl skirt, her camiknickers with the ecru lace trimmings. Always be as nice underneath as on top in case you have an accident. She had had an accident, a terrible accident.

'Terrible, terrible . . .' She found herself saying the words as Anna tucked her into her bed.

'Was Frederick with you?' Her face was close to hers. Trust Anna to put two and two together and make four.

'Yes. They found him. But they covered him with a rug, Anna, they tried and tried but they covered him with a rug. Over his head.' She screamed. She knew she was giving Anna a fine old time with her screaming and weeping until the doctor came and gave her something which would take away the agony for a time.

ELEVEN

THE MARK OF CAIN! On *his* forehead, not hers as she had first thought, the mark of Cain when the rug was pulled down, the death-white face, no love in it, the closed eyes, the purple bruise. Cain killed Abel, Jean killed Frederick, who, full of life, had taken her, who would never again, never again . . .

'Hush, Jean, hush, close your eyes. I've given you something. Try not to think.'

'It's there all the time, on his forehead, nothing will take it away.'

'Hush . . .'

'Anna, my heart is broken.'

'Father's seeing to everything,' Anna said to her after a couple of days. 'The doctor thinks you'd be better to be up and about.'

'A tragic accident,' he had said to the family when they were gathered together in the sitting room. Jean was in a drugged sleep upstairs. 'Do you know the deceased, Mr Mackintosh?'

'Yes. He was a lecturer at the Art School in Glasgow, which my daughters attend. He had come here for a day of painting.'

'Was he married?'

'Yes, he was.'

'He had three children,' Nancy said. She was suitably subdued, but there was a spark of excitement in her eyes. 'He came with his wife to one of our parties at home.' Trust Nancy to get her oar in somehow.

93

'You will have his address?'

'Yes.' Mother looked too composed. Her mind would be working like mad behind it.

She was a good organizer. She had suggested to the Binnies that it was very distressing for them and perhaps . . . They had twigged right away. Anna had met them coming downstairs with their bags. Grace was gracious. Well, she had to be with a name like that.

'We would just be in the road, Anna. Your mother and father have enough on their plate,' and she had agreed. They were waiting in the dining room until the taxi arrived. 'Your father's been very thoughtful. He's arranged for a taxi to take us up to Glasgow.' Mother and Father closing ranks. This terrible business was a family affair. Things might be said . . .

'The police have been informed, naturally,' the doctor was saying, 'and, er, Mr Kleiber's remains are at the hospital. Perhaps if you could give me the address of his wife, er, his widow, unfortunately, and I could pass it on to them.'

'What a blow for the poor soul,' Father said. 'Maybe I should go and see her, I mean, just the police telling her, so —'

'Harsh,' Mother said.

'It would be very helpful if you would. I don't think your daughter could accompany you just yet. She's suffering badly from shock.'

'She'll go when we're back in Glasgow. That'll be soon.'

'It's so terrible,' Mother said. 'You can't believe it has actually happened.' She was sitting up straight in her chair, putting a brave face on it.

'That's the difficulty your daughter's having. But she's young. She'll get over it.'

She'll never get over it, Anna thought. She loved him. Knowing Jean, she would put her heart into loving, as *she* did. But she and Ritchie weren't built for tragedy. Somehow Jean was, that extra something you couldn't put your finger on. A quality of abandon.

94

'If I started off right away before Mrs Kleiber gets to know from the police,' Father said, 'it might be kinder.'

'The Binnies are waiting in the dining room, Father,' Anna said. 'They say you ordered a taxi.'

'So I did. I'll go in it too.' Anna saw the idea pleased him. He was a real Highlander as far as money was concerned, not mean, but he didn't like to throw it away. For some silly reason she thought of those two furry tennis balls. It felt as if that was years ago. 'Mr and Mrs Binnie were our guests,' he was telling the doctor. 'I thought they would be better out of all this.'

'Very wise.' He got up. 'A sad business,' he said, but he was used to dealing with tragedy. Perhaps they became immune.

Anna, Nancy and Mother had some coffee and sandwiches which Bessie brought in an hour or two later. None of them could face a meal.

'Oh, isn't it terrible, Bessie?' Nancy said. She wiped her eyes. Nancy cried easily and still looked pretty when she cried.

'There's nae cause for *you* to greet,' Bessie said. 'It's your puir sister's affair.' Tumshie was standing at her feet. Never one to waste an opportunity, Anna thought, watching the cat as it rubbed against Bessie's legs. Mother hadn't even noticed. Poor Mother, so intent on making everything seem quite joco. Her goodbyes to the Binnies had been masterly. 'We'll get together in happier circumstances, Grace. Maybe at one of our bridge dos.'

When Bessie and Tumshie had gone away she said to Anna and Nancy: 'We'll have to have a talk. What do you know about Jean and Mr Kleiber, Anna? Was there anything between them?'

'Not that I know of.' Then she thought, this is our mother; you can't put her off like that. 'I think she admired him, was captivated by his . . . otherness.'

'His what?'

'He was different. Foreign. Some of the girls in the Art School were dippy about him.'

'Anna's right,' Nancy said. 'They were always giggling together about him. Mary Thingummy said he reminded her of Fredric March, you know, the film star.'

'Ach!' Mother brushed away all that nonsense. She said to Anna, 'Do you think his wife would know he was coming here?'

'Only if he told her. He could have said he was coming here to paint. That's what Jean told us, remember?'

'Well, we'll stick to that. A friend. Just a friend. Coming here to paint. Are you listening, Nancy? Mr and Mrs Kleiber were friends, family friends.'

'We only saw them once, at Father's party.'

'Well, we saw them together, didn't we? Family friends, nothing more.' She looked impatient with herself. 'Oh, I wish I had impressed that on Angus!'

'Father isn't stupid, Mother,' Anna said. 'He isn't going to say he came here to make love to Jean, is he?'

'What a thing to say, Anna! You young people nowadays.'

Anna shrugged. 'He'll be diplomatic. The woman has enough to put up with, without anything else. That's all I'm saying.'

'Yes, you can rely on your father. He's good with people. You two,' she looked from Nancy to Anna, 'choose a man you can rely on in an emergency, not one who has to lean on you. We'll go upstairs and pack ready for Father when he comes back, and we'll tell Bessie to get things together in the kitchen.'

'I asked James for the weekend, Mother.' Nancy looked aggrieved. 'You said I could.'

'Well, now you can't. Get to the telephone and tell him our plans have changed and we're coming home, that there's been an accident. If he's a man at all he'll not press you for information.'

'He'll understand,' Anna said. She had watched the blossoming of love between her young sister and this man fifteen years her senior. They were suited to each other. Nancy needed an older man, a father figure.

Anna was packing in her bedroom when she heard Jean call. Mother had gone into the garden. 'My head is splitting. I need a breath of air.' Mother was no fool. She knew there was a lot to come yet. She would hold herself ready.

Anna went into Jean's room and found her sitting up. She couldn't look pale if she tried, with that warm skin of hers, but her eyes were terrible, the black lines underneath them looking as if they had been scored with a carbon stick.

'How are you feeling?' she said, sitting down on the bed beside her.

'Sort of half-awake, drugged, dead inside. What did that doctor give me?'

'Some kind of knockout pill. I have to give you another.' He had been explicit that a reliable member of the family should take charge of them.

'I don't want any more. Frederick is dead, isn't he?'

'Yes.'

'Everyone was very kind, those men – I can't think of their names . . . Anna, how are we going to tell his wife?' She reached for Anna's hand, gripped it like a vice.

'Father's left with the Binnies. He'll do it. He hired a taxi to take them up to Glasgow.'

'He especially adored the youngest one, Hilde. Oh, Anna, in here . . .' she put her other hand on her breast '. . . the pain . . . I saw a pencil portrait he did of her. She was like a little angel in those Italian paintings. Raphael. So sweet.'

'Yes.'

'The thing is, Anna, how am I going to go about carrying this grief?'

'By thinking of the little girl, maybe. Or his wife.' Jean's eyes were on her as if she were drowning.

'They were married very young. I think they had grown away from each other over the years.'

But *you* are very young, Anna thought. He might have done the same with you.

'You have to get yourself fit to travel up to Glasgow. We'll probably leave tomorrow. Father will hire a taxi again.'

97

'He won't like that.' There was a glimmer of the old Jean.

'Do you want something to eat?'

'No, I'm not hungry. I have no feelings, of hunger or thirst, or of anything, no feelings at all. I know Frederick is dead. That's all.'

Anna made a decision. 'How did it happen?' she said deliberately, cruelly.

'We had been in the woods . . .' Her face crumpled, tears seemed to spurt from her eyes, her grip on Anna's hand tightened.

'Well, you couldn't sail in the woods. Did you decide there to hire a boat?'

'Don't ask me.' Her head moved from side to side as if she was trying to shake something off.

'You hired a boat.' Oh, it was cruel. 'Was it his idea?'

'Yes, I think it was. We were so happy, Anna.' She raised her face to her, submerged in tears. 'We just wanted to be together. Oh, Anna, the love, the love . . . It filled me, I was trembling with it.'

'I know. I feel it too for Ritchie.'

'Ah, but you're sensible, sensible and practical. You wouldn't –'

'What?'

'I don't want to talk. Stop it, Anna. I can see through you. I know you.'

'Would you like to see Mother?'

'Oh no, she's the last one I want to see.'

'Good thing she can't hear you saying that. So you took out a boat?' She would leave the woods meantime.

'Yes, it seemed a good idea. The water looked lovely. The Cowal shore was a watercolour of blue-grey tints, like in a dream. The joke was, he hadn't brought anything to paint with, only a sketchbook, I think. He's mischievous, that man.' The smile through the running tears was a grimace.

'Was he used to small boats?'

'Not really. I rowed. I could watch him that way. The happiness. He's so beautiful ... Then he thought he would like a go. He said it would recapture memories of Vienna for him. He's so pedantic the way he speaks. Anyone could fall in love with him just listening. He stood up.'

'He shouldn't have done that. Father was always telling us –'

'Yes, I thought that too. It would have been all right but there was a wash from the *King Edward*, and suddenly we were both in the water. It wasn't very cold at all.' She wished she would stop smiling. 'I remember thinking that. You know how sometimes when we were young Mother made us go in near Cove, I think it was, and when we came out we were shaking with the cold. My fingers would be dead, white and dead ... Oh no, I shouldn't have said that. Oh God, oh God!' The tears were dissolving her face so that there was none of her sister there, just pain.

'I remember those swims. It was only good when you stopped, when you came running out and Mother would wrap you in a big fleecy towel and give you a sandwich.'

'Frederick couldn't swim. Couldn't swim! Can you believe that? Can *no* one swim in Vienna for God's sake? He disappeared but I found him, and I righted the boat. He helped. He apologized for not being able to swim. Viennese politeness.'

'So then?'

'Then?' She looked mad, this lovely sister of hers, mouth gaping, features ruined with tears, 'Oh, then the other boat came with the two men. I can't remember their names, isn't that ridiculous? I can't remember their names!'

'It doesn't matter.'

'It *does* matter! Frederick had disappeared and one of them dived and got him and they covered him with a rug. On the pier they lifted out Frederick under the rug. "Gone," they said. I asked the doctor to let me see him, to let me see what "gone" looked like, the drowned face, the closed eyes, the mark on his forehead, the mark of Cain!' She was suddenly screaming,

'Gone! Gone! It's too much, too much to bear. I'll die ... die ...'

Their mother was at the bedside. She had a glass of water which she put down on the table. Her face was without expression. She was good at it. Even when she was playing bridge her opponents never had a clue. Self-composed.

'Have you the pills, Anna?'

'Yes.'

'Jean.' Her mother bent over her, speaking softly. 'We know how bad it is. We're breaking our own hearts for you, but we don't want any more of that screaming. It doesn't do you any good. You have to sleep so that you can get back to Glasgow tomorrow.'

'He isn't there! Even if I go back I'll never find him. Oh, Mother, if you knew the pain ...' The word shrieked round the room in a wail.

'Take the pill from Anna. That's right. Now wash it down with this. There,' she was stroking Jean's head, looping the heavy hair over her ears, 'that's my Jean, my bonnie Jean.' She turned to Anna, shaking her head, then went back to her stroking. 'There, there, we're all here, taking care of you. The pain will go, you'll see, the pain will go. Before you sleep Nancy's bringing you something from the kitchen. We're all helping. Bessie's made neat little sandwiches for you with smoked salmon. She's cut off the crusts. Your favourite. And coffee. You like coffee best, don't you? Funny how Nancy and I are the tea drinkers and you and Anna like coffee. And Father's in between, sometimes one and sometimes the other. Don't go to sleep yet, my darling. You have to get your sandwiches.'

Nancy was in the room with a tray decked with a lace cloth, and on it the doilied plate of crustless sandwiches and a cup of coffee. The steam was rising from it. 'Are you feeling better, Jean?' she said. Jean raised her eyelids and looked at Nancy as if she were a stranger. 'One thing, it got rid of the Binnies in double-quick time.' Nancy giggled. 'I was having James for the

100

weekend but that's put off now. Still, I'll see him when we get back to Glasgow, I expect.'

'You can eat those yourself, chatterbox,' her mother said. 'She's asleep.' She tucked the clothes round Jean, stroked her cheek. Lovingly.

TWELVE

A FEW WEEKS LATER Angus took Jean with him when he went again to visit Mrs Kleiber. He had waited until he could rely on her not weeping. Tears were supposed to wash away the grief, but it wasn't so in her case. He could hardly bear to look at her at times, this quiet young woman who sat still for hours, doing nothing with her hands, not reading, just sitting, then, suddenly, getting up and rushing to her room. They would sit listening to the sobs, looking miserably at each other. He would comfort Rose, taking her in his arms although Nancy and Anna were there.

It was now a month since the accident. For the last week or so they hadn't heard that dreadful sobbing. There was a limit to tears.

'I promised to bring you to see her, Jean,' he said, 'but I don't want you breaking down when we're there. It was bad enough the first time.' He had told Rose he would not like to go through that again, not for a million pounds. And those three children, stupefied except for the youngest one, a beautiful little girl who made up to him shamelessly, the way Nancy used to do.

Still did. You spotted it early in children, girl children, this desire to please Daddy. It was a good thing that Nancy and James Pettigrew had hit it off. It didn't matter that he was so much older. It was a splendid match and right for her as well. He would adore her as well as love her, be a father as well as a lover.

They drove out to a row of sandstone tenements near Queen's Park. There was nothing very nice about them, built as they were over a string of ordinary-looking shops, but the park would be useful for Mrs Kleiber as a place to take the children. They were aged nine, eight and three, she had told him that day when he first saw her.

She hadn't wept, he told Rose when he came home. She had gathered the children to her as she sat, and said, 'This gentleman says Daddy will not be coming home,' and then she was speaking in German to them and rocking herself back and forth. She had forgotten about Angus, and after a time he had got up and let himself out. You could stand just so much of that, the sheer inability to help, and the guilt of being the bearer of bad news.

He had knocked at one of the other two doors on the landing and a woman about Rose's age had answered it, nice-looking, capable. She had immediately agreed to go in and sit with Mrs Kleiber. 'Poor soul,' she had said. 'We take our kids to the park together.'

Mrs Kleiber answered the door on this second visit with a silent Jean standing beside Angus. 'I have brought my daughter to meet you,' he said.

'Yash?' She barely looked at Jean. 'Will you please to enter?' She stood aside. 'Funny how important location is,' he had told Rose afterwards. 'The furniture reflected the flat, reflected the area. Show me a picture of an interior and I can make a good guess at where to find it.'

He was keeping his fingers crossed in case Jean broke down. In the car he had said abruptly to her – it was the only way to do it – 'Was there an affair between you and Frederick Kleiber?' She had turned her head away from him. She seemed to be looking at the busyness of Victoria Road. 'Jean,' he said, 'I want an answer.'

Her voice was level. 'I loved him. I will always love him. Will that do?'

'It'll have to,' he said, 'but by God, keep quiet about that to his widow. It's bad enough that you loved a married man without blurting it out to her.'

'I'm not daft, Father.' She seemed to be searching in the street for something.

Now they were in the dingy room with its dark paintwork and its nondescript furniture where one piece had no affinity with another, like furniture which had been bought in a hurry to be purely functional. The two boys weren't there – probably back at school – but the little girl was clinging to her mother's skirts. He thought he had never seen a prettier child, with her black ringlets and piquant face. She had a battered-looking doll in her arms and when Jean smiled at her, she went over to her and said something in German.

'She's asking if you would like to hold it,' her mother said.

'Thank you.' Jean took the doll and cradled it in her arms like a child. 'It's a lovely dolly,' she said. 'What is it called?'

'Say "Leonie" to the lady.' Her mother spoke sharply. 'And in English, if you please.'

'Leonie. Papa . . . ?' She looked at her mother.

'Papa christened it.' The little girl nodded uncertainly, then looked at Jean and Angus. 'Come, Hilde.' The mother took her on her knee. 'You must be a good girl.' She snuggled shyly against her mother's breast.

Angus looked at Jean. She was sitting poker-straight, her face expressionless. There was no fear of her weeping.

'You forgot Leonie.' She handed the doll to the little girl.

Mrs Kleiber must have been a pretty woman, Angus thought. She too had a piquant face, a cat face, broad across the brow and eyes, a small pointed chin. But she hadn't worn well. She was plump and had thick ankles. Her eyes, though, were fine, with clear whites. 'I thought I should bring Jean to see you,' he said, 'so that you could ask her anything which might be giving you cause for anxiety.'

'So? There was the postmortem. There is no anxiety. Only

104

grief. Ah yes, there is grief. Worse because I am not in my home. Would you not grieve, Miss Jean, if you were left with no husband and three children?'

Jean looked at her, a long look. 'Yes, I would grieve. It is a terrible situation for you. I grieve ... all the time. Words can't –' She changed what she was going to say. 'Will you go back to Vienna?'

'I do not know. Perhaps it would be dangerous. Have you not heard of Nuremberg? My husband was a Jew. Everything is being taken away from them, even the right to live. Was that not why we came here? At least, we said, it would be safe. Now that is a joke, yash?' She repeated the word, 'Yash?' looking at Jean.

'Yes,' Jean said.

'Pah!' It was an impatient gesture. Angus thought, her indignation is saving her. 'Here you understand nothing. You are not Europeans. And the French? Pah!' she said again. 'Nobody wants to help us. You are prepared to give Hitler the benefit of the doubt.'

'It is a terrible situation for you,' Angus said. 'My daughter knows that. The loss of your husband, and the situation in your country.'

She looked at him, head on one side, as if she was considering what he said. 'And yet, do you know, Mr Mackintosh, the political situation helps a little? Do you understand that? It takes the edge off my grieving.'

'Yes, indeed,' Angus said.

'I always worried about his safety. That is why we came here. Now, at least, the anxiety is gone.'

'I can see that.'

'You knew my husband well?' Mrs Kleiber said to Jean. She had a darting way of speaking, like a bird, a bird with bright eyes.

'He taught me at the Art School, Mrs Kleiber.'

'And he was charming, yash?'

'He was well-liked.'

'Sometimes you should look behind the charming man. Often there is a selfishness. Their charm is used up outside and they have none left to give at home. Meetings, lectures, days off to paint, no time for his sons. This little one,' Hilde was nestling into her, sucking her thumb, 'this little Hilde he adored. He liked girl children. Tell me,' her head poked forward again, 'did he ever talk to you about me? About Elizabeth, his wife?'

Angus held his breath.

'Yes,' she said. 'I knew about you, and your children. I think he was very proud of them.'

'Did he tell you I was simply a *Hausfrau*? A woman who hadn't nice clothes, who lived in this strange, ugly place?'

'No, he never said that.' Jean was still calm.

'Well, of course I am a *Hausfrau*. Who wouldn't be in this miserable flat which was all we could afford? Frederick did not worry about that. He was seldom here. An art school. A good environment. Doting pupils, girl children grown up. Do you understand that? Do you?'

'I understand how hard –'

'We all realize how hard it is for you in a country not your own,' Angus said. If this went on Jean might break down. 'Very few diversions when children are small. My wife would understand that. Are you musical at all? I always think of Vienna and music together.'

The woman looked less tense. 'Ah, yes, that is so. Yes, in the happy days I sang a little, played the piano a little, flirted a little. That is even more difficult for you to believe? Frederick often said he was enchanted by me. And then we had to leave because he was a Jew. I gave up so much for him. I could have remained with my family, but one must go where one's husband goes. So they said. We are taught in Vienna to put our husbands first. It would be the same here, in Scotland? Mrs Baxter in the next flat says to me, "Let them go to the devil." What do you think, Mr Mackintosh?'

'Well . . .' Angus searched for a reply. He heard Jean's shaking voice.

'I would do anything to change what has happened.'

'We all would.' Angus decided to be blunt. 'Mrs Kleiber, if you are temporarily embarrassed and you would like to go back to Vienna soon, it would be my pleasure to pay your fare, and that of your family, of course. Perhaps that would be a practical way of showing our sympathy.'

'That is generous of you. Why do they say here people are not? I do not see this. Mrs Baxter gives me some of her baking, the scones, and the pancakes. I am waiting for a letter from my mother, then we shall see, yash?'

'Would you like me to tell you how it happened?' Jean said. Silly girl. 'I have found it is better to talk than to hide one's grief. Sometimes I screamed. My sister Anna said it was a good idea. "Scream your head off if it helps," she said. Would you like me to tell you, Mrs Kleiber?'

The woman shrugged, glanced at Angus. 'It cannot make any difference,' she said. 'One day I have a husband. The next day I have not. My children have no father.'

'It was a simple accident,' Jean said, as if she were reading from a script. 'Changing places in a boat, and being capsized by the wash from a passing steamer. I find it difficult to believe. How can I expect you . . . ?' Her voice shook.

Don't for God's sake go any further, Angus thought. It is bad enough as it is.

'What I can't understand,' Mrs Kleiber said, 'is not the accident in the boat. It is why he chooses to go off alone in a boat with you, a student of his. That is incomprehensible to me. Do you understand, Mr Mackintosh?' She addressed him as if she would get more sense from him.

'We can be held responsible there,' he said. 'We invited him to come and paint near our holiday home. Perhaps we didn't make it clear enough that we meant him to bring his wife and family. He might have been reticent. We had guests staying, a crowded house, and Jean volunteered to show him the best painting spots. On the water, in a boat, you get a better view of the coastline, of the hills beyond that.'

'This is so?' She spoke to Jean.

'You do see a place differently from the water. He was interested.' Her voice was stronger.

'I face facts,' Mrs Kleiber said. 'Frederick always had new plans, new interests. I learned not to take him too seriously. This,' she looked round the room, 'was to be temporary accommodation only. He would take me to the best shop in your Buchanan Street and buy me a fur coat. That is how he was, but he was my husband and I loved him.' Her eyes were full. Lovely eyes, Angus thought, really a pretty woman if she were permed and powdered and dressed by Jaeger like Rose.

'We will go now,' he said, rising. 'Come on, Jean. I want you to think of us as your friends. And please believe me, it would. be an honour if you would let me help you to get home to your family in Vienna.'

Jean got up. She went to the woman, bent over and stroked the little girl's cheek. 'Forgive me, Mrs Kleiber,' she said, turning to her, 'please forgive me. I feel so responsible for the death of your husband. I am ashamed.'

'There is no need to feel ashamed, I hope.' She spoke briskly. 'Will you let yourselves out, if you please? I do not want to disturb Hilde.' Jean stood beside her for a moment then followed Angus who was holding the door open for her.

'Well,' he said, when they were rattling down the stone stairs, 'that was difficult. I don't deny it was difficult, but it was right.'

'As family friends,' she said.

He heard the bitterness in her voice. He looked at her. 'Sometimes the plain truth only adds to the sorrow, and that would be selfish. Only *you* know the truth.'

'She, at least, is not in an invidious position. She'll get sympathy and understanding.'

'Which is her right.'

108

'Which is her right.'

When they were in the car he said, because it rankled, 'Besides, your family have rallied round you. And Mother does her best. Sometimes she doesn't understand you.'

'Oh, I can live with that. It's not sympathy for having been involved in a tragic accident I want.'

'What on earth *is* it you want then?' Sometimes those girls were a trial. Not for the first time he wished they had had a son, or better, two. You could talk to boys. You knew how their minds worked.

'Understanding of my grief at losing Frederick, my love,' she said.

He smacked the driving wheel in exasperation. Keep your eye on the road. They were coming to Eglinton Toll, had just passed the Plaza where the firm's annual dance was held. He said, 'He was a married man with three children. You should have thought of that.'

'I did, all the time.' Her voice was hoarse.

He stole a look at her. Her eyes were dry and tearless, but for a moment he saw her as she would be in ten years' time, the best of her youth gone. Something had been extinguished in her, the vital spark. Rose wanted them married, and married well. She might be disappointed in this one. He put a hand over hers which lay in her lap. 'Love doesn't choose, Jean. Maybe that will have to be your penance. Don't talk about Frederick Kleiber to your mother. She wouldn't be able to take it. She is highly moral. As I know.' He gave a short laugh.

'Oh, I don't talk to her. Don't worry.' She lay back in her seat and closed her eyes.

When they got home Nancy and Anna were back from the Art School. 'Mr Brown was asking when you were coming back,' Anna said. 'He says you left some things half finished.'

'I'm going back tomorrow.' She didn't sit down. 'Call me when Bessie dishes up,' she said, and went out of the room.

'Well, Angus,' Rose said, 'how did it go?'

'Better than I expected. Mrs Kleiber is a survivor. I think she'll go back to Vienna. I offered to pay their fares.'

THIRTEEN

1937

'THIS IS WHAT IS called a wally close,' Ritchie said as they climbed the stone stairway. The January wind made the trapped air even colder on their faces. Anna was on holiday from the Art School and Ritchie had gained his degree. Some of his paintings were to be on show in a London gallery along with other outstanding work from various art schools in Britain, and he had decided to try his luck there and would be sharing a flat with Bob McNair, a former student in Glasgow who was working as a commercial artist.

'A wally close?' Anna said. 'I'm ignorant. What is it?'

'You should be ashamed to admit it. See those tiles? That's posh. That makes it a wally close. In Bridgeton you get plaster walls, dark brown paint on the lower half and dirty white above. Great for the graffiti, though. And gas mantles. Do you know what a gas mantle is?'

'I think so.' There was no point in seeming ignorant about everything.

'As a child I thought they were the most beautiful things I had ever seen in my life. A little white bag which you put over the gas. "Don't touch it," my mother would say, "your finger will go right through it." It was like fairy gauze.' He gave a hoot of laughter. 'Hark at me! Once it was safely on, you could regulate the gas by a tap, hence the well-known Glasgow saying, "having your gas on a peep".'

'The wonders of science!' She pointed to the step they were

111

standing on. 'I like the decoration. All those whirly bits. Whoever did that should be at the Art School.'

'My mother, if you want to know. When she washes them she does that with pipeclay as a finishing touch. Her signature, in a way. That's where my talent comes from.' He put his arm round her waist and squeezed it. 'Boldly executed, wouldn't you say? Touch of the old Miró there? He abhorred straight lines.'

'Bold is the word.' She put her head on his shoulder, feeling very much in love.

'I owe my mother a great deal. She's the one that subsidizes me when I'm really broke.'

'When you've spent your Carnegie money?'

'That goes on paint and fees. Every time I take you for coffee in the Regal café it's she who finances me.'

'Oh, that's terrible! You should have said.'

'She knows you're worth it. She trusts my judgement.' He tightened his arm round her, kissed her cheek. 'Will you come and see me in London? If it's a success will you marry me? I could get a flat there. If you hadn't finished your course you could go to St Martin's.'

'I'm still thinking about your mother paying for all those coffees.'

'If you want to feel guilty throw in the University Union as well. There's no false pride between my mother and me. What about it?'

'What about what?'

'You coming to London. Us getting married.'

She looked at him. University Unions or not, she didn't get enough of him. She wanted to be closer than they were on the sofas in the sitooterie – clothes off, flesh to flesh. They kissed. And kissed again. She felt his tongue in her mouth. Ritchie didn't go in for polite pecks, closed mouths.

'I'll drop a hint or two to my parents,' she said when he released her. She was trembling. He always did that to her. It wasn't living in London which sorely tempted her, it was living

112

with Ritchie, being in the same bed, instead of this endless tightrope walking. They were both ready for the Grand Experience. That was what she and Jean used to call it. Poor Jean. She wasn't the same since Kleiber had died . . .

There was a loud bang of a door shutting above them. She looked up.

'It's Mrs Nosey-Parker,' Ritchie said in her ear. They pulled into the side of the step against the wall. The woman coming down had a shopping basket over her arm and a scarf over her head.

'It's you, Ritchie,' she said, stopping beside them, her fat face beaming. 'Ur ye on your way to see yer Mammy and Daddy?' She looked pointedly at the bunch of flowers Anna was carrying.

'Right first time, Mrs Beith,' Ritchie said. 'How did you guess?'

'Well, ye're on your way up, uren't ye?' She shook her head at him. 'Pull the ither yin, Ritchie Laidlaw. My, you're a warrior!' She looked at Anna as if for confirmation. Had she caught a glimpse of them kissing, she wondered. 'And it's nae guid pittin' on yer airs and graces with me. I knew you when you were jinkin' roon the closes, or dreepin' aff the wash-hoose roof. Aye, he was a tearaway.' This was addressed to Anna. Ritchie gave in.

'This is Miss Mackintosh, my girlfriend,' he said.

'Pleased to meet you.' She was satisfied. 'Well, I'll away and get the bus. I'm gawn to Hamilton.'

'Don't let that great metropolis turn your head,' Ritchie said.

She shook her head at him. 'I'll say cheerio, then. Cheerio, miss.' She went on down the stairs, holding on to the bannister, being careful not to step on the pipeclay whirls, perhaps an artist's respect for a fellow artist's work.

'A pleasant interlude,' she said, laughing.

'Aye, it's nice to fraternize with the proles sometimes. Us yins don't put on any side.' They were both stifling their laughter as they went on up the steps. Anna sobered as they came towards the landing. She felt apprehensive about meeting Ritchie's parents, afraid that her form of politeness might seem to them like condescension. Clevedon Crescent gave you a criterion which you would be better without.

They reached the door. 'Laidlaw' it said on the polished brass plate. Ritchie lifted the brass knocker, which was a replica of a castle, and gave a sharp rat-tat-tat with it. Then he took a key from his pocket and opened the door. 'Just to warn them of our arrival,' he said with mock seriousness.

He was his mother's son, she thought, when they went into the lobby and found her standing there. She had the same strong curly hair, his dark eyes. Her dress was black with tiny white spots. It had a very white collar showing over the grey cardigan she wore. She was thin to gauntness.

'Here we are, Ma,' Ritchie said, 'and this is Anna.' The woman smiled nervously and held out her hand. When Anna took it she felt its hard skin rasping against hers. She and Jean used a lot of hand cream. Turps dried the skin. Anna gave her the flowers.

'Oh, they're nice,' Mrs Laidlaw said. 'Carnations, Ritchie. Thanks.' She looked at Anna, pleased. 'We've heard a lot about you . . . Anna,' she said.

'All good, I hope.' No, that was the wrong way to talk. It sounded forced, unnatural. She saw his mother smiling at Ritchie, unsure.

'She's listened to me often enough, singing your praises,' he said. 'Where's Dad? In the front room?'

'No, he's in the kitchen. I told him there was a good fire at the front, but I can't get him to leave the kitchen grate.'

'Come and meet him, Anna.' Ritchie steered her towards an open door. 'He's always at that fire. Always willing to toast a slice of bread, isn't he, Ma?'

'Aye, and get tartan legs with the heat.'

The man who rose to his feet with a poker in his hand was desperately shy. Or unused to social contacts. He wasn't a match for his wife. He had a stubborn look, the stubbornness of the weak. He hadn't gone 'into the front' when he was asked. 'She can take me as she finds me,' Anna could imagine him saying.

'How do you do, Mr Laidlaw?' She held out her hand. He gave it a small shake and dropped it.

'I'm fine, just fine, miss.' He looked at the poker he was holding. It was thin, designed for poking the golden-red fire between the bars of the grate, polished to a rich blackness, the steel trim gleaming. The handle of the poker was shaped like the head of a teasle, made of copper wire.

'Take your father away ben, Ritchie,' his mother said, 'while I make the tea. He just gets in my road.'

'Please don't go to any trouble,' Anna said. 'There will be a meal ready for me when I get home.'

'I was going to give you ham and eggs. It's quick.' She looked disconsolate.

'Oh, no thanks. Bessie will have it ready.'

'Is that your sister?'

'No.' She was ashamed. 'She's our maid. She's been with us for years. More like a friend.' She saw a black cat sleeping on the cushion of a chair. 'She has a cat too. She calls it Tumshie. It tries to slip into the dining room behind Bessie, but Mother won't have it . . .' Mr Laidlaw looked bemused, his wife puzzled.

'She could have given it a nicer name than that. Ours is called Lucky. Black cat for luck. Now away you go the three of you. I've just the tea to mask if you're sure you won't have anything cooked.'

'No, thanks. Thanks all the same. Nothing.'

'Not even a scone, or a pancake?'

'Of course she will, Ma. She's been baking for weeks, Anna. It's as much as your life is worth.' Ritchie had gone to a cupboard and was taking out some cups.

'No, no, Ritchie!' His mother stopped him. 'I've got the best ones laid out. They're there on the tray.'

115

'I'll carry it through. You get on with the tea. Come on, Anna. Come on, Da. We're just in the way.'

The sitting room had so many surfaces made bright with polish that it was dazzling. Anna felt they were all winking at her. The fire gleamed in its setting of Dutch tiles in a frame of black iron. The three of them sat down on chairs which had been placed round it. The chairs had antimacassars on their backs and arms. Mr Laidlaw was still carrying the poker. He looked at it and gave a short laugh. 'Goodness me!' he said to it as if it had grown in his hand.

'Well, since you've brought it,' Ritchie said, 'give the fire a good poke.' His father bent down, and inserted the poker through the ribs. Flames spurted from the dark pieces of coal.

Anna looked round the room, saw photographs of Ritchie at every stage, and on every polished surface. The room was like a shrine. 'You must be very proud of Ritchie,' Anna said to Mr Laidlaw, 'having some of his paintings on show in London.'

'Aye, I am, though I can't say they're much to ma taste. Lizzie tells me they're modern art. She has a book owr there, *The History of Modern Painting*. She pores over it.'

'Have *you* read it?' Anna asked.

'Naw, it's no in ma line.'

'Any luck today?' Ritchie sat down beside his father, having deposited the tray.

'A bit, son. I went to see the gaffer of the foundry and he said they might be taking on more men.' He looked at Anna. 'A foundry would be new to me,' he said. She was grateful to be included.

'What was your job, Mr Laidlaw?'

'A miner at the Gartsherrie pit. Eighteen years I put in there, then one fine mornin' we're paid off. There's gratitude for you.'

'Aye, that was tough,' Ritchie said. Anna looked at him. His eyes were full of sympathy. Did he never feel guilty about his maverick decision to paint instead of taking a job and helping his parents? If he did, he had never said so. He was single-

116

minded. They both were. She was going to marry him even although he wouldn't have been her mother's choice.

Mrs Laidlaw came bustling in. She had put the carnations Anna had brought her into a cut-glass vase which she placed on a table at the window. 'I wanted them in water before I made the tea,' she said. 'They needed a drink.'

'And you've put them at the window so that all your neighbours can see them,' Ritchie said, laughing.

'Away with you,' she turned to him, smiling, and Anna saw how pretty she must have been. The smile lifted her face, her eyes were bright. She was intelligent, Anna thought, you could tell by her quick movements. She was decisive. She laid out the cups and saucers quickly, she found a small table and put it in front of Anna.

Her husband didn't move. He was staring dully at the fire, he didn't join in the conversation, which was centring on Anna's admiration of the china. It showed taste in its delicacy, the gold rim on the fluted cups. Remember the man's unemployed, she told herself. That's enough to break anyone's spirit.

The tea was passed round, the pancakes and scones, the potato scones rolled round slivers of cheese.

'Just in case you get peckish,' Mrs Laidlaw said. Anna took one to please her.

'You have a lovely bright room,' she said.

'Oh, aye?' The woman saw through her remark, knowing where she came from, how she lived. But there were to be no snide remarks, no self-pity. 'And what do you think of Ritchie, going away to London?' she said.

'It's grand. He'll come back famous.' She smiled. 'Are you going down to see the opening of the exhibition?'

'Oh, no.' She shook her head. 'It's too far, and I'm working every day. Are you going?'

'I don't know. I haven't got my invitation yet.'

'Will you listen to the girl, Ma? I've asked her a hundred times. And I've asked her to marry me if I make a success of it.

117

What more does she want?' His mother didn't seem surprised, but Anna caught a quick look from the father as if he were assessing her.

'I'm cautious by nature,' Anna laughed. 'I'll wait to see if he sells any of his paintings.'

'Oh, they'll fall at his feet.' His mother had a sense of humour. 'So *he* thinks.'

'You wouldn't mind if we got married?' Anna asked her. 'I mean, later on.'

'Ritchie's choice is ours too. Isn't that right, Walter?' she said to her husband.

'He's always gone his own way.' There was a glimmer of a smile. 'We'd have a job stopping him now.'

'See how I'm worshipped,' Ritchie said, laughing. 'Have one of Ma's pancakes, Anna. I told you she's been baking for weeks to impress you.'

'Oh no, I couldn't, thanks all the same.'

'Don't press her,' Mrs Laidlaw said. 'I know how I hate to have to eat out of politeness. You're a twin, Ritchie tells me?'

'Yes, Jean, but we keep it dark.'

'They're as like as chalk and cheese,' Ritchie said, 'but Jean's the better painter.'

'Then you've a younger sister?'

'Yes, Nancy.'

'And you're all at the Art School? Your father and mother must be proud of you.'

'They never say. We take it for granted, somehow. My mother went there, and of course, my father, although he only draws plans.'

'What are they for?' Mrs Laidlaw's face was bright with interest.

'For houses, and churches, and public buildings. You name it, he does it.'

'He's a partner in a firm of architects, Mother,' Ritchie said.

'Yes, you told me. But that wouldn't have suited you, son.'

She looked at Anna. 'He's no good at kowtowing. I don't mean *your* father has to do that, but maybe on his way up . . .'

'Has he his name on the door?' Mr Laidlaw said suddenly.

'I suppose so.'

'I've seen that, Lizzie,' he addressed his wife, 'when you go for interviews. What would you say if one day I had ma name on the door?' He was smiling. He's getting used to me, Anna thought.

'I'd say you deserved it, if it happened.' She wasn't a nagger. 'But you need time for that,' she was now speaking to Anna, 'time to read, to study. Walter and me, we never had the time, not when you're working with your hands all day. That's how it's been with us. Leaving school too early. Having to work.'

'She's exaggerating,' Ritchie said. 'How about your ship in a bottle, Da, and your poker work, Ma? They're always doing something like that at night, but they don't think it's art.'

'You don't have to go to Art School to call it art. In my classes there are women who embroider, design furniture, wallpaper, hammer metal like me. There are various disciplines. Could I see your ship in a bottle, Mr Laidlaw?' she asked.

He was embarrassed. 'Oh, it's nothing. When you're oot o' work . . .' He looked at Ritchie for help.

'Let Anna see it,' he said. 'She would be great in a foundry, filling moulds. She has muscles like Tommy Farr's.'

'What a nerve!' Anna said. Mr Laidlaw got up.

'All right,' he said. 'But no laughin' behind ma back, Ritchie, remember.'

He returned almost immediately, carrying a clear bottle with a model of a sailing ship inside. He put it on a table, and Anna got up to look at it. 'It's wonderful, Mr Laidlaw,' she said, examining it. 'I don't see how you do it. Correct to the smallest detail. A mystery to me.'

'It's a trick,' Ritchie said. 'There's a way of opening the bottle down the side.'

119

'Away with you!' His mother laughed at him. 'You know he sits for hours with his wee pliers.'

'Aye, they're a grand pair. That's Mother's poker work,' he said, pointing to a three-legged stool with an intricate design burned on it.

'You should both be at the Art School,' Anna laughed.

'No, no,' Mrs Laidlaw said. 'Ritchie's the painter. Ever since he was a wee lad he's been drawing. You couldn't get a pencil out of his hand. The headmaster spotted him when he was twelve. He'd seen something Ritchie did for a competition.'

They had finished their tea. Anna looked at her watch. It was five o'clock. 'I'm afraid I'll have to be going,' she said. 'It will take me quite a time to get home from here.'

'Yes, it's a long way,' Mrs Laidlaw agreed. 'You aren't near the Botanic Gardens by any chance?'

'Yes, very near.'

'Your father took me there one Sunday,' she said to Ritchie. 'My goodness, that Kibble Palace! That's a sight. I've always wanted a garden and a low door into it. To step right away into a garden . . .'

'They are a lot of work, all the same,' Anna said, getting up. Mother had a man who came three times each week to keep theirs in order. 'Thank you for inviting me.'

'It was nothing. Come into the bedroom and get your coat.'

In the freezingly cold room she said to Ritchie's mother, 'I've drunk so much tea. I wonder if I could use your bathroom?' She saw the woman hesitate.

'Well, the factor's just putting one in for us. It's no' finished. But I keep something here.' She opened what Anna thought was a cupboard door. Inside there was an Elsan closet. 'I'll go out,' Mrs Laidlaw said delicately.

Anna sat down on it with mixed feelings. Needs must. She began to giggle, and had to put her hand to her mouth as the stream echoed hollowly in the steel drum. What would Mother say if she could see her now?

She went back to the front room to say goodbye to Mr Laidlaw. He was relaxed now, smiling as they shook hands. She saw that he was a good-looking man, except that his dull eyes reflected the burden of being unemployed. Anyone would be morose.

Mrs Laidlaw walked with them to the door. She was at ease too, the visit had gone well. 'Ritchie tells me your sister was in an accident on a loch. Is she all right now?'

'Yes, I think so. She's back at the Art School anyhow.'

'I'm glad. I always wish young folks could have a happy time. They don't know what's for them in the future.'

'We'll away then, Ma,' Ritchie said. 'I'll be back later.'

'It'll no' be goodbye then,' she said to Anna.

'I hope not.'

'They're nice,' Anna said as they clattered down the stairs. They stopped on the first landing so that they could kiss. She saw through the window the dingy back court and the row of dustbins.

'That used to be the toilet,' Ritchie said, pointing to a closed door. 'Very romantic, especially if you were in a hurry and Mrs Beith beat you to it.'

'It's a disgrace.' She wanted to say it's ugly, all ugly, but it was Ritchie's home. 'Nineteen thirties and not a bathroom in every house. And why don't they plant grass at the back, put in some flowers?'

'It's not wholly the factor's fault. Half the people in this tenement didn't want the alterations in case he put up the rent. It takes my father all his time to pay it as it is. You can imagine how I feel. At least if I'm in London, they won't have me to keep, and if I'm lucky I might be able to send some money.'

'Did you ever feel guilty, not working?'

'Often. But I represent a better future for them. It would have meant failure if I had chucked painting and got a job in a foundry.'

'Are you a socialist?' she asked him. 'One of Jimmy Maxton's men?'

'No, I'm classless. I'll be judged by my work.' He kissed her again, swiftly. 'I'm happy with you, Anna. Are you happy with me?'

'Yes, happy.'

Nothing could spoil that happiness. They stood in a shelter at the bus stop and shivered with cold. She lifted her face to him like a flower thirsty for rain, she thought, laughing inwardly at such an analogy. Is that what love did to you? She felt no shame as he kissed her in front of a man who had also come into the shelter.

'Don't mind me.' He wore a thin, threadbare jacket with turned-up collar, his hands were thrust into the pockets and the butt of a cigarette dangled from his mouth. It turned up at their laughter. 'If a'm in the road, just say . . . Oh, here's the bloody bus! Ten minutes late as usual. A've got it doon to a fine art.'

They jumped on and he followed them upstairs. No smokers down below. They sat down, she and Ritchie, as close as Siamese twins. 'I'll try to get to London to see the show.'

'And will you tell your parents we want to get married? This state is killing me.'

'Yes, I'll tell them soon.' She felt the same, desperate with love. It came in waves.

In her happiness she thought of Jean, who was a different girl since that terrible accident. They thought Mrs Kleiber had accepted Father's cheque and gone back to Vienna with her children. There had been a brief note of thanks but nothing more. Perhaps she intended to stay there.

The episode was buried now. No one talked about it at the Art School after the first flurry of excitement, sadness – he had been popular – and askance looks at Jean. But after the surprise, sympathy was forthcoming. She wasn't painting well. Mr Brown had had a kindly talk with her and asked her to try to put the tragic accident behind her. 'Put the experience into your work,' he had advised.

Anna couldn't get through to her, the first time she had ever felt a loss of rapport. She was a sister now of long silences, one who had lost her ability to laugh. Jean accepted Robin Naismith's invitations with a dutifulness which was worse than any refusal. He was in love with her, and so eminently suitable that their mother was nearly climbing the walls at Jean's stupidity. And, as Anna knew, her evident happiness with Ritchie must separate them even further. They had always thought along the same lines, had never had any secrets from each other.

FOURTEEN

JEAN WAS IN HER BED when Anna came into their room.
'Good time?' she asked.

'Marvellous!' She plumped down beside her. 'Marvellous!
Oh, that Ritchie! I love him . . . like anything!' She laughed.
'I went with him to visit his parents, Jean. Mother would
not have liked it. The WC's on the landing. She had an Elsan
in a cupboard in her bedroom, for guests. I nearly died of
embarrassment.'

'What are they like, his mother and father?' She didn't sit up.
The old Jean would have had sparkling eyes, would have
laughed with her.

'She's the bright one. His father is an unemployed miner.
Bears a grudge against society, but wouldn't *you* if you'd been
thrown out of your job through no fault of your own?'

'I suppose so.'

'You look wan. Is it the curse?'

'No. So what else?'

'We're going to get married as soon as Ritchie is making some
money. His parents accept that utterly. If I'm good enough for
Ritchie I'm good enough for them.'

'I think you'll find Mother will be the same when it comes to
it. She likes Ritchie. No wonder. He could charm birds off a
tree.'

'He's charmed me all right. It's a lovely feeling, an impatient,
lovely feeling. I'm at the right age for marrying, and the beauty
of it is that Ritchie wouldn't mind if I went on with my work.

He believes in equality. He has no false pride. There are plenty of good shops in London. I might be able to sell my stuff there, or even start an arts and crafts shop. I could sell your pictures, Jean. Frederick Kleiber always thought a lot of them . . .' Her voice trailed away. She was aware that Jean wasn't listening to her, that she had struggled up. She leaned her head on her pillows. She looked terrible, a dirty grey colour.

'Anna,' she said, 'I'm pregnant.'

'You're what?' She stared at her.

'You heard me. You'll soon see. Sometimes I think Bessie has tumbled to it the funny way she looks at me.'

'Oh, Jean!' She leaned forward and put her hands on her sister's shoulders, 'You *can't* be. What are you *saying*?'

'Are you thick? I'm saying I'm pregnant. That the baby is Frederick's. That he is dead. Oh, if *I* could only die.' Her face twisted and she shook herself free.

'Frederick . . . That day?'

'In the woods. Yes, that day. You talk about happiness with Ritchie –'

'But we wouldn't. I mean, that's why we want to get married.'

'You were always cautious.'

'Move over.' She leaned her head on the pillows beside Jean's, put an arm under her neck and pulled her close. 'Oh, Jean.'

'That would be the best solution. To die –'

'What are you saying?' Anna sat up to look at her sister's face, the scored eyes, the despair in them. Had she been looking like that for some time and she had been too preoccupied with her own affairs to notice? 'Don't talk like that. Oh, I wish Ritchie was here! He'd know what to do.'

'There's nothing anyone can do. I'm five months pregnant. I haven't slept properly for five months, lying in terror while you slept in your bed. I'm having to wear smocks all the time.'

Anna got up and sat on the side of the bed. She had to face her properly. Why hadn't she noticed anything? Her sister was a changed girl. And those eyes – she couldn't bear to look at

125

them. She got up and walked about the room, trying to come to terms with this fact, the most factual of facts which nothing could change. 'Give me a minute or two. We'll have to make plans, think what to do. Have you –'

'Tried to get rid of it? When I first knew. When I couldn't cope with the terror. Not any more. It's Frederick's baby.'

Anna thought what it must have been like for Jean, lying night after night, not sleeping, feeling changes in her body. She stopped at the bed. 'You might be mistaken. Let *me* see.' It was a terrible thing to ask, as if she were a midwife. Jean pushed down the bedclothes, pulled up her nightdress.

'Exhibit number one,' she said, with a twist to her mouth.

She wasn't very pregnant-looking, Anna thought, surveying the soft swell of her stomach, but Jean was built on a bigger scale than she was. It wouldn't show so easily.

She took her sister in her arms. 'Oh, Jean, what's going to happen? You'll have to tell Mother and Father. There's no other way. A baby is so . . . inevitable.'

'A fat lot you know about it.' She tried to push Anna away.

'Don't speak like that to me. I'm trying to help.'

'Like sticking a pin in my stomach and letting it all run out?'

'And there's no point in that kind of talk. Let me think what would be best. Father first. He'll take the initial blow better than Mother. Then he'll tell her. Nancy, of course, will have several fits but we don't have to worry about her. She has James Pettigrew. He'll do the worrying for her.'

'Oh, it's going to break their hearts.' She was suddenly weeping. 'I'm glad you know. I've lain awake night after night and listened to time ticking away, listening to my body with Frederick's baby inside it. I've thought of throwing myself under a bus, taking pills, even of slashing my wrists, but the thing is, Anna, I want to *live*. I want to have this baby. It will fill this awful gap in my life since he died. I've thought of that day in the woods, and why something which seemed so right should be wrong, and then, as if it were a punishment, that

126

awful accident. It haunts me, that poor drowned face, the long hair like seaweed. Mr Brown says I've to use it in my painting, but I'm painting chaos because I'm in chaos. And the stupidity of it! Wouldn't you think,' the tears were streaming down her face, 'wouldn't you think that a grown man would be able to swim!'

'Some sailors can't.'

She paid no attention. 'So stupid! So stupid, stupid, stupid . . .'

'Even if he hadn't drowned you would still be pregnant.' Jean's eyes, loaded with tears, looked at her. 'He had a wife and family. What if he couldn't leave them?'

'He said he would.'

'Even that lovely little girl you told me about? Could he have given her up? And his job would have suffered. He might even have lost it.' There was a peremptory knock on the door.

'You twins! Stop all that noise. Some people want to get to sleep.'

'Sorry, Mother,' Anna said.

Jean's tears had dried. She was lying back on her pillow. Poor thing, Anna thought. Anger momentarily flared up inside her against the dead man. It took two. There was that wildness in Jean, that impulsiveness, her boldness, her refusal to think of consequences. It was all in her painting, or had been. I hope that hasn't been ruined as well, she thought.

She began to undress, stripping off the clothes she had been so happy in all evening. She hung her dress on a hanger because she always did, that nice speckled tweed like crushed raspberries, the U-shaped inset of beige pin-tucked silk with a neat Eton collar of the same material. Ritchie had admired it.

She was in no position to condemn Jean. It would have been so easy with Ritchie, but they had kept it light. Frederick Kleiber was Austrian, with that heavy, romantic temperament which was so vastly different from Ritchie's. You should enjoy loving, but watch that your brain kept ticking over. The rule was that you waited until you were married. There was no point in breaking rules.

'Would you like me to come in beside you, Jean?' she asked when she had put on her nightdress.

'If you like.'

Anna put off the light and climbed in. She put a gentle hand on Jean's stomach, fancied she felt a movement underneath it.

'I've decided,' she said. 'We'll go to Father's office tomorrow and tell him. It will make it . . . businesslike. Then he can tell Mother and Nancy.' She said as a joke, 'And Bessie and Tumshie.' Maybe you should have been like Tumshie, 'doactored', as Bessie called it, an unspoken thought, outrageous . . . 'Don't worry. That's what we'll do. We'll tell Father, then just let it happen.' Jean's hand came over her own.

'It would have been easier if I had drowned too.'

'No, never say that. Think how I would miss you.'

'Would you?' She turned to face her. The round stomach was like a cushion between them.

'You know I would, even though you are an awful nuisance at times.'

'But this beats the band, eh?' Her voice broke.

'Yes, it beats the band. Try and get to sleep. We'll both try.'

She did, almost at once, so she was unaware if Jean slept or not. But it was soon morning and they had to get up and face the day. And Father.

'Will you be out on a site today, Father?' Anna said at breakfast the next morning. She felt the glances. They must know about Jean simply by looking at her, but then *she* hadn't until she was told.

'No, I've got a lot of paperwork to get on with.'

'No appointments?'

'No. Why the interest?'

'I was just wondering the same thing,' Rose said. 'Have you a ploy on?'

128

'No, just that Jean and I are going down town and we might look in for a coffee.'

'There's nobody under thirty on the staff now.' Angus smiled. 'We had a trainee who made the typists swoon with delight but he left last week.'

'No one looking in from Pettigrew and Crawford?' Nancy said, looking arch. 'James said he was going to see you. I don't know what about.'

'He wants to stay on the right side of his future father-in-law,' Anna said.

'Anna!' Rose gave her a look of reproof. 'We aren't talking about anything like that. Not meantime anyhow.' When they do, Anna thought, looking at the folded smile on Nancy's face, it will at least make up for Jean. She had a moment of complete disbelief. She had dreamed the whole thing. A baby! Frederick Kleiber's baby! She looked at Jean and knew it was no dream. Had Mother not guessed because it was quite outwith her own experience? Clevedon Crescent had never had to shelter an illegitimate baby, unless perhaps a maid's.

'So that's all right, Father? Around eleven o'clock?'

'Sure.' He smiled at Rose. 'I know what it is. They want a loan. They've spent all their dress allowance.'

'Could I come?' Nancy asked.

'Two's company, three's a crowd,' Anna said. You had to be direct with Nancy. She couldn't take a hint.

'Well, I hope it cheers Jean up.' Rose looked at her. 'I haven't liked to say this, Jean, but you're not looking yourself. I know what happened at Kilcreggan has been very difficult to get over, but you mustn't feel responsible. It's all right for his wife to grieve, but it's not your *place*, if you see what I mean. It was a series of misfortunes, the wash from the *King Edward*, Mr Kleiber not being able to swim . . .'

Jean got up. 'Excuse me.' She was like a figure of stone. She left the room.

'*Now* what have I said?' Rose looked round the table.

'She can't bear you to talk about it, Rose. That's evident.'
Angus folded his napkin and got up. 'Must get on.' Rose turned
away. She hated being corrected in front of the family.

'We'll see you later, Father,' Anna said.

He looked doubtful. 'Do you think Jean will want to bother?'

'Oh yes. She said she would last night.'

'What a row you two were kicking up last night,' Rose said.
'You might have some consideration for other people in the
house.'

'Aye, the bleathering that went on!' Bessie was in the room.
'And Jean's left her toast. Whit's wrang wi' her these days?'

'Maybe she could do with a good tonic. I'm definitely away.'
Angus closed the door behind him.

'I'll go and find Jean,' Anna said, getting up. She was careful
not to catch Bessie's eye. Father had to be told today. Delay
only made the situation worse.

'You give her a pep talk.' Rose looked thoughtful. 'It's five
months since the man was drowned. She can't still be grieving.'

'I'll do my best.' To think I was so happy last night, she
thought. 'By the way, Mother, Ritchie's going to live in
London. Some of his paintings have been selected for a London
gallery.'

'Do you mean there's a chance of him selling any?'

'More than a chance. Mr Brown predicts a great future for
him. He'll be sharing a flat with Bob McNair. You won't
remember him.'

'What if Ritchie becomes famous!' Nancy looked excited.
'Then we could all bask in his reflected glory.'

'It's not "what if", it's "when".'

'Of course you can't see past him, Anna.' Rose was putting
away napkins in the sideboard drawer.

'Well, you like him too. Come on, admit it.'

'Yes, he's enterprising, and he has a . . . presence. He's not
run-of-the-mill. Pity about his background but you can't have
everything.'

'I'm not marrying his background.'

'Who said anything about marriage?'

'Ritchie and Anna talk about nothing else,' Nancy said.

'Would you and Father mind very much, Mother?' Anna appealed to her. 'We're praying his paintings will be a success.'

'Well, we can't stop you marrying, but don't rush into it. There's better fish in the sea than ever came out of it.'

'Not for me. There's only Ritchie.'

'Oh, you girls will always go your own way!' Rose looked exasperated. 'James Pettigrew couldn't be more suitable if I'd chosen him myself,' Nancy preened herself at this, 'but Ritchie Laidlaw is different. It's such a precarious job, painting. It might take him years before he could keep you.'

'No, he'll take a job. Bob McNair does very well as a commercial artist and does his own stuff in his spare time. Ritchie will do the same.'

'That's you and Nancy,' Rose said. 'But what about Jean? Will she see sense and take Robin Naismith, such a nice young man, so polite. I've always liked Kilmacolm people. They care for the same things as I do. Oh, I know you laugh at me, but breeding tells.'

FIFTEEN

THEY TOOK A TRAM which went along Sauchiehall Street and down Hope Street, where they got off at Campbell's, the fruiterers, on the corner of St Vincent Place. It was a cold January morning and Jean looked haggard. Obviously she hadn't slept much last night, if at all.

'We'll walk up St Vincent Street to give you some air,' Anna said, slipping her arm through Jean's, an unusual gesture, but she reminded herself it was an unusual situation. How would I feel if it were me, she thought. Pregnant. She and Ritchie had never talked about children. But then he had a hard core of common sense, and to make her pregnant before they were married was not common-sensical.

Frederick Kleiber had been different. Even in his lectures at the Art School he had shown a type of emotion which was un-Scottish, the difference between a heather brae and a velvet-lined room. He wasn't canny. He was a European, there was a flamboyance in the way he waved his arms to illustrate a point. He was volatile, exuberant, sometimes angry, sometimes beguiling. The girls sat at his feet and he loved that.

She said when they were in the lift going up to the second floor, 'How are you feeling, Jean?'

She shook her head. 'I think I can't feel any more. Even this fighting in Spain. Normally it's something I would feel strongly about, especially the two-year gaol sentence on volunteers, but I can't feel the anger I should.'

A new young girl opened the window marked Reception

when Anna rang the bell. She looked excited. 'Oh, is it Mr Mackintosh's two daughters? He told us you were coming.' She ran to open the door for them and ushered them into the middle of the busy office. Heads were lifted from drawing boards to smile and nod at them. 'The boss's daughters . . .'

Cathy, Father's secretary, was suddenly there. 'Good morning, Anna, Jean.' She had known them since they were children. What would she think, Anna wondered, if she suddenly said, 'Jean's pregnant.' It would be too much for her. Anna saw the neat hairstyle, the round flat face, the thick glasses, too much weight. 'Your father says I have to show you in right away. He's expecting you.' She led them out of the general office into a corridor off which several doors opened. She knocked on one, labelled in black letters, 'Angus Mackintosh, RIBA.' 'Here they are, Mr Mackintosh!' she said with satisfaction.

'Come in, girls. Did you congratulate Cathy on her engagement?'

'No, we didn't, did we, Jean?' You could have bowled me over with a feather, she was thinking.

'We're very pleased,' Jean said. She was calm. 'I don't know what Father's going to do without you.'

'I'll miss him. Maybe the day will come when girls can work after they're married. I was just saying to David –' She turned the diamond ring on her finger.

'Would you bring in the coffee, Cathy, please,' Angus said, stemming the flow. 'That's all they're here for.'

'Oh, I can't believe that, but I'll bring it right away.'

'Wonders will never cease,' Anna said when the girl had gone.

'Aye, there's hope for everybody. Sit down, girls. I have to go out after all, trouble at a site near Nitshill.'

'We won't take up much of your time.'

'You're being very mysterious. What's wrong with asking me whatever it is at home?'

'We wanted you to know first.' Why was Jean not helping her?

'We'd better wait till Cathy brings the coffee.' Jean was still calm, too calm.

'You're making me feel nervous.' Father's Highland intuition was beginning to work. 'Ah, here she is.' He looked up as Cathy came in with a tray. 'That's grand, thanks. Just put it on my desk.'

'I've brought some Jacob's chocolate biscuits,' she said, 'for the girls. They always liked them when they came with their mother. Wee Nancy was a star turn.'

'She still is,' Anna said.

'The draughtsmen spoiled you twins. You're not so like each other as you used to be, maybe because you're not dressed the same now.'

'We soon stopped that.' She was having to do all the work. She looked at Jean's too calm, too sad face.

'Thanks very much, Cathy,' Angus said pointedly. When the girl had gone there was a small silence. He looked uneasy. 'Your mother said you were just run down,' he said to Jean. 'Is that right? We've been a bit worried about you, I don't mind telling you.'

'Jean,' Anna said, 'you'll have to tell him.' The girl's eyes were sunk in her head, she looked gaunt, her face pale in its setting of black, frizzy hair.

'Yes, I'll have to. Father, I'm pregnant.'

Angus's cup rattled in its saucer. It had been halfway to his mouth. He looked flushed.

'For a minute I thought you said you were pregnant.'

'I did.'

'You're saying . . .' His mouth was trembling.

'I've known for ages. You see, I thought if I didn't mention it, it would go away.' She put her face in her hands.

Angus looked at Anna. 'This isn't a joke, is it?' The flush had died away leaving him very pale.

'No. We thought it would be better if you told Mother. That's why we're here.'

'It will kill her.' Jean's voice came from behind her hands.

'Sit up, Jean. And drink your coffee.' His voice was stern. 'It won't kill her. She isn't killed so easily. Nancy's the one who'll be shocked, but we know Nancy.'

'She'll have James to comfort her.' She had uncovered her face.

'And who's to comfort you? Who's the father?'

Anna had never seen him like this before, hard, unfeeling. She looked at her sister. 'Go on, tell him.' Jean would have to do this herself.

'Frederick Kleiber.' She kept her head up but she didn't look at him.

'Frederick Kleiber? My God! But he's gone . . .' He rocked back on his chair, drawing his hand over his face.

'Yes, he's gone.' She wasn't weeping. She might even be finding relief in the telling. 'He was going to ask his wife for a divorce. We would have gone somewhere where nobody knew us.'

'And leave his wife and children to fend for themselves? What nonsense is this you're talking? What kind of behaviour would that have been? Couldn't you have used your head before . . . ? How many children bereft . . .'

'Three. The little girl is called Hilde.'

'I don't care what she's called!' He got up and paced about the room, suddenly opened the door and shut it again. 'Got to be careful. I don't want this spreading.' He resumed his pacing. 'I'm flabbergasted. I don't know what to say. You should have spoken to your mother first. She would know how to handle it.'

'I don't think she would have believed it,' Jean said. 'A young lady of Clevedon Crescent! Her daughter!'

'Watch your tongue!' He stopped and shook his finger at her. 'You're in no position to be critical of others. Your mother's conventional, and what's wrong with that? She's brought you up to be well-behaved, she's always been so proud of you all.

135

Ach!' He shook his head impatiently. 'Drink your coffee. We have to talk, talk sensibly, see if anything . . .' He flung himself into his chair.

He talked, as if the words were choking him, asked when the child was due, where it had been conceived. He wanted to be quite sure, he said, that she wasn't imagining it, that it wasn't a phantom pregnancy. Hadn't she heard of it? There was a girl in Ullapool –

'This was no phantom,' Jean said, 'much as you would like it to be.' She was sitting straight in her chair. 'We were in love, we made love. Then we went out in a boat and he was drowned.' The tears ran down her face. She still sat straight in her chair.

Angus looked at Anna. 'This is terrible.' He shook his head miserably. 'What can I do?'

'You'll have to tell Mother first. Jean can't face her. She knows how she'll react to something like this. It will floor her completely. Once a maid of Grandpa and Granny's got herself into trouble – that's how Mother thinks of it – and they arranged for her to go back home right away. She thinks it's a disgrace.'

'She won't be alone in that.'

'I could go away somewhere,' Jean said, 'so that she wouldn't have to see me.'

'Don't make her out to be such an ogre!' Angus spoke sharply. 'She would worry just as much about that. She's got a kind heart. She would do anything for anybody in real trouble.'

'Real trouble,' Jean repeated.

Anna passed her a handkerchief. 'Wipe your tears, Jean. They'll only make you feel ill.'

'Well, it's no good going on. But it's the total irresponsibility of it all. I simply can't understand it!' He banged his fist on the desk.

'We were in love!' Her voice was a wail.

'I was in love with your mother but I didn't throw her on the ground and –' He drew his hand over his eyes again. 'My mind's in a turmoil. Fill in your time until I finish. There's a

136

good film at the Odeon, Tyrone Power . . . I don't think you girls know how proud your mother and I were when you all went to the Art School.'

Anna felt sorry for him. 'Yes, we do, Father,' she said. 'We appreciated it. And so did everyone.' She smiled. 'They called us The Glasgow Girls.'

'Did they? I knew one or two of them, well, not quite – knew *of* them. On you go, then. I've got to get this finished.'

Anna went into the drawing room later on. She could feel the pulsing of a headache between her brows. 'What's that you're playing?' Nancy was leafing through records at the cabinet gramophone, a handsome machine whose volume could be regulated by opening or shutting the small doors in the upper quarter.

'"The Way You Look Tonight."' She held out her arms beseechingly. And then, 'Where's Jean?'

'She's gone to her room until dinner's ready.' Anna couldn't blame her. The courage she had needed to drop her bombshell made Anna glad she wasn't in her shoes.

Nancy was sashaying about the room in a slow foxtrot. 'It's like a funeral here. Mother and Father have been shut up in their bedroom for ages, talking. What's wrong? You'll have to tell me eventually.'

'Jean's pregnant.'

'Pregnant!' Her mouth fell open. 'What are you saying? She can't possibly be *pregnant*!'

'It's the easiest thing in the world, unfortunately.'

'It's not Robin Naismith, is it? I know he's mad about her. But he's not like that. He has beautiful manners –'

'No, it's someone who's dead.'

'Dead!' Her eyes were round with horror. 'Who is it, who is . . . ?' She stopped and stared at Anna. 'I know. Mr Kleiber. He was always looking at Jean, and talking to her in the corridors.'

'That wouldn't do it. Don't say any more, and remember, don't weep and upset Mother. She'll be here any minute. Put that record off . . . Oh, Mother!' She drew in her breath as Rose came in. If she had been weeping the tears were gone now. She sat down in a straight-backed chair. She had a slight frown.

'Mother!' Nancy got up and went towards her. 'What's happening? You're all frightening me. There's nothing wrong with Jean, is there?'

'Sit down, Nancy. Yes, there is, considering she hasn't a husband.'

'Oh, Anna was right!' She sat down and covered her face with her hands. Her sobs were loud.

Angus came in. He looked pulled together, Anna thought, his hair was freshly brushed. They had come to a decision. They were going to put a good face on things. She might have known. Appearances were of paramount importance to Mother. 'Stop that noise, Nancy!' she was saying now. 'There's nothing wrong with you. You always cry louder than the one that's hurt.'

Jean was there. Anna's heart was wrung by her exhausted appearance. She looked as if she was going to collapse. She said to Rose, as if there was no fight left in her, 'Did Father tell you? I'm sorry.'

'Yes, he told me. *You're* sorry? How do you think I feel? Sit down there.' She pointed to a chair beside her. 'Don't worry. I'm not going to shout and curse as they do in the Briggait. We have to behave like civilized beings although you haven't shown much sign of it. You're lucky, Jean Mackintosh, you don't know how lucky. But you owe us some kind of explanation.'

'She says you're pregnant,' Nancy said in a hushed voice, her sobbing stopped. 'You're not really, Jean, are you?'

'Yes, I am.' She had her hands clasped on her lap, was looking down at them. 'Yes, I am, Nancy. I'm sorry if it shocks you all, but I can't even say that I didn't know what I was doing. I did.'

138

'But you didn't know he was going to drown afterwards?' Rose said.

'No, Mother.' She lifted her head to look at her. 'I didn't know that. Would it have stopped me, you're asking? I don't know. I thought with such a wonderful love as ours it was bound to have a happy ending, that Frederick would get a divorce, that we would all live happily ever afterwards.'

'Like a fairy story?' Rose shook her head in exasperation. 'Oh, we all knew how affected you were by his death. We had only to look at your face, but we never thought there was anything else.'

'I wanted to tell you, Mother. I couldn't find the courage.'

Anna looked at her mother's face, the hard line of her mouth. Had she wept when Father told her, she wondered. And her voice was steady. 'You should know by this time you can't arrange things to suit yourself, that you can't have a child to a married man with children of his own.' She looked round at the others, 'Oh, that's Jean!' Her voice rose. 'Always wanting to break the rules, or bend them to suit herself.' No one can be that cool, Anna thought. She needs to weep.

'I ask myself where I failed, how you ever even *contemplated*, how you ever got yourself into a position where you might have a child to a married man, to *any* man when you're not married to him. You have your father and me as examples in front of you. We've been faithful to our marriage vows. Mr Kleiber evidently hadn't the same principles. You should,' she suddenly raised her fist in the air, colour rushed down her neck, over her face, in her eyes, 'you should be downright *ashamed* to show your face here after what –'

'That will do, Rose,' Angus said. 'The girl's suffered enough and has more to come.'

'People I know, like Grace Binnie –'

'I'm sure she isn't a blameless character if you knew all.'

'I suppose so.' Rose whispered the words. 'I'm upset . . .'

'I'll go,' Jean said.

'And where will you go?' Rose bridled.

'I was wondering . . .' she faltered, 'if I could go to Kirkcud-bright, to Great-aunt Jessie?'

Anna looked at her, surprised. And yet of all people, Miss Craig was the one most likely to understand.

'And shock her too? She's family! No, thanks, we'll keep this to ourselves while we can.'

'Where would you like to hide me, then?' Jean's voice was bitter.

'You are in no position to give me any of your lip, my lady, but there's Cowal View lying empty. If you went there it would give us time to get things settled. Anna could go with you.'

'I couldn't go there, Mother.' Jean began to weep. 'I'd see him everywhere.'

There was a knock at the door. Anna answered it, thinking how secretive they were all becoming. It was Bessie. 'Yes, Bessie?' she said.

'The meal's gettin' ruined, Anna. Whit's your mither thinkin' aboot?'

'Come in, Bessie,' Angus called. She walked in, followed by her faithful four-legged shadow who, sensing a distraction, had seized the opportunity.

'We've disturbing family news, Bessie. It's not everyone we would tell, but you're one of the family in a way. Jean – Jean's in the family way.'

'Ma Goad!' she said, her hand going to her mouth. 'Who's the faither, Jean?' Jean turned away, unable to speak.

'Unfortunately . . .' Angus hesitated, 'he died.'

Bessie's eyes widened. 'Yon yin? At Kilcreggan? As if it wisny bad enough! Oh, you poor soul.' She turned a lugubrious face to Jean. 'An' him a furriner.' And to Angus: 'Don't you worry, Mr Mackintosh, I'll keep ma trap shut.'

'We'll be ready in ten minutes, Bessie,' Rose said. 'On you go, and take Tumshie with you.' She got up and followed Bessie into the hall. 'I want to phone.'

'She's gone to phone Aunt Jessie,' Angus said.

'I'll clear out.' Jean was deathly pale, but dry-eyed. 'I'll go . . . somewhere. I'm not wanted.'

'Don't talk nonsense. You've nowhere to go to, nor any money. You were independent enough when you were with Kleiber but you need your family now. Sit down and let's wait to hear what Aunt Jessie says. And put yourself in your mother's place. It's hard for her too.'

They sat and waited in silence.

SIXTEEN

ROSE AND JEAN sat in the taxi which was bearing them swiftly along Great Western Road on their way to the station.

I would be busy about my usual affairs if this were an ordinary day, Rose thought, shopping here, meeting Grace for a coffee in that new place in Byres Road. What would Grace think if she could see her now, on her way to hide a pregnant daughter from prying eyes? She was aware rather than saw the sullen white-faced girl sitting beside her. The other face of sex. Every married woman since Eve knew the male blandishments even when backed by love. But wasn't it *she* who gave Adam the apple?

There was to be no more rowing nor recriminations, Angus had said, and she had agreed. If breeding meant anything at all it meant not behaving like a fishwife and showing your daughter the door if she got into trouble. But wasn't her plan a polite way of doing that very thing?

'You remember how near we were to it at times when we were courting, Rose,' he had said when she lay weeping in his arms in the big double bed, part of the suite Mother and Father had given them, the traditional wedding gift. Come to think of it, a bed symbolized the whole spectrum of life from birth to death. Where had Jean and Kleiber . . . ? On a bed of damp leaves somewhere in Kilcreggan?

'But you had respect for me, Angus,' she had said.

'If I hadn't been so afraid of your father I believe I might

142

have gone over the line.' And he had added wistfully, 'Do you think Jean should have felt the same about me?'

'No, Jean's different.' She was sure of that. Just as she was sure that Nancy and Anna would never find themselves in the same position. 'There's an air of . . . abandon about her somehow, a kind of recklessness. That's what makes her a good painter. It's a strange thing to say, but I think she and Kleiber were suited to each other. A conventional life like the one I lead would be anathema to her.'

It had taken a lot of courage that night to telephone Aunt Jessie at Kirkcudbright, not from a moral point of view – Jessie knew a thing or two although she had never been married – but it had been her own self-esteem which made the words stick in her throat.

'Aunt Jessie! How are you? We've been meaning to get in touch with you for ages to ask if your angina has been troubling you again.'

'That was kind of you. You're like Mattie,' that was one of the Craig sisters who had died young, 'always considerate of others.'

'I'm afraid I have another reason as well. Not that we aren't concerned about you. It's Jean –' She had stopped speaking suddenly because of the tears choking her. 'Aunt Jessie, she's . . . she's . . .'

Her aunt's voice was concerned. 'It isn't like you to be tongue-tied, Rose. As long as she isn't ill, or hasn't been in another accident.'

'She's having a baby!' The words burst from her. 'It's been such a blow to us! We can hardly bring ourselves to talk about it. You're the only one –'

'Are you telling me that Jean is pregnant?' The controlled voice cut through hers like a sharp knife.

'Yes. She told us last night. I tried to phone you.'

'I was staying with a friend.'

'Oh, that's why. I haven't slept a wink.'

'How about Jean?'

'What?'

'Has *she* slept a wink? How long has she been keeping this from you and Angus?'

'Five months! Can you believe it? It happened when we were on our usual holiday at Kilcreggan.'

'Why doesn't he marry her?'

Rose twisted the telephone flex tightly round her fingers. 'He can't. He's dead. And he *was* married.'

'Oh my God!'

'I know you must be shocked, Aunt –'

'Shocked, no, no. Go on, Rose. What plans have you?'

'We wondered – and just say if you can't, we'll quite understand – we wondered if she could come to you for a month or so until we get things sorted out. I know it's a terrible imposition, but we're desperate.' She found herself holding her breath, pinning all her hopes on Aunt Jessie agreeing.

'It's not the end of the world, Rose. Yes, by all means, let her come here.'

She had hung up the receiver feeling as if she had been put in the wrong.

'I wish the driver would get a move on,' she now said. 'We've only twenty minutes to get to the station for that train.'

'Not long till you get rid of me,' Jean said.

'It's not a question of getting rid of you.' But it was. There was their standing in the community and Angus's position in the city, but most of all the shame lay in the fact that Frederick Kleiber had been married. Jean should have known that another woman's husband was sacrosanct. 'You seem to have no sense of shame,' she had said last night, and Jean's great dark eyes had looked through her, seeing down to her soul, her miserable soul. One had moments of enlightenment. 'It was good of Aunt Jessie to offer to take you,' she said.

'I didn't think *she* would have any difficulty.'

Rose noticed the emphasis. 'You're determined to put *me* in

144

the wrong. It's only till we get a nursing home arranged, either at home or in Kirkcudbright. That might be better. You can join the painting coterie down there. They won't care what . . . state you're in.' She stumbled over the word.

'It isn't a state, Mother, an unnameable condition, it's a baby growing inside me.'

Rose's temper flared, along with a sudden sharp jab at her temples. She had developed a splitting headache. 'Keep your voice down,' she said, glancing at the solid back of the taxi driver. Was it their irrefutable curiosity which made them take on a job like this? They must hear some juicy titbits. She sat back, breathing quickly. Really, there was no gratitude from children nowadays, even when you were prepared to pay for a nursing home for the coming confinement. 'I'll get some kind of job,' Jean had said. What kind of job could *she* do, except painting, and she had even lost her enthusiasm for that? You reared them and lavished money and loving care on them, and then they told you it was your duty and that being pregnant and unmarried wasn't 'an illness', or something like that.

'If I were you, my lady,' she said, pretending to be looking at something interesting as the taxi raced down Renfield Street, 'I would lie pretty low for the next few weeks, and remember that you're there on sufferance.'

'Yes, I'll remember that, Mother.'

Rose looked at her, saw the white cheek, thee tear rolling slowly down it. It was the slowness of the tear which nearly broke her heart. 'Oh!' she said, clumsily clutching the girl in her arms. 'Oh, Jean! Why did you have to spoil everything?'

'I didn't. I loved –'

'We were getting on so nicely, the three of you at the Art School, your father doing well in the firm, looking forward to a long happy time at the Crescent, big weddings for all of you, one after the other, happiness . . .'

145

'Right, y'are, missus,' the taxi driver said, drawing up at Queen Street Station.

It was a different world from Glasgow, Jean thought, as she was driven from Dumfries Station in a hired car. Father might have quibbled at the expense, but Mother was of a different calibre. 'It's a better service and you'll save time. There's some money to see you all right.' She had handed her a fat envelope. 'I don't want you to be beholden to Aunt Jessie.' Jean had been ashamed, and diminished.

The drive through the gentle, undulating countryside soothed her, Lochfoot, Springholm, white-washed cottages, golden-haired cattle, through the bustle of Castle Douglas, then over the hill to drop down into the quiet wide streets of Kirk-cudbright, where no one bustled and they had never heard of pregnant girls whose lover had died and who had to accept handouts from her parents.

Great-aunt Jessie greeted her in an affectionate, matter-of-fact way which saved her from breaking down. 'Now, not a word till you go up and have a wash and then come down and sit at the fire with me for tea.'

'Mother –'

'Not a word, I said.'

Then, freshened after the tiring journey, she sat across from her great-aunt in the familiar little room. 'You're so good,' she said.

'Not me. Now, the whole story, please. I've only heard your mother's side of it.'

'He was called Frederick Kleiber and I loved him.'

'That's a good beginning.' Her great-aunt lifted the silver teapot. 'Go on.'

146

SEVENTEEN

IT SHOWED THE EXTENT of Anna's desire to be with Ritchie that even the upset at home over Jean's pregnancy didn't change her mind about going to see his paintings in London. Her mother had been fretful and pale.

'I don't see why you should decide to go to London when we're all worried out of our minds.'

'The exhibition closes next week. Mr Brown wants anyone who can to go. He says Ritchie's paintings are catching the eye of the critics. He put a cutting from a London Sunday paper, the *Observer*, up on the noticeboard. And I promised Ritchie.'

Rose gave in reluctantly. 'Well, if you insist, but it's only for the weekend, and you must take Nancy with you.'

'But she's bound to be going out with James! All her spare time is taken up by him now. You don't object to that.'

'How could I? She couldn't do better for herself.'

'He'll spoil her to death. He's already doing it – flowers, chocolates, theatre tickets.'

'What's wrong with that? Sometimes I think the young men nowadays are far too casual. It's a relief to me to see how he cares for Nancy. I've had enough of one of you going her own way to last me all my life.'

Anna saw with the words an older Nancy sitting at her writing-desk, fair-haired, pretty, well-named, but a wan rose. She gave her an unaccustomed hug. 'Don't worry, Mother. Take it a day at a time.'

'But the baby's due in May! I can't expect Aunt Jessie to keep her indefinitely. She's too old for that. And what are all our friends going to say?'

'Haven't you told any of them yet?'

'No. I'm having them here for bridge this afternoon.'

'Is Grace Binnie one of them?'

'Yes. I've asked her for lunch so that I could break the news.'

'She'll be sympathetic. She's an old friend. If you can't bring yourself to tell the rest, leave it to her. I should think anyone with daughters will say, "There but for the grace of God go mine." They'll admire you for standing by her.'

'Oh, I'll stand *by* her.' She looked at Anna with young eyes. 'I can understand her too.' And then, quickly, 'But don't think that gives you and Nancy carte blanche.'

'Oh, you're a caution, Mother!' She hugged her again.

Nancy was quite pleased at the idea of a trip to London. 'It will let James see that I lead a life of my own,' she said, looking ridiculously like Rose. 'You don't want to be at their beck and call all the time, do what *they* want.'

'Why not?'

'Look at Jean.'

'She wanted it as well.'

'Wanting and giving in is a different matter. I want to feel right in white when I go down the aisle.' Repeating patterns, Anna thought. Mother all over again. Who did *she* resemble? Herself, she hoped.

'If only Jean had encouraged Robin Naismith it would never have happened. You should always take a cat of your own kind.'

'What about Ritchie?'

Nancy smiled. She looked like a helmeted angel in her toque of sky-blue felt, pulled low down on her golden hair. She was going to have lunch with James. 'Ritchie's different. He's going to be so well-known that where he comes from won't matter. Artists are in a class of their own.'

'Do you read cards as well?' Anna laughed.

148

'No, tea leaves.'

Anna threw a magazine at her, Nancy retaliated with a cushion. They rolled about the sofa together like cubs. Anna caught glimpses of her sister's flushed, pretty face under the toque, now askew, the little white teeth, the eyes which were too pale a blue, generally, but now were deeper and sparkling with excitement. Did she know passion too, with douce James?

The gallery was in Clerkenwell, in the middle of a long dull street with the occasional barbers' shops, newsagents plastered with placards, and large tenement blocks. Bob's flat was in one of these, but they had strict instructions from Angus to occupy the double room he had booked for them in a gloomy respectable hotel in Russell Square, and to take taxis if they were at all worried about travelling on the Tube. In his anxiety about their safety he gave them ample spending money. 'And yet he would walk a mile to save a halfpenny fare in Glasgow,' Nancy said. He also gave each of them a five-pound note which they were to tuck away in an inside pocket of their purses 'just in case'.

'He's afraid of the white-slave traffic,' Nancy said. 'They like fair-haired girls particularly. Keep tight hold of me.'

As soon as they got to the hotel – a big, tasteless, overbearing sort of place, Anna thought – and claimed their room, she telephoned to the gallery. Ritchie had sent her the number.

He answered almost immediately. His excitement was infectious. 'You're arrived! Oh good! What sort of journey did you have?'

'Lovely. We met two very nice young men in the train but Nancy turned them down. She said James would be angry.'

'Oh, you!' Nancy seized the receiver from her. 'Don't listen to a word she says, Ritchie! It was Anna who said there was nothing doing. She talked about you the whole time. What? Bob? Well, you never know. I'd better hand you back to Anna. Her eyes have gone quite green.'

149

'She sounds as if she isn't missing James,' Ritchie said. 'Anna, Bob says you can stay in the flat. He has a sleeping bag I can use and you and Nancy can have my bed.'

'No, we couldn't, honestly! Father would check up on us. He's paid for a room here.'

'Doesn't he trust you?'

'Wait till I tell you my news, then you'll understand.'

'Ah well, foiled again. We'll just have to hope that Nancy and Bob get on together and we can manage some time on our own. I'm dying to see you.'

'So am I.' She listened to his directions about how to reach the gallery. Her heart beat faster, her ears burned at the prospect of seeing him. She hung up reluctantly.

'You were cooin' like a *doo*,' Nancy said.

'Rubbish!'

'You should see your face. It's as red as a turkey cock's.'

'Aren't you getting your ornithology muddled?' She sat down on the bed to change her stockings. Best Milanese. Twelve shillings and elevenpence a pair in Copland and Lye's. They made your legs gleam. She stood up and looked over her shoulder to make sure the seams were straight.

There were quite a few people in the gallery when they arrived. A red-haired girl was sitting at a table at the head of the room and she looked up when she saw them. At the same time they noticed Ritchie in front of one of the paintings with a woman to whom he was speaking earnestly, gesticulating, stopping to point at something on the canvas from time to time. His face lit up as he turned and saw the girls. Anna gave a small wave, her heart lifting with her hand.

'He's with a client,' she said to Nancy.

'Better to speak to the girl at the table.'

'Yes.'

They walked down the length of the room together, Anna feeling rather self-conscious, Nancy looking in her element, eyes bright, her swagger betraying her youth. 'Very smart woman, that. Jewish. Did you see the diamond pin in her hat?'

'Keep quiet, Nancy,' Anna whispered. They had almost reached the girl who had raised her head to watch them. Her eyes were odd, like amber glass, and she seemed to look past them rather than directly at them. 'We've come to see Mr Laidlaw.' Anna stopped in front of her.

'Ritchie?' The eyes changed, flickered. The lashes were thickly dark. 'He's busy with a client.'

'He's expecting us,' Anna said, bridling slightly.

'Is he?' She was cool. 'Well, have a look round while you're waiting.' She returned to her writing.

'She looked sleekit,' Nancy said when they were out of ear-shot. 'Those funny eyes.'

'I think she has a kind of squint.'

'Maybe she has a kind of pash for Ritchie.'

'Could you blame her?' Anna was haughty.

They were looking at someone's 'pyrotechnic squiggles', as Nancy called them, when Ritchie came over. Anna felt him squeezing her arm.

'Great to see you, Anna!' They faced each other, her eyes taking him in slowly, appreciatively. He had changed a little, a question of attitude, manner. It could be the effect of London. He hadn't quite the same ingenuousness. 'Mmmh!' he breathed, shaking his head slowly as if entranced, and, his eyes still on Anna, 'How are you, Nancy?'

'Fine, thanks, but you might look at me when you speak to me.'

'Sorry.' He turned to smile at her. 'I'm bowled over by this vision. I'd forgotten how beautiful she is.'

'More beautiful than that girl at the table?'

'Christine?' He shrugged. 'No comparison. She's a nice kid but odd-mannered at times. You have to get to know her.'

'Oh,' Nancy said with heavy emphasis, 'that's the secret, is it?'

151

'Were you trying to sell a picture, Ritchie?' Anna asked, keeping her face straight.

'She's taking it. Miss Greenbaum, a gallery buyer from New York. She's looking for emerging talent, she said.' He pulled a face.

'I remember you doing it. What is its title?'

'*Necropolis*.'

'Oh yes.' She turned to look at it, taking the opportunity to glance at the buyer, who was still in the room. Very red lips, very dark eyebrows, matt white city complexion, hard mouth. But the picture itself made her heart sing, now that it was professionally hung.

'Miss Greenbaum said it was full of atmosphere.' Ritchie laughed. 'She didn't know I had climbed over the railings at night risking a strolling bobby, and prowled about for hours. It was spooky.' He pointed. 'See that patch of light at the top?'

'Yes. What is it?'

'A floodlit John Knox. He still dominates the place, the old devil.'

'I like it.' She more than liked it, but she wasn't going to fall over herself praising him.

They stopped at the red-haired girl's table on their way out. 'Put a sticker on *Necropolis*, Christine,' Ritchie said.

'Sold another one?'

He nodded. 'To a Miss Rachel Greenbaum. She's staying at Brown's Hotel.'

'I'll make out an account and get it despatched.' Anna felt shut out as if the conversation was more private than its content suggested.

'This is my girlfriend,' Ritchie said, heartening her. 'Anna Mackintosh. And her sister Nancy.'

'Yes, we've already spoken.' Her eyes slid past the girls and back to Ritchie. 'So she liked *Necropolis*? It's my favourite. I'd like to visit Glasgow sometime.'

152

'We live there,' Nancy said. The girl looked sideways at her. There was a little silence which Anna broke.

'Are you able to get away now, Ritchie? We haven't long.'

'Sure. You've got the address, Christine?'

'Oh, yes. Don't worry.' She gave him a lingering look then bent to her writing, ignoring the girls. It was calculated rudeness, or so it seemed to Anna.

Nancy said when they were going downstairs, 'She would never get away with that manner in a Glasgow shop, Christine . . . ?' She looked at Ritchie.

'Bouvier. London's different.'

'She doesn't even *look* at you when she's talking, does she, Anna?'

'No.' She was casual. 'But Glasgow's special. Everyone says the shopgirls are so helpful. They get really involved.' She was thinking of the girl, of her heavy red hair hanging over her left eye like Veronica Lake – funny that Nancy hadn't picked that up – her pale skin, the light scatter of freckles on her nose, but above all, those strange amber eyes which slanted past you. 'Maybe she's skelly,' she said, regretting the word as she uttered it. 'But maybe you've forgotten that word since you came to the great metropolis, Ritchie?'

'Me? What a hope!' He looked a little uneasy. 'Skelly Nelly was a girlfriend of mine at school, I'll have you know.' They had emerged into the street. 'We can walk from here. Oh, it's great to see you, Anna!' He turned to her, and his loving look reassured her.

Ritchie wouldn't hear of their going back to the hotel. 'I've bought in all the food, Heinz beans, sausages, eggs. And a bottle of wine. We'll have a party.'

'What do you say, Nancy?' Anna asked. 'You're my gaoler.'

'You know it doesn't matter a bit what I say, but, yes, I'm game.' Her eyes were bright. Anna wondered if James was going to be too tame for her.

They climbed three flights of stairs to the flat, which Anna thought would give their mother a heart attack if she saw it. She said so.

'I'd have you know this building is owned by the Peabody Trust,' he informed them. 'Do not spurn.'

Inside, a curtain hung over one end of a large room, presumably to hide the sink and cooker. They were shown a bedroom where they could leave their coats. There was a rushing, roaring, rattling kind of noise as they powdered their noses.

'The Tube,' Anna said. 'Ritchie told me it sometimes wakens him. King's Cross is quite near.'

'I don't know about you, but I think I'd rather sleep at Russell Square. At least it's got all mod cons.'

Bob McNair turned out to be an affable, rather shy young man, sandy-haired, with a wide friendly smile, the high cheekbones and broad frame of the true Highlander. 'Fine!' he said. 'You've done us proud, Ritchie. Wine and paper napkins, no less. We can't hope to keep up this standard.'

He was tactful. He didn't allude to the question of the girls staying, but excused himself and went to have a wash. His interest in the gallery when he came back was obviously genuine. 'Any more sales today, Ritchie?'

'My fourth one gone, to a woman from New York, no less.'

'Which one did she buy?'

'*Necropolis*. She liked my palette, she said. What do you think of the Mackintosh sisters? They're on at the Windmill tonight.'

Nancy laughed heartily, glass in hand. 'But we don't strip!'

'If James could hear you!' Anna joined in.

'Pity.' Bob changed the subject. Perhaps it was too risqué for him. 'What do you think of this part of London, Miss Mackintosh?'

'Nancy, please. Well, we don't really know it. Usually we're in the West End with Mother, shopping.'

'You should see the City. It's got a lot more atmosphere than Ritchie's picture.' He grinned at Ritchie.

'I'd love to. Could we go for a walk? We've been sitting in the train for the best part of the day.'

'I'd like to go too,' Anna said. She wanted the opportunity to talk to Ritchie alone.

'I've got strict instructions from Mother to keep an eye on Anna,' Nancy told Ritchie and Bob. 'We've had enough trouble already. Oh gosh!' She put her hand to her mouth, looking embarrassed.

'Don't listen to her,' Anna said, 'she's had too much to drink.'

The City was ghost-like. A mist hung over the buildings, and they had to peer to see the old timbered houses at Holborn, which Bob pointed out to them on their circuitous route to Fleet Street.

Ritchie was sharp. 'What did Nancy mean when she said you've had enough trouble already? Is there anything wrong?'

'It's Jean.' She hesitated for a second. 'She's pregnant.'

'Jean!' He stopped her in his astonishment. They were at the window of an antique booksellers. 'You're telling me she's pregnant! I didn't even know there was anyone.'

'Frederick Kleiber,' Anna said.

'Good God!' She saw his stunned look, and told him the whole story, how Jean had kept her secret from them for so long.

'Sometimes I wonder,' she said when she had finished, 'will we get used to girls having babies without husbands, even having babies to married men? But we've got to shake off that old man first – the one in *Necropolis*.'

'John Knox?' He was grim-faced. 'Yes, he's better where he is, on a plinth out of harm's way, the miserable old hypocrite.'

'Your soul will burn in hell for a remark like that.'

'I'm no' feart. So tell me, what's happening?'

'The situation now? Mother's palmed her off to Great-aunt Jessie in Kirkcudbright while she thinks.'

'Will she not have her home for the birth?'

'I don't know. She's a surprise packet. She can change her

mind in a day and then pretend it's been like that all the time.'

'Jean wants this baby?'

'Oh yes, she wants it. She's relying on it to bring Kleiber back to her, otherwise she would have had a bash at getting rid of it. And I would have known about that.'

'How come?'

'Any pain she feels, I feel. Even a headache. She's the same with me. She knows how I feel about you.'

'How do you feel?'

'Daft about you.'

'Me too. I want to feel like this for ever, turn into an old goat and keep on chasing you round the bed till I'm ninety.'

'Not a bit of it. You'll be chasing your models. Or red-haired girls in galleries.' It was like a little cold wind blowing round her heart.

'Not me. I'm a one-woman man.' His hand curved under her breast as they walked.

'We'll see.' She looked at her watch, and stopped. 'It's a quarter to ten. Time Nancy and I were back at the hotel.' Nancy and Bob had made up on them. 'We'll have to get back,' she said, and to Bob, 'I'm playing the older sister.'

'We can offer you a double room.' He seemed to have lost some of his shyness. 'Not four-star, but clean.'

'No, thanks.' Anna smiled at him. 'We've checked in. They might send out a search party.'

'Righto,' Ritchie said. He looked as if her news about Jean had shaken him. 'We'll all turn back.'

'Oh, that's not fair.' Nancy pouted. 'I never get a chance to see London.'

'We'll walk slower on the way back,' Anna said. 'On you go. We'll walk behind *you* this time.'

Ritchie went back immediately to the subject of Jean as they retraced their steps. 'She must have gone through hell.'

'There's still more to go through. She doesn't know how Mother will come to terms with an unmarried daughter and child, where she will live, what she will live on. I don't see them living with us, somehow. Bringing up children was more a duty than a pleasure to Mother.'

'You're hard on her.'

'I don't mean to be.'

'Let's talk about us for a change. Do you like London?'

'It's exciting, but Glasgow's big enough for me. I prefer the country to towns.'

'That's for when we have our family. I've got a job down here. It's in Bob's firm. It's a printers.'

'Oh, that's great, Ritchie. But you're not giving up painting?'

'No, far from it, but we couldn't live on that yet. I need something to supply the bread and butter. The money I've made from this show will buy some furniture, after I send something home. Things are looking rosy.' He squeezed her against him. 'And Mr Wolf, who runs the gallery, says he would be pleased to be my agent. He thinks he could get me a flat to rent in a month or so. I thought May, Anna, or even sooner.'

'May for what?'

'For getting married. We could go to a registry office unless you hate the thought of that.'

'It doesn't worry me. Mother will have to be content with a big do for Nancy.'

'May, then. Mr Wolf hinted he might get a flat for me at Easter.'

'No.' She shook her head. 'What am I saying? It couldn't be May! Jean's baby is due in May!'

'Won't she be taken care of? You said she was with your great-aunt, or that your mother might have her home.'

She was amazed at his stupidity. 'But it's impossible! I *have* to be there, just as I would like her close to me. We must be close for births, deaths and marriages.'

'You always said you were independent of each other.'

'We are, but not in the deep down things. Don't you see?'

'I see if you tell me it's so. Well, all right, June. I have to get the licence, take in birth certificates, and so on.'

'Mother will be too involved with Jean and her baby at that time – I hope. She had always wanted us to have a double wedding, but since that's impossible now, we'd be better to play it down.'

'You won't be disappointed?'

'No, but I'll wear a white dress. I couldn't be married in anything else.'

He kissed her. 'A June wedding and a white dress. You inside it. Perfect.'

'It must be ten o'clock, Ritchie.' She looked ahead, raising her voice. Nancy and Bob were within hearing distance. 'What about a taxi, Nancy? My feet are aching.' The four of them came together.

'I thought you'd never suggest it,' Nancy said. 'So are mine.'

Anna wished she'd had more time with Bob. Still, she consoled herself, when she was married and living in London, there would be plenty of opportunity.

'There's a man getting out of one!' Ritchie let out a piercing whistle. The taxi driver backed up beside them and threw open the back door. 'Where to, guv?'

'It's only the ladies. They'll tell you.' He bundled them both in. 'Phone me tomorrow.' The girls were thrown back in the taxi as the driver swerved away.

'That was sudden,' Nancy said.

'We've had a long day.'

'You look radiant. Like a bride.' Her face became serious. 'Did you tell Ritchie about Jean?'

'Yes. I have to tell the man I'm going to marry.'

'Knowing you you've told him you'll wait until the baby comes?'

'Of course. He understands that. June. I couldn't leave her on her own. Poor Jean.' She stretched her aching feet. 'I can see that sad white face of hers.'

158

She could also see the stretched thin skin of Jean's stomach, the full breasts, imagine the aching heart as if it were her own.

EIGHTEEN

THE TWO GIRLS were in the drawing room at Clevedon Crescent a week or two after they had come back from London. Nancy said, wearing a Mona Lisa smile, 'I'm not being secretive, Anna. Anyhow, you'll know soon.'

'You're up to something. And you have that poor James wrapped round your little finger.'

'What a thing to say!'

'Well, why is he closeted with them? There's something going on.'

'I told you, you'll soon know. I would have told you before, but there was our visit to London, and then to Kirkcudbright, and James had quite a few enquiries to make and I wanted him to see Mother and Father first.'

'Is it something you've known for a long time?'

'Not a long time, but there was Jean . . . and it's hard to get a hold of you.'

'What's wrong with the Art School?'

'Oh, that eternal jumping around from class to class, upstairs, downstairs. And that freezing library old Mackintosh designed! All those windows. Anyhow, all will be revealed. Just bide a wee.' She smiled wickedly. 'Don't look so suspicious. I'm not Jean. I wouldn't have the nerve.'

'Thank goodness for that.' Nancy saw the anxious look on her sister's face change to tenderness. 'Poor Jean. Didn't she look pale last weekend when we saw her?'

'Yes, the fresh air there hadn't done her much good. She

160

hardly touched her food when Father took us to the Selkirk Arms. Solway salmon. My favourite.'

'You've got an appetite like a horse, Nancy, and you're thin as a reed.'

'Jealous?' She secretly envied Anna's figure which was slim and shapely with a seductive little bottom – the only word for it.

'What a hope! Great-aunt Jessie says she can't get her to eat much.'

'They get on well together, although I wonder for how long. James and I think you couldn't expect someone like Great-aunt Jessie to cope indefinitely. Will Mother have her?'

'She can't face up to it yet. She's still suffering from shock. A Mackintosh girl! No, she's better with Great-aunt Jessie in that cosy house of hers. An artist's dream.'

'And the garden's lovely, a proper cottage garden.'

'Jean's been fraternizing with Great-aunt Jessie's painting friends. Jessie King lives there with her husband, Mr Taylor.'

'She's the one who did that beautiful batik work?'

'There's nothing she doesn't do. She's done the interior of a tearoom there, designed children's toys, illustrated her own books . . . *The Little White Town of Never Weary*. Isn't that a magical title? There's another. You know those prints and photographs Father has in his study?'

'The ones Mother doesn't approve of?'

'Oh, her! There's one that makes me want to weep, by Frances Macdonald. Her husband destroyed most of her work and his own when she died, so Father's lucky to have it. A naked woman standing on a path, a snake-like path. A naked man at the end of it. *'Tis a Long Path Which Wanders to Desire*. It makes me think of Jean.'

'What an idea! Oh, you mean Jean and Mr Kleiber?'

She saw Anna turn away to hide her face. 'She loved him.' She coughed to clear her throat. 'She loved him so much.' The twins had always been like that, *feeling* for each other, cutting

161

her out. But now she had James who would put her first . . .
'She says she sits at the harbour a lot and watches the fishing
boats when they go out and in. I can see her in those old prints
of Father's – isn't it strange how they *fit* her? Jessie King's
illustration of a book of Oscar Wilde's, for instance, *I Had Never
Seen Anyone So Pale*, strange title, drifting, sad, clothed this time,
perhaps in one of Jean's enveloping smocks . . . and the black
hair.'

'Well, maybe. That's what you think. But ordinary people
wouldn't. Father's got a thing about those Glasgow Girls, and
the work they did. It's not like him, somehow, an architect.'

'Maybe it's his other side, a fey, Highland side, a side we
don't know,' Anna mused.

'He should have been more sensible and bought some more
of their work when he had the chance.'

Anna appeared to be lost in thought for a moment.

'Maybe you're right.' She saw suddenly that Jean's affair was
too *raw* for Mother. She couldn't deal with it.

'Anyhow, I hope Jean can get back to painting. That will be
her salvation. Kirkcudbright's right for her. It used to be known
as the most artistic little town in the United Kingdom, Aunt
Jessie says. A lot of the lady artists went there at the same time
as she did, a coterie of Glasgow Girls. Very avant-garde.

'Remember Mr Kleiber calling *us* the same thing? It went all
round the School, "Here's the Glasgow Girls!"' Nancy laughed,
remembering that strange man, so foreign, so handsome. He
could send thrills up and down your spine just by looking at
you. No wonder Jean . . . James was so *solid* in comparison.
But wasn't that what a girl needed in a husband? At least Mother
and Father would have no complaints about *her*. She looked
towards the door, brightening in anticipation.

The door opened. James came in, ushered by Mother and
Father. They were all smiling, James a little more than them,
but then they had to show a slight doubt at the beginning, not
look carried away. Especially Mother. Still, they looked pleased,

and James looked really happy. She got up and went to him, and he put his arm round her. Safe in the arms of Jesus, she thought. Oh, Nancy, that's blasphemous, but, still, even better, James was here and *now*.

'It's all fixed,' he said. His glance was so loving. 'Your parents have agreed.'

'Oh, Mother.' She went to Rose, who was holding out her arms.

'You're a little schemer, Nancy!' She kissed her, and Nancy saw the tears in her eyes.

She said to Angus, 'Had James a terrible time persuading you, Father?'

'Oh, he's as bad as you!' He hugged her. 'What could we say when he came to us with everything cut and dried? I never thought my wee girl would be the first to leave the fold. And only twenty-two.'

'What's going on?' Anna was on her feet. 'Well, it's not difficult to guess, looking at all those smiling faces.'

'Come and join in the congratulations,' James said. He was a fine-looking man, Nancy thought. He would look very imposing in morning dress. 'Nancy and I are getting married.'

Anna crossed the room to them, laughing, holding out her arms, 'Oh, congratulations!' She turned to Rose. 'You're right. She *is* a schemer, my wee sister. And you're just as bad, James Pettigrew.'

'What about giving your future brother-in-law a kiss?' There was a knock at the door.

'That'll be Bessie,' Angus said. 'I slipped into the kitchen and told her to bring in a bottle of champagne. Come in, Bessie!' He strode to the door and opened it, 'Come away in.'

'About time, Mr Mackintosh,' Bessie said. 'My arms were breaking wi' the weight o' this.' She was bearing a large silver galleried tray with glasses and a bottle of champagne on it. Nancy saw Tumshie stepping daintily after her, as if on high heels. She sat down close to Bessie, her paws neatly together. 'Oh, Tumshie,' she said, looking down, 'you know you shouldn't.' Everyone laughed. Tumshie looked round innocently.

'Oh, let her stay,' Rose said. 'It's a special occasion.'

'Would she lap a little champagne in a saucer, do you think?' Father was opening the bottle.

'You never know, Mr Mackintosh,' Bessie said, her broad face with its pug nose breaking into a smile. 'But whit's it all in aid o'?'

'That's what I was wondering too, Bessie,' Anna said. 'We always knew they were getting married.'

'At Easter,' Mother said.

'Easter? Barely two months away?' Anna shook her head, smiling at the couple, James's arm round Nancy's waist. Proprietorially. 'You're a sly puss,' she said, 'and you're no better, James.'

'She's jealous because we're beating her and Ritchie.' Ritchie was handsome, without a doubt, but her James had style, and the look of a man of property, Galsworthy, she remembered. Oh no, she would never have fallen in love with someone as young and untidy-looking as Ritchie.

Father was handing round champagne. 'Here's to the happy couple,' he said, raising his glass.

Bessie sipped, sipped again. 'You can get married every day o' the week, Nancy,' she said, 'if your faither hands oot a dram like this.' She looked down at her friend Tumshie, who looked back with adoring eyes. Nancy felt she was looking up at James in the same way.

The wedding was at Wellington Church. Long ago, when they had lived in Claremont Street, Rose had chosen it because it was halfway between there and Clevedon Crescent where they hoped to live one day. Her parents had worshipped in the city. Also the Palladian front with the flight of steps made a splendid setting, and she had looked forward to having each of her girls married there in due course.

No one appreciated the intensity of her feelings when Angus had told her Jean was pregnant to a married man, not even him. There was the disgrace, of course, the bitter blow to her pride, the realization that she would never see Jean coming down those grand steps. But it was her imagination – the thought of Jean lying partly naked in that man's arms, letting him . . . in broad daylight too. She always told Angus to put out the light, although sometimes he pleaded . . . She pushed the shameful thoughts away, not suitable for someone like a respected married lady.

Anna in palest leaf green with a shady hat of the same colour, although stylish, was eclipsed completely by the stunning beauty of Nancy. James looked enraptured, but City smart. His eyes were bright because he saw a new life stretching ahead of him which would keep him young. He had the maturity which Nancy required. He would adore his young wife, and in her liking for grandeur she would make a wonderful hostess.

They were going to live in Hyndland, so she would be close enough to run in to Clevedon Crescent for an occasional cup of coffee. James had sold the house he had lived in with his first wife, and bought a five-bedroomed terrace house looking on to a small private park for which the owners of the row of houses opposite possessed a key.

Angus had taken James out to dinner a night or two before the wedding in order to have a financial talk, and had been astonished, not at the comfortable state of James's bankbook, but at what he had told him.

'We might have waited a little longer, out of a sense of decorum for Gwen, but having the wedding at Easter was Nancy's idea. She has a good heart, Angus, although she's a bit, well, frivolous. She's just a wee girl to me in some ways. She's written to her sister to say that she and the baby are welcome to make a home with us.'

Angus had been ashamed. Rose would have come round, given time. 'It's very generous of you, James, because I know fine you're at the back of this, but I'm sure things will sort themselves out. It's our responsibility.'

'Maybe so, but Nancy says her mother couldn't face it.'

He had been even more ashamed, knowing this was true. He'd held Rose often enough in bed, listened to her broken weeping, and cursed this awful Craig feeling of 'having to put a face on it'.

'We've taken a bigger house with that in view,' James was saying, 'and, of course, we hope there will be a family of our own in due course. Gwen was unable to have any.'

'Has Jean accepted your offer?' he had asked.

'Yes, Nancy had told Anna and she thought she should. She says if she and Ritchie had been married, she would have done the same. I think Ritchie has been pressing her, but she didn't want to be in London until Jean's baby was born. You have a fine trio there, Angus, they stick together. And don't worry about Rose. When she sees the baby it will be a different matter.'

So, here they were, standing on the steps to have the wedding photograph taken, and then he and Rose joining them with James's mother, a douce widow from Hillhead. Nancy had asked the mothers to wear golden brown or champagne, nothing which would clash with the gold and ivory of her own colour scheme. It was a wonder he hadn't been asked to wear a brown suit. Jean's absence hung over the wedding breakfast and the departure of Mr and Mrs Pettigrew to Paris for their honeymoon.

Anna's smile was brave, and Rose in her golden brown two-piece with little toque to match, bronze courts and a spray of cream orchids on her lapel looked beautiful. But nothing could take away the wistful look from her face, nor the edge of hardness to the mouth. Her wound was taking a long time to heal.

NINETEEN

ANNA WAS SPENDING the Easter weekend with Jean and Great-aunt Jessie at Kirkcudbright, ostensibly to show them the wedding photographs, but really to see how Jean was getting on. She was big now, and yet it was strange, Anna thought, that someone could have such a swollen stomach and look so thin. And pale. The paleness had a blue tinge round the eyes, and on her thin hands the veins were raised and blue.

'Does she do what she's told, Aunt?' Anna asked. They were sitting in what she called the garden room because as well as looking on to the garden it trapped the sun even when it was cold in the shadows.

'No, she tries to boss me.' She smiled, but Anna noticed the drawn look. Was it getting too much for her already? Jean said she had pills to put under her tongue for her angina. 'And Jean wants me to lie down in the afternoon. I said if she promised to have a daily walk I might. The doctor says she has to have plenty of fresh air.'

'I do most days,' Jean said. 'They say it's mild here because of the Gulf Stream, but I'm always cold.'

'Well, you and I will have a stroll this afternoon and Aunt will put her feet up. Now *I'm* the boss.' Anna smiled.

'I'll bake a scone for our tea.'

'Indeed you won't. I'll bring in some cakes and scones from that fine baker's facing the car park. I remember how good they were.'

'Yes, they take a lot of beating.'

Even her smiles are tired, Anna thought.

'Take my arm, Jean,' Anna said, when they were walking slowly along High Street.

'Oh God!' That was more like the old Jean. 'Well, all right. I'm inclined to stagger. They'll think I've been spending too much time in the Selkirk Arms.' She sighed. 'It's a weary business.'

'Not long now.'

'No, not long.'

'Nancy says I've to tell you your room is furnished ready for you. It's a bit frilly for your taste, but it's comfortable and there's a wireless and a good armchair so that you can have some privacy when you want it. She's ordered a cot. She says when she was in the shop they looked at her suspiciously. She was sorry she hadn't stuck a cushion under her jumper!'

Jean laughed. 'Nancy has surprised me.'

'I think James has a good influence on her. It's a rare match, that.'

'I'm glad for her. Does Mother say anything about me?'

'Not much. I think she hates herself, but her pride's still stronger than her love. She'll have to fight her own battle.'

'I can't help her. I've tried. And the last thing I want is to bother Nancy and James when they're just married, but there's the baby to think about.' Her voice broke. 'I'm pinning my hopes to that baby, that it will break the ice in my heart.'

'Just look a little forward at a time. Ritchie and I will be getting married in June, and then you can come to us. You could start painting down there. Ours will be a painting house. Nothing to spoil.'

'What's keeping you back?'

'Mother and Father have to recover from Nancy's wedding. That reception in the Grosvenor will have set them back quite a bit. And I know Nancy's dress was into hundreds. Nothing but the best.'

Jean was looking at her disbelievingly. '*You* wouldn't want nothing but the best. You shouldn't keep Ritchie dangling. He's attractive, and fiery. He'll maybe take up with one of those smart London girls.'

'Not a hope.' But she had a pang of unease as she thought of that girl Christine Bouvier with the strange eyes. 'Maybe I will, when I see you settled with the baby, and strong, and then that would be another place for you to come to . . . though we couldn't offer you the same luxury as you'd get with Mr and Mrs Pettigrew.' She laughed.

'I know who I'd rather be with.'

'Ask Nancy to put some papers down so that you can paint. It will be your salvation. Have you done any here?'

'Yes, a little. Great-aunt's friends encourage me. I've painted in their gardens at Green Gate Close. And sketched at the harbour. Oh, there's plenty to paint. It's a fine place this, full of character and old stone. I believe I could settle here if I had enough money.'

Anna took her courage in both hands. 'Frederick would like you to paint.' Her sister's face became like stone, but she knew it was to hide her grief, not indifference.

'It breaks my heart to even hear his name mentioned. Don't, Anna.' She turned away.

'I won't, but remember, I'm ready . . . when you're ready.'

They had come to the Tolbooth and Jean said as they passed, 'Paul Jones was kept a prisoner there. I had to look up who he was. All I knew was the Paul Jones at dances where you danced with the man who stopped opposite you when the music stopped. Remember that night Ritchie took us to the University Union? You and Ritchie paid no attention to it, but I had plenty of variety.'

'You would. Do you ever hear from Robin Naismith?'

'Yes, he still writes. And he wants to come and see me although I told him everything. He's kind, and gentle, but not for me. We have nothing in common.'

169

Now they were in the old High Street with its fine Georgian houses. I could live here too, Anna thought, but it wouldn't suit Ritchie. He needs a metropolis like London to stimulate him. She thought of his mother who had the same strength of purpose. She must go and see her sometime.

'That's where Mr Hornel lives,' Jean said. 'He's a friend of Aunt Jessie's, and Mr Oppenheimer's close by. I haven't met them yet.'

'Quite a coterie, isn't it? The Glasgow Style.'

'Yes, the women still here are very gifted, though it's past its heyday. They do all kinds of metal-work and jewellery and embroidery, book covers, and all that. Everything they do has their stamp, a delicacy, a kind of feyness.'

'That would suit you fine, or would it? You're bold in your painting.'

'And I think most of them have private means.'

They had come to the Mote Brae. 'Shall we go down here to the harbour?'

'Maybe on the way back. You wanted to go to St Cuthbert Street to get the scones.'

'Oh, yes, so I did. But you're tired, Jean.' The pale expressionless face, like the women on the gesso panels in the Art School, elongated figures, but this one here had a round stomach with Frederick Kleiber's child inside it.

'No, not tired. Weary.' Neither spoke for a few minutes. Anna looked at the castle as they passed it, a ruin, like Jean's life. No, she mustn't think that. There was a new life to come.

'Has it got any easier, Jean?' she said, as they passed the stern front of Greyfriars Church.

'Frederick? No. I'd only tell *you* this. Do you feel it too – we think alike often – a dull, heavy, hopeless kind of pain? I try to be cheerful for Great-aunt's sake, for the sake of the child – misery might affect it – but the effort's usually too much for me. The only time I can forget myself is when I'm engrossed in a painting.'

'That's what Frederick would want you to do. He saw your talent.'

'My talent?' Her suffering eyes met Anna's. 'I relive that scene on the boat again and again. I think I might have done this, that, it's the terrible guilt as well as the terrible grief which is crucifying me. Oh God, you must be fed up with this! I don't talk about it to Great-aunt Jessie. It distresses her. It's not that she's shocked, like Mother – she doesn't care a fig for the pride of the Craigs because she threw it in their faces herself – but she doesn't like to see people unhappy. She admits to that, says it's a sign of age and not wanting to carry anyone else's burdens. And they get set in their ways, those women here. They have "days" for seeing each other, the painting crowd, and I've upset that by being here.'

'I'm sure you haven't. She loves you because she sees her young self in you. In any case, you'll soon be with Nancy and James, and when Mother sees the baby she'll be won over.'

'I don't want to win her over, using the baby as a bait.'

'Well, Miss Difficult-to-please, when you're strong enough you can come to us in London and the baby can model Putti angels for Ritchie. You're right. He's getting fed up. He says I should have been with him by this time, that I don't love him enough.'

'What do *you* say?'

'I say, "Jean needs me." No, don't look upset. It's true. I wouldn't have a moment's happiness away from you just now. You come first with me, always have. You'd be the same with me. Only when I see you all right can I marry Ritchie.'

'Oh, Anna.' She clutched her hand. 'I never wanted to come between you.'

'You haven't. The only thing that will come between us is his painting.' She spoke convincingly to convince herself. 'It comes first with him. I'm entitled to have a first too. But this won't last, this misery. You'll get used to being without

Frederick. Maybe the baby will be like him and you'll have him in your arms again.'

'Aye, maybe. And yet, no man's worth it. Their love is more urgent, sooner over. Ours is deeper, doesn't fluctuate, more lasting.' She paused for a second then said briskly, 'Here's the shop. There's always a queue, but their apple tarts are worth waiting for.'

They walked slowly back by the harbour because neither of them could resist having a look at the fishing boats. They were coming in with their catches and it was all bustle and good-natured shouting.

'It's a hard life they have,' Anna said.

'Yes, I should take a lesson from them. They're cheerful. "Get on with living," Aunt Jessie says. "Don't look back."'

When they were going up the Mote Brae Anna noticed that Jean was panting.

'Stop for a minute. I want to take a look at those old houses. One thing about Kirkcudbright, it's held on to its past.'

'You didn't have to stop. It's only a stitch in my side.'

'When is the baby due?'

'Two weeks. I'll even welcome the pain to get rid of it.'

'Look forward. Are you going into the hospital?'

'I think so. Not for my sake, for Great-aunt Jessie's. And the water baby . . .' Her face was suddenly anguished. 'I mustn't call it that. It stirs up memories.'

'Don't then, call it a water baby. Just think of it as yours and his. Ritchie and I haven't discussed children, but I think he'll want them. He's prolific in his thinking, and his painting . . .' she laughed, 'and his loving. Plenty to spare, nothing mean about him. He'll want children to share life with us, to let them see what a fine man he is. It's all right for them, but we have to contend with the having of them.'

She thought of Frederick Kleiber and how he might have been selfish and irresponsible and seduced Jean with his foreign charm. But, no, it took two to make a baby and she had been

172

deeply in love, still was. No point in thinking about it. It was done and the result would be here as a constant memory.

They went down the close and in the narrow confines, Jean bumped awkwardly against her. Anna looked at the drawn face. 'You'll be glad to get off your feet,' she said, thinking, as she opened the side door, It's not yet. The house seemed very quiet. Perhaps Great-aunt Jessie was having a nap.

'We've brought scones and pancakes and apple custard tarts, Aunt,' Anna sang out. She wasn't in her usual high-backed chair at the fire. 'You sit down, Jean. She's probably in the kitchen getting the tea ready.'

She couldn't open the door. She knew as she pushed against it that some heavy object was preventing it. She inched it open until there was just room to squeeze through. She had to step over her aunt's body, which was slumped behind it. Great-aunt Jessie was lying with a tea towel in her hand with fishing boats printed on it and the word 'Kirkcudbright' in black letters. Her lips were blue. Anna stood for a moment, shocked and trembling, then got down on her knees and felt her pulse. At first there was nothing, then she thought she felt a faint flutter. She got up, suddenly afraid, and went dashing back to the sitting room.

'Aunt Jessie . . .' she said, trembling, then calmed herself, 'I think she's fainted.'

'Oh God! It will be her angina.' Jean looked as if she was going to faint herself. What a business, Anna thought, trying to make light of it to herself, the two of them. 'The number's here.' Jean moved quickly but clumsily to the table, clutching her back, opened a pad. 'I'll do it.' Her voice was steady enough as she spoke into the receiver, though there was pain written on her face. 'Yes, that's right. Dr Whitbread.' It gave Anna time to get her breath back.

'You sit down again and I'll go and cover her with this rug.' Anna took a plaid hap from the back of the sofa. Her aunt still lay in the same position. She looked very old and shrunken, her lips were still blue. Anna tucked the rug round her, took a cushion off a chair and managed to get it under her head. 'Aunt Jessie!' she said softly. 'Come on, Aunt. It's Anna.' She rubbed her cold hands with their dry wrinkled skin. Some day hers would be like that. She was gazing down at the still face when she heard a reassuring masculine voice in the other room. She remembered Jean saying the doctor lived only a few doors away. She went quickly back to the sitting room. A youngish man was there, carrying a black bag. He had a thin, but not a mean mouth, and bright brown eyes.

'Who's the patient?' he said, looking from one to the other.

'It's our great-aunt, Miss Craig. She's in the kitchen, on the floor. I thought it best not to move —'

He was swift on his feet, pushing past Anna. She followed him as he got down beside Aunt Jessie and put his ear to her chest. After a minute he looked up.

'She's in a bad way, I'm afraid. How long do you think she's been lying here?'

'It could be an hour. We went —'

He was up and away again with long strides to the sitting room. When she went in he was telephoning, asking for an ambulance to be sent to their address.

'Dr *Whit*bread,' he said, decidedly, and raising his voice, 'Right away, please!' He stopped for a second on his way back to the kitchen, nodding his head towards Jean. 'Miss Mackintosh is in labour,' he said. 'I'll send round the midwife.'

Anna gasped. 'I thought she was going into hospital?'

He smiled drily. 'One at a time, young lady, one at a time . . .'

TWENTY

THERE WAS THE SMALL bustle of the ambulance arriving –
they looked to Anna in their cheerfulness uncommonly like the
fishermen they had seen earlier in the day – rapid instructions
from Dr Whitbread to treat Miss Craig gently – she was now
in a semi-conscious state – and a clap on the shoulder for Jean:
'I'll send the midwife.' Anna bent over the stretcher and stroked
her great-aunt's cheek. Her eyes were open in a fixed stare.
'You'll be all right,' she whispered. She nodded with a half-smile
which was twisted.

Anna turned to Jean when they had gone. 'Poor Aunt Jessie!
But, Jean, was he right about you?'

'Yes, this is it. I'm not frightened yet, only glad it's you with
me, and not her. I worried about that. What does the doctor
think it is?'

'I don't know. He's a terse man, isn't he?'

'Maybe he makes fewer mistakes that way. I haven't found
him . . . unsympathetic.' Her face screwed up as she said the
word.

'Is it bad, Jean?'

'Bearable.'

'Well, I've to get you into bed and then we'll have a cup of
tea. We both need it.'

Her sister was pitifully thin, she saw, as she helped her to
undress. The upper part of her thighs had hardly any flesh on
them and her calves hung loose, like an old woman's. 'What on
earth have you been doing to yourself?' she said. 'It's not sensible.'

175

'I was sick a lot, and then I had terrible indigestion. I tried to play it down, not to worry Aunt Jessie. How people have eleven of them I can't think!'

'I expect everyone vows this will be the last and then they have another. Maybe they don't have any choice.'

'I had a choice. I could have said no, but ... I lost my reason. I was glad to lose it!' She spoke fiercely. 'I don't regret it!'

'It wouldn't matter if you did, would it?' They looked at each other and laughed. 'I'll go and make a cup of tea.' She took an alarm clock from the mantelpiece and placed it on the bedside table. 'Time the pains and then we'll be able to tell the midwife when she comes.' She felt a vague sympathetic ache in her own stomach. If only she could share Jean's pain.

When she went back to the bedroom with a tray, Jean was lying back on the pillows, her face ashen.

'I think I'm swimming in blood,' she said. Anna put down the tray and folded back the clothes.

'Roll over.' Jean did. 'No, you're not.' She put her hand on the under sheet. 'But it's wet.'

'Oh, it's the membrane rupturing. Dr Whitbread warned me.' She laughed. 'Remember my first period and how I had a spot on my nightie and you were madly jealous?'

'I was not. What nonsense you talk! Turn over and sit up. I'll get dry sheets in a minute. Here's your tea and I've brought a tart. I thought you might fancy one.'

'I couldn't *look* at a tart!'

'Well, I could. All this excitement has made me ravenous. I wonder how poor Aunt Jessie is getting on. She looked terrible, didn't she? She gave me a wee smile, but there was something funny about it.'

'Was there? I was too preoccupied. If it was a coronary she wouldn't have been unconscious, would she? Isn't it terrible to think of her suffering here on her own? If only we hadn't gone out.'

176

'Never mind the "if onlys".' There was a loud peremptory ring on the door bell. 'That'll be the midwife. It's all go here.' She put down her plate and sped away.

The stout body on the doorstep announced herself as Mrs Jardine. 'Nellie, if you like,' she said, bustling in. 'Have you got her in bed?'

'Yes. I was going to get dry sheets. Her membranes have ruptured. Would you like a cup of tea, Mrs Jardine?'

'Thanks. Good and strong. Black. It's my only tipple.'

When Anna came back to the bedroom with the tea, the midwife had her sleeves rolled up. 'You're right. Her waters have broken.'

'I'd better get clean sheets for the doctor coming.'

'He won't be coming, m'dear. He's gone to the hospital at Dumfries with your auntie.'

'Is it her heart?'

'Oh, no! She's had a shock. The toffs call it a stroke. Didn't you notice her mouth? There isn't the same facilities here for dealing with shocks.'

'Oh, that's awful. That's awful, isn't it, Jean?' Her sister nodded. Her eyes closed and tears ran slowly down her cheeks.

'It's bad news for her especially.' Anna looked at Mrs Jardine. 'Is she . . . far into labour?'

'Don't talk as if I weren't here, Anna.' Jean was crying openly now. Anna took a handkerchief and wiped her eyes. 'Don't worry. You'll be going into hospital, won't she, Mrs Jardine?' She turned to the woman.

'No, not unless it's necessary. That was Dr Whitbread's idea to spare your auntie. She's a great favourite of his.'

'I see. Well, is she? Far into labour? You want to know, Jean, don't you?'

'You can't tell at this stage,' Mrs Jardine said. 'I've seen prims who'll go for three days after the waters break. Dr Whitbread doesn't believe in induction. "Let nature take its course," he says.'

177

Jean smiled wanly at Anna. 'Nature red in tooth and claw. That's what it feels like, tearing at my insides.' She had stopped weeping at least.

They changed her nightgown and the sheets, they made her as comfortable as they could, Nellie – they were calling her Nellie now – got her out of bed and told her to take a walk about the house to 'hurry things on a bit'. She had also given her a 'good strong laxative'. 'Good and strong' seemed to be her criterion, Anna thought, placing another cup of black tea beside her to keep her strength up.

'Refreshes,' she said, sipping. 'That laxative I gave your sister. It would move cement.'

Anna nodded and bent to the woman's ear. 'Are . . . things going all right?' she whispered.

She took another sip, considering. 'I think so.' She kept her voice down. 'But the lassie hasn't had a good pregnancy. Well, I don't ask questions, a miss or a missis, it's all the same to me, but you could see she had a load on her mind. If I had been asked I never did think it was a good idea to have her here – well, we saw the result today when that poor soul was carted away. Where was your mother in all this? Couldn't your sister have stayed at home?'

Anna flew to Rose's defence. 'It was a . . . shock to her. And Jean and our great-aunt always got on well together.'

'Did she offer?'

'I don't know. Is Jean all right?'

'Aye, padding about's the thing. Well, yes, I have sympathy for your mother, especially if she had set great hopes. Lassies should bear that in mind, but on the other hand, mothers should think back on what they were like in their twenties. Hot-blooded. I had two laddies. Fishermen. They married early. Knew it was safer.' She got up. 'I think I'll phone the hospital and see if Dr Whitbread is on his way back. Report progress. Will you keep an eye on your sister? She's probably enthroned by this time.'

The bathroom door was shut. Anna knocked. 'Jean!' she called. 'Are you all right?'

'I think so.' Her voice was hoarse. 'My insides are turning inside out. It's hell.'

'Will I come in?'

'No, you know I hate being watched. It's not . . . dignified.' The last word was drowned by a groan which turned into a scream. 'Oh God! Oh God!'

Anna pushed open the door. Her sister was rocking on the toilet seat, her arms round her stomach.

'Something's happening, Anna. I have no control. Something . . . different. Get Nellie.'

Anna went to the open door. 'Nellie!' she shouted. 'Nellie! Come quickly!' The woman came puffing round the corner of the hall.

'He's on his way. What's the commotion, Jean? It's all right. It's only your bowels opening.'

'Get me off this! Get me up!' Jean's face was twisted, unrecognizable.

Together they supported her along the hall, through the sitting room towards her bedroom. Halfway across she broke free of them and crouched like an animal on the floor. 'I'm being torn apart,' she moaned, 'torn apart. Help me . . . help me.'

Nellie was calm, obviously used to *accouchements* of all kinds. 'Get towels and hot water, plenty of towels. And my bag. Look slippy.' She had turned Jean over on her back, pushed her legs apart and lifted the skirt of her nightgown. So undignified, Jean would be thinking . . . Anna sped on her tasks. 'Hurry!' Nellie called after her. 'Fill the kettle again when you've filled the basin. It's singing on the Aga.'

She spent precious minutes trying to locate a basin. Towels, she remembered, were in a chest of drawers in the bathroom. When she ran there the strong faecal odour hit her and she pulled the chain hurriedly. She found several towels, put them over her arm and went back for the basin. She had to stand for a moment to compose herself. Her hands were trembling. What a life – the thought raced through her head – one minute we're enjoying a walk, next we're in the middle of a performance like this, and poor Great-aunt carried away with a stroke. Jean's torture might soon be over but not Great-aunt's . . . She was half running, trying to keep the water from sloshing out of the basin.

'Anna!' It was Jean's voice, shrieking. 'Anna! Anna!' She increased her speed, some water from the basin slopped over her feet, soaking her shoes.

When she went into the sitting room, all she saw of Mrs Jardine was her stout posterior. Her head was between Jean's legs.

'Hold my hand!' Jean clutched at her.

'Mind! I'm holding a basin. The water, Nellie,' she said to the posterior. 'And the towels.' She got down on her knees and placed the basin on the floor, took Jean's waving hand. 'It's all right. I'm here. Soon be over.'

'You haven't my bag.' Nellie emerged.

'Oh, sorry! I'll get it.' She was back in a minute. Some bloody towels were lying on the floor now. How did some women manage to go through this, year after year?

Together they lifted Jean and put a large towel underneath her. She saw Nellie had found some newspapers in the room to protect the carpet.

Jean was moaning now, her eyes half-closed. She appeared to be barely conscious. Anna stroked her hand, humming under her breath an old nursery rhyme which they had used to shoosh their dolls.

'It's dead, Anna!' Jean's voice went up the scale in a shriek. 'Did you know that? My baby's dead!'

'Don't talk rubbish!' She was suddenly fiercely angry. 'Oh, you *are* talking rubbish, you silly girl!'

'Yes, that's what I was, a silly girl. That's what Mother thinks. So silly. Her bold clever Jean, like a servant girl, under the bushes, feet sticking out, legs . . .' Nellie had an amused look on her face, as if to say, 'This is a new one.'

'Yes, Dr Whitbread's been held up at Dumfries,' she was following her own train of thought. 'Well, he couldn't be in two places at once. It'll only take another wee push, Jean. Hold on to your sister.'

Anna clasped her in her arms. 'This is it now, Jean. Hang on to me. Can't you feel it?'

'It's dead, I told you. You . . . can . . . always tell . . . God!' Her voice rose then fell away into silence. Her eyes closed like a china doll's.

Nellie was wrapping a little bloody bundle with the last of the towels.

'The water's here, Nellie,' Anna said.

'I don't need it.' She nodded towards the half-unconscious Jean. 'She's right. The poor wee soul's deid.'

TWENTY-ONE

THERE FOLLOWED a strange time with the two of them in
the flat-fronted house in High Street with its Georgian door
and fanlight. Nothing seemed real, rather like Great-aunt Jessie's
house, which was really a cottage behind the façade which kept
it in line with its neighbours.

Day followed day tending Jean, who lay like a wraith in
bed, hardly speaking. Her faint grateful smiles to Anna were
heart-breaking. Unlike the Kilcreggan doctor, Dr Whitbread
didn't sedate her. His 'let nature take its course' theory seemed
comprehensive, but he spent a long time at her bedside each
day, talking to her.

Her response to the death of the baby had been very different
from that to Frederick Kleiber's. She was calm, she didn't
scream, she wept ceaselessly and soundlessly, day after day.

Once when Anna was sitting with her, she said, 'I hate to see
you like this.' She wiped away the tears.

'I'm sorry, but it's part of the after-birth, Dr Whitbread says.
I don't feel desperate, suicidal, the way I did after Frederick,
just infinitely sad for my poor baby. Giving birth has taken away
my bitterness.'

'That's healthy. That's good.' She looked down on her
sister. She was pale and thin, but her eyes were not dead, and
there seemed an inner glow to her which hadn't been there
before.

'Did I tell you it was a little girl, Anna?'

'No.'

'Dr Whitbread said I had to know that, even christen her in my mind if it helped. I chose the name.'

'What was it?'

'Yours. It was to be my way of saying thanks.'

When she was up and going about the house, Dr Whitbread still looked in. He had a tight-lipped, jokey way of talking, 'risky', Anna called it. He made them laugh. He never sat down, but would perch on the arm of a chair to show he wasn't waiting long.

'Couldn't you give her a tonic now?' Anna asked him once.

'Grief like Jean's is the best tonic I know,' he said. 'Nothing better for clearing out the system. And tears are healthy. There's no bitterness where there are tears.'

'So, I'm signed off now?' Jean said.

'No, you've a bit to go yet.' Anna thought so too, looking at the gaunt face, the saddened hair which has been so full of life. But the eyes weren't dead now, and the intense blueness had returned. 'But once your insides are mended you can have as many more children as you like.'

Rose came to see her, and she and Jean wept together. Anna left them to it. She suspected Rose wept longer than Jean. She was supposed to be relieving Anna of attending the invalid, so that she could visit Aunt Jessie at Dumfries.

Not that the visit would matter much to her great-aunt. She was in a world of her own as well as in a big ward of silent women who didn't seem to have any communication with each other, not grieving, but gazing at something which wasn't there, perhaps their past.

Aunt Jessie's voice had changed. It had become husky, like a man's, as if her vocal chords were damaged. Her left side was paralysed. Also her memory had gone. When Anna told her that Jean's baby had died, she merely looked reflective.

But she hadn't forgotten Jean. 'I have made a will,' she said. 'The house is hers. Don't let Rose have it. She always wanted

Clevedon Crescent. Let her bloody well stay there.' Anna had to hide a smile.

'You'll be home before long,' she said. 'Jean will look after *you* for a change. I'm going to be married in London soon. Ritchie's getting tired waiting.'

'Men are selfish. Let him wait. Jean comes first.'

'We'll see,' she said.

'Look at Jean and what that man did to her. Only thinking of their own needs. Let him wait, that one in London.'

Dr Whitbread said there wasn't much hope for Miss Craig. She would either have another stroke or slowly deteriorate.

'It's vile,' he said. 'Give me a good-going coronary any day. There you have a sporting chance.'

She telephoned Ritchie at his work whenever she got a moment – she was generally too tired to write. His letters were regular, but she noticed, shorter, and he had no telephone in the flat Mr Wolf had rented to him.

'Everything's shipshape now,' he said on one of these occasions. 'When are you coming?' She thought he sounded terse.

'Jean's far from well yet. I couldn't possibly leave her.'

'Sooner or later you're going to have to choose between her and me.' Yes, he was definitely terse. 'I know it sounds cruel, but she's got to get on with her own life. We're into May now. Perhaps June means nothing to you?'

She was surprised and hurt. 'Of course it does! But have you given a thought to what I've had to cope with here? No support from the family except a brief face-saving visit from Mother, which is driving me round the bend. And there's Great-aunt Jessie. Travelling to Dumfries every chance I get. I couldn't desert them.'

'I know. I'm sorry if I sound selfish, but the new flat's all ready and looks really good. Christine helped me furnish it. She knew of a place where I could get second-hand stuff cheap.'

184

'Do you mean to say she helped you to *choose* it?' A flame of anger had swept through her.

'As a matter of fact she did. She's got good taste.'

'Oh really! When is she moving in with you?'

'Oh for God's sake, Anna, don't be stupid!'

'So I'm stupid now!'

'No, it's me! Oh, it's impossible to speak here. I'm bad-tempered. I'm not painting. Some kind of block, and I miss Bob, but I wouldn't have had his company even if I'd still been sharing with him. He's gone to Spain to fight. And have you seen that picture Picasso's done of Guernica?' She could hear his enthusiasm.

'I saw it in an art magazine.' She spoke stiffly.

'It's amazing! I'm envious, not because he's a genius but because of the feeling which inspired him to paint it, that boiling up of the senses which I haven't felt for ages.'

'It'll come back.'

'It would if you'd come to London and marry me.'

'It's impossible at the moment! I've told you. Don't hold a gun to my head.'

'But I'm hanging here like a loose thread, don't know whether to get the licence or not, working in this dreary place, not painting. You've got to think of us, Anna, not sacrifice yourself just because your sister made a damn fool of herself!'

Her anger came back, fiercer than ever. This petulant creature was not the Ritchie she had known.

'What a nerve!' She was boiling with rage. 'When you criticize my sister you criticize me! She nearly died, her baby *did* die –'

'I'm sorry, sorry. My big mouth. I'm cheesed off, missing you like mad. And the phone here, it's difficult . . . I'll write.'

Her heart was beating loudly in her ears. 'I shouldn't bother if I were you,' she said. 'Why not console yourself with Christine Bouvier!' She slammed down the receiver.

That was a mistake, she thought, but it was too late.

* * *

Anna was washing up in the kitchen after supper that evening when Jean joined her. She looked up from the sink.

'I told you,' she said, as she saw her lifting a tea towel, 'I don't need any help. Besides, I'm nearly finished.'

'Sorry.' Jean put down the tea towel but hovered. There was silence. 'Not talking tonight?'

She made a great play of wringing out the dishcloth, draping it over the taps.

'How was Ritchie when you phoned?'

'All right.'

'So why are you peeved?'

'Who said I was peeved?'

'Have you seen your face? It would turn the milk in that jug into soor dook!'

She tried to hide the smile. 'It's the selfishness of men!' The words burst from her.

'He wants you to go to London. You won't go because of me.'

'What rubbish!' She took the dishcloth off the taps and rubbed them to a fierce brightness. 'There's Great-aunt Jessie as well.'

'She wouldn't miss you, poor soul. And I could go and see her soon. But remember, you mustn't stay here because of me. I'm perfectly capable of managing on my own.'

'Oh sure! You're a picture of health!'

'What you're suffering from, you know,' Jean's voice was calm, 'is sexual frustration. That's what's putting you in a bad temper.'

Anna boiled up inside. The bitch! She knew everything that went on inside her, the longings, the writhings in her bed when she thought of Ritchie. Now there would be the writhings of jealousy when she thought of Christine Bouvier. Had she helped him put up the bed? Tried it out? 'You may be an authority on some things,' she had to hurt, put the knife in, 'but sexual *frustration* is not one of them. That's why you're in the fix you're in, and everybody else as well!'

186

Jean's pale face went paler. Her eyes went black as if they were registering the knife thrust. She turned and walked out of the kitchen.

They didn't share a room in Aunt Jessie's house. There was no need to. It was as if they had escaped Rose's dominance and by so doing had gained a privacy which their separate states of mind demanded. Perhaps, too, the birth and death of Jean's child made it essential for her to be alone.

Anna felt glad of the privacy that night. But first she made herself go into the little sitting room where she knew Jean was with her mother. 'I've come to say good night,' she said.

Rose looked up from the small table where she was playing patience. 'What were you two girls shouting about in the kitchen? Jean said it was nothing.'

The fact that Jean had gone back to Rose rather than to her own room touched Anna. Her heart contracted with difficult love. This was a new Jean who was getting on with life, seeking to integrate herself. 'I lost my temper,' she said. 'I don't know how Jean puts up with me.'

'You've quite a lot on your plate,' Rose said, studying her cards, then lifting a five of diamonds with a little sigh of satisfaction.

'That's it.' Anna pulled a face and walked over to Jean. 'Give me a slap. Go on.' She bent down and held out her cheek.

Jean smiled, her old brilliant smile. She was still very pale. 'You're too old for slaps. Get off to bed and have a rest.'

Her throat ached with unshed tears as she undressed, but she was hanged if she would let them come. She was too old for crying as well.

TWENTY-TWO

AFTER THE ROW with Anna on the telephone, Ritchie took
to wandering about Clerkenwell in the evenings. He couldn't
sleep. He was lonely in his new flat and upset because Anna
hadn't replied to his letter of apology. It was an impasse.

He was still not painting, but although he only vaguely realized it, he was absorbing images as he walked, as if he were a
walking camera. Images of the hill were being stored in his
brain, the Italian Church, the shapes of streets and squares. He
had never been a landscape painter. The solid blocks of buildings
took its place.

Little Italy didn't feel strange to him. He was used to the
Glasgow Italians, had been reared on their ice-cream all his life.
'Go to the Tallys' and get a double nougat' was a family bribe
to cancel all bribes. And at the café near his school he had been
used to warming his hands round a steaming cup of pea brae,
a pea soup richly peppered and thick as porridge.

Here he saw the other skills which the immigrants had
brought with them, Chiappa who made organs, the sartorial
expertise of the shops round Eyre Street. To have their hair cut
at Balsamo's would be the equivalent of his double nougat to
the dark-eyed youths whom he saw lounging about the street
corners. He was sorry now he hadn't regaled Anna and Nancy
with some of the salami and cheeses from Terroni's instead of
the ubiquitous Heinz beans.

He found an old map showing the course of the Fleet River
and tried to follow its route, imagining the life which had gone

on round it, the trundling carts and horses, boats plying their craft, men fishing, the London noises of hawkers calling their wares. The wrought-iron work round underground toilets on their concrete islands gave him shapes to conjure with, the discovery of the little Wren church surrounded by trees was like coming across a piece of countryside.

The old pubs intrigued him, and it was in one of these, the Crown, that he came across Christine Bouvier when he went in one night, more to rest his feet than for a drink. They saw each other simultaneously, and she raised her hand, beckoning him to come and sit beside her.

There was no doubt she had been a great help to him in furnishing his flat, but he shouldn't have mentioned it to Anna. She would have been more upset if she had known how often they had strolled round the junk dealers together. He admired her knowledge and expertise. No one else could have bargained so well for him, nor got him a sofa for five pounds, with a wooden knob which let an arm down to convert it into a single bed.

And the double bed had been a find for ten pounds, including mattress. What would Anna have said if she had known that Christine had lain down on it after they had manhandled the mattress on to the frame, then invited him to join her. 'Vi-spring, Ritchie,' she had said, 'a real bargain. Soft yet firm.' She had patted the place beside her. 'Come and see for yourself.'

It would have been churlish to refuse. Ridiculously, as he lay beside her, their shoulders touching, he had felt a distinct erection, and had rolled away from her and got up quickly with pretended casualness. 'Couldn't be better,' he had said, busying himself about the room. When he turned to her, composed, she had been still lying on the bed, smiling, a cat smile . . .

'Surprise, surprise!' she now said as he sat down beside her.

'Do you come here often?' he joked.

'Often,' she said, 'but you're the surprise. You told me you

189

didn't go to pubs. That you spent all your evenings painting.'

'I did. Give me your glass. Same again?' When he went back with two glasses of lager he told her, 'I've gone off painting recently.'

'Why?' She was striking-looking, the matt white skin with its dusting of freckles, the red hair, which seemed darker in the dimly lit pub, the eyes, which seemed larger, more deeply amber. She looked at him, looked slowly away with a secret half-smile as if at a memory. The bed?

'Perhaps disappointment.' He shrugged. 'Anna's put off our wedding. It's a blow. Her sister's been very ill. She feels she's got to be with her.'

'Why?' she said again, sipping from her glass, eyes on him now, patient, waiting to be informed.

'Well, they're twins. They've always been close.'

'Her sister's more important than you?' Her eyes slid away again, her long fingernails tapped the table.

'It's not exactly that. There have been stresses.'

'I wouldn't worry if I were you,' she said. 'You have a nice flat, furnished,' she emphasized the word slightly, 'it will sort itself out. And if it doesn't,' the amber eyes were on him, 'there are other girls.' She smiled at him, lips together.

'No, no, you're wrong there.' He had to say it. 'Anna's the only girl for me. Always will be.'

She was still smiling, close-mouthed, but he saw her eyes change, a feral look. He thought of the cat which had come into his flat one day from the yard at the back, and when he had tried to stroke it, it had reared and hissed at him. Then, still with the closed smile, her look became softly golden.

'Well, if that's the case, do you know what I should do? Stop feeling sorry for yourself. Everyone who came to the gallery was impressed by your work. You know how your pictures sold. Throw yourself into your painting, forget about Anna. She obviously doesn't put *you* first.'

'But I couldn't forget her. You don't understand.'

190

She looked impatient. 'Well, put her to one side until she's ready to come to you. The reason why you can't paint is that you're using up all your energy thinking about *her*. Mr Wolf was just saying to me the other day that it was time we had more stuff from Ritchie Laidlaw. We have to strike while the iron's hot, you know, in the painting world.'

He saw the sense in what she was saying, or maybe it was the effect of the lager which was making everything look mellow, lighting the brasses and making the dark oak of the pub gleam. He had been allowing himself to become gloomy and introspective.

'Perhaps you're right. Look, why are we talking about me all the time? Let's change the subject. You never told me why you came to London.'

'Oh, I've lived around here always, Holborn chiefly.'

'Alone?'

'No, with my parents when I was at school. But they fought a lot with each other. It made me miserable. I was upset often because of it. The doctor said . . .' Her eyes had shifted from him again. She was looking at something which wasn't there, something distressful. 'Then they got divorced and I had to find a place to live on my own. They didn't want me. A friend got me the job in the gallery. It's been better. I've only been off work once or twice. I've tried hard. It isn't easy when you have parents who don't care.'

He felt sorry for her. 'You've had a bad time, Christine. I never realized.' Anna was right. He was becoming selfish. 'Don't you ever see them?'

'No. My father went off to America with the woman he left my mother for. Then she . . . died.' She looked away again in that odd manner of hers as if she was looking through a window at her past. 'Sometimes,' she said, still turned away from him, 'I feel so lonely, so in need of a good friend.'

'I know the feeling.' He didn't. He knew he was the type of person who was incapable of feeling isolated. He filled his own world. He never lost his sense of his own identity, or that it was only a matter of time before he fulfilled himself completely. He longed for Anna, fervently and often, missed his parents from time to time, but told himself that all would be well, eventually. 'I'll walk you home,' he said. He noticed the pub was emptying.

'That would be nice.' She gathered up her handbag and a scarf which lay on the seat beside her, and stood up. 'I'm glad we met tonight, Ritchie.' This time she looked straight at him.

When they got to her door in a long terrace off Farringdon Road, she said, 'You've never seen my place although I've been in yours. Why not come up and have a coffee?'

He was doubtful. 'I have an early start.'

'I see. Now that your flat is furnished you've no further use for me?'

'Goodness, no. Well, just a quick one.'

They went up the narrow staircase in single file. A woman popped her head out of a door on the ground floor as they passed and said, 'Oh, it's you, Christine.' She was as blowsy as the faded cabbage roses on the carpet. 'And a friend.'

'Good evening, Mrs Denton.' She didn't offer to introduce Ritchie.

'Do you remember my picture *Necropolis*?' Ritchie said as Christine was unlocking her flat door.

'The one the American woman bought? Yes. Come in.' She bowed, smiling. 'My humble abode.'

'Looks all right to me. It was seeing the statue of John Knox at that cemetery in Glasgow which started me on it. I bet he thought that to go to a woman's flat was going to the devil.'

'It depends. Was that the man who denounced Mary Queen of Scots from the Edinburgh pulpit?'

'Good for you.'

The room they went into showed taste. There was a boldness of colour in the furnishings, the walls were a Chinese red, the furniture painted black, the dark curtains had an abstract design.

192

She must have put on a record as she busied herself around, for the cracked plaintive voice of Billie Holiday now hung in the air.

She emerged from an alcove with two cups on a tray and put them on a small black painted table, sitting down beside him.

'This is really nice, Christine,' he said, looking around.

'I did it all myself. I like rich colours, can't stand English chintz. Is the coffee all right?'

'I'll sip and see. Fine. I'm sure Anna's going to like our flat. You were a great help.'

'She'll like it if she comes.' He looked at her but she wasn't being malicious, he felt sure. Her expression was wistful, poignant, even, as if she were taking her colour from the poignancy of the singer's voice.

Natural sympathy rose in him. 'You're probably more pessimistic than I am. I don't blame you. But I know Anna. When she's ready, not before, she'll come here.'

'I hope you're right. But she should put you first, not her sister.' She looked at him. 'You haven't told me why it is so important that Anna should be with her. *Is* it so important?'

'I should have been frank. Jean had a child by a married man, but it died.' He saw Christine's look of surprise.

'But that's terrible! And it would have been loved. She would *need* it. I was never loved. That's what ruined my life.' It was as if Jean's calamity had acted as a trigger. 'I felt sometimes as if I didn't exist. All that quarrelling, fighting, going on around me . . . It's left its mark on me. Can you understand that? Sometimes it gets too much to bear, the sense I have of worthlessness.' She had become pale, her eyes seemed to have sunk behind her cheekbones.

'I can see how it would affect you,' he didn't see anything of the kind, 'make you ill. Was that why you were away recently?' His voice tailed off. He noticed the skin round her eyes was mud-coloured, and her eyes had lost their amber colour, becoming a dull, dark brown. She looked at him suspiciously.

193

'Did Mr Wolf tell you to ask me what was wrong? I've tried my best not to be off more than I can help. I need the job to keep up all this.'

'Good God, no. I don't see much of him at all, just to pay the rent. It was only an idea, that you might be ill. I've never been ill in my life. Doctors would starve if they depended on *me*.' He tried to be light. 'The same with Anna. She looks frail, just as you do, but she's tough, inside and out. And stubborn as hell. That's why she won't leave Jean until she's absolutely sure that she's not needed. Of course being twins makes it worse. They'd *die* for each other. I've written to her, but if I went down on my bended knees and *implored* her to come to London, she wouldn't. Jean comes first.' He shrugged. 'That's how it is. Like it or lump it.'

'Which are you doing?'

'Lumping it.'

'As long as you know what you're letting yourself in for. I should have thought . . .' Her voice trailed away. 'Of course in a way I understand. It was like that with my mother. I tried and tried, went back and back, and then, one day, she was dead.' Suddenly the tears were running down her face. She didn't make any attempt to wipe them away, but turned and held up her face to him, suffused, pathetic.

He was discomfited. 'Losing your mother must be sad. Worse for a girl.' He thought of his, and realized it would be sad enough for him.

'It was his fault!' Her voice rose. 'He spoiled her life, my life, ruined everything. No wonder she . . . Oh, I can't bear it!' She threw herself against him and he took her in his arms, moved by her distress.

'Poor you.' He stroked her back gently as she sobbed. 'Try not to let it get you down. You have a lot of talent, and a good job. Mr Wolf is a kindly man. Look how he got me my flat. Don't look back, Christine, make a new life for yourself in your job. Mr Wolf won't let you down. You're creative. I can see it in the way you've decorated this flat, not a bit of English chintz to be seen . . .' He was babbling.

'Do you really think so?'

She drew slightly away from him, her face upturned. She looked beautiful, as if the tears had washed the darkness out of her eyes, revealing again their clear amber colour. There was a strand of red hair, darkened by her tears, lying on her pale cheek. But it was the quality of strangeness about her which intrigued him. She was as different from Anna as night from day.

He smiled down at her, and nodded. 'I'm sure of it.' Holiday's voice running on in the background added to the strangeness, the same strangeness he got from looking at the work of Frances Macdonald. He thought of those thin contained women she drew, their symbolism, their spareness and yet their sensuality. Christine could have modelled for them. Was *she* sensual? He bent down and kissed her. The act was involuntary, and yet curious.

He meant it, partly, as a friendly, comforting kiss, but she clung to his mouth with hers, and he let the immediate sensation run sweetly through him. Damn it, he thought, that was a mistake, as he felt his body harden, heard the blood beating in his ears. He kissed her again, this time fumbling for her breasts with a free hand. She helped him, unbuttoning her blouse while her lips still clung to his.

They fell back on the divan, and in the same movement he rolled on top of her. He felt his body begin to move, let it happen, then with an effort of will, rolled off her again. They lay facing each other, his heart thudding, pressing himself into her through their clothes. 'God, Christine,' he said, 'you're beautiful.'

'Take them off.' He heard her voice through the wailing of the record. She was hitching up her skirt, fumbling at his crotch.

The warmth of it, he thought as their flesh met, the silky, pulsating warmth of it. His head was thrumming like a drum, and he lay for a second experiencing the bloody, immediate joy of it. Suddenly he was cold and flaccid. Their position, lying facing each other, felt familiar, it jogged his memory. This was how he and Anna had lain on those long sofas in the University Union, decorously dressed, but so closely together that it would have been impossible to insert a thin sheet of paper between them. 'My dress,' she had whispered, 'you'll tear my dress.' He had total recall of it too. She had made it herself, navy-blue chiffon over an underskirt of petunia silk with a velvet cummerbund embroidered with silver thread. He collapsed like a spent balloon, rolled away from Christine and got quickly to his feet, hitching his trousers into place, fastening buttons and pulling his belt tightly.

'God, I'm sorry, Christine,' he said. His voice was shaking. 'You must think I'm terrible, a rough Scotsman frae Glesca.' He tried to make a joke of it, but she didn't move. He wished she would pull down her dress, close her legs. 'Sit up, Christine.' He helped her, noting with relief that the dress fell into place. 'That was a terrible exhibition. But you looked so beautiful, and sad . . .' The Holiday record had finished and was clicking monotonously on the turntable. He switched it off, thinking, you're to blame.

He went back to the divan but remained standing above her. 'Forget it, will you? Forget the whole thing. I'm sorry. I don't know what happened, that record, you . . . I'll go now. Christine, speak to me, please.'

She got up slowly and stood facing him. Her eyes were strange. 'You don't understand, do you? You don't understand at all.'

'Understand?' He was flummoxed.

'Why are you so cruel?'

'Cruel? Cruel? Oh yes, you can say that again. It was terrible of me. I've said I'm sorry. I'll repeat it. It won't happen again.'

'You simply . . . don't understand.' She seemed to be searching his face, and yet her eyes didn't quite meet his. It was eerie, as if he wasn't there. 'You'd better go.' He nodded gratefully.

They walked to the door together, and out of embarrassment he kissed her, putting a degree of passion into it he didn't feel. He wanted it to be an apologetic kiss, to show that he cared for her and that his feelings had run away with him but that it was a friendly caring, and nothing more could possibly come of it. And perhaps with a tinge of regret. It was a lot to expect of a kiss.

What a fool he'd been, he thought, mid-kiss. Anna was to blame. But no one else would do. Thank God he hadn't gone the whole hog. It would have been so easy . . .

He could feel Christine's long fingers digging into his shoulders, her slim body against his, slimmer than Anna's, but he was dead sexually. He was Anna's. Whatever pickle he got into, no one else could ever take her place. But for a slim girl, Christine's breasts were definitely bigger than Anna's, he thought with interest, as he released her.

He would write her a decent letter of apology, express himself properly instead of saying over and over again as he had been doing that it was 'terrible'. Every girl needed praise and admiration even if the man had behaved like an idiot.

'Good night,' he said, releasing himself. He found he was wiping his face with his handkerchief as he bounded down the stairs two at a time.

He sat down immediately he got back to the flat, paper and envelope in front of him on the table.

I really feel I owe you a written apology for my behaviour. I took advantage of your distress but it was no excuse, then and now.

I don't usually attack young girls in their own flat, but you were so lovely and my feelings ran away with me. If anyone else is to blame, it might be that singer. She sort of set the mood.

But I'm not trying to shift the blame in any way. You

mean a great deal to me. I think you know that. Please
forgive me, and don't think too badly of me in future.

He wasn't entirely pleased with the letter. He would have liked
to say that she hadn't been exactly discouraging, but that would
have been ungallant. Anyhow, it would have to do.

He put it in the envelope, addressed it and went to bed. He
felt frustrated and unhappy.

Anna's resentment at Ritchie hadn't abated. And she was tired.
Rose's presence was an irritant, and she could see Jean was
being worn out in her effort to maintain a status quo. The scored
lines under her eyes were deeper than ever. They wouldn't be
able to take much more of Rose's carping.

Rose greeted her one evening when she went into the sitting
room. 'I was just saying to Jean that now she's over her illness,'
she persisted in referring to the death of Jean's baby as an illness,
'I'll get home to Father.' Anna saw the relief on Jean's face.

'Yes, I'm all right now, Mother. It was good of you to come.'

'A mother's duty.' She waved her hand. 'But maybe now
you'll change a few of your opinions.' She turned her pretty
rose-tinted face to Anna, golden hair as immaculate as a wig. 'I
don't hear much about Ritchie now, Anna. Is that going to be
another of those fly-by-nights?'

She drew a deep breath. 'If you mean by that remark that he
flew off to London to escape me, you're wrong.' She wouldn't
give her the satisfaction of believing she might be right. Rose
had her seer's look on now. She caressed her cards like a crystal
ball.

'I see life opening out for you two girls. Let bygones be
bygones. You have a sister married and in a nice way of doing.
You could go up for weekends with her and I'm sure James will
know presentable young men, architects and such like. Nancy's
now giving select little dinner parties, she was telling me. I'm
sure she could match you two up in no time.'

Anna exploded. 'What do you think we are, Mother? A pair of Liberty curtains?'

'I wonder what's in this year?' Jean said, straight-faced. 'Baggy eyes or saggy busts?'

Rose tossed her head, looking hurt, and expertly spread out the cards on the small table in front of her. She was quite capable of trouncing a Jack while still talking. 'I've never understood you twins. Goodness knows I've tried, gone to endless lengths –'

'To match us up?' Anna said. Jean giggled.

'You may laugh,' Rose directed an aggrieved look at her, 'but you certainly can't be proud of the mess *you*'ve landed yourself in, miss. If it hadn't been for your sister here, standing by you –'

'I certainly couldn't have relied on you, Mother dear.' In the old days Jean would have flared, but now she was calm, her face drained of colour. She got up. 'Excuse me, please. I'll go to my room where my presence won't annoy you.' Anna watched her as she opened the door and shut it quietly behind her.

'You shouldn't speak to her like that,' she said. 'We were only teasing. She's trying hard to get over Frederick's death and then the loss of the baby. I still hear her crying at nights.'

Rose's hands, pale, rose-tipped, had lifted a card, her neat head was bent in concentration. Was it pretence, or, deep down, was she ashamed? Rose, the enigma, Anna thought. You couldn't tell by her voice.

'Well, she has only herself to blame, and it was God's mercy that the poor little thing didn't live. It would only have been an embarrassment all her life, and ours.'

Anna felt her brows contract, then her throat. She managed to prevent herself from letting out a long, piercing scream.

'And you take your time about Ritchie Laidlaw. No rushing down to London to see how he is. *That* one will get on all right. Full of confidence. I don't want two of you landing yourself in Queer Street. One is quite enough.' The sheer awfulness of her remarks seemed to dowse Anna's anger like a jet of cold water.

'You've always been so understanding, Mother,' she said. 'Such a help in time of trouble.' It was suddenly quite easy not to lose her temper. She would take her cue from Jean. Rose, Ritchie – the only one worth considering just now was Jean, the other half of her. It's easy for me to be calm, she thought. I haven't lost a lover, lost his baby. Ritchie is there when I want him. I'm venting my frustration about him on Mother. That's unfair. She got up.

'Where are you going?' Rose said.

'To Timbuktu.' She smiled. '"Sticks and stones may break my bones, but words will never hurt me." Do you remember that little rhyme you taught us?'

'Did I?' Rose looked up from her cards, smiling, pretty, apparently unaware that she had been less than motherly. Anna liked her at that moment in an impartial, nondaughterly way. 'You used to say it when you were bouncing your ball against the wall at the kitchen window. Bessie worried in case you'd break it. Ah, happy days!'

'Happy days indeed,' Anna said, feeling like this woman's mother. She was impervious. She hadn't *got* it, the implication. How had Father stood it for so long? Was that why he was so nonassertive at home? A decision to ignore? She tried again. 'Do you know what they'll put on your tombstone, Mother?'

'Don't bury me yet!' She looked up, smiling, 'Anyhow, tell me.'

'Here lies Rose Mackintosh. She meant well.'

'That's nice.' She looked down at her cards again. 'Very nice. Well, no one can say I didn't try.' Was her leg being pulled, Anna wondered, was there a thorn in the Rose? She felt reluctant admiration.

She went to Jean's room and got into bed beside her with all her clothes on, only stopping to kick off her shoes.

'What are you up to?' Jean asked. She was lying still and straight.

'Game to Miss Anna Mackintosh,' she said, 'I *think*.' She sat up, taking one of the pillows from behind her and thumped it with all her might.

'What are you *doing*?' Jean said, not moving.

'Only pummelling Mother to death. Matricide.' She lay down again, letting her breath escape loudly. 'But it's no good. She's immune.'

'You've won the battle if you've realized that at last.'

They lay together for a long time, arms round each other. Anna didn't know to begin with whether they were weeping or laughing. When she crept off to her own room later, Jean was feigning sleep.

The next day the letter came, the envelope addressed in a strange spiky handwriting, like angels dancing on a pin, she thought. It had a London postmark.

Dear Miss Mackintosh, *she read*,

You may wonder how I know your name and address, but Ritchie has spoken of you often and described where you live in Kirkcudbright. I knew it was High Street, although I never knew the number, but I gather it is a small town, so this should reach you all right.

I have been Ritchie's friend and confidante for some time. Perhaps you may remember meeting me at the gallery when you came with your sister. I think I can say that I have managed to restore his belief in himself, which was at a pretty low ebb. The enclosed letter he wrote to me recently will show you what I mean.

Anna flicked over the pages and glanced at the one at the back attached by a paperclip. It was Ritchie's handwriting, there was no doubt about that, stubby, black, as if he leaned on his pen too hard. She was still feeling nothing. Phrases jumped out at her, like blows to her eyes, 'written apology' . . . 'took advantage' . . . 'attack young girls in their own flat' . . . 'so lovely'

. . . 'feelings ran away with me' . . . 'You mean a great deal to me' . . . 'Please forgive' . . . She closed her eyes, feeling cold, yet sweating in her armpits. She felt sick. She sat, not moving. For the first time in her life she thought she might faint.

Ritchie. This girl. All the time. Now it was getting through to her.

I don't feel badly about letting you see Ritchie's letter. Even if you tear it up the words will be scored in your brain.

I think I understand him better than you've ever done. People like you who have everything – money, a happy background, loving parents, and a boyfriend as exceptional as Ritchie – don't know how important it is to 'hold fast to that which is good'. A vicar who came to see me recently, at the request of my doctor, strangely enough, quoted that to me. It's probably from the Bible. There has been very little good in my life, and when someone like Ritchie comes along, that's what I did, held fast.

As you will see from his letter, we mean a great deal to each other – sometimes his feelings run away with him, but I understand him, the way you never did. I would advise you to keep out of the way.

Christine Bouvier

She's mad, Anna thought, a complete nutter. She put her head in her hands for a moment, then raised it again. By God, she wouldn't weep for Ritchie Laidlaw! Rose had offered to do some shopping, and Jean was in her bedroom, tidying up. She might hear.

Sick, she thought, sending Ritchie's letter was sick, but Ritchie's intimacy with this crazy girl was the sickest thing of the lot. A flame of anger shot through her at the thought of the two of them together, Ritchie 'attacking' her in his lust,

202

ripping off her clothes . . . She moaned, swaying from side to side, beating the sides of her head with her fists. She was damned if she would weep.

She heard the door shut. That would be Rose off on her morning shopping expedition, her coffee in the fancy little tea-room she had discovered, which Anna and Jean thought too pretentious for words.

She jumped up. She would show the letter to Jean. She sat down again. No, she thought, Jean would tell her she had advised her to go to London. 'I told you so.' But Ritchie should have understood the bond between the sisters, that Jean still needed her support. Men didn't understand, the closeness between women, especially in adversity, didn't understand birth, nor the loss of a baby, nor the loss of a lover. This is my problem, she said to herself. She was busy in the kitchen when Jean came in.

'Coffee?' she said. 'When the cat's away . . .' She had brushed her hair, smoothing the points on her cheeks, put make-up on. She avoided meeting Jean's eyes.

TWENTY-THREE

JEAN AND ANNA were sitting having tea at the fire after Rose had gone back to Glasgow. It had been a rainy, weepy kind of day, Anna thought, in tune with her own state of mind. It was over, then, the great love affair with Ritchie. At times she could scarcely believe he had been unfaithful to her, especially with that crazy girl Christine Bouvier. It suited Anna to call her crazy. Nor could she understand his failure to believe in her reluctance to leave Jean. It was his selfishness which hurt her even more than his unfaithfulness.

'Penny?' Jean's face was lit by the flames. She looked beautiful these days, as if she had been cleansed in some way by her suffering. She had a darting thought that perhaps she, Anna, was taking longer to get over Jean's pain and desolation herself, using it as an excuse, because Jean was improving daily.

Perhaps John Whitbread was helping, Dr John, who still called frequently with his black bag but no longer on professional visits. A blind, deaf and dumb man could have told which sister he was interested in. Had Anna been asked, she would have to confess that she liked him better than she had liked Frederick Kleiber.

Frederick had been charming, but unreal in a way, as if he had strayed from the stage of the Vienna Opera House. He had retained too much his Viennese character and ambience in his larger-than-life gestures which were natural enough to him but strange in a Scottish city where the inhabitants prided them-

204

selves on being the opposite of demonstrative. He had been the love of Jean's life, but Anna doubted if he would ever have integrated.

'Penny?' She looked at Jean. 'Nothing much.'

'Well, it's making you pretty gloomy whatever it is. It's Ritchie, I know it. Something's wrong between you. Anna, listen to me. He paints with his body as well as his mind. If he has a painting block he's so talented that it's only a trough between the waves. But he needs you for his wellbeing.'

'So do you. Besides, I've gone off him recently.'

'I don't believe you. And I don't need you now. I'm grateful for all you've done, but I would have done the same for you. You know that. Get off to London. I'm fine.'

'I'll go when I'm ready and not before.' She looked at Jean. The flames had died down, Jean's face had shrunk, her body had disappeared inside the vastness of Aunt Jessie's plaid woollen dressing-gown. She still looked like someone who had been dealt a mortal blow. Except for her eyes. They were alive now. 'I tell you what, as soon as you can go with me to Dumfries to visit Great-aunt, I'll know you're on the mend.'

'Right. I'm on. Tomorrow.'

'Okay.'

She looked wistful. 'You and she are the only two who have never condemned me.'

'What about Father?'

'He loves me, but he was always doubtful about Frederick.'

'And Nancy offered you a home.'

'That was James, really.'

'Ah well, eat up your cinnamon toast. It's dripping with butter. Otherwise I'll be offering you as a scarecrow to the nearest farmer.' She couldn't bring herself to tell Jean about the letter.

They went to see their great-aunt the next day. There was no change in her, but she was plainly overjoyed to see Jean. She clung to her hand. 'Take my place in the house, Jean. Keep it

205

alive.' Her eyes wandered. There was no trace of the bright eccentric woman who had never looked her age.

'Aunt Jessie,' Jean said slowly and deliberately, 'you know my baby died. Frederick's baby.'

The old lady put on a clown's face of tragedy. Overdone, as if a string had been pulled. 'Frederick's baby?' she repeated, shaking her head sadly. 'Oh dear, oh dear.'

'Yes. So I have only my painting. That's what's important to me now. What he would have liked.'

'Will he be with you in the house?' Her eyes were wide.

'No, he died. He was drowned.'

'It's not the same without a man. I know.' Her eyes glazed over. She tittered, put her hand to her mouth.

On the way home they walked down to the harbour. The boats were coming in with their afternoon catch, rusty, sea-battered working boats, no sleek sailing yachts amongst them. The setting sun gave the scene a pink glow which you could have put a frame round. 'Marvellous, isn't it?' Anna said. 'Timeless. Dying to be made a painting of and called *Sunset in the Harbour*, or *Coming Home*.'

'I'll come down and paint it sometime,' Jean said, and then slowly, 'with my dead baby's blood.'

'Jean! What a thing to say.'

'Don't worry. That was chiefly for effect. I'm not better yet. You'd be surprised at the wild thoughts I have. A lot in me needs to be painted out of my system. It's the only way I know to get rid of it.'

'You should think of going back to the Art School when you feel fit.'

'Yes, I've been thinking that. I need the discipline and the working conditions there. Would you go to London, then?'

'Don't bother about me.'

When Jean was putting the key in the door they heard the telephone ringing. Anna's heart leaped, but she hid any interest.

'Hurry,' Jean said. 'It might have been ringing for ages.'

Anna took her time. The telephone was dead when she lifted the receiver.

'Whoever it was had hung up,' she said when she went into the sitting room.

'I bet it was Ritchie.' Jean looked exhausted. The journey to Dumfries had tired her.

'You've got him on the brain.'

'Only because I think you're hiding something.'

She hesitated, ashamed that she should feel so much resentment against Ritchie whom she had loved so much, and that she should be too proud to confide in Jean. But it had taken *her* five months. They were alike in their stubbornness.

'You're played out,' she said. 'Let's have a sherry.'

Jean advised him to write when he telephoned again. 'She doesn't want to speak to you, Ritchie,' she said. 'I don't know what you've done but she's in a huff.'

He took Jean's advice. Anna read the letter, feeling as if it were from a stranger.

> Anna, what's wrong? I thought you loved me? I can't
> help wondering if it's anything to do with Christine
> Bouvier. I admit she helped me with furnishing the flat,
> and she takes a great interest in my work. It's purely
> friendship on my part, but she's a *brooding* type of girl,
> and maybe she reads more into this than she should. I've
> told her about you, that you're my girl.
>
> Would you like me to come up to Kirkcudbright? I
> could ask for time off. We need to talk. You know I
> love you, always will.

Her reply was succinct. She wrote the letter knowing that jealousy was at the root of it all.

No, I don't want you to come up and see me, thank you
very much. From what you say, you seem to be too
busy to waste your time on *me*!

He was disappointed but not suicidally so. His temperament
was too sanguine. She was 'in a huff' as Jean had said, and he
knew her stubbornness. At the back of his mind he was faintly
uneasy. He hadn't told her the whole truth, that he still saw
Christine, nor about that terrible stupidity of his in her flat. He
was too ashamed. But he knew Anna. There were no half-
measures with her. He would leave her to calm down for a week
or so then try again. And so far as Christine was concerned,
next time, if there were a next time, or even approaching a next
time, he would dash away and take a cold bath. Christine was
odd.

The good thing was that his desire to paint had come back
and he was totally absorbed. His mind was going round and
round the idea of a series of paintings with a corporate theme,
some abstraction or even mélange of the old and the new city.
He began to wander about the streets again in the evenings, to
haunt the galleries in London to see other painters' oeuvres,
how they tackled their problems. He was obsessed, his creative
juices were in full spate, hardly letting him sleep at nights.

He called at Mr Wolf's gallery one evening on his way home
with a degree of trepidation. He had avoided it since the débâcle
with Christine. He liked Mr Wolf, a friendly, kind-hearted little
Jew with a large head of curly black hair and a thrusting chin
on a short neck. What endeared him to Ritchie was his love of
art and his willingness, as Mr Wolf said of himself, 'to put his
money where his mouth was'.

'I know you lot take time to get started,' he said when Ritchie
appeared, 'like a dog going round and round making its own
bed, but once you're away there's no stopping you. You're a
big painter, Ritchie, and I don't just mean in the size of your
canvases. I admit mantelpiece stuff sells easier, but yours have

real quality. Is the pot boiling again? Have you got a fire in your belly?' He gave it a playful smack. 'Remember, I want to go down in history as the man who discovered Ritchie Laidlaw.'

'I've started already, you'll be pleased to know.' He felt good.

Christine made it easy for him. She had been at her table on his first call but hadn't intruded. Now, as he began to drop in more frequently, he found her pleasantly welcoming. She didn't allude to the 'débâcle', and added her enthusiasm to that of Mr Wolf. She was knowledgeable. When he looked in to report progress she took Mr Wolf's place if he was out on his multifarious projects. The money he needed to finance his gallery came mainly from a stall he had in the Caledonian market.

The memory of that unfortunate evening began to fade. Ritchie still thought Christine looked good, with her abundant hair, and her amber eyes outlined thickly in black, her arty black clothes. He was sufficiently provincial to enjoy being seen with her. For she had got into the way of casually picking up her bag and leaving with him.

They fell into the habit of strolling about the City streets while they discussed art and his paintings, and sometimes stopping at a pub to have a drink. She never mentioned personal matters, nor even his letter of apology. It was a closed book. But she fired his enthusiasm, got him canvases and paints cheap from wholesale suppliers and showed an enthusiasm for his ideas which made him itch to get home and back to work.

He would start about ten o'clock in the evening when he had had a rest and food and done a few chores, and would often paint until three or four in the morning. He found himself counting on this new relationship with Christine. He was lonely, he missed Anna. Although he had written again she hadn't replied. Christine was a friend who could speak the same language and was comforting to be with after his many rebuffs from Anna. But that would come right in time, he assured himself. He had to be patient. He was doing this for her.

Christine said to him one evening when they were having a

drink in the Crown, 'Why don't you let me see what stage you've got to, Ritchie? You always say my criticism is valuable.'

Here it comes, he thought. It hadn't died a natural death after all. He said jokingly, 'Aren't you afraid I might attack you?'

She smiled, mouth closed, her eyes slid away from him and back again. 'We were both foolish. Maybe it was too soon.' He frowned at that but let it pass. 'I won't eat you, Scottish laddie,' she said, still with that smile. She made him feel unsophisticated.

'Don't be daft,' he said. 'All right, come on.'

She had a good eye. She saw what he was after, picked out the thin thread of the river, the candy stripes of the shop awnings, the cobbles, the tunnels like round black eyes in the grey and brown blocks which were houses. She understood the general references, the meditative abstraction which had gone into the work, and he was heartened.

She also saw the clutter of dirty dishes in his sink and insisted on washing them 'because I like order,' she said. 'Obsessionals can't stand chaos. There's too much of it in their own minds.'

It seemed churlish, then, not to make her coffee, and from there, since it was now supper time, not to suggest bacon and eggs, which she cooked swiftly and expertly. The atmosphere was relaxed between them as if they had agreed on a new start. He found himself telling her about his early life at home with his parents, how he had climbed the brick walls in the back courts, fished for minnows with a bent pin and a jam jar in the slow-running burn at the back of his tenement, and later, the impact of the Art School, of meeting Anna who was so different from anyone he had ever known, and so beautiful.

'I miss her,' he said. 'God, how I miss her. Maybe looking after Jean has got her down.' He smiled shamefacedly. 'And she gets the mistaken idea that while she's buried in Kirkcudbright with Jean I'm having a fine old time in the great metropolis, with girls.'

'Which girls?' She frowned.

'Well, to be frank with you, Christine. I made the mistake of telling her how you helped me to furnish this flat and I think it rankled with her.'

'Well, she's easily offended.' Her face was calm. He noticed one side of her mouth was lifted.

'She isn't usually, not Anna. But once her dander's up . . .' He laughed. 'I remember telling her that was why she had taken up metalwork. It was so that she could hammer the living daylights out of a poor innocent piece of copper or brass. She won't even speak to me on the telephone, and she won't answer my letters. It's as if she knew that you and I –'

'Were more than friends?'

He didn't like that remark, but decided to ignore it. He went on. 'You see, she's fair, quick-tempered, but fair. And intuitive. That's what worries me. She's unique, Anna. If I searched for a hundred years there would never be anyone else but her.'

'You aren't very complimentary.' He cursed that he had fallen into the trap again. She was unpredictable, this girl. He looked at her. Her mouth had that peculiar sideways lift, her eyes had lost their clear amber colour and become clouded.

'Sorry. I'm rude. I appreciate your interest in my painting. You've been a great help to me. I'm sure Anna will come round in time to seeing –'

'Anna! Anna! Can't you talk about anything else? All I ever hear is Anna! You don't understand me, me! You have everything – this Anna, a loving family, friends at the Art School you can see any time. I just wanted to be . . . included.' She put down her knife and fork. He saw her mouth was trembling.

'You're not seeing straight, Christine.' He would be matter-of-fact. It was safer. 'I'm not all that lucky. Or rather my father and mother aren't. No silver spoon in *my* mouth. He's on the dole and she has to go out and work, scrub closes.' He saw the puzzlement in her eyes. 'Oh, you don't know about that! Dirty old drunks spitting, worse, even. But, yes, I'm lucky because they love me. My mother is the salt of the earth. It's her hard work that's paid for my tuition all those years I was at the Art School. How do you think that makes *me* feel?'

'At least she didn't commit suicide,' she said. She pushed back her chair, her face twisted, looked around wildly for a second, then went stumbling to the wall facing them, where she stood, her back to him, her head in her hands. The noises coming from her were frightening, odd, prolonged moans.

'Christine!' He got up, alarmed, went towards her and took her in his arms to comfort her. It was a natural reaction. He felt again the boneless feel of her, unlike Anna who was whippy and pliant. 'Don't,' he said, 'please don't upset yourself like that. I can't believe what you've just said. Did your mother really . . . ?'

'Did your mother really . . . ?' Her voice was a sneer. 'Yes, she really did, you with the wide eyes. Haven't you ever heard of suicide before? She took a cushion and put it in the oven, lay down, put her head in and turned on the gas. I found her. I've never forgotten the look on her face . . . a kind of triumph. It haunts me. I can't get rid of it. "Take that, you bastard!" she was saying to him. I thought if you and I were . . . close, it would blot it out.'

He held her to him, stroking her head. Poor thing, poor lassie, he thought. 'Try and put it behind you, Christine.'

'How can I? I wanted you to help me.' She raised her face to him. 'You could, you know.' Her eyes were swimming. 'Stop thinking about Anna all the time.' The tears had washed them into their clear amber again.

'I'll do what I can to help you but . . .' he had to face up to it, say it, 'it's not much, only friendship. I've apologized to you for that night. I found you attractive, you seemed to like me, it went on from there. But there's Anna, always will be. I'm sorry.'

'But you don't understand!' She freed herself and battered with her fists against his chest. 'You don't understand. I need love!' Her voice wailed the word, then she bent her head against

212

him and sobbed, heartbreakingly. He held her, his mother's son, feeling pity and sorrow.

He made her coffee, but she barely touched it. She sat hunched up in the corner of his sofa, occasionally taking deep indrawn breaths in the aftermath of her weeping. She didn't speak. When he thought she was calmer he took her back to her flat.

At the door she said to him, seemingly calm now, 'You won't leave me, Ritchie, will you? I won't break down like that again. It was telling you, remembering.' Her face was pale, thin, as if she had lost flesh in the last few hours. Her eyes were strange. He was afraid, of her and for her.

He told himself it was the feeling any ordinary person got when faced with a situation outside their control. But, also, there was a strong feeling of guilt, as if he might be partly to blame. Was that the hold she had on him, that if he left her, he might be held responsible for . . . anything which might happen?

'We're friends, Christine,' he said. He wanted to say, 'just friends'. He thought he'd better wait for another time.

TWENTY-FOUR

IT WAS SUDDENLY like summer in the little town. Unexpec-
ted roses nodded over fences, and the women painters in the
street scurried up and down sharing plants and cuttings and
discussing gardening instead of their work. Jean came in for a
share of the largesse, and for the first time in her life discovered
the link between grubbing with her hands in the soil, and painting, a kind of harmony with nature.

The porch at the back became filled with boxes of compost
in which she was propagating seeds such as sweet peas, and
begonia corms. Life was calling to her, she realized. Once, early
summer had simply meant longer evenings, tennis, leaving off
jerseys and scarves. Now it signified a kind of rebirth. She
imagined she could feel the pulse of nature as she handled the
soil.

For the first time since Frederick and then the baby had died,
she felt a lightness of spirit, the blood coursing freely through
her veins. Even her last period had been fresh, no longer slug-
gish and evil-smelling nor accompanied by slow dragging pain.
It was like emerging from suffocating darkness into light. She
wished she could tell John Whitbread – she had confided many
things to him at her lowest ebb – but details about her menses
seemed inappropriate now that she regarded him as a friend
rather than a doctor.

He had looked in to see her this afternoon. These visits when
he was out on calls had become *de rigueur*. Anna was in Dumfries visiting their great-aunt, she told him.

'As long as I'm not compromising you,' he said, smiling at her in the hall. 'I must admit looking in here is a welcome break in my daily toil, and my wee black bag makes it all right.' He was teasing her.

She smiled back, seeing him as a man for the first time. She saw that he had an air of distinction, as if he had good ancestors, the narrow face, the high brow, the straight-set humorous eyes. She imagined she had never seen them clouded with anything else but concern for her.

'Come into the sitting room,' she said, feeling embarrassed also for the first time. 'You know you're always welcome.' It was strange she should feel embarrassed now, when he had seen her in all kinds of invidious positions, held her hand while she wept, stroked her brow when she was vomiting that black bile after the baby's birth. Doctors had to be versatile. And remembering his remark, 'Compromise is a meaningless word to me, John,' she said, 'after Frederick.'

He sat down and she went to bring the tray. It was always kept ready for him, Aunt Jessie's oak-galleried tray of the lace tray-cloth, her Clarice Cliff china as bright as spring flowers. When she came back with it he jumped up.

'I'll make the tea. Let's pretend you're an invalid today, now that you aren't.' He was back in a minute or two. He was quick and dexterous.

'It's how to persuade Anna that I can manage on my own, that's the trouble,' she said, pouring out the tea and handing him a cup.

'Ah, yes.' He looked at her. 'Do you think it's *all* devotion?'

'No.' She met his eyes. 'How did you guess?'

'She's edgy. When you were in dire straits she was superb. I should think there would be no better person in an emergency than Anna. Now when she has virtually nothing to worry about, when she should be winging back to Ritchie in London, she doesn't choose to go.'

215

'Perhaps she's fallen in love with you,' she said.

He smiled. His left eyebrow quirked. 'Now Freud could make something of *that* remark. However, let it pass.'

She struggled against a blush, sent it back where it belonged. 'Or perhaps she's grown to like it here.' She was able to meet his eyes calmly. 'We're happy together. It's tempting – at least it is to me – to stay in this little corner together, safe from alarms and incursions after the storm, resting in the shallows, you know the sort of thing.' She smiled. 'It's a very special relationship we have. Perhaps she's reluctant to give it up.'

He shook his head. 'No, it won't do. You are two healthy girls now. Sex will win every time.'

'Do you think so?'

'It did with you.'

'Touch, as we used to say in the Art School.' She smiled. 'But she sees where it got me.'

'Sadder and wiser, but that's not a bad thing. Life isn't over for you by any means, Jean. Is it?' He looked her in the eyes.

'If you had asked me that last week when there was a snell wind blowing up from the harbour I would have said yes, it is, but now . . .'

'Is Frederick still with you?' His eyes were sympathetic.

She sighed. 'No. He went with the baby. Now it's a corporate sadness hardly distinguishable, but, sometimes, I get a flash of memory. I see him with all his dark charm, his way of speaking English, the big hat he wore, pulled to one side, and my heart weeps. But it goes. I'm lost in admiration for the way life operates, that grief goes . . . and there's only the sorrow left.'

'That's your mind and body emptying itself, getting ready for someone else.' He looked confident, Dr Know-it-all.

'What rubbish!' She smiled gaily at him in case she had inadvertently looked seductive, God forbid. She went back to the safer subject of Anna.

'They're at odds just now, Ritchie and Anna. Sometimes I

216

see a green glint in her eye. She and Nancy met a *femme fatale* in the gallery Ritchie frequents. I told her she was frustrated and she didn't like it.'

'Frustration's healthy.'

'I'm frustrated just now, John. No, not that kind.' She put down her cup. 'I want to get ahead with my life, my painting. I'm alive again. I could sit my Diploma at the Art School at the end of term. I've done all the work. I could stay with my parents – my mother's quite willing to have me now that I don't have a little bundle.' Her mouth twisted and she looked away. 'Anyhow that would convince Anna I could manage without her and then she could get off down to London and vanquish Delilah.'

'I should think Anna could vanquish any Delilah. But do you really feel up to going back to Glasgow and trailing to the Art School every day?'

'It's only for a month. Yes, I do. You've seen me at my worst moments. I'm better, thanks to you. And Anna. At least I'm learning to cope. I need the stimulus of the school, the competition, the atmosphere to help me to get going. I have a lot to say, in paint.'

'You sound decided. You sound like an artist. I'll miss you, you know that.' His eyes held hers for a second before she looked away. No, no more of that . . . But this one was different, unmarried, straight as a die, had been a very present help in time of trouble, faithful . . .

She turned to him. 'I'll be back. This is me reinstating myself in my own eyes, the school, the Diploma, if I get it. Great-aunt Jessie has given me this house, remember. I'm going to settle down here and become one of the Glasgow Girls, at least a poor imitation. I'll get a wee wumman,' she laughed, 'to do the rough.'

'Don't plan too much.'

'It's good that I can. Good that I can talk to you like this. I'll never forget what you did for me.'

'I'm not going away,' he said. 'I'm a fixture. I'll be waiting.

You must know how I feel about you, Jean.' He leaned forward and took her hands. 'I've been very circumspect. I can't keep it up for ever. Everybody in Kirkcudbright is agog, except you.'

His smile was charming, the word came naturally to her mind although it had always been monopolized by Frederick. There seemed to be some kind of river swirling round her heart, breaking the ice. But *she* was going to be circumspect this time, think only of her painting, at least for the present.

He released her hands as if he had followed her thoughts. 'Don't look fearful,' he said. 'Take your time. I'm here when you want me. And I'm not likely to rush off to the other end of the world. Kirkcudbright suits me fine.'

'I quite like it myself.' She smiled at him, feeling happy, and released. He had said he wouldn't rush her.

'I must get on,' he said, getting to his feet. 'Mrs Thompson in Kintyre Street wants her prescription before the chemist shuts. Thanks for the tea.' He lifted his bag, his wee black bag. Did he sleep with it at nights? He said at the door, 'You think your plan will convince Anna that her services are no longer required?'

'Oh, I think so. We're close and I know she's crazy about Ritchie. She'll rush away down to him.'

'Well, I should think neither you nor Anna is going to be an old maid.'

'You don't think so?' She laughed at him, full-throated, enjoying this particular kind of laughter which had been strange to her for a long time. The future seemed quite . . . interesting.

When Ritchie delivered his finished picture to the gallery, there was only a cleaning woman there, a sharp-nosed, sharp-eyed Cockney. She could well have been behind a whelk stall on his eighteenth-century river bank.

'Miss Bouvier ain't in yet. She's always late, that one. Takes advantage when Mr Wolf's in that there Amsterdam. Comes

218

dragging in with a face blotchy and white like a pan o' boiled tripe.'

He was surprised, therefore, when Christine telephoned him in the afternoon, her voice bright with enthusiasm. If she had been ill, she seemed to have recovered. 'Your painting was here when I got in, Ritchie! And you said your juices had dried up! Far from it.' She was gently chiding. 'Your palette's the best yet, muted, but glowing like pewter. It *sprang* at me when I came in. Mr Wolf's sure to like it. And that silver thread of the Fleet River running through the whole composition like a leitmotif, drawing the eye. I like it, I really like it.'

He demurred, 'Ach, away . . .'

'You're too modest.' He knew he wasn't. 'Come up tonight and have supper with me and we'll talk about it. I owe it to you for your bacon and eggs. And your sympathy.' He was astonished that she should ask him after the last time. Surely she must remember how she had behaved, how she had broken down and told him about her mother's suicide, how she had wept?

'No, thanks, really. I'm too busy.'

'Well, Saturday, then.' He frowned, wondering what he could say to put her off. It was dangerous. 'Let's make it a little celebration for the first picture of the series. I'll cook something really special. You can bring the wine.'

'I don't think it's a very good idea, Christine,' he said. 'The last time . . . you were upset. I don't think it would be wise.'

'Oh, that? Don't hold it against me, Ritchie. I was abreacting. Do you know that word? My . . . my doctor uses it. It means letting yourself go, clearing your mind. You did me a lot of good, just listening. I'm inclined not to confide in anyone and it all builds up. I'm absolutely fine now. I promise you it will be different. I want to thank you properly for your help, and to cook you a decent meal. I'm a good cook. Surely you can't refuse poor little me?'

He felt trapped. Maybe he *had* done her good by listening.

She didn't have many friends, and she had gone through a bad time. In any case, Anna wasn't showing much interest in him, holed up in that godforsaken little town with her sister, putting him out of her life.

'Okay,' he said. 'Thanks a lot. But I can't stay long. I'm working solidly in the evenings now.' That at least was true.

When he got back to his flat the idea of painting gripped him to the exclusion of everything else. Without stopping to eat he began laying in the broad outlines of the next painting, then working obsessively in one corner of the canvas as he usually did, setting up the standard he wanted to maintain. He forgot Christine, forgot Anna. It was hunger which made him stop at about two in the morning.

He made himself some scrambled eggs, and when he was eating at the kitchen table he flicked over the pages of a magazine someone had given him in the office. His mind was still with his painting. Suddenly an illustrated page leaped out at him, and he scanned it, shaken and appalled.

They were photographs taken in the north of Spain, near Bilbao, horrifying pictures. One was of a man in priest's robes sitting at the roadside. His face was gaunt, blackened, his legs were awkwardly spread out – or what remained of his legs. He could see black blotches, which must be blood, on what looked like sticks poking through the torn robe.

He swallowed, sickened, and turned his glance away. But now it rested on the little group of children near the priest. Their faces were again black-splotched, these mouths made anguished black squares in their tear-stained faces. Their hands were held out in supplication. The caption underneath read, '*Aviónes, Bombas, Mucho, Mucho.*' He shut the magazine and pushed away his plate of eggs, his gorge rising at their vivid yellowness.

Painting, he thought, while Rome burned, but this time it was Spain. Christine, Anna, but always himself, absorbed in self. He should have been with Bob in Spain instead of fiddling away here. 'I've got to join them. It's a fight for democracy.'

He remembered Bob's words. He had packed up and gone, quietly, no heroics. Ritchie felt ashamed. He snatched up a piece of paper which lay on the table and began to write to Anna.

It's two o'clock in the morning. I've been painting and I've just looked at some magazine pictures of the Civil War in Spain. They're unbearable. Maybe I'm keyed up after painting – you know the feeling, your nerve endings tingling – but that's how it seems to me, unbearable. I've been going about wrapped in a cocoon of gauze, 'Me-gauze.' Bob was always politically minded, and I would listen to him, but it was a case of in one ear and out the other. Once when he talked about Hitler depriving the Jews of citizenship I was moved, but that was because of Jean and Frederick Kleiber. Spain didn't ring a bell.

Of course I knew about the formation of the International Brigade. I knew people in the office who went, Bob was the first. But the whole thing didn't really impinge on me. I was wrapped up in my own affairs.

I had to admit I had a bad dream once. I was walking down Argyle Street, my dreams are always based in Glasgow, and I thought I heard the stomp, stomp of Nazi boots behind me. I hid in a shop door – it was Stewart's, the jewellers – then fell in behind them, up Union Street into Sauchiehall Street, well behind. I hid again when they broke into shops, smashing glass with their bayonets. I watched while they raped women. Can you believe it, and do you get the analogy, me standing by and doing nothing?

There was another man standing beside me, a man in a large hat with a dark kind of cloak round him, operatic. A German soldier came lunging at us, and I thought, this is it. Serves me right. But he turned and ran his

221

bayonet through the man in the cloak – and it was
Frederick Kleiber . . .

I woke up in a sweat, thinking, thank God, it was only
a dream. Then morning came, life went on, and I did
nothing, hardly read the news.

He tore up the sheet of paper and dropped it on the floor. It
was bad enough having dreams like that without passing them
on. He crawled into bed shivering with cold and lack of sleep,
but couldn't sleep. He mind was a welter of colours and shapes
and figures derived from his painting and the reliving of the
dream. I'm a self-pitying mess, he thought. I've made it worse
by becoming involved with a neurotic girl whom I haven't the
guts to shake off because I felt sorry for her. What she needed
was professional help. He couldn't solve her problem . . . Suddenly he was asleep.

But when he looked at the painting in the morning it pleased
him, even in its early stages. It was in harmony with the first
one, and yet it was different, more advanced. It was going to
be a good series. He was on the right track.

His other worries could be sorted out. First of all, he wouldn't
go again to Christine's flat. He would make a clean break. Then
he would telephone Anna, or send a telegram, if necessary, and
tell her he was taking the express train to Carlisle on Saturday
morning and then the bus or train to Kirkcudbright. It was so
simple when you became decisive. Anna was his love. Once they
saw each other all would be well. For the first time for weeks
he was happy.

He telephoned at intervals to Kirkcudbright all that day with
no result, and in the end wrote out a telegram: 'Arriving Saturday morning. Love Ritchie', then tore it up again. Obviously
the house was empty. There could be several reasons. They
could be visiting their great-aunt, or they could be spending
the day with the painting coterie there. But he would still go
to Kirkcudbright on Saturday. He would soon find Anna.

222

He raced from his office at half-past five to the gallery. He had to apologize in person to Christine, tell her that he couldn't come to her flat on Saturday. She wouldn't like it but it couldn't be helped. She was at the table at the end of the room, and when he looked up he thought she seemed paler than usual. Her eyes didn't seem to recognize him until he was quite near her, and then they came alive, and she was smiling.

'Oh, Ritchie! I'm glad you caught me. I was thinking of going home. I haven't been well today . . .' Her voice trailed away, her head moved as if she was orienting herself in some odd fashion, and then she said brightly, 'But that's enough about me. You must have come to see your picture. It's been properly hung now.' She swivelled round in her chair towards it. 'It really fills the room, doesn't it?'

He could look at it objectively now that he had been parted from it. It had gained a presence. For a time he had thought that compositionally it hadn't come off, but it had settled down now into its theme, the one which he was following in the second one. The colours and shapes were happy with each other. He felt elation. It was his 'thing' after all, the thing he knew deep down he had, a painting voice. It had strength, and purpose, and, he was sure of it, appeal. There was only that bit in the left-hand corner – he could afford, in his pleasure, to be hypercritical now. It needed to assert itself more, be brought out from the shadows – perhaps he could get it down and alter it.

'Has Mr Wolf seen it yet?' he asked her.

'No, he comes in tomorrow. I've spoken to him on the telephone and told him that your painting monopolizes the gallery. He said he's prepared to believe it. And, what's more, he's brought back a friend with him, a Dutchman, who wants to commission a series of paintings for a bank in the Hague. He thinks this might be what he's looking for, and he's bringing him in. Isn't that terrific? Like fate, a buyer before it's been up a day!'

223

'Hold on, Christine.' But he'd borrowed a little of her excitement. 'It's not sold yet.'

'It will be. I feel it. Aren't you glad I encouraged you to start painting again?'

'Yes, very grateful.' He added, 'Thanks.' Of course he was grateful, but he should have started again in any case. But there was no doubt about it, it was a chance in a million. He tempered his rising excitement. 'It's a pity they're coming tomorrow. I'd like to alter that bit in the left-hand corner.'

'But there isn't time! He's only coming for one day, this man. Anyhow, you can meet him tomorrow and see what he thinks.'

He shook his head. 'That's not possible, Christine. I'm afraid I shan't be here.'

'Shan't be here?' She looked mystified. 'Tomorrow, Ritchie, *Saturday*!' She laughed. 'The excitement's going to your head. You're coming to me in the evening. Remember?'

'I'm sorry, I can't. That's what I came in to tell you. It's rude of me, damned rude, but I've made up my mind to go to Kirkcudbright and see Anna. It's important. I've got to go. Maybe you could tell Mr Wolf that I'm sorry, but –'

She interrupted him: 'Does she know you're coming? You never said a word to me when I invited you. You implied you'd be painting all the time but you could come.'

'I know I didn't say at the time, and, no, she doesn't know, not yet. I've tried and tried to get her on the phone but I'm bound to get her this evening –'

She looked impatient. 'Since she doesn't know yet, couldn't you change your mind and decide *not* to go? You're going to disappoint Mr Wolf and this friend of his. Don't think it's myself I'm thinking about although you *did* accept my invitation at the time. It's just such a chance for you!'

He looked at the girl. On the face of it what she was saying was perfectly reasonable. It was the chance he had been waiting for. Chance was a good thing, in painting as in everything else.

He saw her lip was trembling. The familiar feeling of apprehension returned to him.

No normal girl – Anna, for instance – would take it so badly. Or wouldn't they just lose their temper, not look as if they were going to burst into tears? Maybe comparisons were odious, because Anna might well have the right to take it personally, but not Christine, surely? His conscience pricked him when he remembered that night when things had got out of hand, but surely she wasn't going to blackmail him about that?

'No, Christine,' he said. 'I must go. I should have gone to see her long ago. I've been stupid. I know I'm letting you down, not to mention Mr Wolf, but this is more important to me. It's not realizing that which has been so stupid.'

'But the chance you're missing, Ritchie, the chance to become famous!'

He shook his head, laughing. 'That's going a bit far. I'm really, really sorry, for letting you down. If you knew me better, you'd know me for the most pig-headed fool you're ever likely to meet. Anna's the same, not a fool, but stubborn. We're two of a kind. But once we're together, once we even see each other, everything's hunky-dory. It's a kind of . . . magic.'

He watched her tidy the papers on her desk, head bent, square them neatly, lay a pencil on top of the pile. He wished she would speak. She looked up at last. She was smiling. But her bottom lip was moving in a strange way now, more than merely quivering. And the tears were running down her cheeks. The familiar apprehension filled him. But nothing would make him change his mind.

'I'm sorry, Christine. And don't worry, if I never see Mr Wolf's friend again, I'll blame myself, right up to the hilt.'

She nodded, still with the mirthless smile, as if she was unmoved. But the tears were still coursing down her cheeks. 'That's right,' she said, 'you blame yourself, right up to the hilt.'

There was nothing else to do but to walk away from her

table, up the length of the gallery and go out through the swing door.

He didn't manage to get Anna on the telephone when he tried later. Nor again. Nor again. It only made him more determined. He had to see her.

TWENTY-FIVE

ANNA HAD GONE for a walk on her own, 'a Greta Garbo walk,' she had said pointedly.

'Okay,' Jean said. 'I know when I'm not wanted.'

Anna had been moody and unapproachable for the past week or so. It was to do with Ritchie, she felt sure, and it was more than a simple case of jealousy about that girl in the gallery Nancy had told her about. Something more had hurt her. She would have to wait until Anna felt ready to tell her.

She went into the garden and walked down to the foot to lean on the wall. It had become a favourite place of hers, the view over the estuary, the changing light. If she had to choose between the elegant West End of Glasgow and this, she would choose this every time, she thought. Closer to nature. Some day she would like to do a series of paintings viewed from here, the way Monet had painted his haystacks or his churches, variations on a theme according to the time of day.

We could be very happy here the two of us, she thought. Men get in the way. She didn't really mean that. Frederick had been her love, her life. It would never be the same without him. Could anyone ever take his place, she wondered. She meant physically, the closeness, the warmth, the quiet before the storm of emotion, the memory of which even yet made her tremble.

Now there was, or could be, John Whitbread. He had made it clear in many ways, but wasn't he too self-composed, too conventional, too detached ever to arouse her? He had been a help in time of trouble, but to feel gratitude was not enough. Would that be fair to him?

And there was her painting. He would want children. You had to give yourself to that, to looking after a husband and a busy doctor's home. Would there be time for both?

There had to be space for contemplation as well as execution in painting. How many hours had she spent at this wall, planning, feeling her way in before she even put brush to canvas? Nancy's painstaking methods were not for her. Nancy accused her of being slapdash. She didn't realize that in her head was where most of the work was done.

'Jean! I've been looking for you.' She turned and saw John striding down the flagged path towards her. 'The house was deserted,' he said as he came near. 'I thought the birds had flown.'

'We're both in pensive mood today.' She smiled at him. 'Anna's gone off for a walk.' Why didn't she feel any turbulence when she looked at him? Regard, even a kind of tenderness, but no excitement. In the Art School, if she knew Frederick was standing behind her, she had begun to tremble even before he leaned forward to speak to her. 'I thought this was your supper time. Mrs Bruce will be wondering where you've got to, won't she?' Mrs Bruce was his elderly housekeeper who was, in his words, 'a devil for punctuality'.

'Damn Mrs Bruce!' he said. She looked at him, eyebrows raised. His eyes were very bright. He was slightly out of breath, which could have been caused by walking down from his . . . No, that was ridiculous. The garden path was level.

'Well, well,' she said. 'What would your patients say if they could hear their nice Dr John damning his housekeeper?'

'Could we sit down?' He was clearly agitated.

'Is there anything wrong? Have you been running?'

'Yes, I had to get to the shops before they closed.'

'But I thought Mrs Bruce did all your shopping?'

'Not this kind.'

228

'You sound mysterious.' She had allowed herself to be guided towards the gazebo, as Great-aunt called it, a little stone building with seats facing a low part of the wall, where one could see the sun setting.

She saw him put his hand in his breast pocket. The hand was trembling. It came out with a small square box. Her heart missed a beat. Her sapphire ring had been in such a box, her twenty-first birthday ring.

'This is for you.' He thrust the box into her hand in a clumsy fashion, unlike his usual deftness. 'Please take it. I chose the best in the shop and I knew you had a sapphire ring so this one's opals and diamonds, in a sort of crown.'

She was lost for words. Opals are bad luck, she thought, as she opened the box. It was a lovely ring, the stones beautifully matched and set, and rising in a crest, a princess ring. 'What is . . . ? I don't understand.'

'Jean,' he said, looking agonized, 'I know it's sudden, but will you take it? I just couldn't bear the thought of you going away. It's an engagement ring. Could we get married as soon as you finish at the Art School? If you'll promise before you go back to Glasgow then I'll be able to sleep at nights.'

'I can't believe this.' She was staring at the ring. 'You didn't say a word. The whole idea is far too sudden. We're not nearly at this stage.'

'Aren't we? It was the thought of you going . . . going back into circulation, and you might *not* come back.'

'Oh, John, the Art School isn't full of rampaging men!' She made the mistake of laughing. 'I've only begun to think of you as perhaps more than a friend. But another man in my life, so soon . . .' She handed back the box, shutting the lid. The click it made sounded very final. 'Besides, you should have asked me first. We should have talked about ourselves, the possibility . . . We should have gone on walks together.'

'You mean, courted?' He looked exasperated. 'You know I haven't time for that sort of thing. I thought you realized I was in love with you, that you were the one person I wanted to marry.'

'How could I when you never said? The whole thing's far too sudden.' She was annoyed now. Frederick had been different. There had been no doubt about how *he* felt.

'I'm too casual, that's what it is. It's a bit of a pose, really. When I took over from my father I felt . . . raw. I had to pretend. But I credited you with seeing through that, that you *knew* me.'

'In a way, but I wasn't sure where the kindness stopped and the other thing began. It was stupid of you to dash away and buy a *ring*.'

'Maybe.' He held out the box again. 'Won't you at least wear it while you're in Glasgow, get used to the idea of . . . belonging? It wasn't such a bad idea, really.' He was opening and shutting the box as he spoke. The clicking little noise irritated her. He shouldn't have done it this way, it was too sudden, too presumptuous. Do you want to be *wooed*, for heaven's sake, she asked herself, but he should have asked her if she could *entertain* the idea . . .

'I'm not such a bad catch in Kirkcudbright,' he was saying as a joke, and that was even more irritating. 'And you like it here, don't you? You've made friends already. I'm seven years older than you, but that's all right. Better for the man . . .' She hadn't even known Frederick's age. 'And the house is fine, it was Father's and Mother's, and Mrs Bruce will stay on to help. You'll need her. We'll probably have —'

She had to stop him. 'I can't marry you,' she said. 'I can't marry anybody. Frederick . . . It wouldn't be fair. I can't replace him. Yet. What we had was special, unique.' She saw the pinched look around his mouth, the grimness in his eyes. He put the little box back in his pocket. 'It was a bit precipitate of you, you know. Buying a ring, choosing the stones, even, deciding everything, never consulting me, or how I felt, and there's Anna. She's perhaps broken up with Ritchie. I have to think of her. We might live here together for a time, join the painting coterie . . . the Glasgow Girls,' that was going too far, 'but most of all I haven't completely got over Frederick, nor the tragedy of the baby –'

He interrupted her. His voice was harsh. 'It was terrible for you, the whole thing, of course, but there is nothing unique about it, in fact there is nothing unique in the whole world. There's only a small set of circumstances, happenings which get played and replayed – love, marriage, birth, death. The only thing that makes it different is the people and how they react. You were brave, but you've had your tragedy, Jean, right up to the last encore.'

She was speechless with rage for a second, and then the words burst out from her. 'What a nerve,' she said. 'What a hell of a nerve to speak to me like that!'

'Is it? Or is it the truth? Think.' He was as angry as she was. 'You've been supported by your family, particularly your sister, by your great-aunt. And by me. Yes, by me. My heart ached for your sorrow, and then as I began to fall in love with you I began to resent this man whom I'd never met, who gave you such sorrow, whose baby you had. I mourned with you when it was born dead –' She tried to interrupt, he held up his hand. 'No, don't speak. There are other people in the world. Don't begin to *enjoy* your unhappiness. I have girls coming to see me every week saying they've been "caught", that's how they describe it, nothing highfalutin. But their excuse is the same as yours: "I loved him". Is their love any less than yours? Not to them. And as for tragedy, often they had been kicked out by an irate father, sometimes they ended up on the streets of Glasgow, and one I know died from a botched abortion. I have had it up to here with your tragedy!'

She shouted at him, hands to her ears, 'I hate you! Leave me. I hate you, hate you. Posing as my friend . . . !'

He stood up, white, grim-faced. 'I can see I've cooked my goose now. Clumsy, and stupid, because I was fearful of losing you. I thought if you were wearing my ring . . . So stupid. Maybe you're right and Anna would be best for you. You'll never replace your lover, never allow yourself to love.'

He turned and went striding down the path. She saw the burnish caused by the setting sun on the leather patches at his elbows and on his dun-brown hair, turning it to red, fox colours, she thought, rich fox colours.

She felt terrible. But the assumption, the masculine assumption, that she would fall into his arms, a 'good catch'. Mother would agree. But he'd been hurtful. He had been too near the bone. He had made her squirm and that would take a lot of forgiving. She stoked her indignation as the tears ran.

They had dried when Anna came back, walking down the path with her neat figure, her neat head poised neatly on her shoulders. 'You'll get cold sitting there,' she said, stopping at Jean's side. 'I've thought it out. I'm coming back with you to Glasgow. I don't see why I shouldn't have my Diploma as well as you.'

She looked at Anna coldly. 'I don't want you,' she said. 'This was *my* thing.'

'My fees are paid. Try and stop me.'

'What about Ritchie? Are you going to let *him* down?'

'I don't see John Whitbread exactly shouting for joy at *your* departure. Haven't you noticed him positively drooling over you when he ever so casually drops in?'

'Leave him out of it!' Halfway through their flaming row they saw Elspeth-next-door pruning an unnecessary rose near their communal hedge. They looked at each other, swallowing their smiles.

'Good evening, Elspeth!' Jean called.

'Oh, good evening, girls! I didn't see you.' The grey head bobbed at them. 'I get so engrossed with my pruning . . .'

232

TWENTY-SIX

THE ELDERLY LADY with the drooping hemline had a peculiar form of hairdressing. Her grey hair was tucked uniformly inside a black velvet ribbon which encircled her head, making it look as if she was wearing an inverted pot with a rolled rim. She had a large silver buckle fixed to a belt under a substantial bosom.

'I heard you knocking,' she said to Ritchie. 'Are you looking for the Misses Mackintosh?'

'Yes, I am.' You would have been very deaf if you *hadn't* heard the row I was making . . . 'I've come from London to see them.'

'From London!' She raised her hands as if a spider had swung in front of her.

'Yes, I phoned several times.'

'But you got no reply?'

'That's right.'

'They've gone to Glasgow, you see. They left on Friday, all of a sudden. Jean was agitating to be off.'

His head swam with disappointment. 'When will they be back?'

'Oh, it will be at least a month!'

'A month!'

'Yes, until the end of term. They're enrolling at the Art School to finish their Diplomas. Staying with their parents at Clevedon Crescent in the West End, a most salubrious address, I remember. Perhaps you know it?'

'Yes, I'm a friend of Anna's. You're sure they've *both* gone?'

'Yes, quite sure.'

His heart was beating with a slow, sickly thud against his ribs. If Anna had gone back to the Art School to get her Diploma did that mean she had no intention of getting married to him, ever?

'Did Jean *want* her sister to accompany her?' he asked.

'No, no, far from it! But Anna is *so* caring. Nursed Jean back to life, you know. Anna is a very determined young lady.'

'I know.' He could scarcely speak.

'They've left me in charge. I have the key and I have to forward any mail. Anna carried the big suitcases to the taxi. Wouldn't let Jean do a thing. A lovely pair of twins, don't you agree, Mr . . . ?'

'Laidlaw.' He could have wept.

'They'll be back, of course, Mr Laidlaw. Jean assured me of that. "This is my home now, Miss Cochran," she said to me.' She pushed out her long chin at Ritchie. It had a slight fuzz of hair. 'A safe haven for the poor lass after life's battles. Would you like to go in and have a seat? Or come into my humble abode and have a cup of Earl Grey with me? So refreshing.'

'It's very kind . . .' He looked at his watch. There was a train back to London in an hour. And no doubt there would be one to Glasgow. But Anna had chosen Jean instead of him, without even letting him know. 'No, thanks,' he said. 'I'll just make my way back to the station.'

Sunday was a lacuna of disappointment and desolation. He lay in bed most of the day, only getting up to make some food towards evening, then walked round the streets for hours in an effort to tire himself out. He passed Christine's flat but scarcely gave her a thought. If he had offended her perhaps it was for the best. His mind was full of Anna.

The old biddy, Miss Cochran, had said they would come back

to Kirkcudbright once they had their Diplomas. Surely it wasn't to live there together permanently? Jean, he knew, had never been a competitor for Anna's affections, but had the tragedy she had experienced made her more dependent upon her sister? Or Anna more protective? Against that, he didn't think either of them was cut out to be an old maid. He remembered how Anna's eyes had brightened with love when she saw him, how she had always been as lusty as he was, chafing against the mores of the time, but unlike Jean she'd had a core of cautiousness which he'd had to respect.

Had she been jealous of Christine ever since she had seen her in the gallery? She hadn't Anna's friendliness, and might have offended her by her manner. And perhaps he had allowed Christine's name to slip into his conversation more than it should. But what about him? 'If you prick me do I not bleed?' he thought wildly, his mind going round and round. Nothing made any sense.

He went back to his flat and fell on his bed exhausted. In five minutes he was fast asleep.

He was given a message at the office halfway through the following morning by one of the staff, John Cox. 'A Mr Wolf telephoned, Ritchie. He would like you to go round to the gallery, he said, right away.'

'I don't know if I can do that. I'm busy.' He was surprised. Mr Wolf had never telephoned him here before.

'He sounded excited, agitated. Said it was very important.'

'Okay.'

Masters, the boss, wasn't around. He got his jacket and went swiftly out of the office and along Farringdon Road towards the gallery, speculating as he went. Had Mr Wolf's Dutch friend been interested in the picture? But John had said 'agitated'. That didn't fit.

Mr Wolf met him at the door. He didn't look like someone who was about to give him good news. His sallow face was moist with sweat, a strand of his black hair was streaked across his forehead, his dark eyes were full of an odd mixture of horror and apology.

'Ritchie!' His little moustache quivered as he spoke. 'Thank God you've come! I didn't know how to tell you. I thought you'd better see for yourself.' He was pushing him into the gallery in front of him as he spoke.

Christine wasn't there, which relieved him somewhat. He didn't want to meet her. And then he saw her table was a mass of torn brochures, papers and magazines. Pens and pencils spilled out of their containers, her chair was overturned.

'What's been happening, for God's sake?' he said. On the edge of his vision he knew there was something else, a greater confusion, an additional horror. He swung round and saw his picture, or what remained of it. The canvas hung in tatters, it was spattered with red paint as if a pot had been flung at it by a wild arm. A knife had been used to make a cross, and the indentation was filled with half-congealed red paint.

'Did someone break in? Was she attacked?' He was staring at the mess.

Mr Wolf's hands were half up to his face as if he would like to cover it. 'I almost wish . . . No, no. I'm pretty sure *she* did the attacking.'

'Christine!'

Mr Wolf nodded. 'Even in my wildest nightmares –'

'Have you any idea why?'

'She must have a grudge against you, Ritchie.' He was a picture of Jewish misery, persecuted. The possible reason struck Ritchie like a heavy blow to his head. He almost reeled.

'Oh God! I cancelled a date with her, to go to Scotland. But surely you wouldn't expect a reaction . . . like this!' He turned to look again at the ruined picture.

'Not from a normal person. Maybe I'm to blame, partly –'

'No, no. I don't think that.' He had to reassure him.

'A friend asked me to take her on. She'd had a nervous break-

236

down and, well, I felt sorry for her. She told me about her background, her mother.'

'Yes, she told me too. Terrible.'

'Some days she didn't come in. But I was lenient. I had a hard time myself when I was her age. I wanted to give her a chance.'

Ritchie nodded. 'Don't reproach yourself.'

'And the thing is,' Mr Wolf put his small plump hand on Ritchie's arm, 'I had practically sold it for you. At a splendid price. My friend from Amsterdam was very taken by it.'

Ritchie's mind shifted gear. 'Perhaps I could do something to patch it up. I don't mean for your friend, but so that it wouldn't be totally lost.' He walked up close to the picture, Mr Wolf trailing at his heels.

It was finished. No amount of work would ever make it right again, nor would he want to try. How could he ever paint out the venom? To be at the receiving end of such hate, such malevolence, was a new experience. It shook him.

'It's my Guernica,' he said. It was like a blind going up, or fog clearing. Decision came with the word. Mr Wolf was chattering on. He doubted if he had heard him.

'I have a feeling for painters. That's why I started up this gallery. I know the work that goes into it, the hours and hours. I've always wished I could paint, used to dream about it. But it wasn't possible. At least my parents taught me how to look, in the old days –'

'Don't upset yourself.' He turned to the man.

'But I have to. I can't recompense you. My insurance is non-existent. I couldn't pay my last two premiums.' His face was tragic.

'Don't worry. I'll come back to the series. It's just a setback. Not for a while, but when I do I'll make a much better job of it.' Too diffuse, he thought as he looked again, too packed with trivia, St John's Gate, St John's Square, St John's Church, monks, shields, knights, striped awnings, Uncle Tom Cobley and all. 'Please don't worry about the picture as far as I'm concerned,' he repeated.

'You're very decent, Ritchie.' His little plump hand was again on Ritchie's arm. 'You've taken a load off my mind.'

'Tell your friend from Amsterdam there will be more in the pipeline if he's interested. By the way, where *is* Christine? What's happened to her?'

'That's a sorry tale. Someone telephoned. A neighbour, I think. Apparently she'd had some kind of brain storm and caused quite a commotion. They had sent for the doctor and she was admitted –'

'Admitted! My God!' They walked back to her table together. 'Poor soul. I hope I'm not the . . . I didn't realize she would mind so much . . .'

He was attempting to tidy the papers on her table as he spoke, putting the pens and pencils back in their containers. A sheet of paper with words scrawled in thick black crayon lay in front of him: ANNA IS TRASH RITCHIE LAIDLAW IS A COMMON OAF TOTALLY WITHOUT TALENT!!! The three black exclamation marks following the words seemed to jump out of the page, hissing at him. He thought of the feral cat which had come to his flat.

'That's . . . that's . . . terrible!' Mr Wolf said.

'It doesn't matter.' He was surprised how calm he was. 'I'm going to Spain in any case.'

Mr Wolf nodded, as if it made sense. 'They're all going. Well, good luck to you. Come back and paint.'

'Thanks, I will.'

'I'll keep the flat for you as long as I can,' he said wistfully. 'I'd go myself like a shot but the wife wouldn't let me.'

Ritchie was surprised at how calm he felt as he walked home. I had this coming to me, he told himself. I need Spain more than it needs me.

TWENTY-SEVEN

THE MAN IN CHARGE of the group was Syd Sharp of Sydenham, a staunch WEA worker and a poet. They were told to behave like tourists – Ritchie wondered if many tourists travelled with a brown paper parcel containing a toothbrush, clean shirt and socks – and sent on the train to the South of France. Their presence was an open secret. The French people seemed to be strongly on the side of the Republic. There were often cheering crowds at the stations they passed through.

Ritchie's group collected at Céret and were taken in a taxi to the foothills of the Pyrenees where they were met by a swarthy guide – probably a smuggler, Syd said – told there was to be no smoking nor talking, and began their march in single file up the mountains.

The silence was a relief. On the train journey Syd had given them a pocket WEA course on political philosophy, Marxism and the evils of Fascism. Now, stumbling along in the darkness, Ritchie was free to think of Anna and wonder what on earth he was doing here at all. 'A noble crusade,' Syd had told his captive audience, 'to help the young Spanish Republic in their fight against a corrupt political system.' Well, he would see.

He fell in love with Barcelona because it was so like Glasgow. They were both 'parading' cities, possibly because the Catalonians and the Glaswegians had the same warmth and conviviality, the same need to be in contact with humanity, the liking for show.

239

He remembered how when he was a child his mother would take him to Argyle Street when Anderson's Polytechnic had a sale, and how, as a great treat, they would go to Miss Buick's for a cup of tea and a chocolate liqueur cake. He remembered with exactitude the consistency of the coffee-flavoured cream into which his teeth sunk, having cracked through the delicate outer shell. And licking round his lips with a searching tongue for a last delicious crumb. Miss Buick had been a devotee of the great Miss Cranston. She had understood what Glasgow women needed in the way of rest and refreshment . . . and hangers-on like himself.

Barcelona and Glasgow had the same cheerful bustle in the streets, the rough good humour, the beggars with their wares slung around their necks, the street musicians, the generosity of the people with their few spare coppers and their lively appreciation of the buskers.

Glasgow's Argyle Street was like a second River Clyde, a river of people, the Ramblas of Barcelona seemed to combine the elegance of Sauchiehall Street with the *joie de vivre* of Argyle Street, although neither of the Glasgow streets had bird fanciers' stalls with thrushes singing their hearts out behind bars, nor the beautiful Canaletes Fountain, nor the Aladdin's cave of La Boqueria. But then the Ramblas didn't lead to Barrowland with its promise of riches if one looked hard enough, a doubtful Sam Bough, a green velvet jacket with ruffles, a lidless Doulton teapot, a wally dug door stopper.

After they had contacted the Brigade headquarters and been told where to pick up the train going to the base at Albacete tomorrow, he set off to explore.

He had a beer at the Plaça Reial and let Barcelona flow past him. You would never get palm trees in George Square, he thought, nor that Barcelona smell – warm, musky, a faint odour of cat. Nor fountains, nor music. George Square had decided on a petrified gathering of worthies, and Queen Victoria on her plinth still kept an eye on the proceedings. But Glasgow's sky was pierced with church spires, a fine sight if Dixon's blazes were flaming the sky at the same time. He didn't think Barcelona had any foundries which opened their furnaces at night and made the sky pink.

An islander's urge led him to the sea where he sat on a wall in the seamen's quarter and then in a dock-side café. He thought of his ruined painting, and dismissed it. The next one, the Spanish one, would be better, ochres and aquamarines, city faces from the Plaça Reial, stronger faces from here – poets, peasants and sailors, Glasgow and Barcelona in a glorious jumble. This was a city where he could work and live. But he was here to fight.

He ordered a paella and then a fish fry, remembering Syd's injunction. 'Have your last decent meal. From now on it'll be beans and olive oil. And don't drink the water.' He had plenty of wine instead.

TWENTY-EIGHT

ANNA AND JEAN had worked hard since their return to Clevedon Crescent. They were nineteen again in one sense, sharing the same room, falling easily into their mother's way of running the house with the assistance of Bessie. They both admitted to having missed Bessie and Tumshie. The latter seemed, with the passage of time, to have given up her territorial ambitions, and spent most of the day gazing dozily at the kitchen fire. Bessie's comment was that Tumshie was 'nae sae gleg as she used to be'.

Bessie took their return with equanimity and would not have admitted to being the writer of the painfully worked-over letter which had come to Jean at Kirkcudbright and made her weep. She had shown it to Anne.

Dear Jean,

I was right sorry to hear about the wean not living. That must be hard for you to bear but maybe best in the long run.

It's a good thing you have your twin beside you. I have never had a sister, and often envied you three. Maybe that's why I'm so fond of Tumshie.

Things are going all right here, although your mother often has a wee greet to herself, but she cheers herself up with yin of her bridge dos, and Mr Mackintosh takes her out when he gets in, a tower of strength your Da is.

And then there's Nancy running in and out with a new

costume on every time and a twin fox fur if you please, *two* heads with glinty glass eyes set in them, not to mention a dyed musquash for Sundays.

I'll hope to see you looking fine and bonny if you come back here, and your great-aunty not any worse, though sometimes with that disease they're better to snuff it.

Yours sincerely, Bessie

Angus had welcomed them both and said it was still their home. 'You both look thinner,' he said, 'but then you always do everything the same.'

'You've lost your wee corporation too,' Anna said, noting also the veins which were purple against his pale cheeks. He'd lost his youth as well as his portliness.

'Aye,' his eyes were worried, 'the firm's not so good these days. The depression's hitting us like everyone else. Everybody's pulling in their horns when it comes to building. Have you recovered, Jean?'

'Yes, Father,' she said. 'I'm back to normal if you can call it that. But try and convince Anna. She mothers me like an old hen.'

He looked at Anna. 'How's Ritchie? You don't seem to have seen much of him recently.'

She was cool. 'No, he's working very hard in London, too hard for visiting or visitors.'

'So you thought you'd fill in the time by taking the Diploma with Jean?'

'Yes. It will stand me in good stead.' He looked at her wryly but made no comment. Mother had probably expressed her opinion to him about the suitability of painters as husbands. Father wasn't one to rock the boat.

Jean, now that they were installed in Glasgow, had given up her objections to her being there too. She seemed to have other things on her mind.

'Are you missing John?' Anna asked her one morning when

243

they were on their way to the Art School along Sauchiehall Street.

'Painting comes first with me,' she said. 'I'm not so sure about you. You know Ritchie has a flat waiting for you in London. Are you sure you aren't getting at him through me? If you are, that's stupid.'

'That coming from you is a joke.' She looked at the shop window they were passing. Aunt Jessie's shoemaker. Sad.

'Oh, I admit I haven't shown a great deal of sense in my life, but I think you should tell Ritchie what you're doing. It's only fair.'

She was ashamed. She knew there were bitter lines round her mouth. 'Leave me be, Jean,' she said. 'This is the way I want to do it.'

'Are you keeping anything from me?' They were climbing the incline of Renfrew Street, and she put her hand under Jean's elbow to help her. 'We've always shared everything.'

'Like waiting five months before you told me you were pregnant?'

'Touch.' Anna looked at her as they climbed the flight of steps to the swing door. Students pushed past them. Had too much happened to them to be here? And Jean was a different girl, frailer, older, not happy, but determined. Maybe it was true she didn't need her.

They went to dinner at Nancy's house in Hyndland and saw how she pouted when she spoke to James and how he doted on her.

'I knew it,' Anna said. 'He's spoiling her and himself. He's got a silly look on his face that he didn't have before they were married.'

'You're becoming a shrew. It's love.' And when Anna made a face: 'Have you forgotten what that means?'

'A snare and a delusion.'

Jean turned away.

*　　*　　*

244

They took turns in visiting their great-aunt. She scarcely knew the difference between them now. Sometimes one or the other of them took Rose along, and she mistook Rose for Nancy, which wasn't surprising. Since her marriage to James she had grown more and more like her mother every day.

There had been frequent letters from John Whitbread, Anna had noted, although Jean made no comment. But on one of her visits to see the invalid Jean took Rose to tea at his house.

'It's very kind of him to invite me,' Rose said on their way there. 'Do you think –'

'Don't read too much into it, Mother,' Jean said, but she was smiling as she turned away, a new softer smile.

Rose found him charming, the house old-fashioned but solidly built with plenty of room for improvement, and Mrs Bruce, although old-fashioned in her ways, a good solid body of the right kind. 'No, Jean, there's nothing that couldn't be put right with a younger woman installed there.'

'Our kind,' she said with satisfaction in the train going home. Dr Whitbread had insisted on driving them to Dumfries to catch the Glasgow train, a distance of twenty-seven miles. It was most considerate, she had commented, and said she would be quite happy sitting in the back seat.

'Funny a young man like that not being married,' she said to Jean as they were steaming along. He had supplied Rose with *Scottish Life* and *Good Housekeeping*, which she had accepted graciously.

'Yes, funny,' Jean said, admiring the Galloway landscape as it slid past the window. And thinking of John.

When Rose had been 'freshening herself' upstairs in John's substantial mahogany-furnished guest room, he had apologized to Jean for his former clumsiness with the ring. 'Maybe I didn't do it right in the letters I wrote. I seemed to take leave of my senses that day. It was the fear of losing you. I knew, you see, that my happiness rested with you, would always rest with you.'

245

Her resentment had vanished as she looked at his face, the rock-like steadiness, the love in it. Steadiness. Frederick Kleiber hadn't had that. She had an outrageous thought for a second of asking him if he could swim . . .

'Maybe we can start at the beginning again, John,' she had said. 'I'm not proud of the way I behaved either.'

She felt tenderness overcoming her now as she looked at the passing fields and hedgerows. The softness and tranquillity of the landscape soothed her. It and John seemed to her to be one and the same thing.

When she got back from that visit she said to Anna, 'I heard from John who heard it from Elspeth that Ritchie came to the Kirkcudbright house the day after we left for Glasgow.' She was interested, and pleased, at the astonishment in her sister's eyes.

'John must have been mistaken, or Elspeth. She gets wandered.'

'John's reliable. She told him on one of his rounds. Ritchie came off the London train and was terribly disappointed when she told him we had left. "Bowled over," she said, apparently. He even refused her Earl Grey. He went right back to London, very cast down, she said. Quite a presentable young man, she said to John, with Botticelli curls, she said.'

'Will you stop saying "she said"!'

'Temper, temper. Oh well, if you refuse to believe it I can't do any more. But I've told you, whatever's happening between you two I still think you're being very stupid.'

'If he came to Kirkcudbright and didn't find us why didn't he write and say so?'

'Maybe he did but the letter wasn't forwarded.'

'Elspeth would have sent it on. You know she loves going into your house, poking about in it, being in charge.'

'Well, I've told you. That's all I can do. Anna,' she took a step towards her, seeing the misery on her face, 'look how good you were to me when I was down. Let me help you.'

'I don't know what you're talking about.' She went out of the room, cutting Jean short.

Stubborn bitch, Jean thought, and felt better for having thought it.

At the Art School Anna worked assiduously on her clock face although intermittently her attention wandered. Sometimes she thought she might have experienced a kind of catharsis at the same time as Jean, and that there could be a physical explanation for this since they were so close. Had Jean's anguish about Frederick and then the baby lit up *her* jealousy of Christine Bouvier so that it became abnormal? That meant there was even a psychical explanation for the lowering of her spirit. She had to search in the dictionary for that word but felt it fitted.

They had only been at Clevedon Crescent for a fortnight when Ritchie's letter arrived one morning. She tore it open, then, seeing Jean's eyes on her, languidly took it out from its envelope. Her eyes devoured it.

I came to see you at Kirkcudbright but you had gone. The lady next door, Miss Cochran, I think her name was, told me you were in Glasgow so I'm sending this letter to your parents' house.

Life seems to be knocking me sideways these days, so I felt I had to come to a decision. Spain had been hovering in the back of my mind, a guilt about it, that I ought to be there. So I packed up. In fact, I'm writing this on the boat going over to France. I know I've made the right decision. What's the use of having principles if you're not prepared to fight for them? I'll write again when I'm settled, although 'settled' doesn't seem to be the right word.

You should have told me you were going back to the Art School, Anna. I would have understood that. You haven't been playing fair, and the same goes for me. I've been kind of friendly with Christine Bouvier, but you can put that down to missing you, treat it as a compliment. But if you think she ever came close to being the love of my life, you can think again.

Yes, she helped me with the flat, and yes, I was grateful. I showed it, too much, but I can tell you, I regret that. But, thanks to her encouragement and belief in me, fair's fair, I got over my block, painted a picture I really liked, put my heart and soul into it, and – you're never going to believe this – when it was hanging in the gallery she slashed it to pieces! To ribbons.

I think, no, I know she was jealous of you, and furious because I told her I was going to Kirkcudbright to see you on the same say as I had promised to see her. I had accepted her invitation to a celebration dinner for the completed painting. I shouldn't have let her down out of politeness if nothing else, but suddenly I had to see you, knew that if we saw each other we could mend the rift between us.

But she didn't have to slash my picture. It was like slashing *me* in the face with a knife. You, any normal girl, would never have done a thing like that. It was then I realized that I had got myself mixed up with a neurotic, unhappy girl.

The disappointment when I found you had left was enormous. And at the back of my mind I felt somehow I deserved it. But, all the same, you shouldn't have gone off to Glasgow without telling me. That wasn't like you. Altogether, I felt I had to give myself a good shake-up, get myself straight, and the best way seemed to be to go to Spain and think of something else for a change.

You'll be busy studying, I'll be busy fighting. We'll see each other clearer when we're far apart. Because I want to spend the rest of my life with you. No one else will do.

Ritchie.

She sat stunned when she read the letter, and then, with it in her hand, excused herself from the table and ran out of the room, aware of the curious glances. She was lying on her bed staring at the opposite wall when Jean came in and sat down beside her.

'If that was a love letter from Ritchie,' she said, 'it's having a funny effect on you. I thought you would be jumping for joy.'

'He's in Spain,' she said. 'He's gone to Spain without telling me.'

'Spain? My God!' She blew out her breath. 'And yet it's like Ritchie, somehow. He couldn't have borne not joining up, being in there with the idealists.'

'But not telling me!' The tears were running down her face.

'Well, you decided to come here without telling him. Isn't it a bit like tit for tat?' She stroked Anna's ankle lovingly. 'Cheer up. You'll soon be dead.'

'But I was in the right! Besides, he was having an affair with that girl in the gallery.'

Jean stopped stroking. 'How do you know that? You never –'

'You always thought Ritchie could do no wrong. That's your trouble. You trust people too much.' Anna sat up and scrabbled for her handbag under the bed, found it, went quickly through its contents and produced a letter. She held it out to Jean. 'Read that and you'll change your tune.'

Jean read it slowly and handed it back.

'She's deranged. It's got a bad smell about it.'

'Is that how it strikes you?' Anna was mopping her face, blowing her nose.

'Definitely.'

'I believed it at the time. After all, she enclosed Ritchie's letter –'

'It's ambiguous. You read too much in it.'

'Maybe I did. He says in his letter she slashed his picture to pieces.'

'An act like that proves she's deranged. You should feel sorry for her.'

'But he practically admitted in his letter –'

'It depends how you read it. You were suspicious, fed up. You're generally clear-sighted. This isn't like you, Anna. We're talking about Ritchie. You love each other.'

'Yes . . . Jean, I've been very foolish.'

Jean gave her a hug. 'It's much better when you spill the beans. Now we're about equal. I waited for five months.'

'And the baby died.' She leaned against her sister. 'Oh, I've wasted a lot of time. Maybe Ritchie will –'

'Ritchie won't die. You're both lucky. I'm the tragedy queen around here. Or was until John told me it was time I took my bow. He's offered me a new role.' She got up quickly and went to the door where she turned a glowing face to Anna. 'Now I'm being coy.' She laughed. 'Put some powder on and come back and finish your breakfast. Mother will be on tenter-hooks.'

'Okay. I'm glad for you, Jean.'

'I'm glad for myself. Now, if I were you I'd tear up that letter and forget it.'

'Yes, miss.'

Oh great, she thought when she was powdering her face, absolutely great!

Anna went steadily on with her work. She worried about Ritchie, but not deeply. The thought of him in uniform and a gun was comical. Besides, she knew he would have to be trained first and that was safe enough. If there had been a war here he was more likely to be a conscientious objector. Spain appealed to him, was romantic, a crusade. He was a great one for crusades, it was his own personal war.

His first letter, when it came, was brief. He had left the training camp at Albacete and now was with the International Brigade at Aragon. 'Life has become very simple,' he wrote.

'There are only two states.' Awake or asleep? Alive or dead? A seed of anxiety was planted in her and she wrote immediately.

I feel like asking you to be careful, but that would be stupid. This escapade of yours is beginning to worry me. At first it seemed like a joke. I thought of you as the one who would be out of step in any brigade. But this is serious stuff. I can't give you a row for scarpering off when I did the same thing, but now that you've done it, watch your back, as the kids shout in the Saturday matinées.

I'm truly sorry about your picture being ruined, and also sorry about the girl's state.

Perhaps she would tell him about Christine Bouvier's letter when he came home.

I think we're both acting in character, really. You're a bit of a Don Quixote, and you know me, what I begin I always want to finish. It seemed the right thing to do at the time, and Jean needs me yet to give her a bolstering from time to time. She's been through hell. We're both modern in thinking. We're finishing the Diploma because we want to establish our identities.

She couldn't bring herself to write anything more loving. The thought of him lying in bed with Christine in that flat still rankled, still hurt.

But she counted the days between his letters, which didn't tell her much about the fighting but a lot about the people and the terrain. He was clearly enjoying himself. You could always count on Ritchie to do that.

Work, as always, was the answer for her. She concentrated on the clock she was making for her Diploma examination, a brass wag-at-the-wa' with the face garlanded with icanthus and the Scottish rose. She put the emblem of war between the garlands – partly hidden crossed bayonets – and to symbolize Spain, waving fronds of palm, which Ritchie had told her grew in some of the Spanish squares.

Rose was happy and busy. Life was as it had been before those annoying men Frederick Kleiber and Ritchie Laidlaw got in the way. Neither of them had been suitable, and if there was a gap now it would give things time to settle. She favoured one of James Pettigrew's architect friends for Anna and John Whitbread for Jean. There had never been a medical man in the family, but there was always a first time.

Angus worked steadily in his office at St Vincent Place but seemed to have lost his verve. He no longer had his morning walk up St Vincent Hill. The girls discussed it, were worried by it, although he had been checked by his doctor, who thought there was nothing organically wrong.

'He's halfway through life,' Jean said. 'Maybe it's traumatic for a man.'

'Could it be,' Anna suggested, 'that you reach the stage when you take account of life and find it's not what you meant at all?'

'We'll have to be careful,' Jean said, with those new, lovely eyes.

It was coming near the date of the examination. Jean's submission was an abstract of Kirkcudbright harbour, deep aquamarine colours and dashes of rust red which were the fishing boats. The black perpendicular strokes were the spars. It had a unity which pleased her; the composition gave her increasing satisfaction as she developed it. She and John wrote regularly to each other, 'courting by letter,' John called it. Anna kept her worries hidden about Ritchie.

The day arrived. The last time we'll plod up those stairs, Anna thought, sit in the library, which always seemed light even on a grey Glasgow day, work in cluttered studios, be part of a motley bunch of young people who took delight in their artiness, their undisciplined hair, their short skirts or baggy trousers. They both admitted to feeling older, a different breed.

The Great Hall. 'Shush!' someone said as the lecturers came on to the platform, followed by the Principal. 'Shush! Shush!' The students took it up all round the hall.

Now the list of names was being read out. Yes, theirs was there, thank goodness. 'Please come up in turn.' Give a thought to Rennie Mackintosh. European Symbolists being fêted while he died in obscurity. Rustles and whispers. Latecomers squeezing past, 'Sorry . . .'

All the names on the list had been called, one by one, the owners had mounted the platform to receive their Diplomas, except Anna and Jean. A pause. 'Oh, what a panic's in thy breastie . . .' Pressure of shoulder to shoulder. Tenseness, apprehension, disbelief, a black umbrella of despair over the two of them.

'And now,' the booming voice silencing the rustling and whispering, 'it is my pleasant duty . . .' A grown man with a pin, torturing butterflies, '. . . to present diplomas . . .' Machiavelli and Rasputin combined and hidden behind the benign front of the Principal, '. . . to two young ladies whom you know, the Mackintosh sisters!' Burst of clapping growing, reverberating round the hall, even a wolf whistle from some badly reared genius from the Gorbals.

'You may wonder why I single them out. Well, they have a great name, one we revere here of all places, but it is for their personal contribution to the school.

'Jean Mackintosh has grown in stature since she came here as a pupil. We believe she will go on to great things. But it took her sister, Anna, to identify herself more closely with our own Glasgow Girls of honoured memory, in whom her special talent is securely based. We are proud of them individually and as an entity, those wonderful craftswomen of the late nineteenth century.

'Originally, as some of you will remember, we had three of

the same family here, and our tutor then, Frederick Kleiber, whose untimely death we still regret, had the happy thought of calling them our *present-day* Glasgow Girls. Jean and Anna, now there are two, are none the less worthy of this appellation.'

They squeezed out of their seats to the applause, the embarrassing applause. They walked down towards the podium together. They didn't look at each other. Jean was beckoned first to come forward.

'Jean Mackintosh's landscape shows more than promise. Its boldness and assurance reminded the committee of that other gifted student, Ritchie Laidlaw, at present fighting in Spain.' She stepped back with her cardboard tube.

'Anna Mackintosh's clock face in brass is a striking work, and I mean that in both senses.' The titter was thin. But then it was a thin joke. 'The decoration is interesting, transitional Art Deco allied with modern symbolism, an unusual and original design.' Anna stood back beside Jean. An imperious lifted hand prevented them from turning away.

'Those two young women are a good example of all that is best in the school, both so different in their approach. In one we have a fine painter in embryo, in the other a fine craftswoman, their work disposing of the line often drawn between art and craft. Both have shown in their work during the last part of this term a surprising maturity which their various tutors have commented on. We congratulate them!'

They went back to their seats singly, their minds twinned in embarrassed pleasure.

Bouncing back on the tramcar along Great Western Road Jean said that was awful, wasn't it, and that she had been afraid to look at Anna.

'I was the same. What would you have done if we'd caught each other's eye?'

'Laughed, maybe. Cried.' She still didn't look at Anna. She had her hand up to her face to hide it. She's thinking of

Frederick, Anna thought. I wonder if she felt him there, heard that charming, husky, foreign voice, imagined his arms round her again. She thought she heard a small sound from Jean, like a moan. Her throat filled, and she leaned forward, pretending to peer at the passing shop window.

'Did you see that? A *huge* notice. Cooper's have tuppence off their Blue Mountain. We'll have to tell Mother.'

TWENTY-NINE

1937–38

CHRISTMAS WAS SPENT at the Pettigrews, since Nancy wanted to show off her house seasonally decorated, and Rose was quite glad to hand over the catering to her. There were plenty of young people there, but it was a subdued affair for Jean and Anna.

'I'm happy when I'm painting,' Jean told her when they were back at Clevedon Crescent, 'but I feel like a skeleton at the feast at Nancy's parties. Too much has happened.'

She was also happy when she returned from a New Year visit to Kirkcudbright. She had seen their great-aunt, who still lingered on, and also John Whitbread. Anna thought Jean's inner glow was more pronounced.

She had received a disturbing letter from Ritchie which was occupying her mind. In it he said they were being fêted like fighting cocks and visited by notables such as Atlee. Now she felt real fear for him. She could see that it was no longer an amateur scrap for idealists; it could deliver death as surely as death had been delivered to Frederick Kleiber on a quiet Scottish loch. This time the fear and involvement were her own, not stemming from Jean.

Rose arranged parties to allow them to meet suitable young men. The past didn't exist for her, except that she had decided they would sell Cowal View and buy a house in Arran where Angus could indulge his new-found passion for golf. Anna, being vulgar, said he now preferred Bobby Jones's plus fours to Rose's camiknickers. But they stayed at Clevedon Crescent that winter because they felt they owed it to their parents, although the scales had fallen from their eyes.

Grace Binnie came to the parties, of course, in steel-grey satin to match her steel-grey hair. (It had 'gone' early and she wasn't going to make a stick to beat her back by having it tinted, oh dear, no.) She looked quizzically at Jean and said, 'Well, a new life for you now, Jean,' and gave her a 'I wouldn't dream of mentioning anything' nod.

Jean, because of her dramatic sense, played up to her parents' friends by acting the eccentric bolder daughter, wearing lots of jewellery round her neck, in her ears and on her fingers, which clinked and clanked as she moved. Nancy was generally there to advertise her pregnancy, and it was quite like the old days with their parents' friends saying, 'My, you are lucky, Rose Mackintosh, with three such lovely daughters!' Angus beamed but Anna noticed he had a purple-red flush over his cheeks and on the bridge of his nose, which might have been acquired at the nineteenth hole.

Now that Anna no longer worried about Jean, Ritchie took her place. She scoured the daily papers. Everything pointed to a big battle in the offing. There had been no letters from Ritchie since before Christmas, which added to her anxiety. She set off one morning to see his mother. She should have done it long ago.

It was Mr Laidlaw who opened the door. One look told her he hadn't got a job. He wore a collarless shirt and grey trousers which were baggy at the knees, and he looked even more defeated than before. He was clutching a pink racing sheet in his hand.

'It's Anna Mackintosh, Mr Laidlaw,' she said. 'Do you remember me?'

'Aye, Ritchie's girl. Ma wife's no' in. She's got a job at the grocers for two hours to help oot.'

'Oh!' He hadn't asked her in. 'When is she due back?'

'Ony time noo. I was just reddin' up for her.'

'Would you mind if I waited?'

He shook his head. 'Ach, no. Come in!' He hesitated in the narrow dark hall. 'I think Lizzie would like you in the front room.'

He showed her into the parlour, which was as highly polished as the last time she had been here. Fortunately it wasn't a cold day because there was no sign of a fire.

'Sit down, Miss Mackintosh,' he said. 'Take a load off your feet.' He half laughed, blushing. She remembered he was painfully shy.

'Anna,' she said, 'not Miss Mackintosh.' She smiled at him. 'Thanks.' She sat down. 'I was wondering if you'd heard recently from Ritchie. I haven't.'

'Aye, jist the ither day. Wait and I'll get it.' When he came back with the letter in his hand he sat down opposite her at the fireless grate, looking more at ease. 'I don't know how you put up with him.' His face broadened in a smile.

'Oh, I'm used to him. But I got worried.' There was the sound of the door opening and she heard Mrs Laidlaw's voice.

'I'm back, Walter!'

Her husband jumped up, and went out. She could hear the whispered conversation in the hall, then they came in. She was wearing a bulky coat of grey herringbone tweed which looked too big for her. It had a jumble look, good material, but out of date.

'Well, well, Anna!' She had more composure than her husband. 'This is a pleasant surprise.'

'I'm staying with my parents just now. Jean and I have been at Kirkcudbright in my great-aunt's house. She's in Dumfries hospital. She had a stroke.'

'Oh, that's bad.'

'She's not making much progress, unfortunately. But I really called to see if you'd heard from Ritchie recently.'

'Aye, two in a row. The post from there's all to pot.' She sat

258

down opening her coat and revealing a white apron underneath. 'In the first one he said he'd had a nice Christmas, in a village in Aragon. The only bad thing was the weather.'

'Twenty degrees Fahrenheit,' her husband said.

'You always think of Spain as hot.' Anna looked at him.

'They'd cut slits in their blankets to make them into ponchos,' Mrs Laidlaw said, 'as a protection against the terrible winds. They got full of snow. When they were doing their training their guns jammed with the ice. Even the food was frozen.'

Mr Laidlaw smiled. 'He said the only benefit was that the lice didn't bite.'

'Trust Ritchie to see the funny side.'

'Aye, but even at school he got chilblains holding his slate. Do you remember, Walter? I knitted him mittens and he said they made good hankies.' His mother smiled, shaking her head. 'He didn't finish that letter – said he was being moved up nearer the Front.' She leaned forward and touched Anna's hand. 'Stay and have tea with us. I could have it ready in a minute.'

'No, thanks all the same. Mother will expect me back for . . . ours. I only looked in to see if you'd had a letter. I should have come long ago.'

'Yes, I see that.' She lifted a battered-looking atlas lying on a small table beside her. 'Ritchie's. Look at the blot. That's him all over. And the blot!' She smiled. 'See, here's where I think he is. There's Madrid,' she pointed, 'right in the centre. And there's Teruel, nearer the coast, and Valencia south of that. Lovely names, aren't they? I'd like fine to go to Spain, those dancers with frilled skirts stamping their heels and a rose tucked behind their ears . . . Get the last letter, Walter.'

'It's here. I got it before you came in.'

'Well, you read it, Anna. It'll make up for yours going missing.'

'Are you sure?'

'Aye. You're his girl. You'll be missing him.'

'I didn't expect him to dash off to Spain.'

'He had to have his war one place or the other.' She smiled, and Anna thought, she's sharp. 'But don't you worry. He'll settle once he gets his win' oot.'

She began to read.

. . . now we're in the thick of it again after resting near Alcañiz. At least wounds don't bleed so much here because of the cold. We had to wade across the Ebro. It was quite shallow, but colder than those blocks of ice in the fish shop. I thought when I got to the other side my toes would drop off, but the blood came rushing back. Some of the men weren't so lucky and got frostbite.

. . . Then we've been fighting perched up on a cliff for three days. As steep as Ben Nevis. The noise stupefies you. You don't know you're in the thick of it until the noise stops and what looks like half-stuffed sacks all round you are your pals. That's enough of that. I only wrote it for Da. The Spanish Commander commended us . . . the ones that were left.

What strikes me is that it's mostly *working* men from Spain and other countries, but amongst the British there are quite a few toffs, and they're the only ones who talk about what they're fighting for. And God, how they talk! But I think we've all got our own Spain in our hearts although we can't write poetry about it, about freedom, and fair shares for all, and finding out about yourself, and in my case missing Anna like mad and grudging her being with Jean.

I hope you aren't working too hard, Ma, and that Da has got a job. Tell him I'm fighting for him as well . . .

She handed back the letter to Mrs Laidlaw, having difficulty in keeping her mouth from trembling. 'Thank you,' she said. 'It was good of you to let me read it.'

'Fair shares for all, Ritchie said.' She smiled. 'Now are you

sure you won't take tea with us? I've got a shepherd's pie ready
to heat up.'

'No, thanks. Mother will have mine ready. I'll get away home
now and let you get on with yours.'

At the door Mrs Laidlaw said, 'How's your sister? Jean, isn't
it?'

'Didn't Ritchie tell you what happened?'

'No, he's close, Ritchie. Like his father.'

'She was going to have a baby to a married man, but he
drowned when they were in a boat together.'

'He drowned!' She looked shocked. 'But she . . . knew?'

'No, not then, you see, they had . . . just . . . that day.'

'Oh dear, dear!' She took Anna in her arms. 'Oh, the poor
thing! I know you'd be good to her, comfort her. Oh, what a
terrible thing to happen.' She released Anna. 'I'm *that* sorry.'

'The baby died. It was dead in the womb.'

Mrs Laidlaw's face whitened. She put her hand on Anna's
arm. 'Awful. Has she got over it a bit?'

'I think so. You never know with Jean.'

'Don't you grudge any time you've spent with her. Blood's
thicker than water, and with twins it's extra thick. You tell
Ritchie that.'

261

THIRTY

1938

ANNA LEARNED A new word that spring, 'pogrom'. Hitler had driven into Vienna surrounded by cheering crowds, young men had broken through the police cordons and shouted for '*der Führer*'. Jews still resident in the city trembled and saw no hope.

Anna purposely didn't comment on the news, but, sitting up in bed, Jean said, staring into space, 'For the first time I'm glad Frederick isn't alive to see what is happening.' For the war was drawing nearer. Now they could see Spain as a preliminary, a mirror held up to the world.

Their decision to return to Kirkcudbright was mutual. They had given Rose a fair crack of the whip in making themselves exhibits at her parties, and bait at Nancy's gatherings of architect friends of James's. Robin Naismith, much to Rose's chagrin, had got himself attached to the niece of a titled lady, and Rose had reluctantly agreed that John Whitbread might do – if he got himself a better tailor – and wondered why the girls laughed.

She took their departure calmly. She and Nancy were engaged on a trawl through the Glasgow shops for maternity dresses, long before she needed them. 'Your house would certainly be a good stop-over for us when we come to visit Aunt Jessie, and a change of pace for Daddy. He's quite worn out with worrying about this war they keep talking about and the effect it's having on the firm. Luckily, Clevedon Crescent is in my name.'

Kirkcudbright seemed to share their mother's sanguinity

about the future. No gloom hung over it, and soon the girls were once again absorbed into the painting fraternity.

Anna was invited to share a barn which had been converted into a workplace by a few men and women interested in silver-smithing, metal work and jewellery. It was in one of the closes near the Tolbooth, and she had a bench with a view down the garden to the Dee. There was something very comforting about the studio with its interior walls of rough round stones, its beamed ceiling and huge stove which they kept bouncing with heat. The calm acceptance of her presence helped to subdue her anxiety about Ritchie.

She felt younger amongst them. For a long time she had been responsible for Jean, and it was pleasant to be called 'girlie' by elderly Mr Rawlinson, and to be teased by the ladies because he brought her a cream sandwich cake which she was careful to share at the tea-break.

At that time the old-fashioned stove would be thrown open, the firelight would glow on their faces and dance off a piece of silver or reflect in the raised design of the Venetian mirror she was making. It was her retreat, and while working she could think of Ritchie and turn over some of the phrases from his last letter.

It's no longer simple, a war of the peasants against the landed proprietors. It's become sullied. The names, and aims, of the various factions on either side have become elastic, almost interchangeable. All wars must be the same.

The thing which surprises me is how easily the Spaniards have taken to killing. It's like an infectious disease they've all caught. Killing comes naturally to them – someone said to me that there's a black spot in the heart of each one of them – and yet they're noble and warm-hearted. They'd share their last crust with you, or bowl of lentils. Don't mention those things ever to me when I come home . . .

At the end of the day she would walk along the High Street, picking out the Queen Anne houses or peering upwards to see the ship on top of the tower of the Tolbooth. She would imagine she smelled a sea smell.

Jean would be in her studio which they had converted out of an old stone wash house at the back. Great-aunt Jessie had painted at Green Close along with the other women painters, but Jean's canvases demanded lots of room. Sometimes Anna would find her pacing about the wash house, oblivious to everything, and when she came into the house she would look at Anna without seeing her.

Once when Anna got home she found her at the foot of the garden in the dark, leaning on the stone wall which separated it from the fields running down to the river. The sadness in her face was such that she turned away and went back to the house. The rape of Vienna by Hitler had perhaps upset her.

They visited their aunt most days. She had given up trying to walk, which John accepted. 'She's chosen this way,' he said. 'Let her be.'

He and Jean took walks together. Sometimes, if he had time, they drove to Dumfries and had dinner there. She loved him, Anna felt sure. It only needed a small step. Once when Anna told him how patient he was, he smiled wryly. 'I can wait,' he said. 'I don't want three in a bed.'

'It saddens her,' she tried to explain, 'that she has to say goodbye finally to Frederick. I think she realized it the day Hitler marched into Vienna.' She looked at him as a painter might, saw the thin face as if it had been honed by constant caring, the finely drawn mouth, the hair which grew far back – he would go bald early – the air of quietness. He knew how to wait. Jean was lucky.

One particular day, which she was spending at home in order to shop and write to Ritchie, Jean tired her with her restlessness. She was in and out of the house several times, finally throwing herself into a chair, her legs stretched out. 'Sometimes painting isn't enough. I can do nothing today.'

'Well, read a book for goodness' sake,' Anna said. 'You're like a hen on a hot griddle.'

The doorbell rang, and John walked in unannounced. They never locked the door during the day, a country habit which wouldn't have been permitted at Clevedon Crescent. 'Hello, John!' Anna said, looking up. 'Are we glad to see you. This one's driving me mad with her restlessness.'

She looked from one to the other. Jean was on her feet, looking at John as if her ship had come home. He was looking at her. Anna felt she didn't exist, had been wiped out, as if by the stroke of a paintbrush. She got up. 'Excuse me,' she said, and walked towards the door. She doubted if they heard her.

In the kitchen she started leisurely to make a ginger cake. She had been given the recipe by Miss Winter, one of the ladies at the studio. She carefully measured out the ingredients, taking a pleasure in assembling them, the flour, the preserved ginger, the spices, the butter, the fruit. From the sitting room came the steady hum of voices, once Jean's laugh, and then silence, a long, significant silence.

When she went back to the room John said to her, 'We're going to the Murray Arms at Gatehouse tomorrow evening for a celebration dinner. Come with us.' He seemed to be having trouble containing his joy.

'No, thanks,' she said, 'two's company.'

'Oh, come on, Anna,' Jean said. Her joy was slightly sheepish.

'No, I've a lot to do. It's good of you, but I want to write again to Ritchie. Keep him up with things here. Chamberlain's speech.' Her anxiety came back. 'Franco's battering Barcelona to hell, and Ritchie's holed up in the mountains meantime. He never talks about the conditions, typical Ritchie. Franco's got the Republicans on the run now. He's taking hundreds if not thousands of prisoners. I'm worried sick about Ritchie. Maybe he's been captured.'

'He'll be all right,' Jean said. Grandly.

'How do *you* know? Just because *you*'re all right, grinning there like a Cheshire cat?' Their eyes darted fire at each other.

'Hey, hey, you two!' John said, amused. 'If it's to be another war, I'll hold the coats.' They looked at him, then at each other, and exploded with laughter.

'That's better.'

'Then you said Great-aunt Jessie's worsening. I want to go and see her.'

'She's tired of her state.'

'I'd be tired too, in chains.'

'Then we'll *both* go,' Jean said.

'No, leave it to me. John would be furious if you missed your celebration dinner.' She emphasized the two words, and smiled a downwards smile. She noticed that the kind, brown-eyed, caring John didn't seem to bat an eyelid, nor try to persuade her to change her mind.

'Then, that's settled.' He gave Jean a lingering look, took a step towards her, thought better of it, and went towards the door. He put a hand on Anna's shoulder as he passed her, as if to say, 'Thanks.'

That evening, when they were sitting having supper together, Anna said, 'Your eyes are a deep midsummer-night blue.'

'I'm not used to such happiness.' She got up. 'I think I'll go for a walk.'

So much for the Art School's own special Glasgow Girls, Anna thought, as she went to her room and began a letter to Ritchie, her first proper love letter.

I should have been writing like this long ago, to bring myself close to you. So should you. We're both too damn practical. Maybe if I try hard I could manage. It seems Jean and I do everything together, and we've both decided at the same time that love comes first. So here goes, my own dear love . . .

266

THIRTY-ONE

ALWAYS WHEN he had seen the Orange Walk swinging along the streets of Glasgow, the black bowler hats, the embroidered purple and gold sashes, the shining red faces, the pipe bands, he had imagined he would feel ridiculous marching behind any emblem, but here he was, kitted out and in his right mind, marching joyously – it was the only word for it – behind both the Catalan and Republican flags, chest pushed out like a pouter pigeon's.

It wasn't long before he was doubled up, running and zig-zagging to escape the Fascist bombers. This was no Orange Walk, where all you might get was a broken bottle pitched at you. This was injury and death, men writhing in agony in your path, like being in a bowling alley with a demon bowler on the loose. No ambulances had as yet managed to get across the river. He saw the wounded or the corpses being dragged away to be ferried across in boats. The screaming and the groaning echoed in his ears.

He had heard it before at Teruel, where he had been so petrified by fear that he had soiled his trousers. Even disgust at his own weakness hadn't obliterated his fear. But here he was impervious. He recognized it as a dangerous state, a battle lust which might make him foolhardy. But it was also exhilarating. He felt terrific. He wished he were Syd and could write a poem about how he felt.

After six days he didn't feel so good. The heat was sweltering, the rope-soled *alpargatas* he'd been wearing were cut to pieces on the rocks. Worse of all was the stench of bodies, both men and mules, which fried in the sun. His gritty-eyed, light-headed exhaustion made him step over dead men without a qualm, once or twice on an upturned face. He was deafened by the continuous roar. The steel raining on them from the Fascists' machine guns was like being caught in Argyle Street on a wet night without an umbrella. Absurd thoughts like that passed through his brain.

The battalion was withdrawn, having failed to dislodge the Fascists, and they got a chance to catch up on sleep under the shade of the olive trees and to bathe in the Ebro. He walked amongst the men, searching for the tall, loping figure of Syd. No one had seen him.

In eight days they were in the thick of it again, and this time he was no longer invincible. No one could be optimistic in the face of such constant bombardment and the deadly accuracy of the new German 88-mm gun. They were losing their grip; it was the Fascists who were invincible.

He kept an image of Anna in his mind to prevent the worst of the fear, the short dark shining hair, the white skin. Was he going to be killed before he knew if it were white all over? His head swelled, his eyes bulged, the stench of death sickened him as it grew hotter, as did his resentment. He hadn't had his future yet, he hadn't painted that new picture for Mr Wolf, he hadn't given Anna children . . .

It was when he was standing up to fire that the 88-mm gun roared again, rock splinters danced in the air like arrows, and he felt himself being pole-axed by a blinding pain.

He wakened in a dark cavern, which at first he thought was hell until he saw the white figures flitting about in the swinging light of hurricane lamps. An orderly took off his trousers and splashed some stinging liquid on his leg which made him shout and curse. At least it was *there*. 'Nothing to what it will be like when you're having this chunk of rock dug out, mate.' They were a sharp-tongued lot, these Cockneys.

He was right. The surgeon said he was lucky it hadn't gone into his groin and he might still be a daddy. 'How long have you been here?' he asked.

'In this cave?' He started up in fear. 'What's that God-awful noise?'

'It's a train backing in. The seriously wounded are going on it to Barcelona. But there's no need for you to go. How long –'

'Since June 1937.'

'With no leave?'

'No.'

'Well, you seem to have done your stint.' The young surgeon was smiling down at him. He had a refined voice. 'It's time you got home.'

'I can go home?'

'Unless you want to finish it single-handed. Prime Minister Negrín is withdrawing the International Brigade.'

He wiped his eyes with the back of his hand. 'You must think I'm soft in the head, bubblin' like a wean.'

'No, I feel the same. Patching up bodies just to send them back to be killed ad infinitum isn't doing as much good as being in the Edinburgh Royal.'

'I thought you came from Edinburgh.' He grinned. 'You speaking fancy like.'

'We're a superior race, of course.' His eyes were twinkling.

'Or a different kind of nonentity.' He suddenly went to sleep, missing the surgeon's guffaw.

Inside, the train was like a Bosch painting or one by that daft loun, Dadd. The white of the bandages and plasters glowed in the dim lighting, the air was heavy with cigarette smoke, and he was happy.

'Where are you bound for?' he asked the man beside him who had one arm sticking straight out like a signpost.

'Kent, but it's Middlesex Hospital for us first to get our clearance.'

'You didn't meet a man called Syd Sharp? He came from Kent too. I haven't seen him since we went up to the Front together.'

'I hadn't time to socialize.'

'Where did you get yours?'

'Fuentes de Ebro . . . wait a minute. Was he a tall lanky poof?'

'You could say that.' He wouldn't.

'I remember him now. He was a great one for spouting poetry. He was shouting and singing when we charged, "Where are the lads of the village tonight . . ."'

'". . . Where are the nuts we knew?" My father used to sing it. It's from the last war.'

'Anyhow, that was the last of your pal . . . God, what's that?' The train had ground and crunched to a halt. 'Typical,' the man said. 'Wouldn't you know? We're bloody stuck in a tunnel.'

Everybody was talking, some singing, 'Oh dear, what can the matter be . . .' It died down. People stopped talking. Ritchie put his head back on the seat. No good worrying. He was on his way home anyhow. If they were stuck in a tunnel between Port-Bou and Cerbère they were bound to get out eventually.

It was stifling. Everyone was tense and smoking twice as much, and he found it difficult to breathe. He had never smoked himself, but had never considered it a virtue since he liked his dram. He would buy a bottle of the best Spanish wine for their celebration. Anna . . . He took a piece of paper out of his pocket and began scribbling a note to her, *I'm on my way home now* . . .

One hour passed, then two. The talk rose and fell, but Ritchie with his eyes closed thought of it as the wind when he and Da had sometimes walked on the moors beyond Hamilton. No wonder they built the TB hospitals there – the sharp sweetness of the air. Da had been a great walker, Meikle Earnock, Ferniegair, Tinto Hill, names . . . He remembered the larks

270

singing . . . There was a sudden angry outburst from the men, louder than before, then a voice shouting above it.

'Well, who's game, then? They can't make fools of us like this. It's the bloody French authorities.' Another voice. 'That's right. Come on, we'll ask Corporal Thomas. What d'you say, Corporal?' Ritchie heard his tired voice. 'I can't stop any of you lads who want to go. I'll have to stay with the badly wounded. You're able enough, Graham. You can lead.'

The man with the signpost arm nearly knocked Ritchie's head off as he swung round. 'Not bloody likely. I'm staying put.'

'I'm going.' He didn't have to think.

The man Graham was now giving instructions. 'The French at the front, then those who can walk fairly well, then the crutches. Come on, lads, we're off!' He turned round and waved his beret at the men left in the carriage. 'See you in Piccadilly, chaps!' Ritchie fell in with the straggling group.

Everything he had been doing for the past few weeks seemed at one remove, but this beat them all, a long, straggling procession of the lame, the halt and the blind, some with arms in splints, some legs, some minus an arm or a leg. It took its place beside the other pictures stored in his brain.

A long way ahead they could see an arc of light which grew bigger as they tried to hasten their steps. 'There's a crowd gathered there.'

'Well-wishers.'

'What a hope!'

'The French troops.'

'A hope we urny gawn to be shot noo. That would be ironical.' The sing-song of a Glaswegian.

As they grew nearer Ritchie saw that the French soldiers were armed.

'Keep going!' Graham commanded. 'Don't hesitate!'

The French troops now had their rifles to their shoulders. They looked fierce. Ritchie fixed his eye on the face of one of them.

On they went, limping, swinging on crutches, no one was speaking now. The troops stood firm, but Ritchie saw the little black moustache on his man's lip quiver a fraction. The others moved on their feet, looked uneasily at one another, and then, as Graham and his band came slowly on they fell back and made way for them.

'*Merci bien*,' Ritchie said, passing the small moustache, feeling like a European, a man of many tongues. Glasgow wouldn't hold him now.

Two days later he was bedded down in Middlesex Hospital after an uneventful trip through France and being put on the ferry at Calais. They were interrogated at Dover by a pedantic plain-clothes policeman. 'Look, chum,' he heard one of their lot say, 'I didn't do this for a lark.' He waved his empty sleeve.

He had to wait for his wound to be examined by a surgeon and be declared fit to travel on his own. He had time to think of his battalion still fighting in the Sierra Pandols against terrible odds, and of Syd. Maybe he would join the WEA sometime and study Lorca's poetry in his memory.

He ran a temperature after all the excitement and had to be put to bed. When he was able to sit up again he wrote to Anna.

When I think of you my whole body swells in anticipation. It's as if my skin was too small for me. I can hardly wait . . .

Was this *his* first love letter?

And we'll go and see my parents. A priest in the cave where I was taken told me that the last word on a man's lips before he died was usually '*Madre*'.

He thought of his mother's thin face, her bright intelligent eyes, and how in all the years he had known her she had never once complained about his father although he was more out of work

272

than in. *Los pobres y humildes*. The poor and humble. The salt of the earth. His mind was full of Spanish images, Spanish words. It wouldn't settle on home yet. People, yes, but not the place. Spain was more real.

He remembered a conversation he'd had with a man when they were swimming together over the Ebro, as if they had met in the street. He had escaped from a Spanish prison.

'Do you know what the Fascists do if they find you?'

'No.' Ritchie had spat out a piece of seaweed.

'They force you to lie down on the road and then they run their lorries over you, iron you as flat as a pancake.'

And how once he had recited a poem to Syd in their brushwood hut in Chavola Valley. It lay at the top of his memory because it made him think of lying thigh bone to thigh bone on one of the University sofas with Anna.

> 'O luely, luely, cam she in
> And luely she lay doun:
> I kent her by her caller lips
> And her briests sae sma' and roun . . .'

'Greek to me,' Syd had said. ' "Luely"? What in God's name is that?'

'Lovely, luesome.' He'd had difficulty in speaking because of the thickness in his throat.

> 'A' thru the nicht we spak nae word
> Nor sinder'd bane frae bane:
> A' thru the nicht I heard her heart
> Gang soundin' wi' my ain.'

'Ach, never mind,' he had said, seeing the dazed expression on Syd's face. 'You great skinny-ma-linky-longlegs. You remind me of a whippet at the Carntyne Races.'

*   *   *

Anna was waiting at Glasgow Central when his train came in. When she saw him coming limping along the platform she started running. He couldn't run very fast because of his lame leg and his knapsack. He had scarcely passed the news kiosk when they met. She nearly knocked him over.

'Have a heart, Anna,' he said.

'I have,' she said. 'That's why I'm here.'

'Just a minute.' He put down his knapsack and took her in his arms. His head swam as he kissed her. 'My head's swimming,' he said, releasing her. God, she was beautiful. *Luely*. Older-looking, but even more beautiful.

'Hold on to me,' she said.

He lifted his knapsack and she took his arm. They began to walk.

'I don't deserve this,' he said. 'When can we get married?'

'Soon. Very soon.'

'What made you change your mind?'

'Jean. She chucked me out. She said the Glasgow Girls were not for us.'

'I could have told you that. But some of them were married.'

'I know.' She stopped so that he could see her face. She was radiant, crackling with love. Sparks were flying out of her eyes. 'She's getting married to John Whitbread. You should know by this time that we do everything together.'

'Yur hawdin' up the traffic,' a man said, pushing past them.

THIRTY-TWO

1938–39

THEY WERE MARRIED in September of that year, the day Chamberlain flew back from Munich with the promise of 'Peace in our time'. Ritchie didn't believe it, and thought they should get hitched up while the going was good.

Anna persuaded Rose that it would be bad taste to have a big wedding when times were so out of joint, and although Rose placed no credence on that as an excuse, she said she had lost some of her enthusiasm since her great wish to see the twins married on the same day wasn't going to be granted. 'Jean should watch her reputation living alone and Dr Whitbread popping in at all hours,' she said, and wondered why Anna laughed.

Nancy, to her regret, couldn't be there as she had just given birth to their son, Gordon James Pettigrew, and was luxuriously installed in a private nursing home in Great Western Road. 'You should have put it off for a month or so, Anna,' she said, cradled in pink organdie pillows and rose-spattered eider-down in her room. 'I'm simply dying to get into Daly's and buy myself a decent dress after six months of those dreary maternity things.'

The wedding was held in the parish church at Kirkcudbright and the reception at Jean's house. Rose and Angus stayed at the Selkirk Arms and had invited Lizzie and Walter Laidlaw as their guests, a kindly gesture on Angus's part. Miss Craig had died that summer, or rather, had slipped away from what was left of her. No one could pretend to be sorry. For once, the euphemism, 'a blessed release' was just.

John Whitbread poured the champagne in his official capacity as Jean's fiancé. He said to Anna when they were standing together, 'Is your mother disappointed you and Jean didn't have a double wedding?'

'Yes.' She smiled at him. 'But Jean and I didn't think it would be a good idea. It would have made you and Ritchie look like accessories after the fact.'

He smiled back. 'I shouldn't have minded.'

She put a hand on his arm, 'I'm sure you wouldn't, but it gives you more time to do your courting. Jean's enjoying it. She'll tell you when she's ready.'

And the same word could have been used to describe her state when she and Ritchie were in their London hotel for their honeymoon. Ready.

She had never known such happiness and joy, at times such ecstasy. The first night they came together it was as easy and natural as if they had been loving all their lives. Their bodies were like magnets to each other. When he entered her she groaned with joy and said, 'Oh, that's it, Ritchie. That's it!'

'You are supposed to swoon,' he said in her ear, but his voice was hoarse.

'No, I might have missed it then.' Her tears of happiness were a small warm river running between their faces. Now she understood Jean.

'God knows how we kept apart.'

'He's the only one who does.' Her throat was gagged with desire.

They weren't romantic lovers. They were frantic, frank, sometimes clumsy in their loving, and there was the hidden thought that they must make the most of it. God also knew how long this pseudo-peace in the world would last and they would be allowed to enjoy such happiness. There was a heavy kind of apprehension in the air.

Jean married John the day before war broke out, 2 September 1939. As Anna said to her on the telephone, we're the very devil for choosing important dates.

'Well, we're important people. And John said he was losing patients right and left while I dithered. He cut off someone's leg by mistake last week.'

'Jean!'

'You don't like the macabre touch? Marriage must be making you soppy.'

'Wait till you feel the joy that comes with living together. And loving.'

'Well, you haven't wasted any time for results. Will you be able to come to the wedding?'

'Try and stop me. Anyhow, the baby isn't due for another fortnight. If it's a girl I'll be able to tell her that she's the first antenatal bridesmaid I've known. No, fire and flood wouldn't keep me away.'

Jean wore a white dress, short, as Anna's had been, but, true to type, with gold dangling earrings instead of a veil. Her dark hair was brushed back from her forehead and ears. She had never looked more beautiful, a different kind of beauty from her girlhood. The trembling vulnerability had died with Frederick Kleiber and been replaced by a new serenity.

Even Rose was impressed. 'There's always been something about Jean,' she said shakily, and Angus put a comforting arm round her.

'Well, you have them all married now, Rose. That's what you wanted.'

She wiped a delicate tear away. 'That's right. And I'll have more time to look after you now, Angus.' Perhaps she had noticed how he wheezed going up the Mote Brae.

Once again the reception was in the house on the High Street, but this time there was a waiter pouring out the champagne as John seemed to find it necessary to stand close to his bride. It would have been difficult to prise him away from her, Anna thought, seeing the joy in his face.

She put up her hand to hide the tear – pregnancy made you sentimental – and found her brow wet. It coincided with an odd, light-headed feeling. She said to Ritchie who was sitting beside her, 'Do you find this room hot?'

He turned to her, his eyes dancing with good humour and champagne. 'Hot? I hadn't noticed.' He took a look at her. 'Are you all right?'

'Yes, I think so.' Her vague feeling of uncertainty was splintered as she spoke by the sword which sliced through her body from head to foot, its point coming to a stop on the carpet between her feet. The agony ebbed away in a slow surge of pain, then merely discomfort. 'Oh God!' she said. 'Ritchie, it's it!'

'It?' He was slow because of the champagne. 'It? Oh, you mean, it! My God!' He took a quick look at her, got up and went straight to John, still standing beside Jean with a bemused look on his face, and caught his arm. In a second they were both at her side, followed by Jean.

Through the haze of pain she knew that John was mopping her brow and murmuring reassuringly. 'We'll carry her upstairs,' he said, and to her, 'Don't worry, Anna.' The bemused look of love he'd been wearing had been wiped off and replaced by one of professional assessment.

'It's so embarrassing.' She was vaguely aware of the hush in the room, the turning of heads, 'No, don't carry me. I can walk. Ritchie will help me.' Somehow she was out of the room and stumbling upstairs where she was quickly undressed by Jean. Ritchie was hovering, holding her hands, rubbing them, getting in Jean's way, being frightened to death.

'Give Jean room,' she said, and he fell away hurt. She would make it up to him afterwards.

Now John was bending over her. His grey morning coat had been abandoned, and he was in his shirt sleeves, he was examining her, very professionally for a new brother-in-law. 'Your labour is well advanced, Anna,' he said. 'We'll all help you. Don't worry.'

The rest was incoherence, pain, and then quite quickly, but when she'd had more than enough of this, something soft and moving like a kitten was between her legs, and in another few minutes it was put into her arms. Joy. She looked up into Jean's smiling face, and then Ritchie's, who was crying and kissing her like a child who has been left on his own too long, and then into the calm, reassuring face of John. 'Well done, Anna. The quickest birth I've known,' he said.

They called him Hamish, avoiding offending either grand-parent. The name was suitably Scottish, even Highland. Ritchie said it made him think of bagpipes, but that he heard them skirling in his ears in any case, every time he looked at his baby son.

Life was good, in spite of the war, which seemed at the moment to be emulating a damp squib. The West End had never been gayer. The stringent blackout didn't deter people from flocking into the theatres to see Ivor Novello's *The Dancing Years*, nor the Lambeth Walk musical, until they turned and flocked like lemmings to the latest ENSA show, which at least reminded everyone there was a war on, although in the jolliest way imaginable.

Ritchie said it was a spirit of desperation which was activating everyone, but didn't demur when his agent put on a show of his latest works in a prominent gallery in Bond Street. It seemed the whole world then flocked to see *it*.

On the opening night when Anna went with him – a Clerken-well neighbour had volunteered to look after Hamish – she met Mr Wolf who had first put Ritchie's pictures on show, and when Ritchie was whisked off for photographs, she and Mr Wolf walked round the gallery together.

'I know Ritchie will always be grateful to you for the faith you had in him,' she said.

'He does not forget old friends, your Ritchie. I believed in this boy, fresh from art school, and I was right. That is good.' He looked around the walls. 'What a feast to the eyes! The power jumps at you. That was how I knew he was going places. The power. And his experiences in Spain have left their mark on him. Do you see that?' He pointed. 'Struggling horses in a river. The Ebro perhaps. He must have his river. *Spain*, it's called. He did well to go.'

'And come back.'

'Ayee, ayee. And come back.' He sighed, his Levantine face sad, and then, his eyes ranging about the salon, 'You know, the Scottish painters have borrowed from Europe more naturally than the English. Colour and power. Like my homeland. Like Russia.'

'I'm so happy for him,' she said. She put a hand on his arm. 'One gets selfish. If only this war doesn't spoil our happiness. Do you think it's going to fizzle out?'

'No.' He patted her hand. 'But then I'm a Jew. For you,' he shrugged, 'well, I don't know. Perhaps they will make Ritchie an official war artist instead of –' He stopped. 'A day at a time. This is your night, and Ritchie's. Go and join him. He will want you by his side.'

She walked down the long room to where he stood in the centre of a group of people. There was a buzz in the air apart from the voices, a buzz of excitement, of heightened awareness. This was their hour. Ritchie turned and saw her. He held out his hands, his face alight, his eyes brilliant. 'Come and be introduced, Anna!' he called. 'Everyone wants to meet you.' She reached him and his arm went round her.

'What's your secret, Mr Laidlaw?' a black-haired woman asked, a notebook in her hand.

'Ask my wife,' he said. He bent and kissed Anna and she felt confident as well as happy. A day at a time, Mr Wolf had said.